MW01628213

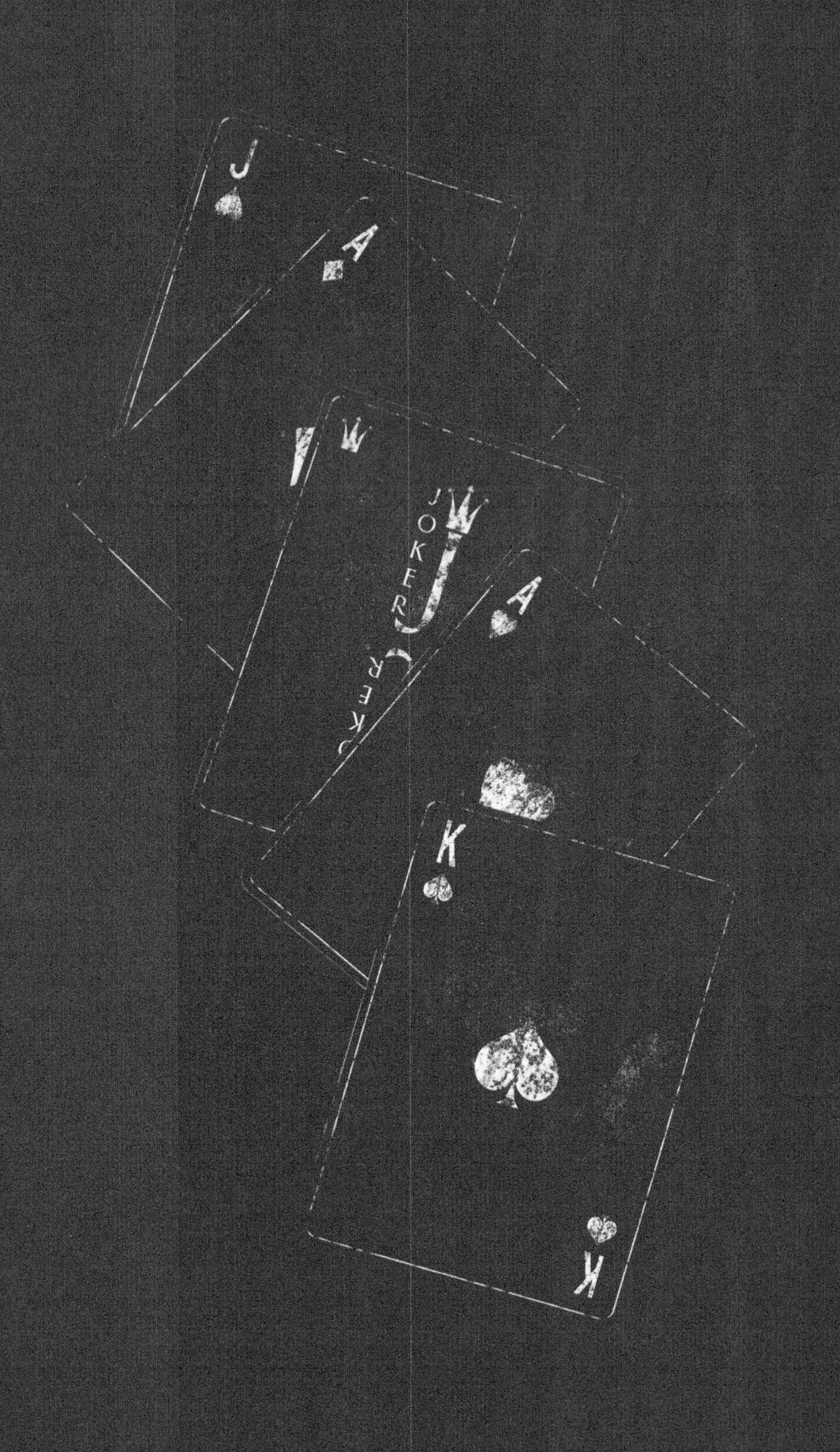
JOKER

QUEEN

of

Wildcards

HELEVA RISQUE

Queen of Wildcards

To all the girls whose dark trauma drives them to read about other women suffering, conquering, and healing to cope with their own pain.

I hear you.
I see you.
I am you.

Let us heal together, ladies. And then, we'll take over the world.

WILDCARDS *playlist*

PRBLMS
6LACK

KILLER
VALERIE BROUSSARD

IN THE DARK
SHAKER, COBRA

PARTY MONSTER
THE WEEKND

MOUNT EVEREST
LABRINTH

DARK RED
STEVE LACY

505
ARCTIC MONKEYS

HIGH ENOUGH
K. FLAY

HAYLOFT
MOTHER MOTHER

PLAY WITH FIRE
SAM TINNESZ, YACHT MONEY

SUCKER FOR PAIN
IMAGINE DRAGONS & ETC

2:55 4:38

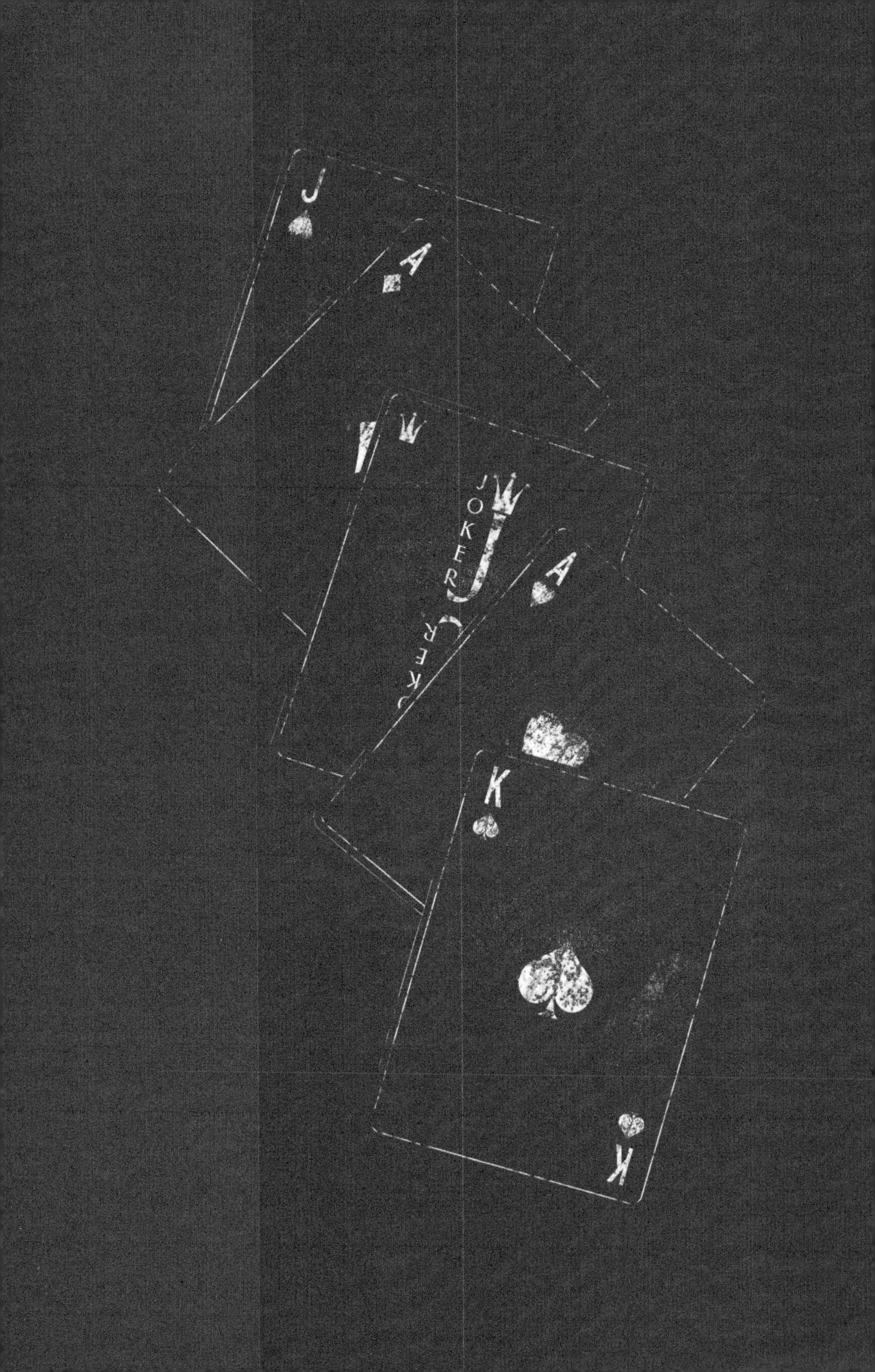
JOKER

CHAPTER ONE
JOKER

"I told you this was a bad fucking idea, you numbskull."

Ace growled through the phone at me, his voice laced with a sigh that would make any dom trainer proud. I was beginning to think my kink was pissing him off by being a brat.

Would make fucking sense.

I tossed the bag of jewels over my shoulder and slung a leg over the expensive Maserati bike I'd bought myself for a birthday present. *Hey, it's not every day a man turns twenty-eight. Might as well enjoy life while I'm still living.* The matte black paint on this metal beast cost me a pretty penny, but it gives me an extra layer of anonymity, a benefit for every successful thief.

Today was my biggest haul yet.

Ace could suck a dick; when I unloaded these diamonds, he wouldn't be complaining as I stacked fat wads of bills in his hands.

"Listen," I grumbled into the receiver, "I know what I'm doing." I jammed the key into the ignition, casting a careful glance around the parking lot. I shot out the street lights when I arrived, so I was bathed in darkness for the moment.

Ace's sigh was audible through the phone. I could almost see the irritated furrow of his brows through the line, could practically feel the irritation radiating off him as he spoke slowly, like I was a child who didn't understand the rules of the house though they'd been explained a hundred times over.

"Joker, we have a system, and you can't just run roughshod all over it." I could hear him typing furiously at his keyboard, probably preparing some boring memo for the bosses. "When you deviate from the plan, bad things happen."

I didn't bother contradicting him. "I'm leaving now. I'll be home in a few minutes." The sound of another bike echoed in the alley behind me, and my thighs instinctively clenched around the huge mass of metal between them as I slipped my helmet off the handlebar. "Hey, I've got company. I'll see you at home."

I could hear him sputtering some directive or another as I hung up and pocketed the little square that kept me so connected with the rest of the world. I wasted no time slipping the helmet over my head, and the bike roared to life beneath me as I peeled out of the lot and into the slow traffic of four in the morning.

The city slumbered at this ungodly hour, but not us criminals. We never slept, not in the underbelly of this festering slum. You had to be on your toes, even when you were some of the city's most prolific, infamous criminals.

My bike purred like a dream and handled spectacularly as I wove in and out of gaps between cars, careful not to draw too much attention. I could hear the bike behind me gaining ground, though, which was disturbing at best.

At worst? It could be someone who'd been watching me, come to lift my haul from my shoulders and put it to good use elsewhere. *And we couldn't have that.*

I'd cased that fucking joint for *months.* Countless hours of work, and an infinite amount of patience as I watched every little thing about the store. Days of hunkering down in my car as if waiting for an imaginary wife to exit the nearby stores. Hundreds of dollars in coffee and energy drinks and takeout. Thousands, maybe.

The payoff would be worth it, as long as I made it home with my haul.

I wove through another couple of cars and banked a hard left, slingshotting myself into an alleyway tucked between two buildings. I pulled my bike into a dark alcove and killed the engine, counting slowly as I ran my hand over the Sig Sauer at my hip.

One.

Deep breath.

Two.

Sounds like they kept going.

Three.

Four.

Five.

And then I heard it. The sound of my tail's engine grew louder, and suddenly it was nearly on top of me.

I realized with a start that the fucker managed to loop around without me noticing and slip up behind me. He had me dead to rights; if he were armed, I wouldn't make it ten feet without being shot.

Looks like the only way out is up.

I ran directly at the rider, and in a split second of confusion, he bailed on his bike, giving me the opening I needed to launch myself up onto the nearby dumpster, then up again, to the dangling fire escape ladder on the side of the building. I scrambled up and around as I heard the ominous click of a safety switch, followed by the typical bad guy warning shout.

"Freeze, or I'll shoot!"

I laughed, perhaps a bit too eagerly, as I rounded another set of stairs and started on the next one. "You shoot me now, you're more likely to catch a body inside the apartments than connect with my gut. Sorry, sister sledge, but I win this round!"

He popped off a shot, and I grinned wildly as it ricocheted off the metal grating of the stairs. My feet pounded up the next floor of the fire escape, and with a cry of victory, I crested the rooftop and took off like a bat out of hell.

The Maserati was a sad casualty, but it was insured. I'd report it missing, and they'd replace it. Simple as that. It was very likely my pursuer would take it or junk it. I'd send someone back to check for it later.

I cleared the three feet of space between the first building and the second, and my feet slapped the tarred surface of the next building's roof as I huffed and puffed, trying to orient myself.

Look for the tower, stupid.

I cast my eyes left and right, but there was no tower in sight. I groaned, skidding to a stop as I turned around and caught sight of the fucking hulking metal monolith—back in the direction I'd come from.

There's no way I can risk turning around now.

If the asshole who'd cornered me followed up the ladders, there was a very real chance turning around could cost me my life. I had no choice but to find a way down and get the fuck out of here.

Out of this neighborhood, out of this fucking shit situation. If I made it home safe and sound, I'd even apologize to Ace for being so reckless this time.

I redirected and raced for the nearest reasonable gap, leaping onto a diagonal building, taking a bit of the impact in my poor knees as I fell about ten feet and tried to keep on my feet. With each step, the bag over my shoulder grew heavier, but I wasn't about to drop it. No fucking way.

They'd have to pry it from my cold, dead hands.

Or check it in as evidence.

The diamonds sloshing around in the leather bag on my left arm were stolen goods. An old friend of mine had heard about a shipment coming in, some hot jewelry our rival gang planned to melt down and disperse as raw material. They'd pulled all the gems from the various pieces, and they'd been conveniently repackaged and prepared for the black market buyer they lined up for the following day.

Except when they showed up to make the swap, they'd find their safe empty and the gemstones conveniently missing.

I was nice enough to at least leave them the gold and silver.

On the side of the short building was a ladder, and I didn't bother to check the damn height of the thing before I scrambled down it, aiming for the alleyway at the bottom. But when I ran out of ladder to descend, I found myself dangling a neat fifteen feet, at least two stories up. There was no convenient dumpster at the bottom, either. Just a few bags of what I assumed was trash, and hard concrete.

Gotta take that L sometimes, buddy. It's either that or risk climbing back up.

The sound of a loud *thud* above me, followed by a groan of pain, determined it for me. I swore colorfully and released my hold on the rusted metal bar, bracing for impact.

I didn't expect to catch a sleeve on a metal pipe sticking out from the wall. Or for the damn thing to slice my arm open, elbow to wrist.

Fuck, fuckity fuck, fuck.

I frowned at the blood pouring from the gash in my arm and stood on shaky legs, dusting off the grime on my clothes. I readjusted the bag with a grimace and tucked my arm against my torso, running for the place I'd left my bike. I just prayed my pursuer hadn't had time or foresight to take the keys or tip it. I wouldn't get it up with only one hand if it were lying down.

And the other arm was useless right now.

I rounded the corner and found my bike where I'd left it, kickstand holding the fucker up like some divine gift. I groaned in relief and swung my leg over the damn thing, swearing profusely when I tried to lift my injured arm to grip the handle.

There was blood everywhere.

Probably shouldn't be riding this bike while I bleed out, but no time for regret now.

Regret later.

I twisted the key with a wince and adjusted the bag, prepared to peel out and bail before the other guy came back. In a spur-of-the-moment decision, I kicked out with my leg as I passed his bike and sent the thing toppling to the ground, the satisfying crunch of metal easing my anxiety as I sped off into the night.

As the blocks turned from slum central to a less run-down warehouse district, I picked out the tower in the distance and shook the lingering dizziness from my brain.

Only a few more blocks. A few more minutes and I could fall over at the front door, and the guys would come out and pick my dumb ass up off the ground, drag me in, and bandage me up just in time to have my almost failure rubbed in my face by Ace.

"Fuck," I muttered, pulling to a stop at the nearby light. The concrete felt a bit further away than usual when I moved my foot out to support me, and the lights of oncoming vehicles were blinding, the shimmering glare wiggling around and blurring dangerously as black spots edged in on my vision.

I swore and kicked off the ground with less push than I had hoped for, and the bike moved across the intersection before my hands slipped from the bars and I bailed, hitting the ground with a groan. The bike kept sliding; thankfully, it hadn't pinned me. I lamented the loss of the beautiful beast for a split second, and then my worst nightmares came to life as a police officer pulled up and began to hustle in my direction.

Get up, get up, you idiot, you're about to get busted!

I couldn't make my body move, and everything was swimming now in front of me. With all the energy I had left in my body, I reached into my pocket and pulled out my phone, dialing the last number I had called.

Pick up, fucker.

Just as Ace answered on the other end of the line, my vision went black, and I drifted off unwillingly with the sound of sirens in the distance.

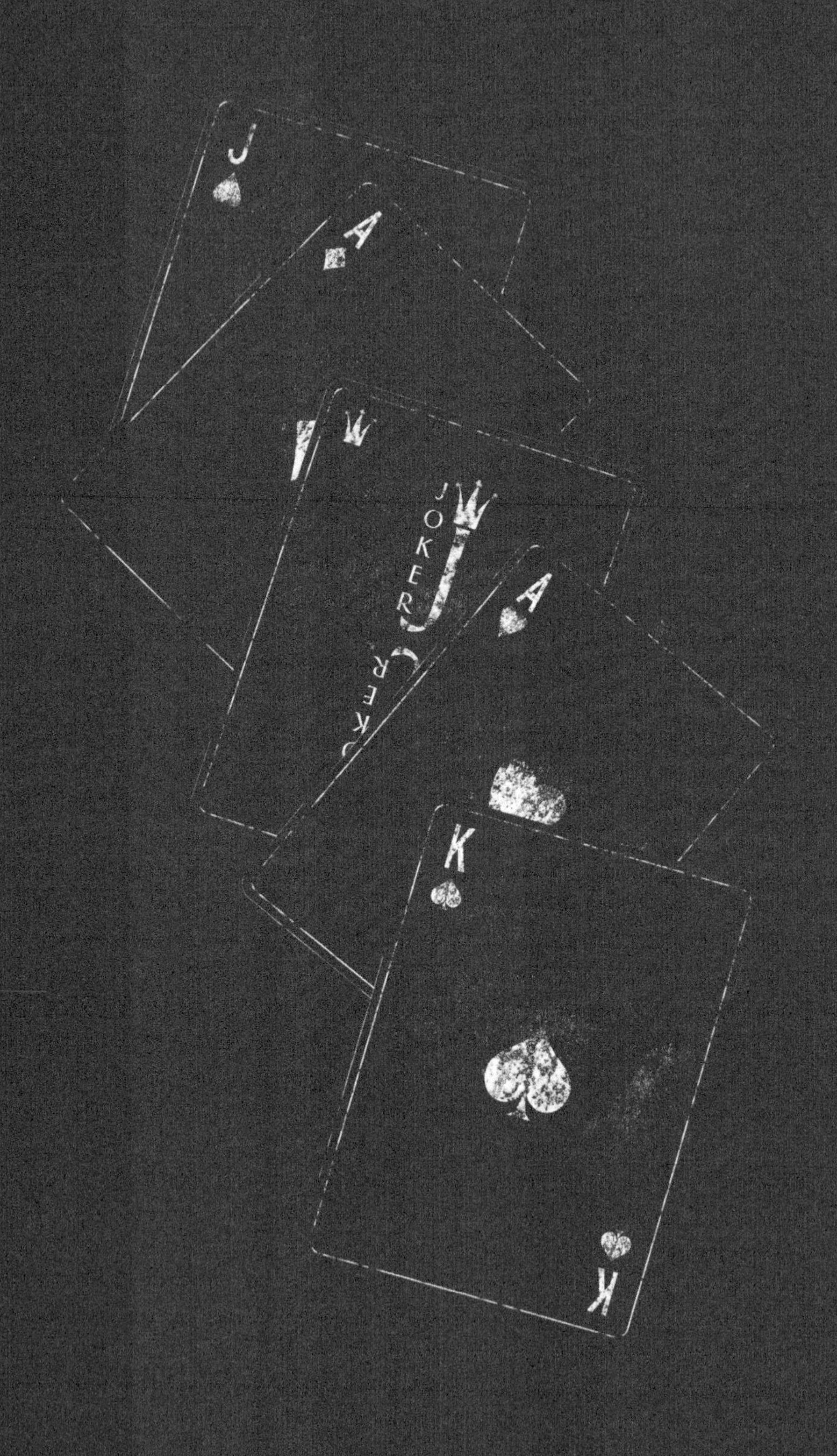
JOKER

CHAPTER TWO
MALLORY

"Seriously, Mal, I don't think you should be living on your own on that side of town," my father grumbled through the phone as I circled the kitchen, on the hunt for the spatula I'd sat down earlier. "It's not safe for a woman on her own."

"You didn't seem to have the same opinion when you left mom and I here alone while you ran your rackets, daddy dearest." His end of the phone went silent as I padded around my kitchen, looking for the cutting board. "But that's neither here nor there." *There it was.* Hanging beside the sink *where I left it, of course.* "Have you been going to your court-mandated therapy?"

He groaned like he did every time I asked him that. "I don't understand why you recommended that shit. I hate talking to people about my business."

I shrugged, not caring that he couldn't see me. "Well, it was the only way they would let you see the light of day again." My hand closed around the smooth handle of my blade, and I set to work chopping the garlic for my sauce with my phone cradled against the shell of my ear. "And besides, your counsel should have never pulled me in as a witness, anyhow. You put me in a precarious position. I could have lost my license for you!"

I nearly had. When the office I worked for as a therapist caught wind of my father's defense attorney's shenanigans, they told me in no uncertain terms that I was not a good fit for their practice anymore. My professionalism and unbiased stature were in question, and they didn't want any such association tied to them.

I could understand it. After all, even as a therapist, as someone who went to college to study how the human mind works and how to fix them, I still couldn't fix myself. I knew why I had issues with codependency with a man who'd been nothing but a piece of shit and passing fancy in my life. I lacked a dad in my formative years, so now, when he was ready to reconnect with his grown daughter, I was powerless to refuse him. The inner child in me wanted Daddy Dearest's approval.

So I'd stupidly forgotten to mention that the criminal I'd been called to testify on behalf of was my own father.

It's not like we shared a last name. It's not like he was on the birth certificate—he wasn't. And since he'd given my mother a fake name, and their marriage paperwork was forged, she hadn't been able to track him down for child support.

Hell, I only found out when he showed up at her funeral. As much as I wanted to deny being related to the arrogant, smug bastard, he had the paperwork to prove it. A DNA test confirmed the rest.

Not that any of that was on the books. But if one looked hard enough, one could find the faint blood trail that led to this shark-in-the-water criminal that was my dad.

"You might hate sharing your business with a therapist, but it's not like they're gonna go and out you to the world. There is such a thing as patient/doctor privilege. It's like a marriage—can't testify against your spouse." *Chop, chop, chop.* The garlic turned easily to diced chunks as I brought the blade down, over and over, perhaps with more force than necessary.

My father's crackly sigh permeated the air as my cheek slipped and switched him to speakerphone. I cringed, but setting down the phone made more sense than tilting my head uncomfortably, so I switched things up.

"So when are you going to visit your dear ole dad, huh?"

I rolled my eyes. "When hell freezes over, you pig. I'm only holding this key for you because I need the money to pay the bills. There's no love lost between us, and there never will be."

"I had hoped for an actual relationship with ya, but if you're gonna be that way . . . "

I didn't bother to answer; instead, I let the steady *thunk* of the knife as it hit the cutting board fill the air around me. In the distance, my ancient stereo echoed out the faint stirrings of a nocturne by Chopin, the melancholy piano chords making an already dreary evening even worse. If the moroseness of my mood and the rainy, overcast atmosphere outside didn't drag down the entire vibe, the piano definitely brought it right into emo mode.

It felt dangerously reminiscent of the vibe I'd drowned in before I went to school for psychiatry and psychology, so I could not only help myself, but others in need.

Right before I tried to off myself in the most cliché way possible.

Fucking stupid. I was the walking poster board of someone rising above and coming back stronger, but all I wanted to do right now was write myself a script for some anti-depressants and crawl over to the couch to veg out for a week or more.

"I *am* going to be that way, dad," I huffed as I turned to dump the diced garlic in the sauce, forcing myself to finish cooking my meal. "I told you from the beginning that I'd accept the blood money for rent and hold this key to your safe deposit box under mom's name, but not to expect some reconciliation from me. You shortsighted me and cost me my job." I took a deep breath and pinched the bridge of my nose, trying to remain calm and failing miserably. "A job I loved."

His answer was to scoff at my plight and probably roll his eyes on the other side of the call. I knew I got my attitude from him; mom had always been so cool, and I was . . . *not*.

"Sure thing, sweetie," he placated, pretending to be the doting, jilted daddy once again. "You go on and live your life, take that check every month that I send you, and pretend that you haven't sold your loyalty to me."

And there came the claws.

"This conversation is over, *Jim,"* I ground out from between clenched teeth, eyeing the phone on the counter with distaste. "Whatever game you're playing, I'm not in the mood for it."

He *hated* it when I called him Jim. If he had his way, I'd still call him daddy like a good little girl and pander to him like he was the patron saint of parenthood. He wanted to be worshipped, and when I didn't give him that, the only thing keeping him from withdrawing his aide was a court order.

Bet he was pissed he ever signed that agreement to support me after costing me my job.

Rent in this town was astronomical, and though I was getting monthly checks from his estate of two grand, a quarter of that went on his books every month so he could be comfortable in prison. A quarter of it paid his lawyer's retainer. And the rest was for me, though I always spent at least a hundred on phone calls from the jail.

Guess he didn't count that commissary money toward his call allotment.

"You just remember who's paying for your upkeep, you little ungrateful bitch—"

"Goodbye," I said smugly, disconnecting the call with a flourish of my slightly sticky hands. "And good riddance."

Calls with Jim were like that sometimes. One minute he wanted to play house; the next, he was busy trying to remind me who I belonged to.

I knew he wouldn't risk throwing away all of his belongings and everything he'd managed to amass as a result of all his criminal dealings just to spite me, so the rent would inevitably get paid every month until he was out on parole, and I jumped ship to get away.

I couldn't risk being around when Slim Jim himself walked free once more. Losing my job was peanuts compared to what he could do to ruin my life.

I just had to keep saving up from my jobs on the side, every penny I could scrape up.

My phone vibrated on the counter, and I realized that my scheduled shift as an online therapist was fast approaching. I usually tried to take calls in the office, but it wouldn't be the first time I'd taken one while making dinner or sitting in the living room.

I still had an hour to go, though—time to check in with the real world.

"Siri, call Gemma."

The nifty AI on my phone dialed up my only remaining friend, and I smiled silently to myself when I heard her pick up.

"Hey, Mal, how goes it?"

"Oh, you know, same shit, different day." I stirred the sauce on the stove absently as the rain outside picked up. "And you?"

Gemma squealed on the other end of the line like a teenage girl. "Oh. My. Gosh. You're not going to believe this, but I've got a second date tomorrow with that hottie from the dating app—"

"Gemma, what did we say about those apps?"

I could practically see her in my mind, flopping into her bean bag chair with a flourish and an eye roll. "Okay, *mom,* we agreed that I would be careful, not that I would stop using them."

The oven blasted me in the face with a gust of hot air as I tugged the door down to check on some garlic bread. "So what steps have you taken to make sure the environment tomorrow is a safe one?"

Gemma groaned. "Are you really playing therapist on me right now? I thought you'd be happy for me and help me wig out over what to wear, not that you'd slide in here all mopey and serious and demand to know how safe I planned to be."

"As a friend, Gemma, I want to make sure you don't end up—"

"What, end up like my sister?"

Gemma and I had bonded a long time ago after going to group therapy sessions together. Her dad left when Janice, her older sister, was kidnapped during a night out. She was only 19.

It had been seven years since then.

I didn't want the same for my friend.

"Listen, Gemma, I know I come off as a bit condescending at times, but I worry about you." My fingers clenched around the hand towel on the counter, and I tugged the perfectly-toasted bread from the oven, taking a big whiff as I moved to lay it out on the stove. "So humor me, please."

"We're having the date at Alonzo's Ristorante," she finally grumbled. "The reservation is for six, which is their busiest time, and I've got a ride to the restaurant and home from our last venue for the night already scheduled with a regular driver."

Gemma used the ride-share apps so often, she knew most of her neighborhood drivers by name. And they knew her well enough, too. I'd even met a few.

"Okay, so you know your drivers, and they know to expect you. I assume they know well enough to call if you don't cancel a ride on your own." The pot with the noodles was boiling over onto the fire, so I tugged it out of the way and scrambled one-handed for a strainer, scalding myself in the process with the thick steam. "Shit, that stings!"

Gemma's bubbly giggle erupted from the receiver. "What did you do, smartass?"

"Just a little burn," I assured her as I fought tears back. It was more than a little burn, but nothing I hadn't seen before. "Keep talking."

"We're going to a movie in the park, and I checked to make sure there was adequate security around, and I'll be sharing my location with at least two contact people, so that there will be someone aware of my location at all times." She hesitated for a second, then cleared her throat. "I also packed some condoms, just in case—"

"Jesus, Gemma, you've been on one date with this guy. You're really gonna trust him to stick his dick in you already?"

I winced when I realized I'd essentially called my best friend a whore.

"I'm sorry. That was uncalled for."

Gemma shuffled around on the other end of the line, and I realized I was being dismissed. "Sorry, Mal, but I've gotta go get ready. I'll touch base with you when I get back?"

"Yeah, sure," I muttered, but she was already gone, the heavy *click* resounding in my ear.

It wasn't until I was in my bathroom minutes later, wrapping up the minor burn on my wrist, that I realized she hadn't asked me to sync up for location. Hadn't even mentioned it.

So who had she planned to location share with?

You're not her only friend, a little jealous voice in the back of my head echoed faintly. *She's normal, not codependent on one or two people like you.*

Gemma was allowed to have other friends. They probably didn't pester the fuck out of her like she was a teenager still like I did. They also probably didn't know her like I did, but that was beside the point.

I just wanted to protect those I loved. That was it.

It was my greatest flaw.

And one I was sure I'd eventually come to hate.

JOKER

CHAPTER THREE
SPADE

Tonight wasn't gonna end well. It wasn't that I could predict the future or anything, or that I had insider information.

Call it a vibe.

And tonight had some seriously hinky ones.

I'd been tasked with picking up Joker's dumb ass from the jail after Ace pulled no shortage of strings to get him out. Of course, the first thing this moron would do was pickpocket the keys and drive us straight to a bar.

Joker drunk wasn't always a good time, either. And from the downturned lilt to his lips, I could tell tonight was gonna be a rough one.

Sure, it wasn't my place to have his back, and I might not be a drinker, per se, but I'd stick it out nonetheless since someone had to. We were a family, no matter how fucked up some of us *were.*

Some of us being all of us, really.

The pad of my thumb ran absently over my knuckles, the faint sting from the open wounds like a pleasant thrum in my body. I had to beat a man near to death before this, and the guards had given me some weird looks when they saw my split knuckles, but they wisely said nothing until we were well out of earshot.

Joker, however, didn't have the kind of filter needed to discern he shouldn't open his mouth about it.

So of course, he did just that.

"Where's the fight tonight, pal?"

The smug bastard tossed his luscious blonde hair out of his eyes and beamed at me like I hadn't just had to rearrange my whole night and a torture session to deal with his stupidity. Unfortunately, ignoring him would only prove fruitless and irritating, so I passed on that plan.

"Already over. Had to cut it short." I gave him the once-over, looking at him from tip to perfectly polished toe. Even after several nights in jail, he still looked like a million bucks. As put together as ever.

I sort of wondered how many dicks he'd had to suck to get such luxurious treatment.

Not enough to ask, though.

We moved into line as Joker tossed a peal of laughter over his shoulder at my brusque tone. "Come on, Spade, join me in a night of celebration!"

"Revelry isn't my forté, Joker," I ground out, cringing as the women all dressed to the nines in their skimpiest clothing brushed up against me as they passed. "I'll have one drink with you, but then, we're going back to the damn compound, deal?"

He sighed dramatically, waving his hands in mock defeat. "Sure thing, pal. Say less." He wiggled his eyebrows suggestively and turned back to the line, where several of the girls in front of him were now openly adoring his gorgeous, lean figure. "Ladies, ladies, to what do I owe the pleasure?"

These whores are all the same, falling all over a pretty smile. I'd rather gouge my eye out than fuck any of them.

I knew it was a bit dramatic of me, but in reality, I couldn't even stand the idea of entertaining a vapid, shallow club bunny like these ones. It made me feel slightly ill to think of one clinging desperately to me like her meal ticket.

I withdrew in on myself tighter and tucked a single, loose strand of electric red hair behind my ear. By the grace of gods that I didn't believe in, somehow I managed to sneak into the tightly packed club without touching one of them, and there was even an empty spot at the end of the bar.

Perfect. I could put my back against the wall and watch the place.

I wasn't one for casing joints, but my skill was enforcing, and fighting when needed. If there was an incident brewing, I wanted to know about it before things got hot and heavy.

They always did, with Joker around.

Speak of the devil . . .

The bastard in question decided now would be the perfect time to drag two buxom bitches to the bar and pay for their shots. I winced when the blonde one turned to me with her predatory, lustful grin.

"Hey there, sexy, are you with him?" She pointed to Joker, and I frowned, my arms sliding across my chest to cross in irritation.

"I'm off the menu," I growled, hoping she'd get the hint.

She didn't.

Her hand moved out to caress my bicep, and I literally bared my teeth and growled at her like a bear about to attack. She flinched back with a nervous chuckle and returned her attention to Joker, where it fucking belonged.

Keep away, bitch.

Don't get me wrong — I loved women, and I loved sex; I just didn't appreciate the first when all they expected from you was the latter and money. If I was gonna take a woman to my bed, she'd better be there for me, not for my wallet or my dick.

Well, okay, so being there for the dick was partially a must.

But a man had to have his standards, and, well, I had mine. And none of these hangers-on met the minimum bar for entry to this ride.

To my immediate right, Joker and his gaggle of horny hookers were laughing boisterously, daring each other to take the shots the bartender set in front of them. Three shots disappeared in an instant, and my scowl deepened as Joker's mouth opened only to play tonsil hockey with first one woman, then the other.

Fucking disgusting.

I couldn't imagine being so uninhibited in such a public place. So free, so uncaring. I didn't have much of a reputation to protect, but I had my dignity, which was more than I could say for Joker.

Dignity, he lacked in spades.

I watched on in silent horror as he proceeded to demand the girls make out with each other for his amusement, which they moved to do so quickly it left my head spinning. These women, who'd previously been fawning all over the prince in question, now pawed at each other, their hands dancing sensuously across each other's bodies. Slight disgust curled deep inside me as the blonde grabbed the brunette's ass and they started to grind against each other, lost in the performance that was no longer just a show, but a full-blown woman-on-woman floor orgy.

Joker smirked at me over his shoulder. "This shit never gets old, huh?" He reached down and blatantly adjusted his raging hard-on, staring at the women with a feral grin. "I bet I can make them eat each other out before I fuck them tonight."

"I bet they ditch you for each other before the night is through," I bounced back, irritation lacing my words, making them harsher than I intended. I wasn't trying to cock block him, but it was a realistic assumption, with as excited and lost in each other as the women in question seemed to be at the moment. It was as if Joker had ceased to exist, and it was honestly funny to watch. His face had fallen a fair bit now that his eyes caught sight of the girls moving away to a quiet corner.

"Hey, ladies, don't forget about me," he pleaded, wandering off after them.

I settled in at the end of the bar and called for a soda, prepared for a couple hours of dry amusement.

IT TOOK EXACTLY two more hours for Joker's plans to go to shit, and for that hinky feeling of mine to double.

Joker stormed back to the bar, minus two women, and the dance floor had cleared out significantly since his disappearance. That rogueish blonde shoulder-length hair looked like he'd run his fingers through it a million and one times, the faint lines dividing it where he'd blazed temporary tracks in his agitation.

One could always gauge his mood by the way he wore his hair and the height of his smile at the edges. The wider his smile, the worse his mood. Conversely, the more messy his hair, the nastier the fallout would be.

And tonight was amping up to be a doozy.

"Back so soon?" I teased, unable to resist the urge to jab the knife in a little further. After all, if he hadn't fucked up so spectacularly, I could be pounding in skulls, getting answers to the questions Ace had on his list. Instead, I was babysitting an unhinged and slightly manic wild card at the bar, stuck watching him nurse his pride after being deserted by his horny hotties.

Such a shame, really, that he needed such validation from others.

I cracked my knuckled as Joker slapped the bar, demanding the bartender's attention quite rudely. "Can I get some service down here, yeah?" My hand instinctively reached out to pull his away from the counter, but he jerked said hand out of my reach, nearly smacking into the man on his other side in his haste. "Fuck off, mate, I'm having *fun."*

"Doesn't look that way from where I'm sitting, pal," I eased, knowing another drink or two would have him really spoiling for a fight. Ace wouldn't be pleased if I damaged pretty boy's face, so I simply flexed my fists and waited for him to continue his rant.

In true Joker fashion, he ignored me in favor of the pretty girl who'd been sent to tend to him, unknowingly becoming his newest victim. She offered him a teasing, flirtatious smile, and he gave her one right back, though it resembled more of a shark's dinner grin.

"Ah, what can I get you, sir?" she asked cautiously as she leaned back to put some distance between her and Joker.

His eyes caressed her tits, then moved to the drinks. "Give me a double of your top-shelf tequila, and make it quick. No lime, no salt, just straight burn."

I almost pulled him back, but I figured it would be easier to drag him to the car fully sloshed. The barf I'd have to clean up later would be easier to deal with than fighting him in a bar full of people. He'd cause a scene, for sure, and I wanted to avoid that if at all possible.

The less memorable, the better. Let him go down in their minds as a desperate drunk man whose buddy had to take him home.

He downed both shots and threw me a look. "Hey Spade, any chance you can grab this round? I left my wallet at home, and I'm all out of cash."

I rolled my eyes and handed a fifty to the bartender. "That enough to cover the drinks and a tip?"

She smiled and nodded appreciatively, taking that as her cue to head off. Joker watched her perfectly round ass with unconcealed lust, and I began to think maybe my eyes would forever get stuck in the back of my head with as much as I rolled them around him.

The arrogant princeling slumped onto an empty stool and leaned his elbows against the bar, staring down at the countertop for a moment. When he looked back up at me, there was nothing but empty, forlorn self-hatred in the depths of his gorgeous, bright blue eyes.

"Why am I like this, Tyce?"

I sat in stunned silence while he hung his head in shame, resting his temples in the cradle of his upturned arms, the tips of his bottle-blonde hair grazing the sticky countertop.

No one had called me by my real name in quite a while. So long, in fact, that I'd almost forgotten how it sounded.

Sure, we all knew our legal names, but when you're in a criminal organization, you get used to calling people anything the government can't quantifiably trace. That means code names all the way. I was Spade, and he was Joker, end of story.

I'd never called him Cassian, and I was fairly sure he'd never once in all the years I knew him called me Tyson, let alone the shortened version he used now. I told myself it was the booze talking, that he'd be embarrassed in the morning when he remembered what he called me in public.

Had to be a slip-up. Had to be the booze. The alternative was too strange to contemplate.

I followed forlornly, deep in thought, as Joker slipped dejectedly from his perch and stumbled outside, his face tilting up to greet the night air and buzzing fluorescent streetlights like an old friend.

Old friends, indeed.

JOKER

CHAPTER FOUR
MALLORY

Tonight's evening of therapy callers had been profitable, and I eyed my balance with the hosting website with glee. Finally, I'd be able to pay off the arrears on my storage unit, where I kept all my things from the last house downgrade. I couldn't bear to part with some of the antiques my mother had carefully amassed during her time alive, because they were the only things I had left of her. And since my new apartment was tinier than I'd have liked, I had to opt for a long-term storage facility with climate control, to preserve the past I was determined to drag along with me.

I was three months behind, thanks to an influx of extra jail phone calls and higher bills. This one evening of work would more than pay for the outstanding debt.

Just as I moved to log off for the night, a notification popped up in the corner of my screen.

New patient request. Video Chat—Urgent.

The client's color was red, which meant he was at risk of suicidal thoughts and actions—possibly a danger to himself and others. Intake flagged him, and they took that shit seriously. But there was nothing saying I couldn't just close the laptop and pretend I hadn't seen it. The call would bounce to the next person in the queue, and I could end my night.

At the last second, I leaned forward and hit *answer,* straightening my posture in anticipation of a standard talk-down call.

I should have known last-minute calls were a bad idea.

Instead of a typical client, I was greeted with a full-screen image of what appeared to be a very drunk woman leaning against the wall of a dimly lit alley. I cleared my throat and pasted a soft smile on my lips, prepared to introduce myself.

"Hello there, I'm Mallory, your TherAnon therapist. Can I ask who I'm speaking with?"

There was no intelligible answer. Instead, I got a pain-filled groan, and then they disappeared from the screen as the sound of horrid retching filled my living room.

Drunk. Great. Last patient for the night is a suicidal drunk.

I squared my shoulders and tried again. "Are you okay? Do you need medical attention? I can send an ambulance to your location—"

The figure returned on screen, pulling their hair back from their face as a hand swiped across pale lips. "No, no ambulance. I've been worse off before."

Dear heavens, it's a man. A gorgeous man.

I blinked stupidly at the screen as he fought back tears and gagged again. *A wildly drunk, semi-suicidal, totally gorgeous man. And a client.*

I forced myself to wait patiently as he composed himself and was rewarded with a megawatt smile when he finally glanced back up.

His eyes sparkled like the ocean at night, and I nearly forgot how to breathe. "Well, hello there, gorgeous. I didn't expect my therapist to be so young and alluring."

His lips curled in a smile as mine twitched absently. It wasn't the first time a client flirted with me, but something about how he did it made me feel cheap, like he talked that way to all the girls. I opened my mouth to diffuse the conversation, to steer it to what he needed help with.

What I meant to say was, *"What brings you to my video channel this late?"*

What I *actually* said was, "You're not too bad, yourself, buddy."

What the fuck was wrong with me?

I had never in all my days acted so unprofessionally.

His answering chuckle sent shivers down my spine that I staunchly ignored. "Feisty. I like that in a woman." He paused for a second, glancing over the top of the phone as his eyes narrowed suspiciously. "I suppose this is where I tell you why I'm calling, and you help talk me off the ledge, or whatever."

I nodded slowly, careful not to edge the conversation in any specific direction for fear I'd upset the precarious balance he seemed to have on himself. "If that's what you want to do, then I'm all ears. Sometimes, patients ask me things, like hypotheticals, which gives them a way to disconnect from the whole process. Sometimes it's easier to pretend it's not happening to us."

His dull laugh filled my ears with a melancholy sadness. Something about the jaded lilt behind his smooth, seductive voice left me wondering how broken the man behind this obvious mask truly was. Sometimes, it was the ones most put together on the outside that were most scarred underneath.

"Okay, doc, I'll bite," he slurred, listing slightly to the side. "Let's say, hypothetically, that I knew a guy who did bad things for a living."

I folded my hands in front of me and steepled my index fingers against my chin. "What kind of bad things does your friend do for hire?"

He hiccuped drunkenly and picked up the phone from wherever it'd been sitting this whole time, stumbling down the alleyway. "All sorts of bad things. Sometimes he's a thief. Sometimes he's just the informant. On occasion, he hurts people. But mostly a thief, I suppose." He frowned as he peered into the screen from chest height, his long locks of hair framing his image like a curtain of light gold silk. "He already sounds like a shitty person."

I shrugged, knowing it was very likely he was talking about himself. "He sounds complex."

"Haha, funny, doc; complex?" He panned his camera, and I got a glimpse of his body from tip to toe before he refocused the camera lens on his face. "Does this look like the body of a *complex* man to you?"

"Looks can be deceiving, you know," I eased, hoping he'd catch his own shifts from the hypothetical and either get more comfortable or switch back without incident.

"Looks are all I've got, precious. The rest of me ain't so pretty underneath."

His words were laced with self-hatred and a sort of resignation I didn't like to hear in anyone. It told me wherever this man had been in his life, he'd never been adequately validated or loved.

I sank back into the familiar role of therapist, glad to have some sense of normalcy and control in this conversation. "What makes you think that?"

He waved a hand in the air beside his head, and I noticed another man over his shoulder, gaining on him fast, with a scowl drawing all his features down like he'd swallowed a sour-ass lemon whole. As he stayed a few steps ahead of his pursuer, the drunken man continued on, not a care in the world. "Where do I start?"

"Where do you *want* to start?"

"How much time do you have?" he quipped, flipping his hair out of his face.

"How much money do you have?" I retorted, pleased to see a small smile spread across his lips.

"Ah, sweet cheeks, I've got money aplenty, but not enough to fix the fuck up I am now."

I eyed my apartment in mock outrage. "You know, I *have* been meaning to move to a more upscale locale, splurge on a bigger space for myself and my two cats."

His breathing had started to even out, and it looked like he'd regained some of the color hidden beneath the pallor of intoxication from the beginning of our call. *It's true, what they say about a good puke after too much drinking—better out than in.*

"So," he began slowly, his eyes steadily on the road ahead, "I've been a criminal for a long fucking time. A real piece of work. But I try not to steal from the little guys, ya know?" He sighed dramatically. "I don't figure you *do* know. But to sum it up, I thought myself a right little Robin Hood, until —" He glanced around, and I could see the guy from earlier still following him, though further back. "Seriously, Spade, the fuck is wrong with you? I can walk just fine, asshole. Go cramp someone else's style."

I could vaguely hear the other man off in the distance angrily grumbling something to the man on the screen, but I couldn't see him anymore, and I wasn't sure if that was a good thing or a bad thing. The blonde Adonis turned back to me, all smiles again, though I knew them to be fake this time.

Someone who wears a mask on a daily basis gets pretty good at spotting them on others.

"So, you see, there was this job," he drawled on, staring pointedly into the camera now, "and I fucked it up. I got greedy. Wanted someone to give 'ole Cass a pat on the back, a good ole *'look how useful you are'* and yada yada. But I made mistakes. Got caught. And now they all fucking hate me."

I watched as this drunken, beautiful man broke down in front of me, a complete stranger, and I remembered why I did this job.

I needed to help people before they got so desperate to make it all go away that they tried to end it. I needed to save as many people like me as I could.

It was the only way I could atone for the karmic balance of the world, by giving back when I'd been given the gift of a second chance at life.

Call it superstitious, but it felt right. And this man here reminded me of why I did this, why I took the last-minute calls on late, lonely nights.

"Who hates you, Cass?" I assumed the name he'd used earlier was his, and his eyes blew wide when I said it, like he wasn't used to hearing it out loud.

What kind of a life is that?

"Say it again, sugar," he groaned, his eyelids dropping to half-mast. "Say my name again."

The request almost felt dirty, but the way he looked at me like I was the only good thing in his life right now, I couldn't have denied him a fucking thing.

"Cass," I nearly whispered, and my cheeks colored when I heard the next moan.

"Oh, man, I haven't heard my name on a woman's lips in so long, it almost feels surreal." He slowed his pace, and I watched the phone shift as he swapped hands and leaned against a wall. His back flattened against that grungy brick, the dim fluorescent streetlights above him bathing him in an unhealthy orange glow. But when he tilted his face up to the light, he practically sparkled, and I sucked in a breath, my thighs clenching almost painfully.

"Why . . . why is that?" I breathed, nearly forgetting the fucking question because I was so turned on by this man's breathy moans and smooth voice. *Get a grip, you idiot; this is work!* My brain screamed logic at me, but the wires had been disconnected, and I found myself gripping the sides of my chair in an effort to redirect my thoughts.

Cass grunted in the back of his throat, and the phone began to shake slightly. "Why what? You asking about my sex life, doc?"

Now it was my turn to let out a breathless moan at the idea of this man fucking *at all.* I could practically picture it, though I knew I shouldn't. He was built for the big screen, all angles and jawline, and just enough sass to make you melt. He could have been a model, or a porn star, with looks like those.

Instead, he was a self-proclaimed criminal.

Lusting after criminals now. Guess it's true what they say—girls end up with men who remind them of their fathers.

His jostling of the phone sped up, and with a sudden jolt, I realized what he was doing.

His breathing was more shallow now, and he looked dead at me through the screen as he spoke. "You know, I get fucked, doc, that's not the problem. The real problem is that I don't get anything out of it. The heists are just heists, the whores are just whores," he lamented, "and they blend into one another. But your voice, those pretty lips wrapped around my name . . . " he paused, his eyes fluttering closed as he bit the swell of his bottom lip. "That voice does things to me, doc. You sound like you really care, and it's been a long time since anyone's cared about *me.*"

I wanted to stay silent, to wait and see what would happen next, but I was rarely able to keep my mouth shut. "I care about you, Cass," I heard myself say. Mental me was swearing up a storm in my mind, but I didn't give two shits. "Talk to me. Tell me anything. I'm all yours."

I'm all yours?!? Really?

I'd meant to say *'I'm all ears,'* but, like usual, my words got tangled up in my head with another phrase I used often, creating a much more dangerous, unprofessional phrase. And from the way his screen was shaking and how labored his breathing was, I'd say it affected us both in somewhat the same manner.

He had an excuse, though. He was drunk. I was not.

I should know better. Should end this conversation. But I couldn't bring myself to walk away.

Cass slammed his head against the brick wall, a feral groan leaving his lips and echoing around me like a sinful podcast brought to life. It was like I was starring off-screen in my own porn show, and for some fucked up reason, I liked it.

I liked it a lot. My panties were drenched.

But he didn't have to know that.

This broke so many fucking parts of my Hippocratic oath it made me sick—but not sick enough to stop.

And besides, it seemed like Cass was getting *something* out of this.

"Fuck, sugar, you know just what to tell me, don't you? You have no idea how bad I—*unghhhh,"* he moaned, the shaking turning to a steady jerk before stopping entirely. "You know, I called you to confess that I'd robbed one of the most prolific crime syndicates in Khula City, stole millions of dollars worth of gems and jewels and shit, thinking it would ease my soul. Instead, your voice got me all hard, and now I'm about to get a public indecency charge to go with that rap sheet."

I gasped at his revelation. Sure, I suspected he'd been jerking off, I was no blushing virgin, but I hadn't realized the ramifications of the action in a dimly lit alley until it was too late.

I just sex chatted with a client in public, I realized with a sort of jaw-dropping horror.

"Oh, my god, I'm so sorry, this was *highly unprofessional—*"

He started to chuckle even as I scrambled to readjust my seat and regain my sanity.

"Don't sweat it, sweets. I got my money's worth. And maybe I'll star in the feature program when you get *yours* later, yeah?"

I blushed scarlet from my toes to the tip of my forehead. "I don't know what you mean."

His laughter was damn near maniacal as he stuffed himself back in his pants. "Sure you don't," he teased. "Sorry, sugar, but the party's over. The warden's here to take me home. You've been a great help—"

The line went dead, and I sagged against my chair like I'd run a marathon.

What the actual fuck was that?

JOKER

CHAPTER FIVE

ACE

"Listen, you're not going to like this, Ace . . . "

I stared at the phone in my hand like I could change the words emanating from it with sheer willpower alone. I yanked the damnable thing back to the side of my head with a snarl. "I don't like any part of what you just said. Let's try that again."

On the other end, I heard Spade clear his throat. Nothing rattled Spade; he was like a solid stone monolith, unmoving, unyielding, sturdy, and reliable. So for him to be palpably nervous was concerning.

No, scratch that, it was downright frightening.

"Well, for starters, Joker drove us to a bar—"

The muscles in my neck tightened perceptibly. "Excuse the fuck out of me? Why was Joker driving, fresh out of jail?"

Spade grumbled something that sounded suspiciously like *'pick-pocketed me,'* but surely he hadn't let someone like Joker get the upper hand on him.

Right?

"Surely you're toying with me." I stood and paced back and forth in the warehouse's office, staring out over the garage, where Joker's battered bike stood in one corner. *To think I actually got it out of impound for the disgraceful fucker.*

"I wish I was, boss, but that's not even the half of it—"

"Har dee har har, Spade. Not even half of it? Tell me he didn't—"

Spade sighed. "He did. Plastered. Walked out into the alley and puked his guts out; serves the fuckface right for making me pay his tab at the bar—"

"He did *what* now?" My fingers pinched the bridge of my nose as I closed my eyes and tried counting backward from ten to regain my calm control. "Okay, that's ungentlemanly." I paused, and my eyes opened to mere slits. "What *aren't* you telling me, Spade?"

The other end of the line was deathly silent for a hot minute. Then, so quietly I almost didn't hear it: "He called one of those therapy video lines and told some shrink his real name, then jerked off to their conversation in the alley."

If I gritted my teeth any more, clenched them any tighter, they'd probably crack. "What *else* did he tell them?"

Spade grumbled incoherently, and there was a shuffling on the other end of the line. Joker's nauseous groans filled my ear, but I was well past sympathy.

"Go ahead," Spade demanded, "tell Ace what the fuck you've done."

I held my breath in annoyance and anticipation. I wanted to put my fist through a wall. Or through someone's face. I wanted to drink until I couldn't stand upright, forget all about this shit show in motion.

There would be no such reprieve for me.

Joker coughed, spit off to the side of the receiver, and grumbled at Spade as he took the phone and his voice grew closer. "I may or may not have spilled details about the heist, okay? That what you wanted to hear, that Joker fucked up again? I don't remember what all I said, I was drunk, for fuck's sake—"

"When you get back here, you're going to dry out and cut it cold turkey, you ignorant fuck. I saved your ass on those charges, the least you can do is not run yourself and the rest of us into the ground in gratitude."

I wasn't normally so brusque with Joker. He meant well, he was just a little reckless sometimes. Predictably unpredictable, he'd once called himself, and I had accepted the challenge of taming him and turning him into a working team member, a hell of a heist thief. But lately, something was off with him. It was like the boy from the streets was surfacing once more, his insecurities driving him to do unhinged shit like he was invincible.

He'd nearly died on the sidewalk when he tried to hightail it back here with that haul. And now there was an unknown variable out there, hunting us down for what he stole that the police confiscated.

Of course, they were only allowed to hold it for thirty days unless someone claimed them, as I'd managed to forge some solid shipment documents claiming we'd purchased them, and a doctor's note blaming his blood loss and recklessness on bipolar disease and a lack of his medication. *He simply hadn't noticed he was bleeding out, riding on a manic high,* I'd told them, and they ate it all up.

But this.

This was serious, and this was a loose end. We couldn't afford loose ends. Especially not random therapists who, for all we knew, could be halfway across the world or affiliated with our worst enemies.

"Spade, Joker, get your asses back here. We have some damage control to do." I didn't wait for an answer and flung the phone against the nearest wall with all the force I could muster, laughing darkly as it shattered into a million tiny pieces. "And you," I muttered, turning to face the fourth member of our little gang, Blackjack, who stood in the doorway, eavesdropping. "I need his phone records. I need to know who he called, and where we're going to find them."

Blackjack's lips quirked up in a smirk. "What did the idiot do this time?"

I shook my head, my anger simmering in the wake of the phone smashing. "He called a therapy hotline and spilled his guts to a shrink, that's what."

Blackjack winced. "A clean-up, then."

"Yep." The air in this office was stifling, but I wasn't eager to leave the safety of my office. I disliked chaos in any form, and every time I turned around lately, someone was causing it for me. At least in my office, I had control over things. I could breathe deeply without worrying I was about to be shot or followed, or that someone was watching over my shoulder for me to fail.

If only my father could see me now.

Dear dad was a first-generation Japanese immigrant to the states, and he'd been fleeing the negative impact my grandfather's past dealings with Yakuza had on the whole family. When I realized crime ran in my blood, I abandoned my father's lofty ideas for me to go to medical school and started up the Wildcards.

We weren't anything special, but anyone who's anyone knew for the biggest jobs, you called us.

We didn't work for anyone we didn't want to, and we stayed out of gang politics, happy to stay far away from the bullshit. It's part of what kept us alive.

Blackjack took the seat behind my desk and leaned back in the expensive office chair, kicking the heels of his combat boots up onto the pristinely polished surface. I winced as caked mud flaked off the soles of his shoes and fell across the marble surface.

He regarded me with a raised eyebrow as if he were the leader here and I was but a pawn. "Spade will be happy."

I shrugged, my eyes glued to his feet. "Depends on what we find. No point in killing someone right off. And if they talk to the cops before we get to them?"

A single brow on his pristine face arched upward. "Highly unlikely." He stood, careful not to get too close to me. Blackjack didn't like to be touched. He had a hate/hate relationship with skin-to-skin contact, and I didn't want to know why. He never offered, and I never asked. Sometimes, a man had to have his secrets.

This one was his to keep.

I flicked my hand in the direction of the door, turning my back to him. "Clean out the cage. We're about to have a new house guest." I cleared my throat as he stood and waited until he was all the way to the door before tacking on the last bit. "Oh, and make sure you grab the masks, too. We'll need them."

Blackjack lifted two fingers in mock salute and marched out the door, whistling a pop tune as he disappeared into the belly of the warehouse.

For the life of me, I couldn't figure out what had all the guys on edge. Blackjack wasn't usually so voluntarily helpful, and Joker wasn't usually this unhinged, this desperate, this *uncontrollable.* Spade had been a bit grouchier lately, probably due to being banned from the gym he used to frequent, and less need for heads to be beaten in. His anger and frustration were culminating in a giant ball of fiery bullshit, and I didn't much care to see the fallout.

And then there was me. Hell, I'd actually entertained a call from my *father* the other day, just to be berated for my lack of drive.

Even in death, I wouldn't be able to please that man.

I sighed and cracked my knuckles, settling in on my office couch to await the arrival of my less-than-intelligent thief and his current incompetent watchman, our handy enforcer.

I DOZED for about a half hour before the sound of the automatic garage door rattled noisily around the metal warehouse. With a groan, I straightened and smoothed my hair, mentally fortifying myself to deal with the shitstorm headed straight for us.

My hand moved to the edge of my desk, searching for a phone that wasn't there until I remembered the poor, demolished carcass of the little technological wonder was lying across the room in fragments, thanks to my earlier temper tantrum. I scowled at the empty room and sat behind my desk, the frustration only building.

I couldn't be without a phone for long. It was inevitable I'd be forced to procure one in the next day or two, and I hated going out in public. I could handle it, but the general populace left me with a nasty feeling that crawled over my skin for days after.

The metal steps to the enclosed office were the only warning I got when several pairs of feet started climbing in my direction. I counted the *clank clank* of each step and smiled calmly when the door swung open to admit a very pale, haggard Joker, a very irate Spade, and a smug Blackjack.

Spade took his customary position with his back against the wall, staring out at the room, the door to his left, me to his right, but only slightly, his arms crossed petulantly. His permanent scowl had taken up residence on his face, and the thirty-yard stare he'd perfected was busy burning a hole in my opposite wall.

Blackjack tossed himself flagrantly into a nearby armchair, his legs dangling haphazardly over one side as he picked his teeth with a toothpick and stared at his phone. One foot bobbed up and down, and I smiled to myself, the motion of his leg reminding me of how a child swings their legs back and forth when they're sitting somewhere their feet don't touch.

Joker looked like shit. Whole and complete shit. He leaned over the side of the couch, and while he didn't look like he was in danger of puking anymore, I still subconsciously inched my foot toward my desk trash can, ready to punt it in his direction should he need it. Clumps of his blonde hair hung matted against his face, and the low moan that rolled out of his throat made me cringe.

Poor guy was in need of some fluids and a good rest.

Unfortunately, we didn't have the time for all that.

I leaned forward, propping my elbows on the desk ominously as I steepled my fingers before me. "So," I started, "who wants to tell me what the fuck we're doing to solve this problem?"

Spade growled, Joker groaned, and Blackjack's smirk grew wider. The latter spoke up first.

"Phone records," he muttered, handing me his phone with a look of wariness. "Website's locked down, but I sent a pretty convincing request through the legal channels."

I lifted a brow; it wasn't often that Blackjack took the legal route first. "And the illegal route?"

"Non-sequitur."

Sometimes his vocabulary made my head spin. I shook it off and turned to Joker. "How about you? Anything to say for yourself, anything helpful to add to the conversation?"

Joker squinted against the light and struggled to sit upright. "I'd like to start by saying tequila and I are getting a divorce. It's not working out, and I'm tired of the hangover after a fight."

Crickets. Fucking Crickets.

Of all the times to land a joke, he chose now.

What a motley crew I had here.

"Jokes aside, you buffoon. What were you *thinking?!"*

He winced at my tone and withdrew further into the couch. I had no time for his hijinks, though, and slammed my palms flat against the top of my desk. "Dammit, Joker, you're putting us all at risk here! First, you take this job, which we all agreed was suspect, and it turns out our initial decision was *correct.* Then you get yourself injured mid-heist, drive off into the night with a bag of stolen jewels on your back, and get picked up by the fucking *authorities.* You nearly *died,* and yet your first instinct after being released from jail—which wasn't easy to do, by the way—is to go get plastered, nearly catch a public indecency charge, and spill your secrets to a complete stranger." My chest heaved with the force of my words, and I fought the urge to clear my desk and strangle him. "Does that about cover it, Joker?"

He had the common sense to look properly cowed, but beneath that apologetic grimace, I could see a storm brewing. When he sobered up, there'd be a fight, or something close to it. And when Joker started a fight, it got bad, really, *really* fast.

I made a note to try and head him off one-on-one later, before that pot boiled over.

"So, what are we going to do about the situation?"

For the first time since walking into the impromptu family meeting, Spade cleared his throat and let out a little chuckle. "Why do I get the idea you've got a fucked-up plan already working?"

My answering smirk was confirmation enough.

"We're going to kidnap them and see what they know."

J
A
JOKER
A
K
K

CHAPTER SIX
MALLORY

After Friday's late call with the handsome, drunk exhibitionist, I'd been flustered as fuck. Nothing could calm the buzzing feeling that ran rampant beneath my skin, not a hot shower, not a cup of coffee, not a shot of whiskey, nothing.

Okay, so the vibrator on my bedside table had helped a little.

A lot.

Still, when I woke up the next morning, refreshed, alive, and with a thankfully empty email inbox, I thought that was the end of that. My superiors wouldn't go snooping through the recordings unless absolutely necessary, so the only two people who could ever access that transcript were me and the idiot who'd jacked his dick to the sound of my voice.

I had high hopes that he woke up ashamed of himself and embarrassed enough not to pursue the matter.

I moved about my kitchen all morning, cleaning up while I had free time. My calendar was blissfully open, and I hadn't scheduled a single call for the night, so it was almost like fate reached in to rearrange my peaceful night when my phone rang for the first time that day.

I answered it without checking the caller ID, too preoccupied with feeding the cats to bother.

"Hello?"

I heard a breath on the other side, but nobody spoke.

"Hello? Is anyone there?" I tried again, hoping this wasn't one of those prank calls. I'd taken steps to make sure my cellphone remained unlisted, but it was impossible to make it through life without your number being leaked to some telemarketer or another. "Listen, if this is a joke, it's not funny, asshole!"

I hit the disconnect button and set the phone on my dining room table. The second time the voiceless breather called, I threatened them with the cops. By the third time my phone rang, I was at my wit's end and frustrated with the whole day. I was also bent over the washing machine, struggling to remove a few socks from the bottom of my top-load washer.

I marched into the living room and yanked the phone off the table with no little amount of aggravation. "Listen, fuckface, if you're just gonna breathe in my ear all night, let me save you the time—"

"Easy, killer, who pissed in your cheerios?"

I relaxed immensely at the sound of my best friend's voice. "Oh, shit, sorry, Gem. I've had one of those heavy-breathing weirdos calling me all day."

I juggled the phone as she laughed on the other end. "That's ridiculous. I'm glad I don't get those calls. You've gotta stop working therapy for that sketchy website.

I smiled as I thought back on my last call. "It's not all bad, and I seriously doubt this is related to my job as a tele-therapist. Besides," I hedged, "our info is private on there. I'm not in any danger."

Gemma chuckled. "Famous last words, friendo." I heard her shuffle around in the background, cursing at something. "So, I'm calling because I want you to go out with me tonight. Let's cut loose together, have a good time."

My lips pursed as I rolled that idea over in my head. "Where would we go? I don't know if I have an outfit suitable for some of your swankier clubs." The dryer dinged pleasantly as I closed the door and started the cycle, and I moved slowly into the next room with a full basket of clothes I knew would probably wrinkle horribly before I managed to fold them.

"What if I told you we'd just go to a local joint?"

I paused in the hallway outside my bedroom door, the basket balanced on my knee. "Maybe I could come up with something suitable."

"Maybe I'd tell you to wear something sexy. Slayted is playing live tonight."

Slayted was Gemma's favorite band, and she never missed an opportunity to see them in person. And if we were being honest, the band members weren't bad looking in the least.

I could suffer through a night of loud music and drunk idiots for Gemma. And I hadn't been out in forever, so it might do me good to leave this apartment and cut loose for a night.

"You know what? I'm in, Gem. Just tell me when and where to meet you."

Her excited squeal on the other end was ear-splitting, but I simply winced and smiled. It made me happy to hear her excited to spend time together. To be honest, there was a solid ball of anticipation building in me, too. I had a feeling tonight was going to be wild, and I wanted to enjoy the ride.

After exchanging details, we hung up, and I set to work clearing the dreaded laundry task off my schedule. If there was one thing on the planet I hated more than laundry, it was dishes, and at least I had a machine that did most of the work for me there. The washer and dryer cleaned clothing, sure, but that left folding and putting it all away, and I dreaded the constant back and forth.

I skipped dinner since I'd had a late lunch and made a promise to myself to grab food after the concert. Then I dove headfirst into my closet until I found an outfit suitable for a grunge bar featuring a rock band.

The miniskirt barely hit mid-thigh, but the zipper that ran up the front of it was a nice touch, and the chains that draped the waist made me feel like I'd stand out less, ironically, considering the company. The fishnet stockings I slipped on underneath just made me feel more badass. I paired it with a sheer black top and a sexy lace bra and yanked on a pair of combat boots I hadn't used since college. I almost felt a bit ridiculous, wearing all the metal and dark colors as I slipped on a few chains, but black had been my best friend once upon a time, so it was like slipping into the embrace of an old friend.

It was worlds apart from the nice lavender blouse and beige pants I wore for my therapy sessions with clients. But there was the professional me, and there was the real me. I just wished society would catch up sooner rather than later so I could merge the two and be comfortable as I was.

I felt powerful in the outfit, regardless of the skin it showed off, and I knew I could defend myself against a grabby guy if necessary.

To reinforce the point, I double-checked my purse for the trusty bottle of mace and found the thin pink tube exactly where it should be. It wasn't much, but I could run in combat boots if I had to, and I could throw down if cornered. Mom and some solid self-defense courses had guaranteed that.

The sun began to set outside my apartment windows, and I basked in the glow of the evening for a moment in my kitchen, just taking a moment to enjoy the quiet calm of the onset of dusk. The birds had begun to calm on the power lines and windowsills, the street was mostly quiet, save for a car here and there, and the apartment above mine was thankfully empty of the tenants who had harbored a pet elephant last month.

All was right in the world.

Tonight would be a good night.

I could feel it in the air.

The auto feeder for the cats was freshly filled, their litter changed, and the water nice and cool, ice cubes topping it off like the spoiled bastards they were. Still, they stared at me as if I were about to abandon them to the wilds and never return.

Just like they did every time I left to go out somewhere.

I reached down and patted Alpine on his furry white head, smiling when he turned and abandoned me for the comfort of his window seat. "Okay, asshole, you know I'll be back tomorrow." He didn't respond except to twitch the tip of his tail, so I turned to his brother. "You'll miss me, won't you, Rocky?"

The two of them were the only steady thing in my life. I adopted them when I got my first apartment and realized I didn't like living entirely alone. They were just enough of a presence to remind me I wasn't wandering alone in a void, but not enough of a presence to cause me any annoyance. They wouldn't ever leave their socks ten miles from the laundry basket; they wouldn't piss all over the toilet seat and leave the fucker up in the middle of the night. They never ate the last of my leftovers and never put a swallow of milk in the carton back in the fridge for me to find. All in all, I'd had worse roommates.

I grabbed my purse as the first strings of the nighttime symphony of the city started up, closed my open window beside the kitchen sink, and grabbed my house keys. As a last thought, I stuck my trusty butterfly knife in the inside liner of my right boot and nodded to myself.

Last line of defense, if the mace wasn't enough. A girl could never be too safe.

The hall light of my floor flickered ominously as I slid the deadbolt into place and checked my doorknob, satisfied when it didn't budge. Months of abuse reflected itself in the sticky, dark, mottled pattern of stains that painted the hall carpet like a camouflage. It made me cringe, and I made another mental note—call the leasing agent about having a cleaner come up here and take care of it.

I wouldn't set a bag of groceries on the floor while I unlocked the door, it was so disgusting. I could only imagine the things that had coagulated between the threads of the ragged, thin excuse for flooring.

The walk down the stairs was no better. The railing had lost its old glossy finish, and the wood was fractured in places, peeling in others, the user as likely to get several splinters as they were to slip and fall on the moist metal surface of the stairs. There was no rhyme or reason to why the steps were wet all the time, but it was as if there was a leak somewhere in the wall that just seeped out into the carpet and the walls and leaked down the side of each step until you got to the bottom, where the water just . . . disappeared.

It was one of the many mysteries I didn't get paid to answer, so I shook it off and walked away.

The cool evening air made the skin on my arms and legs pebble with goosebumps, but I shook it off and steeled myself against the sudden gust, waiting it out. Sure enough, the wind ebbed away, and the residual heat of the summer night was once again stifling.

I pulled my phone out of my purse as I began the short trek to the bar where I was supposed to meet Gemma and one of our other friends, a girl named Sacha, whom we'd gone to school with once upon a time.

As I wove in and out of the rest of the bodies on the sidewalk, some dressed like they'd just left work, others looking somewhat like me—dressed up for a night on the town in one form or another. I paid them little mind except to move between pairs here and there. The wind kicked up again, and couples leaned into one another for body heat.

Honestly, it made my heart give a little pang of longing.

I hadn't the best track record with men, but I wasn't bad off. I just had some standards. The last guy I dated was a real A-1 Asshole, capital A and all. But he was great in bed and had what my mom called a 'sustainable job.' He wanted kids, too, somewhere down the road, so there was a mutual understanding of a future plan.

But he had a temper, and he liked to put people down when he was angry.

After being called needy for about six months, I handed him his walking papers and signed a new lease elsewhere. Even took the cat.

Man, I loved that cat.

A shiver crawled down my back, even though it was humid and hot, and the wind was missing from the air once more, and I glanced around as a hand went to the back of my neck. The hairs there were raised, and the creepy feeling I'd had when the phone calls had consisted of only breathing earlier today returned with a vengeance.

Against everything I stood for, my body froze, and I scanned the people walking behind me, looking for someone else who'd stopped suddenly, but I found nobody. Not a single person on the walkways paid me any mind, and I shook it off.

I was just letting those phone calls get to me, that's it.

Snap out of it, woman.

I shook my head and reached inside my purse, my hand curling around the can of mace in a reassuring gesture. I walked like that the whole way to the bar and didn't stop to look around again until I walked through the doors of ShockWave.

JOKER

CHAPTER SEVEN
JOKER

A day of rest and recuperation made a world of difference in my demeanor, and a small part of me was secretly thrilled that we were about to do this.

I hadn't planned to see those beautiful amber eyes in real life. It didn't matter that she'd be bound and gagged and tossed into a metal cage befitting a fucking circus bear. I'd get to see her and that was all that really mattered.

A part of me felt ashamed of the situation. I felt bad that this unsuspecting woman would end up a captive because I got wasted and she happened to be unfortunately assigned to take my spur-of-the-moment, drunken call of shame. But then I remembered the ramifications if she went to the police and reminded myself it was a necessary evil.

We had to make sure she wouldn't spill what she knew.

Had to find out how much I actually told her, cause I didn't remember.

All I remembered about that video call was that her voice sounded so pretty when she said my name that I was harder than a rock thinking about how it would sound in my bed, as she screamed it loud enough for my little gang family to hear.

Maybe I'd get to fuck her before the guys did her in, or whatever they had planned.

I really hope they didn't kill her. I would forever hate myself if the only way to keep my guys safe was to end her. Something so pretty shouldn't be snuffed out.

I wriggled in the backseat and glanced at Blackjack out of the corner of my eye. He sat behind the driver's seat, where Spade currently sat, and his eyes were trained on his phone screen as the city sped by outside. The lights got dimmer with every block, and the traffic thinned out substantially as the seconds slowly ticked by.

In the seat before me, Ace cleared his throat and rotated to face us. "Location, Blackjack?"

His brows furrowed as he swiped his finger across the screen. "Most recent ping is a bar called ShockWave."

I instantly perked up. "ShockWave? There's a new local band playing there tonight. Bound to be busy up front, plenty of bodies to blend into."

Spade *hmph'ed* from behind the wheel. "Also means increased security. A secure rear entrance for the band. Lots of cameras."

I rolled my eyes so hard into the back of my head that it made my temples throb. "And since when does a little challenge scare *you,* Spade?"

"Never," was his curt reply.

I turned to Ace, but his scowl was that one all of us knew meant he wasn't pleased with the situation.

Ace hated having to improvise on the fly.

"We need a new plan." His eyes moved to BlackJack, but he was busy staring at his screen again, watching the little red dot flicker impatiently. "Any suggestions?"

BlackJack was usually content to let the rest of us come up with the plan. He was more of an order taker, in the long run. But something felt different about tonight, and it bowled us all over when his head lifted to stare pointedly out the window as he spoke.

"We could watch her until she leaves the bar. Pick her off the street somewhere less obvious. Perhaps herd her into a dark alley."

I blinked stupidly at him. It wasn't that the idea was a bad one—on the contrary, it was brilliant. If we could strategically lead her away from the crowded sidewalk, there would be no chance of witnesses, no chance we'd have to take several hostages instead of just one.

But it was the first time he'd volunteered a plan.

I wasn't the only one reeling. Spade looked up into the rearview mirror with wide eyes and raised brows. Ace just stared with his jaw hanging there like some sort of unhinged cabinet door. I was sure whatever look sat on my face was a truly stunned one, as well.

BlackJack didn't even bother to look at us. He didn't volunteer any more info, either.

We were all dressed to the nines in black, some of our outfits a bit more ostentatious than others. Ace was draped in a black trenchcoat with dull silver buttons and rivets, a pair of tight leather pants, and some fancy-ass black boots with small heels. Out of all of us, he was the least concerned with his image, but most concerned with it at the same time. He didn't care if people threw slurs in his direction, because his presence spoke for itself. And if all else failed, well, Spade could smash someone's face in to drive home the point that you don't fuck with us.

Spade had on a pair of torn-up black jeans, a black tee, and a hoodie over that. His sunglasses were pretty obviously out of place at night, but they only added to his wildly unhinged persona. He even had a pair of leather gloves that he slowly slid on at the next light.

Spooky, but not too wild.

BlackJack was an enigma in and of himself. His clothes looked like he'd walked out of an old emo-punk clothing store. His black boots had an inch of sole on them and reminded me of the curb stompers from American History X, just darker. He had on tight black jeans, a solid black tank top, and more bangles and bracelets than I could count. You'd definitely hear the guy coming from a mile away.

Then there was me. I had tossed on a pair of black cargo pants, some old-school Chuck Taylors, and a long-sleeved black turtleneck. Basic and forgettable, which was what I thought we were going for.

Apparently, I missed some sort of memo.

The SUV pulled into an empty alleyway a block down from the bar, and Ace gave us all one more glance as we steeled ourselves for the mission. Tonight, we weren't just stealing some jewels, lifting a safe, or pulling a con. Tonight, our target was a living one, something we'd sworn never to cross over into. Tonight, we broke one of our cardinal rules and stole a human being from the streets. It was very possible it ended in a murder, too.

"Spade, you stay close to the ride. Watch the main exit in the front in case she slips out without our notice."

Spade nodded and slid his seat back a tiny bit as he lit up a cigarette, the glowing red ember the only light in the cab of the vehicle.

Ace cleared his throat and turned to us. "Blackjack, you take the bar. Keep some sort of drink in your hand, but please show more self-control than Joker does when faced with alcohol." I blanched but didn't back down. Ace turned to me next, a little frown on his lips. "You stay along the walls. I don't want her to see you if I can help it, but you're a shit getaway driver, and you know it."

"And what about you?" Spade grumbled, tossing a nonchalant glance in our leader's direction.

Ace grinned mischievously. "I'm going to slip into the crowd and mingle."

AN HOUR AND A HALF LATER, not only had we failed to pick out the target in question, but the place was uncomfortably packed, and the volume level was intense and headache-inducing. I could use a stiff drink or two, but Ace and BlackJack headed me off both times I tried to slink away to the bar. Finally, I felt a tap on my shoulder and turned to see Ace with a scowl on his face, a very puzzled BlackJack at his side.

"What's up, guys? Still haven't found her yet?" I teased, bobbing my head to the beat of the screaming rock band.

Blackjack's jaw ticked. "I know she's here." His eyes cast back to the phone screen again, which he zoomed in and showed to me.

Sure enough, dead center of the square, a red dot flickered, surrounded by three closely-grouped blue dots, which I assumed were us, and one a slight bit away, which had to be Spade. As we watched, the band in the background died off, replaced by a DJ, and the red dot moved toward our three blue dots.

Blackjack made a beeline for the wall, where he could avoid the biggest crush of bodies as everyone either rushed for drinks or a bathroom break. Intermission was never long, so it was every man and woman for themselves. Ace and I quickly scanned the crowd, but I didn't pick out the amber eyes I'd been enamored with from the start.

And then I heard it.

Heard *her.*

"I need a drink, Gem, don't go far. I'll be right back."

My whole body whirled to face the source of the voice, dick already hardening behind the zipper of my pants at the flash of memory from the night before when I'd stroked it to that same voice.

There she was, her gorgeous black hair draped over one shoulder in a long ponytail, dressed head-to-toe in black, like us. Her long legs were wrapped in fishnets and tucked into some serious platform boots, and my eyes followed the trail of small squares up her legs until they ran into the bottom hem of that salacious miniskirt that gripped her hips like a second skin.

"Ace, I found her," I stage-whispered over my shoulder, and his eyes followed my gaze until he saw what I saw, too, and his jaw dropped almost comically.

"The one with the see-through shirt and sexy as fuck bra?" he breathed, his hands balled into fists at the sight.

"That's her."

He frowned, glancing over at me. "How can you be sure? She doesn't look the same as the photo BlackJack found."

"Once you've come to the sound of a woman's voice alone, you tend to remember that particular sonata when it's played back to you."

That gave him some pause. "Fair enough."

Her friends waved her off to the bar, and I watched the two girls she'd been in the middle of talk together in hushed whispers until a couple of guys wandered over and caught their attention. They looked like part of the band, not that I'd know one from the other in here, and I scowled as these 'friends' abandoned the vixen in black at the bar to trot off with their newest flings for the night.

One glance to the bar revealed their third already knew about their flighty escape, and she slammed a bill on the counter as Ace and I watched, downed three shots of whatever she'd just ordered one after the other, and wiped at her ruby red lips before marching pointedly to the front door without a single glance over her shoulder.

Now was our chance.

"Let's move," I whispered to Ace before I flipped my phone open and dialed Spade.

He picked up on the first ring. "Go for Spade."

"She's on the move, and she's ditched her friends. Ace and I are in pursuit."

I hung up on him just in time to see BlackJack appear on my left. Without a word, we tailed our target into the night air, the three of us splitting up at the corner to trail her from safe distances. With Ace on one side of the street, me on the other, and BlackJack circling around to head her off, there was no way she could get away from us.

Was there?

J
A
JOKER
A
K

CHAPTER EIGHT
MALLORY

I'd had a strange feeling all night that something was very, very wrong, but I couldn't shake it, no matter what I did. Even when I was safely inside the bar, wedged in the middle of the girls, the lingering feeling of being watched remained embedded in my very bones.

When Gemma and Sacha suggested that we hit a second bar with the band, I politely declined, though I thought they'd stay with me until I left. But they bailed at the first opportunity, and I really couldn't be mad. I wasn't the wild, daring friend they wanted me to be. I was super careful and always cautious about strange places with strangers. They wanted to fly by the seat of their pants, rushing through their twenties like wild children in search of themselves.

So that left me, now slightly buzzing from the three shots of tequila meant for us to share, walking on my own in a seedy part of town at two in the morning.

Fucking fantastic.

I walked a bit faster as the people alongside me thinned out and slipped my hand into my purse, gripping that can of mace like my life depended on it. I probably wouldn't need it, I'd made this walk a million times, but the thought of being unprepared was too much to overcome.

I relaxed a bit at the next light, but the sound of someone coughing behind me made every hair on my body stand on end. I took a chance, slipped my mace into my purse, and pulled out a makeup compact. I flipped it open just high enough to look behind me, and all the color drained from my face.

Standing a few feet behind me, his eyes piercing and hard, was a man dressed in all black.

At first glance, he could be anyone from the same concert I had just come from. But something felt off about the way he stared over me, like the whole point was to look less conspicuous. It felt like someone trying too hard. His silver hair was immaculate, not a hair out of place, the tone and shine to it marking the dye job as salon-level, not some rush job in your cousin's bathroom over the sink. His trenchcoat gaped open to show a mesh top and perfectly tailored pants, the whole thing a little *too* put together for a grunger at a bar concert in the inner city.

I cringed as a car at the light blew its horn at me, and I started to walk across the road without looking.

A split second before it hit me, I heard the second horn, saw the blinding glare of approaching headlights; I had a second to think *well this is ironic,* and then I was being yanked back onto the sidewalk by a firm grip on my arm. I fell with a groan of pain and quickly raised my hands in apology to the passing car. The driver just ignored me and drove on, obviously putting me in the rear view of his car and his mind. Before I could get up, the guy with the clean-cut looks stood before me and offered a hand up, a disarming smile on his lips.

"That was a close one, miss. Let me help you up."

He tilted his head and waited patiently, but something about the angle of his smile screamed *predator,* and I knew better than to ignore the feeling bubbling in my gut.

I waved his offer off and smiled hesitantly. "Thank you, but I'll be alright."

His eyes narrowed slightly. "No worries. I'm just glad I was here."

Yeah, I just bet you are. If it weren't for him, I wouldn't have run like a skittish bitch into an intersection with a green light. *"Me, too,"* I tittered nervously. "Well, thanks, and, uh, see you around," I mumbled, rushing off without another word or a backward glance.

I upped the pace and hustled across the road and down the block, making a note of the street sign as I passed it.

Three more blocks to my neighborhood, another two after that to home.

I could make it.

I took a deep breath and reached back into my bag to grab my phone. If I could just call Gemma, or even give the appearance that I was on the phone with someone, I could deter anyone from following me. I could make myself less of a target.

I didn't get the chance. Across the street, a lone man turned in my direction, and with a sudden, sickening feeling in the pit of my stomach, I realized how fucked I was.

I recognized that man.

He was the man from the video therapy call.

Shit, shit, shit.

I took off at a dead sprint, pulling the can of mace from my purse once more as blondie darted across the road and headed straight for me.

Fuck.

My lungs burned as my boots slammed against the ground, but I pushed through it, noticing with a start that the man who'd saved me from the car was now running behind me, gaining ground with frightening speed. His eyes were no longer even slightly warm and welcoming, the whole vibe he gave off reeking of a predator chasing its prey.

I refused to be prey.

I could get away. I was fast. I could fight.

There were only two of them.

Three blocks from my building, I darted into a small alley that would cut the distance in half. The two pursuers would have to follow me down the narrow road to catch me, but I knew I had enough of a head start to make it out of the alley before they got close enough. And there was a 24-hr convenience store directly across the road from where the alley popped out, so as long as I could make it to the end of that cobblestone hall and launch myself across the street, I'd be home free.

I clutched my mace tighter and took a deep breath, preparing to kick it into high gear the second I plunged into darkness. My old days of running track waxed fresh in my mind as I breathed in through my nose and out through my mouth, careful to take deep, slow breaths in an effort to not tire out early. I let my focus narrow to each step on the pavement, each breath I took, and every inch of distance I covered. I blocked out the sound of the two men on my heels. I couldn't afford to let the panic set in, or I'd slow, and my body would surrender before I could escape.

Ten more feet to the end of the alley.

I was almost there.

And then, the universe opened its eyes and decided, for whatever reason, to fuck me hard with no lube, and my foot caught a loose brick in the cobblestones and slid out from underneath me. My pace stuttered for only a minute, but the damage was done, and a hand clamped around mine, long fingers curling around my thin wrist and tightening ominously.

"Fuck you, buddy!" I screamed, turning my body to the side as the hand with the canned mace swung around to point straight at him. With a triumphant yell, I pressed the button at the top and let loose the painful pepper spray directly into his wide-open eyes. His painful howl was like music to my ears as his grip loosened and he released me to claw at his eyes.

I didn't stop to see if the therapy session man stopped to help his *friend*—because there was no other explanation. That *had* to be one of his buddies. I kept on running, dropping the now empty can on the ground in my haste.

Five more feet.

I let out a triumphant whoop as the realization that I was about to get away, that all of the training and preparation and nervous habits had all come together to save my *fucking life.*

Take that, Gemma. Bet you'll never underestimate my location tracker shit again.

And then it all came crashing down around me as a blacked-out SUV pulled in front of the entrance to the alley, the same one I barreled toward, and stopped on the curb. The driver's door opened and a tall behemoth of a man stepped out, his wild, long, red hair flying in the breeze. My brain short-circuited as his eyes settled on mine, a feral grin splitting his face in half as he slid across the hood of the massive SUV and headed straight for me, even as I skidded to a halt and tried to circle the rear of his vehicle.

"Catch her, Spade!" someone behind me yelled, and I yelped as my body arched in an attempt to dodge his hands, but I wasn't fast enough, and his meaty fist wrapped itself around my bicep and yanked back, sending me off balance for a split second. I registered the smug smirk of satisfaction on his lips as he decided he had won. It only lasted for a second, though, as I twisted in his grip and planted a boot in his chest, climbing him like a tree. I cleared his shoulders as he struggled to get a grip on me, and I took that opportunity to use my weight and send him to his back.

The dude I'd maced was being helped down the alley by his blonde compatriot, and they weren't far away now.

I was well and truly cornered, but they wouldn't catch me going down without a fight.

Dude on the ground with the fire engine hair groaned, but his hands reached up and gripped one of my boots, holding me in place. He glanced up at me, and I watched him blush—*since when did criminal kidnappers blush?*—as he caught sight of my skirt and then proceeded to look up it.

Pervert.

I twisted my foot, but his grip held, and at the last second, I decided to reach down and yank the hidden blade from the side of my captive boot, flipping it open with insane speed. I grimaced and slammed the damn knife straight down, gagging a little as it slid into his shoulder like fucking butter.

He hissed in pain, his face sickeningly pale as he dropped me, and by the grace of gods I didn't believe in, I managed to fling myself forward and resume my escape. I turned for the back of the SUV, determined to outrun the now-mostly injured team of criminals.

That's it! I'm home free! I could practically reach out and graze the taillights with the tips of my fingers. My whole body lightened with relief. I was going to make it out alive. I was going to escape.

And then a fourth body appeared seemingly out of nowhere in front of me, and two solid arms wrapped tightly around me in an embrace, tugging me against the lean, toned torso of a man who stood a foot taller than me. I felt one of his hands clamp around my mouth, and he turned me around to face my assailants with a chuckle.

"What happened to you three?" he asked with an air of disinterest, like he couldn't care any less what their answer was.

Mister Mace, as I'd decided to call him, looked fit to kill me as his eyes crawled over my immobilized form with fury. "More trouble than you're worth," he spat, his eyes still watering.

I waggled my brows at him, mumbling insults behind the hand over my mouth.

Blondie chuckled and peered around me and the tall guy to his friend with a knife in his chest, who was now on his feet. "That looks painful, Spade."

"Serrated butterfly," he grunted in acknowledgment. "Hurts like a sonofabitch."

The knife man moved to stand in front of me as he gripped the handle of my favorite knife and yanked it from the meaty flesh of his shoulder. I smiled as he groaned, but my glory was short-lived as I watched his dick harden behind those tight pants on his hips.

Sick fuck was getting hot over being hurt.

He brought the blade to my face, and I flinched away as much as possible in the iron grip of *Jack and the Beanstalk* behind me. The cool metal warred with the warm blood on its surface, and he dragged the damn thing down my jawline, over the pulsing artery in my throat. The trail of blood it left wasn't my own, because he didn't push the blade hard enough to break my skin. Still, his wild eyes fixated on the path the knife tip blazed, and I grimaced as he leaned in and licked his blood off my skin, waggling his brows at me as he pulled away.

"I don't think I've been this hard for a woman in a long ass time," he groaned, rolling his hips into me pointedly. "I hope you fight us the whole way."

"Back off, Spade," the maced one ordered, and his obedient lap dog moved back with a dejected whine, pocketing my fucking butterfly knife.

The one holding me moved the arm that held me in place and dragged me into the backseat of the SUV. The injured one climbed in behind the first guy, and the two I'd outrun took the front seats. Mace man was busy trying to flush his eyes with a bottle of water in the passenger seat as blondie started the SUV and peeled out, carefully sticking to the dark alleys and back roads.

The last thing I saw before a bag was slipped over my head was the look of apology blondie shot me in the rearview mirror.

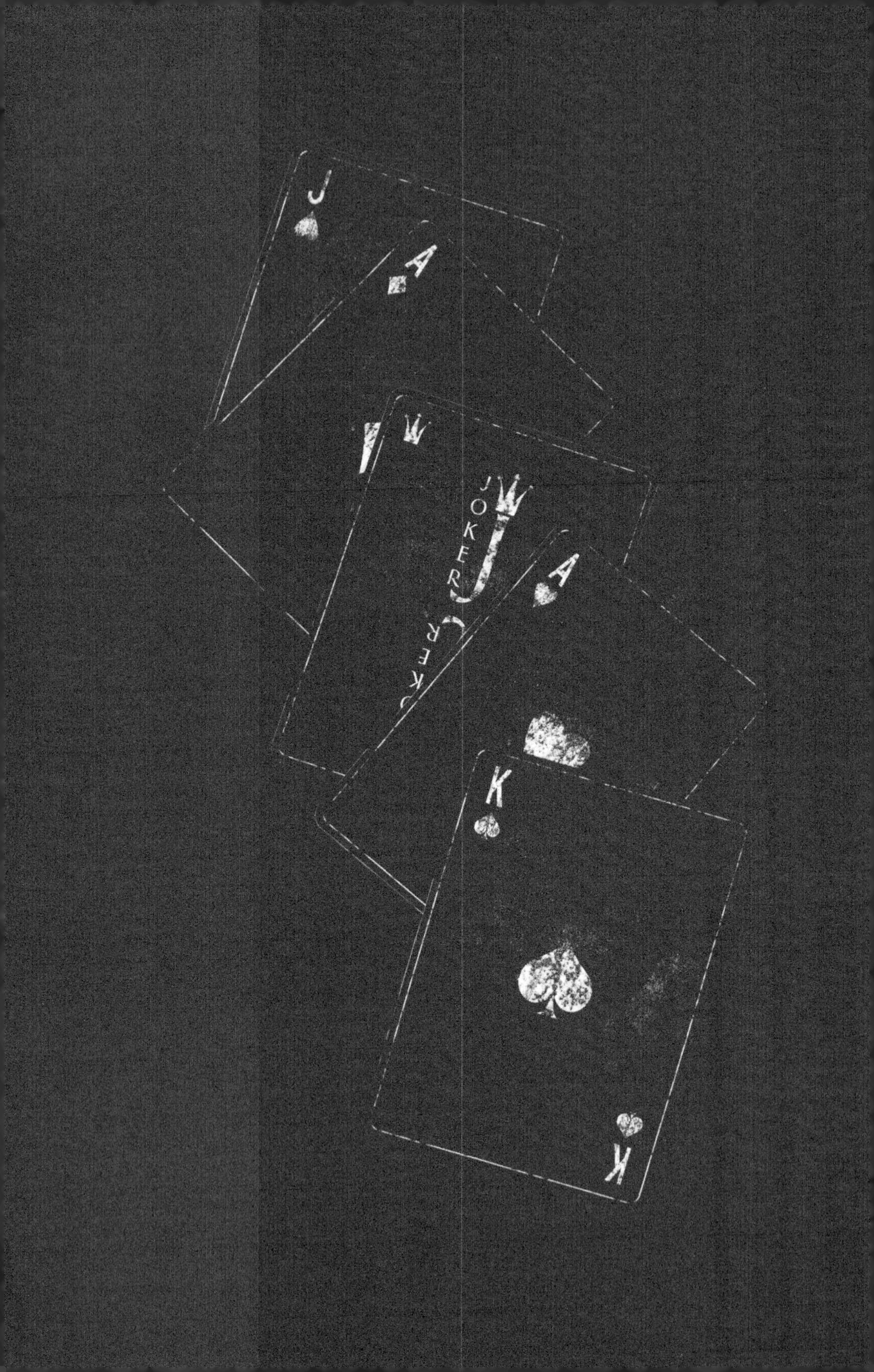
JOKER

CHAPTER NINE
SPADE

The gaping hole in my shoulder hurt like a sonofabitch. It bled freely into the threads of my black tee, and thankfully, the color of my shirt managed to mask most of the damage.

Didn't mean it wasn't painful as all get out to move the fucking thing.

I hadn't been injured by a target in a long ass time, and I certainly hadn't pegged this girl for the type to carry a blade in her *boot,* for fuck's sake. The damn thing was gonna need stitches, and I'd be lucky if I hadn't done lasting damage when I ripped the fucking serrated edges from my muscle. Still, I had to commend her survival instincts. It'd be a shame if we had to off her now. Girls like that were rare.

I watched her kick at BlackJack as he slipped the hood over her head, smiling when he groaned and cupped his balls in pain.

"Better watch her; she's got a hell of a fire," I drawled lazily, grunting as the next pothole jostled my arm painfully. The fucking thing hung there at my side, limp and useless, but I couldn't even be mad at her.

I felt alive, perhaps more than I had in a long time. I didn't want to analyze the feeling too closely yet, so I settled in for a bumpy ride and let BlackJack handle the spitfire in question.

As the lights grew brighter, then spaced themselves out in wider gaps, I watched the familiar streets of our neighborhood go zipping by. Behind the bag, the girl we'd kidnapped was eerily silent, which was not only odd for someone who'd fought so spectacularly, but worrisome. I signaled for BlackJack to swap me seats, and he shot the girl a scowl before nodding, probably eager to be away from the hellion's dangerous feet.

I carefully positioned my injured arm away from her range of motion and laid my free hand on top of hers in what I assumed was a reassuring move. The speed at which her hand yanked back away from mine devastated my ego.

"Fucking hope we have something at home to take out the sting," Ace mumbled from the front seat, shaking his head like a dog as tears streamed from his closed eyes. "Good thing this isn't my first rodeo being maced, and whatever she had in that can wasn't a full-strength solution."

"Companies that water down a self-defense mace for women should be ashamed of themselves," Joker quipped as he swerved to avoid another pothole, hitting two for his troubles. "Could you imagine?"

Ace stared at him wordlessly through thin slits of eyeballs. "The irony in the air tonight is thicker than fuck."

BlackJack snorted beside me. "Idiots, the lot of you."

When we finally arrived back at the compound, I made to pull the girl out of the car but was jerked back by BlackJack, who gestured to my arm.

"I'll take her. You get the door."

I shook my head in stunned silence and did as he commanded, slipping out of the car behind him with a grunt of discomfort. The pain radiated throughout my whole shoulder, and the sinking feeling as I realized I'd be immobile and half-worthless for a few weeks really hit hard. BlackJack moved around the back of the SUV quickly, but Joker beat him to the girl's door and was busy pulling her out of it.

BlackJack scowled but said nothing and turned on his heels to follow me into the finished half of the warehouse. Ace stormed off to his room, probably in search of something to clean off his face with, and BlackJack wandered into a nearby bathroom in search of a medical kit. I didn't expect him to stitch me; hell, he'd already touched the captive so many damn times with literally no recoil or sneer of disgust that it had us all confused and reeling.

Blackjack never touched *anyone.* It was part of his creed at this point. So for him to voluntarily step in and handle the chick . . .

Weird, at the very least.

Cause for concern, maybe. One never knew with him.

Joker had the girl from the SUV cradled in his arms like a blushing bride, and I chuckled at the sight they made, her with that burlap bag over her pretty head, him with a semi-permanent grimace from a muscle cramp. I'd venture to bet it had been a very, very long time since he'd had to chase someone like that. Probably damaged his pride a bit to be bested by a chick.

I know it would aggravate me, the knife to my shoulder, if she hadn't looked so fucking hot and badass while doing it.

Something told me if she'd had that knife in the other boot, if I'd have reached for that foot instead, I'd probably be dead.

The thought sent a thrill racing through my bloodstream, and I groaned and reached down to rearrange myself as my cock decided that was the hottest thing it had ever heard.

Good to know I got off on my own mortality. Maybe I could get her to stab me again while I fucked into her tight little body—

Anywhoo.

I hobbled over to the cage we dragged to the center of our commons area and took a seat on one of the nearby couches that had been unceremoniously shoved against the walls to make room. My eyes followed Joker as he eyed the cage with some disdain before he finally crouched and walked inside with his captive.

If he felt so damn bad, maybe this would teach him to keep his mouth shut.

Talking meant casualties.

Every. Damn. Time.

The girl let herself be deposited on the floor of the cage, the fight leeched out of her like a slow leak in a tire. I narrowed my eyes and watched her as Joker backed out of the metal prison and closed the door almost apologetically. The girl's legs were pressed tightly together, but her knees were bent, and the skirt rode up to the swell of her ass, showing just enough of her thighs to make a man wanna cream. Before I could stop myself, a flash of what she'd look like bent over a desk while I peeled those stockings from the luscious thighs she clenched tight ran rampant across my mind. I stifled a groan and readjusted my dick once more, catching BlackJack's disapproval as he took a seat behind me, medical kit in hand.

I eyed him warily. "Where's Joker?"

He pointed a thumb over his shoulder toward the kitchen. "Helping Ace."

A man of few words, indeed.

"So that means I'm stuck with you, eh?" I tried to chuckle and was rewarded by a stinging tug at the edges of this damn puncture wound. "Ow."

"Sit still, you buffoon," BlackJack muttered, his fingernails scraping my rigid abdomen as he tugged my shirt over my head with quick efficiency. His lips curled up in distaste at the contact as he flung the shirt away, and I breathed a sigh of relief at the familiar reaction to touch from the stoic man.

BlackJack could always be relied on for three things—few words with maximum effect, paranoia, and an aversion to skin-on-skin touch. When he willingly held onto the captive girl, it sent a huge shockwave of questioning and confusion through the whole crew. But this, his hissing recoil as he poked and prodded at the soft, fleshy wound on my shoulder, the way he gingerly held himself away from me as far as possible, his narrowed eyes as he dumped some water over my sore skin to wash away any dirt or grime, it was all a familiar reaction from the man I'd worked with for the last three years in this crew.

Perhaps I was making a big deal out of nothing.

We were all keyed up in our own ways, and I'd been stabbed. Maybe this was shock setting in. Maybe I would die here simply because I couldn't stop worrying about why BlackJack was touching people all of a sudden.

Not now, dick.

I shifted in the chair, and BlackJack slapped me upside the head for my efforts to rearrange subtly. "Sit still, asshole; I'm nearly done."

He stuck two butterfly bandages on my shoulder to hold the wound together and slapped a gauze pad atop it, the force of which made me wince. He made quick work of the bandage wrap in his hands, tugging it around my shoulder and upper arm until I was covered and secure.

"How long will I be like this?" I complained as he reached back into the bag and pulled out a fabric sling. "Oh, no. You're not making me wear that—"

"Try to lift your arm, idiot," he ground out, waiting patiently for me to be a recalcitrant asshole and do it. I knew what the result would be. I'd hurt, and I wouldn't even lift the fucker halfway. But I wasn't about to let him win the pissing contest, so I lifted that arm all the way over my head and grimaced as the room started to spin around me.

I let him put the damn sling on me and settled down after that.

Ace marched into the room just as the last bandages disappeared into the bag where they'd come from, holding a dripping towel and an ice pack on his face, Joker leading him by the arm. His voice was raspy and interspersed with a slow wheeze, but he was otherwise understandable.

"My entire face is screaming in pain right now." He turned to me, a scowl turning his lips down even though his eyes were closed. "Spade, how's the shoulder?"

"BlackJack put me in a sling," I whined, though we both knew it was all in jest. If I didn't want to do something, I didn't do it. "I'm not happy, but it's necessary."

He twisted in the general direction of the cage. "She say anything yet?"

BlackJack shook his head. "Nothing."

She hadn't made a single sound since being deposited on the

floor, which immediately screamed at me in warning. I had been so wrapped up in my own shit I'd missed the obvious signs of psychological shock.

"Take the bag off her head," I demanded of the others, and when nobody leaped up to acquiesce, I launched myself off the couch and against the bars of the cage, my good hand fumbling with the latch.

Ace scowled and motioned for Joker to stop me, but I managed to get inside before he could do a thing, and then I was on the floor beside the girl, tugging at the bag over her head with urgency.

"Spade, what are you doing?" Ace demanded, but I ignored him and breathed a sigh of relief when the girl's head emerged from the bag and her stunning, deep eyes met mine.

The amber in those wide orbs arrested my heart, and I swallowed thickly, raising my good hand to brush her hair back from her face. She flinched away from me, but Blackjack managed to get some zip ties around her wrists in the car, so she couldn't do much to prevent my advance, and she couldn't escape me in the tiny confines of the cage.

She didn't whimper, she didn't mumble, she didn't even cry. I had to commend her; she was certainly a hell of a brave woman. But at the end of the day, we needed answers, and we wouldn't get them from a girl in the throes of shock.

"Hey there, sweetheart," I crooned softly, letting my hand drag along her jawline. "Remember me?"

Her eyes shot to my bandaged shoulder and then back up to my gaze. There was a new fire in them, one of triumph.

Yeah, she remembered me, all right.

"Good, good," I quickly hedged, moving on before she could get any ideas. "We need to ask you some questions, and if you answer honestly, well, it might go easier for you." I pulled her knife from my back pocket, flipping it open pointedly with no lack of skill in handling one. "If you're bad, they'll let me carve you up in whatever way I see fit to get the information from you."

I watched her eyes follow the knife as it flicked back and forth in my hand, the shiny metal glinting against the light overhead.

She knew what was in her best interests. She was a smart girl, this one.

But I was smarter.

"You know why you're here?"

Her eyes moved to Ace, who'd asked the question with a grumble of irritation.

"No," she whispered, trying to find her voice. "I don't know. Please," she begged, turning back to me, "please don't let them hurt me! Let me go; I won't say anything about tonight. Not a word."

BlackJack laughed from his perch on the side table. "You're not leaving here."

Her eyes were wild with fear now, and the shock made way for the fight or flight, the rush of adrenaline to renew itself as she tugged against her restraints. "This is insane; my friends—"

"Your friends ditched you at the bar," Ace growled. "We were watching you."

She shivered violently. "Let's just forget this all happened," she tried again. "Please, I'm nobody to you; I'm somebody's daughter—"

Ace's smirk looked out of place behind the curve of the moist towel, but no less threatening. "Unfortunately for you, those psychological tactics won't work on any of us here." He pointed to Joker, his finger slightly off-center, but the direction was solid. "You got her into this, now explain to her what's going to happen."

Joker cleared his throat, and I winced when the little whimper slipped from between her lips. As the man stepped closer to her cage, she withdrew backward and inevitably scooted closer to me.

Not the wisest choice, typically, but something in me ached to save this little fiery goddess locked in our gilded cage.

I wrapped my arms around her, tugging her body behind mine as I stepped to the entrance of the cage and went toe-to-toe against Joker.

He knew as well as I did that if it came to blows, I'd be the one coming out on top at the end, injured arm or not.

"Come on, Spade, move out of the way." His hands moved to my good arm, and I whirled on him with fiery fury, headbutting him so hard it made his nose bleed. When he retreated, I stepped forward another foot or two, completely outside the cage now, face to face with the idiot who put us all in this situation.

And then I turned to Ace with a withering sigh.

"Family meeting, right now."

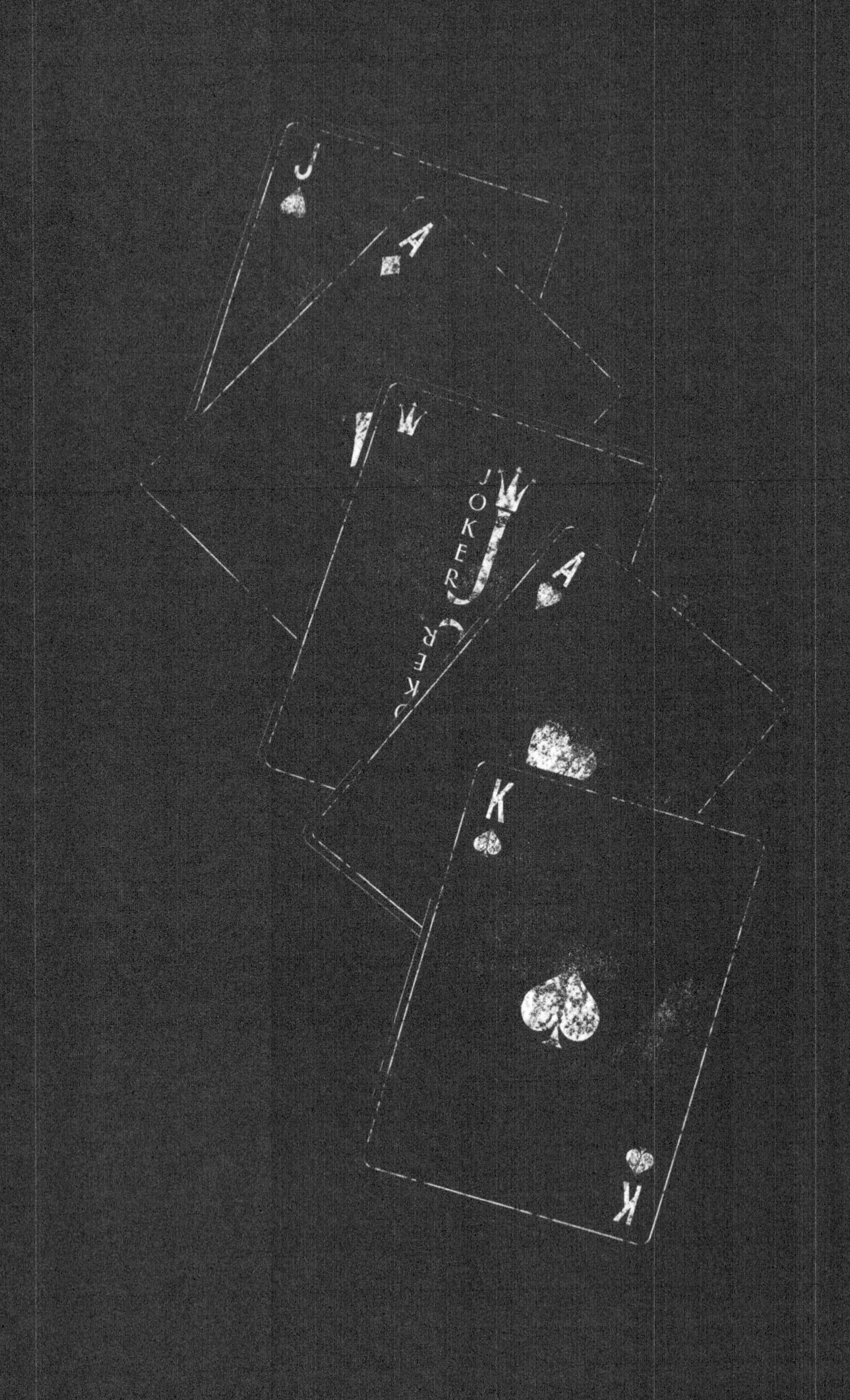
J
A
JOKER
A
K

CHAPTER TEN
BLACKJACK

This was by far the worst one of Ace's plans had gone off the rails. There were some close calls before, but nothing like fighting between members of the crew.

Now the ever-obedient lapdog Spade was calling for a fucking family meeting like he didn't just assault Joker over a captive. One that, by all indications, he was eager to take a blade to.

And yet, I wasn't surprised. Something about this woman made my skin crawl, made my muscles ache beneath this skin suit I wore. I wanted to strip off my clothes and take a frigid shower, and I wanted to touch her again, even if it was just to move her from point A to point B.

I didn't want to touch *anyone*. It was one of those residual trauma responses that I hadn't been able to kick after my father's torture.

So why did something deep inside my being ache to feel the softness of her hair against my arm again? Why was I sitting here seriously contemplating breaking one of my cardinal rules for a stranger?

Shake it off, fool. You're broken. Best to stay that way.

Ace looked rough, and I caught Joker trying desperately to stifle a chuckle as our leader pulled that towel away to reveal a beet-red face with nearly swollen-shut eyes. His low groan of discomfort lent a sense of seriousness to the whole affair, but even I cracked a slight grin at his obvious discomfort.

Ace was so good at being in charge, at being in control; it was humbling and satisfying to see him brought so low, his entire world upended by a waif of a girl in combat boots with nothing more than a can of watered-down mace and a prayer.

"You have the floor, Spade," Ace mumbled, grimacing as he fought his eyes open a smidge more.

"We can't kill her," he said simply, as if that explained everything.

"And why is that?"

I really had to give it to Ace; he was holding his composure well for a dude whose skin was on fire.

Spade ran a hand through his scraggly hair, his jaw ticking. "Because we don't murder innocents, Ace. Never has been our gambit."

I blinked stupidly with my jaw wide open, unable to believe what I'd just heard come out of Spade's mouth. Spade, the man with a deadly addiction to blood and pain and danger. The man who put his fist *through* a guy once for spitting on the boss.

We can't kill her, Ace.

"You're kidding, right?" I interrupted, struggling to understand what was going on here. "So you wanna let her go? Put us all in danger?"

Spade just grinned like an idiot, flipping a knife in the air in one hand while he picked his teeth with the other. "Nah, I don't wanna let her go. She's probably seen too much, knows too much, that whole thing."

Joker cupped his nose, which now sported a healthy splash of red beneath it. "So what the fuck do you propose we do, you maniac?"

Spade's lethal grin split his face like a fucking circus act. It gave me the shivers, the look in his eyes like he was delivering a life or death ultimatum without so much as a by your leave.

"I say we keep her."

The room was so quiet you could have heard a mouse sneeze. Nobody moved; nobody dared to even breathe. My eyes surveyed the inevitable wreckage Spade's suggestion left in its wake, from Joker's pale face to Ace's raised brows, even Spade himself's wide, confident stance and sure grin.

Ace was the first one to speak, his quiet, rough voice no less imposing than usual despite the difficulty he was undergoing actually articulating the thoughts in his head.

"You want to *keep* her as what, a pet? A housemaid? A toy?" His upper lip curled in a sneer. "How do you suggest we go about this? Keep her in the cage when we leave the house? Tie her up like a dog?"

"Cuff her to a bed," Joker muttered, and I choked on my own spit.

Spade just shrugged. "I'm out of commission for at least a week with this gaping wound. I could keep an eye on her until then."

Ace laughed, then groaned. "And whose purse is supposed to fund her upkeep, Spade? Yours?"

"Joker's the reason she's tied up in all this," he pointed out. "I say he funds at least half of it, if not all."

Joker sputtered to life like a diesel engine beside the boss, his cheeks regaining their color as he flushed with outrage. "Now wait just a minute, Spade; who said you could make those kinds of decisions—"

"It's not a bad idea," I interjected lazily. "Spade will need someone to help him while he recovers. She can keep him occupied. We can give her a choice she'd be stupid to refuse—death or life as our captive."

All the eyes in the room turned on me, and Spade lit up like the sky on the fourth of July. Joker seemed once again stunned that I'd interjected myself into the conversation, but my time was precious, and I didn't plan to spend it standing around while they measured dicks and debated the intelligence of keeping a human like one would argue with a spouse over a kitten they found on the side of the road.

"Alright, alright, listen," Ace rasped, "we'll talk about it in the morning when I've had the chance to sleep off most of this bullshit." He gestured to his inflamed face and grimaced. "She stays in the cage overnight."

Spade balked at that, which of course piqued my interest. "What if we—"

"Cage, Spade," Ace warned. "No arguments." His eyes crawled over each one of us as well, surveying the atmosphere. "Anyone in disagreement about the subject, at least for the night?"

I shrugged, and Joker sagged into the couch with relief. Clearly, neither of us was about to argue.

"It's settled, then." He turned to Joker with a frown. "You're the reason she's in this situation; just remember that."

Joker had enough self-preservation to cringe and look apologetic. "I'm sorry, Ace."

Ace's eyes were hard, and my heart went out to Joker. He was feeling the full force of our leader's ire today. "I don't want your apologies. I want you to find a way to fix it."

He stormed off with a growl, headed in the direction of his own bedroom. The warehouse operated more like a compound than a house, but it worked for us. Joker slinked off after Ace, probably in search of some vodka to assuage his guilt.

If he were smart, he'd stay away from the shit. It's what got him in this mess in the first place. Joker was many things, including very lacking in impulse control and common sense, so I knew that'd never happen.

Spade stared me down when only the two of us remained, and I suddenly felt like a rabbit being sized up by a very large and dangerous cat. A large, dangerous, *hungry* cat. So I did my best to appear unconcerned. After all, predators were deadlier if you let on that they worried you. And most days, Spade didn't worry me in the slightest.

"Something you wanna say?" he growled at me, his arms crossed over his muscled chest.

I shook my head. "Your funeral."

Spade grinned like a wild man. "I'll only enjoy it if she fights me the whole way. I haven't ever met a woman who matches my chaos like she did." He stepped closer, and if I hadn't had my back against the wall, I'd have instinctively backed up. "She took down Ace and stabbed me in the shoulder. And then she kicked you in the balls for your trouble," he added, his eyes wandering south to make his point.

I cringed as I remembered the pain her little knee shot through me during the car ride. She had a hell of a kick, and we'd be wise to keep that in mind. "She sounds like a hassle."

"She sounds like a fucking dream, bro; live a little." He glanced at my balled fists, took in the frown on my face and my tense stance. "We could all benefit from a little eye candy around here, anyhow."

I didn't bother to respond. I had no desire to entertain his whimsical fantasies. For starters, it wasn't likely that someone being held captive would take too kindly to the idea of being the sexual fantasy of the four men holding her hostage. Secondly, I didn't have any sort of desire to get close to anyone. Not even the pretty girl sitting in a tiger cage on our common room floor.

Especially not her.

"Lighten up, BlackJack," he chuckled, "she hasn't bitten anyone yet."

My jaw clenched so hard I could practically hear my teeth cracking. "Yet."

His smile only grew wider. "Oh, if she bites, I hope I'm the first victim." He pretended to swoon as he sauntered past me, an unhinged peal of laughter bubbling up from his sick and twisted gut. "Be still, my beating heart."

The weird vibe of the room left with him, and not for the first time, I wondered what really went on up in his skull. Was he always like this, or did something—or someone—turn him into this?

I wouldn't find out here. Only thing I could do was continue on my merry way and hope that he didn't snap on me.

My body leaned toward the doorway leading to the commons, but my head pulled me onward in the opposite direction to my overly small crash pad. I climbed the metal stairs like a panther, silent but no less dangerous for it, as I thought about this crew I'd found myself a part of.

I had long forgotten how long we'd known each other, but the guys were all a different flavor of the wildest ice cream I'd ever savored. Ace was quiet, like me, reserved in his own right but commanding when he needed to be. His office and room bordered each other and were dead center of the second level. His living spaces were tidy, organized, and bland, much like the persona he wore daily.

Spade's little hidey-hole was a bit of a mystery, as he didn't really let anyone in to see what went on in there. Hell, even Ace himself had never seen the dregs of that particular pit. I only knew that whatever he had inside it was probably coated in old blood spatter. His room was connected to it by a single door, and his room was almost all dark colors that swallowed any light whole.

An accurate representation of his soul, one would imagine.

My quarters looked pretty mild, with neutral colors, a small full-size bed, and a desk, which was like my home away from home when we were planning a heist.

Joker—now his room was wild. Color everywhere, a whole mess strewn from one side of the room to another. He was chaos personified, and it wouldn't surprise me if there were old thongs from previous trophy fucks interspersed with empty alcohol bottles stuffed under his bed.

Sometimes, I was truly thankful for my little space. My quiet place where I could escape these warring fronts.

And other times, like now, I wondered why the damn tiny space still managed to feel so empty. So vast, like I was swimming in an Olympic-size pool with no end in sight.

I yanked a towel out of the hallway closet and padded down to the huge communal shower we'd installed when we moved into this place. Ace insisted it was for beating the tension out of sore muscles, but until today I hadn't had a reason to test his theory.

But right now, I would encourage any reprieve from this sinking feeling in my gut that this would all go sideways very soon, and eliminate the crawling under my skin that wouldn't leave me be.

Something wicked this way comes.

JOKER

CHAPTER ELEVEN
MALLORY

I had done some wild things in my youth, but never had I ended a night out on the floor of an animal cage in the belly of what could only be these criminals' hideout, in a very revealing outfit, surrounded by four men who obviously were at war over what to do with me.

Three things were very clear.

One—they were worried I knew too much.

Okay, that one's fair. I did know a fair sight more than was safe for me to know.

Two—the one I'd injured with the blade was a little unstable.

Understatement, but I wasn't about to split hairs over it.

Three—it was still a toss-up on whether I lived or died.

I had to come up with a plan to survive. If I didn't, if they caught me unawares, it would be over in a second, and that's all she wrote. I wasn't sure why they'd called a side meeting, but I was wasting time.

Think, Mal, think!

All my training, all those years of preventative therapy, of training others to handle a captive situation, was gone in an instant, the knowledge somehow evaporated like a fucking puddle on a hot summer day. I sifted through the shifting sands of my faulty, fragmented mind, fighting the remnants of the booze and the fallout of an adrenaline rush, but there was nothing valuable or helpful on the other side. Just pile after pile of basic knowledge that did me no good in an escape.

When they brought me in, I had been bound and hooded, so I didn't remember much, but the way the exhaust had rattled off the walls made me think we were in some sort of metal building. Maybe one of those corrugated steel barns or a small warehouse. And since they'd carried me in, I hadn't felt the flooring beneath my feet. I hadn't felt what direction we walked, so finding my way back to the car would be damn near impossible.

I'd been alone long enough to contemplate my uncomfortable bladder and need for some fluids when the sound of footsteps re-entered the room. I cast my eyes over to the door, and there stood the weird one I'd stabbed in the alley. He waggled a few fingers at me and smiled, creeping me out even further. He could have taken a seat on the couch or kept moving to god knows where they all slept, but he didn't.

Because of course he didn't.

He stopped right in front of the door to my cage and slipped a key inside, and the stupid fucking door swung open with a sadistically loud screech. I winced, he winced, and then he was clambering inside with me. I mean, sure, it was big enough, but I didn't want anyone in this damn cage with me.

Especially not the man I'd almost maimed.

Murdered.

Whatever.

"Hey, now," he soothed, reaching a scarred hand out to brush against my cheek. "Come on; I won't hurt you."

I really tried hard not to roll my eyes, but it slipped out, much to his amusement and my complete terror.

Great going, Mallory, you're insulting the crazy one; smart.

His deep chuckle did things to my insides, and a lock of his red hair slipped out of the low ponytail he had it slung up in. "Okay, considering the events of tonight, I could see where you might have that misconception. But I don't *want* to hurt you."

I didn't trust myself to speak. If I opened my mouth this instant, I knew without a doubt that I would say something to get me killed, regardless of how much he claimed he didn't want to.

His eyes were strangely soft now as he stared into my soul, perhaps reading my mind in the process. "The guys don't know what to do with you." His gaze fell to his hands as a grimace flitted across his features. "I don't hurt innocents, and I don't hurt kids—only two rules I have. Typically, I don't *have* to kill people. Non-lethal methods that leave a lasting reminder usually work as a better deterrent of repeat fuck-ups."

My eyebrows were damn near in my hairline now, but as my gaze flicked back and forth between his eyes, I started to realize how truly fucked I was. Not that I hadn't assumed I was fucked before, but now—

Now it was a for sure feeling.

I knew then and there that I'd do whatever it took to make it out of this alive. I'd never wanted to live more than I did at that moment.

He continued as if I hadn't had an epiphany in front of his very eyes. "You're not to blame here, sugar. That's Joker's bad call. But he told you some things, and it's gonna be easier for all of us if you tell the truth about that in the morning when Ace asks, you hear?"

I nodded as if I knew what he meant by an Ace, as if I was confident I'd make it til morning. My throat was dry, and as I swallowed, I damn near choked on the air I breathed. There was no moisture in my mouth, no relief to be had by swallowing my own spit, as it didn't exist.

He watched me carefully as I choked and sputtered noisily, and I jerked my hands toward my throat, pantomiming my needs.

"You need water?" he guessed, and I nodded enthusiastically, nearly crying in desperation. He rose from his crouched position and moved to the door of the cage. "I'll be right back with some. Don't move—well, not that you could."

When he left the room, I sighed heavily, my whole body going slack at the emptiness left behind in his absence. I missed the feeling of quiet occupation my cats gave me when I was home, and then a new panic spread as I realized they'd only be okay for a few days without someone checking on them. And I hadn't gotten particularly close with anyone I trusted with my key, so it wasn't like they could just phone someone and ask them to deal with the cats.

It felt stupid to sit here worrying over two cats when my life was on the line, but the idea of them trapped in my apartment was enough to send me into a fit of panic. Now I wasn't just choking on my own dry throat, but actively swallowing dread and terror that I couldn't get a grasp on. The booze had all but worn off, and my headache was in full force, compounded by the nausea onset and regret for every life choice I'd made up to now.

When the crazy one returned to the room, I forced myself to calm down, or at least to assume a mask of perceived calm. I thought I was doing a good job pulling it off until he lifted the cup of water to my lips and I nearly drowned myself.

"Easy now," he whispered as he tugged the cup away and set it down, just out of reach. I whimpered at the loss, but his hand gripped my chin and forced my gaze to meet his. "What's got you riled up?"

I shook my head and stared past him at the cup of water. He chuckled, brought it back, and let me drink half of it down before he pulled it back again. I let out a low whine, and his grin turned to concern as the mug disappeared behind him.

"Talk to me," he urged, but really, how do you talk to a kidnapper about your *fucking cats* and the unhealthy attachment you have to them?

You rip the fucking bandaid off, that's how. "My cats—"

His brows shot up so fast it was nearly comical. "You are in a fucking metal cage on the living room floor of a pack of criminals, sitting with a man you stabbed, and your first thought is your pets?"

I stared sheepishly at the floor as he chuckled. I was fucked up and a bit unstable, but in my line of work, who wasn't?

He shook his head wordlessly, a smile, genuine and soft, spread across his full lips. In that second, I could see the handsome man underneath the crazy façade, could actually imagine him being an average guy on the sidewalk who smiled at me as we waited for the light to turn green. And just as suddenly, that man was gone, and the reckless criminal was back.

So his next words really shocked me.

"I'll take care of your cats, sugar. You just tell me what they're called and where to find them."

I blinked stupidly at him, stunned near to speechless at his strange yet somehow genuine-feeling offer. "You'd do that?"

He shrugged. "No innocents, remember? And what's more innocent than a house cat?"

I rolled my eyes, a chuckle building in my throat despite me. "You haven't had a house cat before, have you?"

He moved from his squat to a seated position, his legs stretched out behind me as we sat side by side, facing each other. He reached out his hands and gripped mine, pulling them toward his lap. I let him but ran out of length pretty soon, so I ended up bent over my own knees, chest pressed against my thighs as he held onto my wrists. The zip tie dug into my skin, and I hissed in pain as he fingered it absently.

"If I cut this off," he asked curiously, "you promise not to try anything sneaky?"

Oh, fuck, if he freed my wrists, I'd do whatever he asked.

Build a rapport.

Make yourself appear more like a real person and less like a victim.

All these valid and reliable tips ran through my head, but I couldn't bring myself to think about the long-term ramifications if I didn't escape.

I nodded slowly, trying hard not to appear too eager at the idea of having my hands free again. Just as he pulled my knife out of his pocket and slipped it under my restraint, a chuckle came from the other side of the room.

A familiar chuckle.

"I wouldn't do that, Spade. She'll probably give you a matching stab wound on the other side of your chest."

The one I'd dealt with on the phone smiled as he strolled into the commons area, his eyes on Spade and I in the cage. I filed away the crazy one's name for future use—Cass, Joker, whatever. If I started calling them by their names, maybe they'd be less likely to hurt me.

A girl could hope.

Spade grumbled and pocketed the knife again. "I hate it when you're right, fuck face." He rose and released me from his grip, moving to the door of the cage. "Sorry, sugar tits, you heard the man."

I whimpered pleadingly at him, but he shrugged and locked the cage with a frown, like a kid whose favorite toy had been taken away. The blonde man patted him on the shoulder like a pet and handed him a beer.

"Here, man," he muttered absently, watching me over Spade's shoulder. "Go relax and unwind for the night. This is my mess; I'll watch her."

It was then I noticed he was no longer wearing the black clothes he'd kidnapped me in, but had swapped them out for some basic sweatpants and a hoodie, a pair of socks the only thing encasing his feet.

He looked almost human. Which, okay, it sounded stupid, but when a man is capable of kidnapping you, jerking off to your voice in an alley, and killing people, you start to view him less and less as human and more as a monster.

The imprint at the front of his sweats indeed alluded to the monster vibe.

Spade hesitated for a moment, his eyes cast back over his shoulder at me. "You try anything, Joker, and I'll cut off your dick, you dig?"

My new babysitter shrugged noncommittally. "I dig."

Spade wandered out of the room without another backward glance, and I watched my chances of release go with him. Joker was an unknown, a wildcard I couldn't pin down. All I knew about him was that he had issues—chief among them, alcohol abuse.

And that was enough, really, when I thought about it.

People who abused alcohol turned into a person they weren't;

some would even say they turn *more* into themselves when intoxicated. My experience with alcohol was limited to my father's abusive tendencies toward it and a few ex-boyfriends that emulated his whole aesthetic far too much.

They do say women with daddy issues are attracted to the same type of men that their father is. And boy, did I have those in spades.

The man before me flopped noisily on the couch nearby, cracked the lid of his water bottle, and downed it in one go, his eyes cast lazily over the plastic, locked in on me.

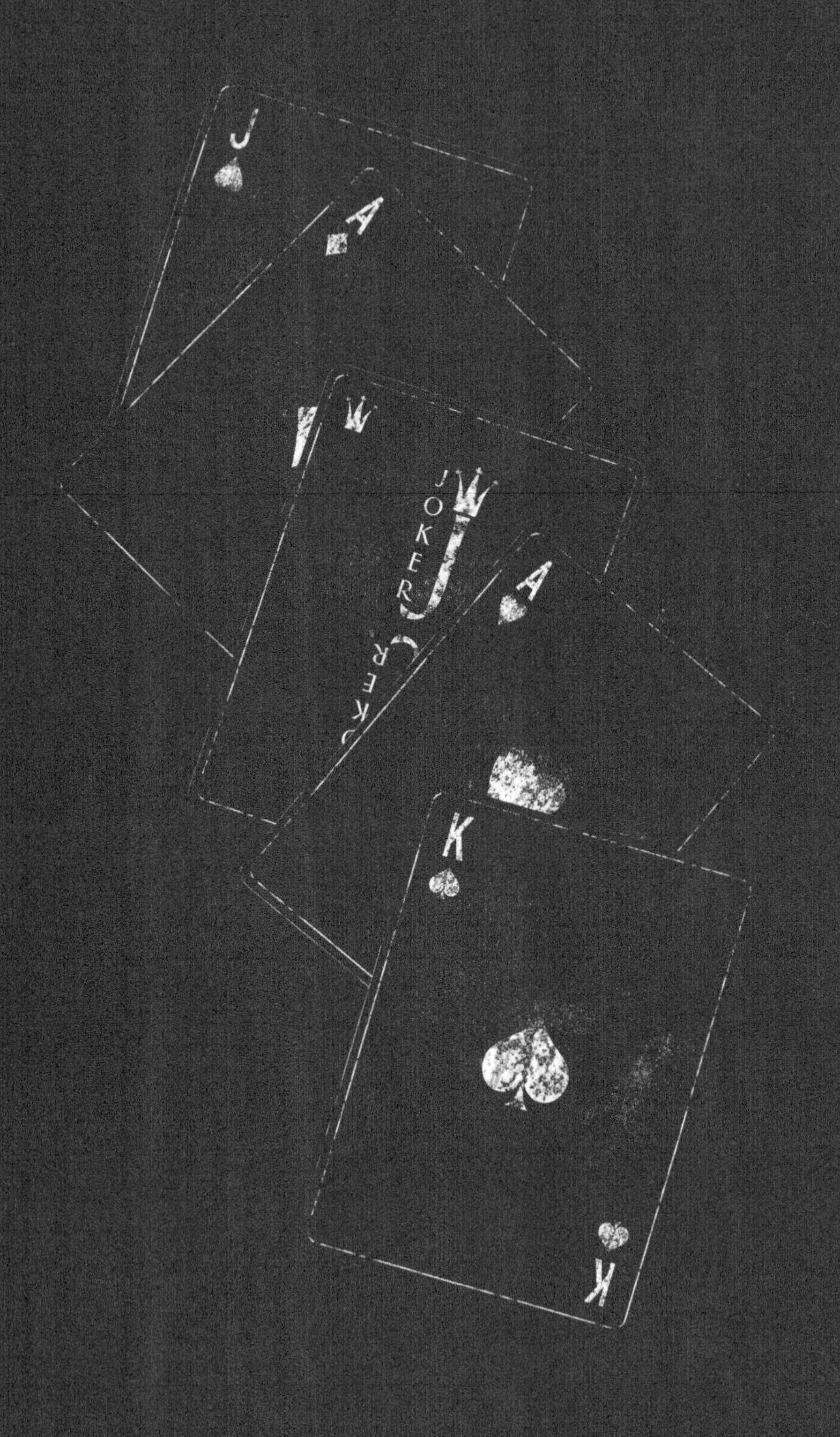
JOKER

CHAPTER TWELVE
JOKER

She was quiet for most of the night. And by quiet, I meant deadly silent. You could have heard a pin drop in that room. When she finally slipped into unconsciousness, that's when things got not-so-quiet.

Seemed our little therapist was prone to nightmares.

My whole body protested as I leaned forward with my hands on my knees, moving for the first time in hours, muscles screaming at the injustice. She lay on her side now, skirt hiked dangerously high on her thighs, breathing rapid and broken as she mumbled and twitched. Nothing that came out of her mouth was intelligible, but I had no doubt whatever she was dreaming about was doing a number on dream-her.

My lips parted with a sigh. "What are you afraid of, sweetheart? What fills your head with fear and your dreams with panic?"

Was it us? Was she reliving the kidnapping in her slumber?

Possibly. We weren't gentle, and she'd put up a hell of a fight, which meant all the more traumatizing when she was finally caught. Anyone who'd been through the night she had was justified in sleeping a tad tumultuously.

Her mumbles and sobs turned into a frantic gasp for air, and with a scream, she jolted awake and scrambled upright, her legs kicking out in front of her until shoulder blades met the back of the bars. She scanned the room, eyes wild until her gaze fell on me, and she gagged.

Well, I'd never had that effect on a woman before.

She took a deep breath through her nose and closed those gorgeous eyes, hiding their depths from view. I counted to ten and hoisted myself off the couch, realizing this was going nowhere unless one of us took the initiative and made the first move.

My movement must have caught her off-guard because she winced and tried to make herself even smaller inside that damned cage. As I closed in, those stunning eyes widened, swallowing me whole in their depths. They followed me avidly as I slipped the key in the cage's lock, swung the door wide, then stepped back.

"Come on out, beautiful. I bet you've got to use the bathroom, and stretching your legs will do you good."

With her hands still bound behind her waist, the trip from one side of the enclosure was long, but she made it, and even refused the hand I offered to help her rise from the floor. Like a stubborn mule, she frowned at my smile, rolling back on her heels to let momentum rock her forward enough to engage her core and lift up on her feet.

And then she swore at the pins and needles as her legs gave out beneath her.

With not a second to spare, I reached out and caught her around the waist, preventing her complete collapse at my feet, and the dizzying scent of her perfume invaded my nostrils, heady and sweet, just like her voice.

"C-Cass?" she mumbled, shaking like a leaf in my embrace.

She sounded so small, so frail, like the girl in her dreams had bled over into the present and was slow in dissipating as she regained herself. Something deep in my soul twitched painfully at my name, and I buried it for the time being, trying desperately to will my cock to behave.

"I'm here, doc," I crooned, wishing we'd learned her name in the online search that had turned up her information. "Joker's got ya."

"Joker?" she blinked up into my soft gaze, and something clicked behind the depths of those fiery amber orbs. "Wha—"

The momentary loss of feeling in those long, fishnet-clad legs must have dissipated because it took her all of two seconds to stand on them herself and pull away from my arms as if I'd scalded her.

My laughter was genuine at her complete one-eighty.

"Come on, doc, let's not get off on a bad foot this early in the relationship. I've got a reputation to protect." I winked salaciously at her and was rewarded with a pretty blush across her cheeks. "There we are. Now, here's the deal—I'll cut the zip ties and let you handle your business as long as you promise to behave." Complete and utter silence met my demands, so I continued, frustrated that she wasn't fighting as she had earlier in the alley.

She'd damn near gotten away—four of us, bested by a woman.

What kinds of horrors had she faced in her life to be so slippery now?

"After you take a piss and wash up, I'll find you something to eat and get you a drink. Maybe even let you sit on the couch with me instead of staying in that horrid little tiger cage."

The reaction I got was the one I expected—confusion. She stared up at me like I had morphed into a completely new being before her eyes.

"Why are you being so nice all of a sudden?" she hedged, wariness creeping into that sultry voice I'd dreamed of since the first time I heard it. "You kidnapped me right off the street, threw me in a cage, and tied me up. You can drop the nice guy act, you know."

"Call it penance, doc," I muttered, turning to lead the way. "Follow close, and keep your mouth shut. If the guys find you out of your cage, it'll be both of our asses."

Silence. I took it for acquiescence.

I padded quietly down the hall in nothing but socks and sweats, the floor absorbing any sound my movement made as we left the commons behind and entered the part of the warehouse that *looked* like a home. For all intents and purposes, it *was* a home. Just not one a normal person would grow up in.

The walls were corrugated metal in the commons, but here, Ace had put up actual structure and walls, soundproofed the torture room, and made our quarters to each of our liking. Walls were finished and painted how we wanted, floors carpeted, and doors heavy with locks on each one.

Not that a lock would keep half of us out of anything. It was more of a formality than anything else. Except for the ones on BlackJack's door. Those, none of us even dared to pick. And I doubted we'd be able to get through one.

We had our own en suite bathrooms, so I took her to mine at the end of the hall. The door swung wide—I never bothered with locks when I was home—and I heard a shocked little gasp escape the pretty doc's lips behind me as she caught her first glimpse of my den.

"It's something, isn't it?" I teased, throwing my arms wide as I stepped aside to permit her entry. "This is my little slice of criminal heaven. Bathroom's the door over there on your right."

The need for a bathroom visit must have temporarily abated because this girl was *not* moving. Motionless in the center of my room, her eyes fanned over the personal space like she was trying to psychoanalyze it.

Fuck, that's right, she's a shrink. She probably ***was*** *trying to decode me.*

The walls of my room were all colorful, not a single muted or neutral shade to be found. The wall the door was built into was a deep green, the left and right were vibrant yellows, and the far one, where my bed sat pushed up against, was covered in the biggest tapestry I could find. It was a beautiful piece of art that depicted the teachings of the Kama Sutra in vivid detail from multiple angles and positions. I watched the doc roll her eyes at that and move onto my bed, which was unmade and full of pillows and silk sheets.

"You don't lack for opulence, do you?" she muttered to herself, turning to the desk along the wall by my closet. "I bet your closet is as chaotic as the rest of it."

I quirked a brow at her observations. "Playing shrink now, are we?"

Her soft smile could light up the darkest pits of hell, especially when it was genuine and playful, like now. "I never play at my profession, Cass."

Her voice was a breathy whisper and barely audible, but my ears picked up every word. There was something there, something I was missing, but now wasn't the time to dive into her psychoanalysis bullshit. "Okay, come here, and I'll deal with those restraints."

Took her damn time joining me, this one. I wasn't usually an impatient man, but the doc pushed even my buttons. When she finally came to stand before me, she spun and faced the wall with the sex tapestry hanging on it.

Have a little fun, Joker.

I grabbed a decorative knife from my dresser and flipped the blade open, but before I placed it in the small space between her wrists, I let my free hand move to her neck, gripping it loosely, holding her in place.

"Before I do this, let's go over the rules, shall we?" I brought my blade up and twisted it so the light glinted off the cool metal blade. "If you try to run, try to fight, try anything but what I give you permission to do, I'll tie you up and hand you off to Spade. And he's downright mean with a blade." My lips moved against the shell of her ear as I leaned in and smiled. "Considering you've stabbed him already, I doubt he'd show you mercy, either."

She went stiff beside me, her spine rigid. "I won't run," she declared as if the very thought were beneath her. "Now, can you take these off?"

I ran my blade down the dip in her spine, pressing just hard enough for her to feel it through that sheer top of hers that still teased my eyeballs. The blade came to a stop when it encountered the waistband of her skirt, and she let out a low whine when I pulled it further down, to her wrists.

"Hold still. This thing is sharp."

The ties came apart with a clean swipe of the blade, and she immediately yanked her hands in front of her, rubbing the ache away from her wrists.

I watched her shuffle off to the bathroom without so much as a thank you. When the door closed quietly behind her, I decided covering the temptation might be a good move, so I rummaged in my *lost and found* from one night stands and managed to put together a pair of sleep shorts and a t-shirt that would no doubt be too large for her frame. Still, it was better than nothing, and she'd be more comfortable.

It wasn't the guilt talking.

Or was it?

After all, I was the one to blame for her kidnapping, her forced captivity, and her imminent survival or death, depending on which way Ace's pendulum swung. Start to finish, if I had just kept my mouth shut, if I'd never gone to that bar, she'd probably be off in her little apartment, tending to her cats and minding her own business.

She'd have a future ahead of her.

Water kicked on in the bathroom, the sink, from the sound of it. I sat on the edge of my bed and stared blankly at that door until it finally opened, and she walked back out.

Her face, once covered in black makeup to match her outfit, was now washed clean, and she looked just like I remembered from the video call.

"Cass."

Fuck, she sounded so much better in person.

"Cass?"

I eyed her from head to toe, drinking in every inch of skin showing in the peepholes of her stockings. The way her skin pushed against the restraint, especially on her thighs—

"Joker!"

That got through to me, and I shook off the dazed thirty-yard stare I'd been wearing, putting on a mask of indifference once again. "I've got spare clothes you can wear if you want—"

"Nah, I'm good, thanks," she rushed out, her eyes averted from me, staring intently at the door to the hallway. "You gonna put me back in the cage?"

"Depends," I said flippantly, "on whether or not you plan to behave." I looked her up and down once more, for good measure, and to unsettle her, as she'd unsettled me. "You look like the type of girl that tends to become a problem for men."

Her smirk shot straight through to my heart and made my cock twitch behind these flimsy sweats. I think she did it on purpose, too.

"Depends on the men you ask," she teased, moving to stand directly in front of me.

"That sounds like a challenge, beautiful," I growled, leaning in until our faces were but an inch away. "And I like challenges."

JOKER

CHAPTER THIRTEEN
MALLORY

A bathroom break, a face scrub, and five minutes of humanity really did the body good. I felt like a human again, not an animal, and I would be damned if I did anything to encourage them to cage me again.

Or tie me up.

Joker—*Cass*—whatever his name was, he seemed like the most stable of them. He was also the only one I hadn't injured yet, so he was really my best option.

But that crazy one with the knife fetish—the one I stabbed—he promised to take care of my cats, and he said he didn't hurt innocents or women. I fit into both of those categories, so maybe *he* was the better target.

Build a rapport. Make them aware of your humanity.

Joker put that blade to my spine and dragged it down to my ass with a purpose. And by all rights and intentions, that should scare me—his willingness to flirt with danger like that was hands down frightening. They were all dangerous men, and I needed to remember that.

The manic man beside me, who'd gone radio silent, flopped down on the couch in the commons, an old, peeling leather thing that had definitely seen better days. He gestured with a wave of his hand for me to join him, and I took shelter in the corner furthest away from me, curling in on myself to make sure there would be no way I'd accidentally touch him.

I wasn't sure what would set him off and what wouldn't, and until I got a solid read on these men, it'd be in my best interests to play it safe.

He shot me a glance and reached over to the short stand where the remote to the tv sat, old and battered but still working. Mindlessly, he flipped it on and started to scroll through streaming services, his brows furrowed as he searched for something.

I had to bite back a snort of laughter when he settled over Vampire Diaries and smirked, hitting the play button.

"Vampire Diaries, really? Are you sure you're some badass criminal?"

His eyes narrowed as he turned to me, and I gulped down the fear, cursing my inability to shut my fucking mouth.

"I suppose you think men can't enjoy a good tv show, huh?" He handed me the remote and leered at me, letting his eyes trail down my chest to the black lacy bra I wore under the sheer top. "What would you rather watch?"

Suddenly, I wished I'd taken his offer to change out of this outfit, but it was too late for regrets. I'd dug my hole, might as well jump in.

"This is fine, but True Blood is better."

He grinned from ear to ear, leaning back against the couch, his arms spread side to side in an impressive display of his wingspan. If he stretched an inch further, he could wrap his hand around the back of my neck and choke me if he so chose.

Okay, Mallory, disturbing and twisted. Dial it down.

No, if he were going to do anything, it wouldn't be that; I was sure of it.

I handed the remote back hesitantly, not wanting to spook him before I knew where the line in the sand was. I figured now was as good a time as any to try and get some answers out of him, like what their plans for me were or what to expect.

It took me two episodes of the damnable vampire show to work up the courage to ask him a thing, and when I did, it was to ask him for a drink.

He shot me a sideways glance but got up off the couch and disappeared without even a warning to stay put. My mind whirled a million miles an hour when I realized if ever there was a time to escape, now would be it, but I wouldn't get far. I had no idea how to get out of here, and the chances I could get to someone, a populated place, or a payphone—if those even still existed—were slim to none. For all I knew, we could be in the middle of nowhere or on the edge of the city. I hadn't heard the railway once, and I didn't feel the familiar thrum of the subway beneath our feet, so it was a sheer coin toss as to our location.

I seriously doubted they were still in the neighborhood they picked me up in. Too affluent, too showy for a criminal gang to hole up conspicuously.

Right?

Before I could overthink our location or an escape much longer, he returned with two bottles of water, one of which he handed to me. I made it a point to meticulously check the whole bottle for a needle hole, twisting it this way and that while squeezing pointedly, looking for any sign of a leak.

If I was going to get roofied, I'd like to know about it in advance. Or drugged in general.

Joker quirked a brow at me quizzically, tipping his head sideways like a confused puppy. "Problem?"

I frowned and turned the bottle upright again, cracking the lid. "Nope."

He watched me lift it to my lips, as I guzzled a quarter of the bottle, even followed the movement of my hand as I twisted the lid back on. Then, without warning, his lips parted, and he leaned over, brushing a thumb over the last drop or two of water clinging to my bottom lip.

My throat went drier than the Sahara, and my lashes fluttered, matching the fluttering in my stomach at his brazen move.

He brought the errant thumb to his own lips, and I watched,

transfixed, as his tongue darted out to lick the slight moisture clinging to his digit.

Fuck, okay, that was hotter than it had a right to be.

"You know, I think those therapy sites need to change their motto, doc." His hand moved to shove a chunk of hair behind my ear, and I swallowed the lump forming in my throat at his flirtatious actions. "They told me those sessions were anonymous, and here you are, making house calls."

His face was so serious as he said it that it took my brain a second to reconnect its synapses and start back up. The second it did, I snorted in a very unladylike manner and fell sideways on the couch, laughing hysterically at his unintended jest.

If he thought this was a house call, he wouldn't like me when I started *really* using my therapist skills.

"A house call; you're joking, right?" My laughter bordered on crazed and deranged if Joker's look was anything to go on.

"They don't call me Joker for nothing, you know." His cheesy grin spread over two perfect, plump, kissable lips, and I stifled an inward groan at the sight of his tongue running the length of the split.

"Why *do* they call you Joker, Cass?" I found myself asking as I wiped the tears from the corner of my eyes from laughing so hard.

He sobered instantly, his earlier, playful mood gone. "Not important."

I sensed it had more to do with the fact that he didn't like the reason his moniker was Joker than using his real name, so I dropped it and smiled, hoping to get back on an even keel with him. "Sorry." I turned back to the screen and put my hands in my lap, inching back into the corner of the couch, curling in on myself as much as possible.

We sat there in silence for another hour before I felt my eyelids start to sag. I fought the sensation as long as I could, but it was futile in the end—the events of the day not only had me drained, but the drinks I'd indulged in at the bar were finally out of my system, and the loss of liquid courage had me crashing hard, now that my brain could more adequately decipher the situation.

I was alone in the common area of a warehouse turned gang hangout with a man who'd jerked off during a video therapy session with me. A hardened career criminal who'd done things so bad, who also told me about said things, that they felt the need to kidnap me and possibly kill me for what I knew. I was definitely not going home anytime soon, and I had very few people who might miss me now that I was gone.

Just Gemma, and she'd abandoned me at the club to run wild with her less stringent, uptight friends.

Go figure.

My forehead rested on the armrest of the couch as I let my eyes close, fighting back the tears at the hopelessness of my situation. I heard him shuffling beside me, but the sheer exhaustion that overcame me made caring a chore. Resignation set in, and it was all I could do not to sob hysterically when faced with my mortality.

I was so emotionally drained it took me no time at all to pass out, my brain determined to shut off until I was more capable of processing everything logically.

MY CONSCIOUSNESS STIRRED at the sound of an argument, albeit a quietly-whispered one.

"You know he's going to be pissed you let her out," one voice—the crazy one, maybe—muttered, a low grumble running beneath the surface of the words. "And I am *not* saving your ass this time."

"You never *do* save my ass, Spade; you dig me a bigger hole and then kick me in." Joker. Had to be.

I felt like I should have been sitting upright, considering I'd fallen asleep hugging the side of the couch, but there was something beneath my cheek, and I couldn't tell what it was, but it wasn't the couch. It moved, and though that should disturb me, it didn't. My brain wasn't lucid enough to comprehend or put the pieces together.

"I'll remember that next time you need bailing out of jail." Spade's voice moved around the room like he was pacing, and my ears perked up as it grew closer. I felt my feet be lifted from the couch—so I was definitely stretched out across it, not curled up n the corner like I'd planned to stay all night. The person whose hands were on my ankles slid beneath them and replaced them on what I assumed was their lap. Those solid, calloused hands remained on the skin just above my boots, sending a shiver down my spine at the contact.

"Don't wake her, Spade," Joker muttered, and I realized with a start that my head was in his lap.

In. His. Lap.

My ear lay against the soft cotton of his sweatpants, and when he shifted, I distinctly felt the outline of his semi-soft cock against my ear, sending a flash of arousal straight to my core. I squeezed my thighs together just a smidge, attempting to alleviate the pressure building inside me at this blonde deviant's nearness to my face and the clear lewdness of my position.

I felt the fingers around my ankle tighten almost imperceptibly, but enough to know he'd noticed my not-so-subtle attempt.

Shit.

"Ace will be up soon. Don't you think she should go back in the cage before he gets out here?" He started drawing circles around one ankle as he spoke, soothing the burn of the suggestion.

"Fuck the cage," Joker growled, his whole body tensed, ready for a fight. "She's not going back in the cage. Stayed here all night on the couch with no problem. I even gave her a chance to run, and she didn't."

So his absence had been planned. I filed that away for later, noting with a small smile that this goofball whose lap I lay in was really quite cunning.

"She didn't run?" Something in Spade's voice made me stop and wonder why he wasn't surprised I didn't flee at the first opportunity. I didn't have the chance to do a full analysis of it, though, before footsteps echoed down the hall behind the couch, and I heard another voice join the fray.

"Of course she didn't. She's not stupid. She probably ran the chances of escape through her head and decided she'd be better off not wasting her energy." The couch dipped in the back, the weight of the person leaning over it shifting the cushions as his finger brushed against my jaw and moved some hair from my face. I remained still, trying to remember to take even breaths as his touch electrified me. "Isn't that right, Miss Stanton?"

My eyelids fluttered open as if he'd commanded them himself, and I twisted my head a fraction to the left, our eyes locking as he leaned over me with a leering grin.

The man I'd maced last night looked pretty rough, the skin of his face still ragged and raw from its run-in with the peppered concoction in my can. Still, his haunting gaze held mine, a fierceness in those cold depths that instilled fear in me rather than the arousal the others' touches did.

This was a man you didn't cross unless you wanted to die.

"Right," I murmured, lifting my head slowly from Joker's lap to face my jailer—the one I had a sneaking suspicion it would all come down to.

After all, they all looked to him like he was the boss. Even the quiet one on the far wall bowed to his demands.

"The truth. Good," he purred, his lips curling slowly in a knowing smirk. "Perhaps you're smarter than I gave you credit for. Lying will get you nowhere with me."

The only thing I knew for sure was I had to get out of here before this man decided I wasn't worth the trouble.

He rose and left me lying there, still halfway in Spade's lap and Joker's arms, painfully aware that I was now the center of attention. My body spun around and sat up straight, prepared for whatever this red-faced man had in store for me. He took a seat in the chair directly opposite me and stretched out comfortably, his hands on his knees, legs spread, deadly gaze locked in on me.

"So, let's have a little chat, shall we, Miss Stanton?"

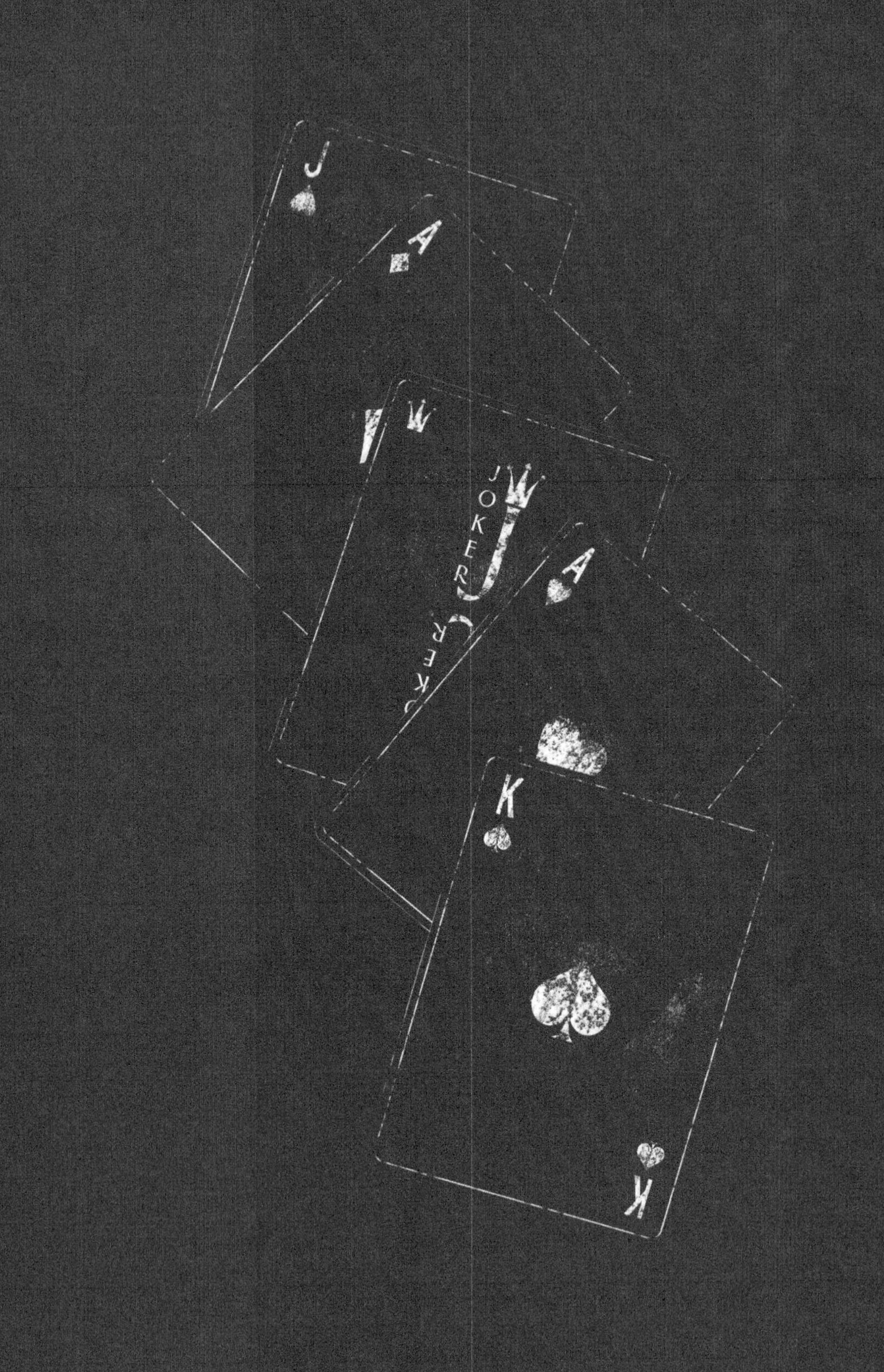
JOKER

CHAPTER FOURTEEN

ACE

Her posture was rigid and tense, like a frightened rabbit in a corner, faced with the fox, but beneath that surface level, there was something there I recognized, a familiar look that struck a chord in me. It was one I knew well, as I'd spent years trying to get it off my own face.

Defiance.

Beneath her shaken resolve, there was a warrior brewing, a survivor hardened to the worst this world had to offer.

What had this little minx endured to hold such a heavy burden beneath her outer shell?

I shook my head, hating the momentary weakness that was my curiosity. I didn't have time to dissect her emotionally. And considering she was a shrink, there was no doubt in my mind her little brain was running double-time trying to find a way out of this.

Too bad for her she wouldn't get the chance to escape. I didn't allow loose ends, and she was like a slowly-unraveling string at the end of a knot. One little tug by the wrong hand and all our secrets were fair game. That put us all in danger, and that was unacceptable.

"Mallory Stanton, mid-twenties, licensed therapist." I lifted the dossier BlackJack put together for me and thumbed through the papers nestled inside, making a point to gaze up at her as I flipped page after page of information I already had memorized. My eyes still stung, and the skin of my face and throat ached something fierce, but I didn't need my eyes to hear her quick intake of breath, see her tense posture, or smell the fear rolling off her. Years beneath my grandfather and uncles in tutelage to the Yakuza had honed my other senses. You learned quickly that should you lose one sense, you needed to be able to rely on your remaining ones to fill the gap. An unprepared man was often a dead one within seconds.

My eyes rose to hers again, locking in on that warrior underneath, the survivor. Perhaps it would be quickest to appeal to the side of her she thought she could hide from me. "Your father was a piece of work, wasn't he?"

Her eyes flickered with shame and hatred for a split second before the mask came down over her eyes, guarding all her secrets. "I don't know what you mean."

Too bad you already told them to me, sweetheart.

"Surely you know I'm talking about Slim Jim himself. The man is a legend in the underbelly of our city. Though that's one man greased by too many wheels, if you catch my drift. Not to be trusted."

I studied her reaction, but the girl determined to win this battle of wills had come out to play against what I could tell was her better judgment, and she wasn't holding back now. "That man is not and has never been my *father.*"

"Ah, but he is something to you, then. Those emotions all over your face make it hard to hide."

Mallory screwed those pretty lips up in a mulish frown, breaking my gaze to stare at the floor. "Fuck him. And fuck you." She looked back, and the fear was all but gone now, replaced by acceptance and anger. Raw, unfiltered anger. "If you're going to kill me, just fucking do it."

I couldn't resist leaning forward and grabbing her by the throat, tugging her body toward me aggressively, reminding her she was literally in the den of a cobra, my fangs waiting to strike. I let her see the hood of the monster, squeezing her windpipe just enough to make her gasp for air. Her eyes widened, the whites rolling dangerously as her hands reached up and clawed at my fist around her neck.

"I know you're new here, but around this place, I'm in charge. I take orders from no one, especially not you." I gave her a single, meaningful shake and released her, letting momentum carry her back toward the couch.

Her back slammed into it, and what remained of her breath left her with a harsh grunt. Joker twitched to help her, but when I shook my head, he froze in place, knowing to offer her support now would sign his own death warrant. I was in a mood, and none were safe.

Spade didn't have the same compunction, and he was off the couch in a flash, his brooding glare staring daggers into me as he lifted her from the floor and curled protectively around her, his hand moving to cup her jaw tenderly. "Are you hurt?"

"Spade," I barked, eyes narrowed at his defiance. "Let her go. Mallory's a big girl; she can handle herself, can't you?"

Spade blatantly ignored me and put himself between her and I. "You don't have to be a dick about it, Ace. She didn't do fucking anything but her job. Not her fault Joker's a fucking idiot when he's drunk."

Joker had the good sense to look chastised, but there was still the issue of Spade's defiance. "Let her go and let me get on with it, or I'll find somewhere else for you to be." I quirked a brow and cast my gaze out the window briefly. "Permanently."

The oaf grumbled in argument but took his seat, pulling Mallory down beside him. The doctor seemed uncomfortable with this display of possession, and to be honest, it shocked me as well. Our enforcer was unstable at the best of times, and I wasn't sure what his aims were with her, but they couldn't be all that wholesome.

But as long as he didn't muck this up, I didn't care what sort of obsession he had with her.

"Now, where were we?" The folder was still open on my lap, and I shuffled my weight to open it slowly, mulling over the contents. "Ah, yes, we were on the topic of your life story." The power shift in the room rattled my brain, so I looked to BlackJack for reassurance that at least one of my men had common sense left in his head. If there was anyone I could trust not to lose his head over a woman, it was him.

BlackJack studied Miss Stanton with narrowed eyes, his gaze sweeping her for any sign of weakness, no doubt. His analytical mind and attention to detail were likely running in tandem, trying to get a grip on what made our captive tick. I was thoroughly pleased with his calm exterior, confident that if something were to happen, he would handle it the way I wanted.

"Your mother is dead, and you have no siblings," I continued, uncaring of the fleck of pain that crossed her features at the harsh reality I reminded her of. "No close friends to speak of, unless you count the ones who ditched you and made our job easier."

BlackJack shifted against the wall as Joker gripped the couch's armrest like he wanted to do it harm. Beside him, Spade leaned forward and tugged a knife from his boot, absent-mindedly running his thumb over the ridges. Both of them refused to meet my gaze, but I knew the score. They might let me grill her, but they were already too attached. And separating Spade from her would be like pulling teeth and probably involve chains and restraints.

"Tell me, Miss Stanton, why didn't you go to the police with what you knew?"

Her answer was nothing like what I expected to hear.

"Why fucking bother? I'm not an idiot. I know the second I squeal, I'm fish food." She shoved her hair behind her, letting it fall over one shoulder as she leaned back and winced, probably bruised from her fall against the couch. "I have better things to do than chase criminals around with the police. If they can't catch you, that's their problem. I have plenty of my own."

"Smart girl," BlackJack murmured from the back of the room. His brows were lifted high in shock, but he still stood with his back to the drywall, a foot propped against it, knee bent, arms crossed over his chest. If anyone had to guess who the last line of defense was in a room, you wouldn't pick him, but that's what made him so dangerous.

"So, it appears we're at an impasse, then, young lady." Her brows raised at my use of the term to describe her, but she remained silent, waiting for me to continue. "You know too much for us to let you go. So, for now, you'll remain with us indefinitely until we decide if you're more trouble than you're worth—"

"I can't just drop everything for you deranged fucks!" Her hands flung in the air, and she leaped from the couch, pacing back and forth in front of me like an angry tiger.

Perhaps the cage *was* fitting for her, after all.

"I have a life to live, a job, people who depend on me, rent to pay, and cats to feed—"

"We will see to it your job receives a notice of resignation, effective immediately," I rambled off, inspecting my nail beds lazily as she fumed before me. "Your cats will be taken care of, rent will be paid, and anything else that needs done. As for people who depend on you, as of now, they don't matter anymore."

"Please, just let me go," she pleaded, switching tactics carefully, hoping to garner sympathy from me now. "If I were gonna tell your secret, I would have already."

"She's got a point," Spade pointed out, shoving the knife in my direction for emphasis.

"If I wanted your opinion, I'd ask you." My hands clenched into fists on my lap, the irritation pushing me to a breaking point encouraged and enabled by the sharp sting of my near-failure from the day before. "There will be no argument on the subject. From here on out, you're ours, and that changes only when I say it does. Your only other option is death, and I seriously doubt you're suicidal."

She froze directly in front of me, and her jaw dropped. "You can't just kidnap a whole ass human being and expect—"

"Expect what, Miss Stanton? Expect you to behave? Expect you to comply with my demands?" I rose to tower over her, my trademark smirk of satisfaction crossing my lips and crinkling the skin at the corner of my mouth. "That's exactly what I expect you to do, sweetheart. And you will comply, of that, I have no doubt." I leaned in next to her face, our cheeks nearly pressed together as I brushed the hair back from her throat so I could whisper into her ear.

"Because if you don't, I have the power to make your stay a whole lot shorter."

"Fuck you," she spat, with all the fire I expected from her now that I'd put a chink in her armor. "I'm not a fucking dog you can keep as a pet. People will miss me, and they'll go to the cops. Somebody's gonna ask questions."

"And that's why BlackJack will send your people a text when they inevitably reach out to you in guilt, letting them know you're taking an extended vacation due to the pressure of all the overworking you've been doing." I pulled away but left my hand in her hair, gripping it just a tad more tightly than necessary as I tipped her head back and brought her face right beneath mine. "We cover all the bases here, Dr. Stanton. Perhaps you shouldn't have taken that last call after all."

My gut roiled at the sight of tears springing to the corners of her eyes, though I knew there was anger behind them, not sadness. How could someone be sad to leave behind basically nothing?

I wasn't an abuser. Hurting women brought me no joy. But Mallory Stanton didn't understand pretty words and reassurances. This woman knew pain, made it her friend, her close companion, and surrounded herself with it like a shield. All that would get through to her was more pain, so that's what I gave her.

So when I released her hair and strode out of the room, why did my heart sink into the pit of my stomach and make me feel like a piece of garbage at what I'd just done?

JOKER

CHAPTER FIFTEEN
MALLORY

These men were ruthless, really and truly. If I stood a chance at surviving, I would have to tame my fast tongue and get on board with being a good captive.

Fuck that, the inner voice in me screamed. *They might have kidnapped you, but you can cause problems for them, make them regret assuming you'd go quietly.*

The side of me that was my father's child relished the chance to torment them right back, cause problems where they expected me to offer none. But that wasn't who I was. Not anymore.

I made a promise to myself a long time ago not to let the darkness back in, and my entire self depended on me keeping that promise.

Their leader and his silent monolith of a man wandered from the room together, and the brief look exchanged between them in the doorway had me wondering if there was something more there. Were they closer than the other two? Was there some sort of shared understanding between the two? Maybe a past moment that defined them as closer to one another.

The couch was starting to get uncomfortably crowded, what with the blonde pretty boy on one side of me and the injured but no less scary enforcer on the other, still flicking that pocket knife open and closed, over and over, his eyes a million miles away. Ace hadn't told them to tie me up again, and I assumed if they could put together a file on me in a few days, they probably had a security system to prevent me from leaving here without alerting them.

Might as well get comfortable.

Spade's knife flicked closed with a final jerk of his wrist, and those faraway eyes focused in on Joker over my head. "You got work to do today?"

Joker's nod was slow but pointed. "Running some interference with BlackJack today at the docks. Your job falls to us in your absence, so get better fast." His eyes flicked to me, and I winced at the implied meaning behind them. "And try not to let her stab you anymore, or I'll have to let the guys down at the ring know you were bested by a woman."

"You'll do that if you wanna add to your collection of scars, pretty boy," Spade snapped back, a shit-eating grin spread over that dangerous demeanor. When he turned to me, that dangerous glint in his eyes was downright unsettling. "You know what that means for us?"

My shoulders lifted briefly as I shot him a curious look. "Means you're going to hide the knives from me, for starters."

His barking laughter was contagious, and my lips curled into a small smile at his amusement.

"Nah, nothing of the sort. I trust you not to stab your only ticket to freedom right now."

As he leaned back on the couch, my confusion was only amplified by his strange comment. "Ticket to freedom?"

"Sure." He sat forward again, reaching for me with a feral grin. When his good hand grabbed me by the waist and tugged, I let out a little yelp, but I was on his lap in a heartbeat, his muscles barely flexing as he lifted me, positioning me where he wanted. "You don't wanna sit around for days in *that* getup, do you?" His grin widened as I blushed, realizing what I still wore. "Course, I don't mind—you look like a little badass, and I'd love to see how that thing looks in tatters around your shoulders."

I tugged at the sheer silk top, offended at his suggestion. "This is a Yves Saint Lauren exclusive. It cost me three months of overtime to afford it. If you even *think* of coming near it with a pair of scissors, I'll gut you permanently this time."

He chuckled and stood from the couch, offering me a hand up, which I took, albeit a bit hesitantly. "If I take anything to that top, it certainly won't be scissors, sweetheart."

Somehow, I didn't doubt he was serious about that threat.

TICKET TO FREEDOM, as it turned out, meant he was planning to sneak me out of the compound. I wasn't sure how I'd lucked out like this, but when he led me into a garage and popped the trunk, I stared at him like he was stupid.

Surely he didn't expect me to get in there.

When I suggested as much to him, his warm chuckle ran over my skin and warmed me as much as it chilled me to the bone. "Of course I do. You're gonna hop in here like a good girl, and when we're closer to your side of town, I'll holler back at you to pull the tab to drop the backseat, and you can climb up into the cab so we don't draw attention when we get where we're going."

I balked at the idea of being crammed in a tight, confined, dark trunk. I wasn't claustrophobic, but I also wasn't eager to turn into a sardine. And who knew how many dead people they'd transported in this trunk, how much blood had stained the carpet before they'd detailed it and erased the evidence.

The thought of another body in there, lifeless and cold, twisted my stomach, and I dry heaved in response, trying to fight back full-on sickness. "I can't," I breathed, feeling light-headed already.

"Sure you can. I do it all the time." He patted the carpeted interior, and I winced at the insistence in his voice. "It's plenty big enough to fit you comfortably. And you won't be in there long."

I backed away from the trunk another step, hands clawing at my throat as I swallowed the bile rising up my esophagus and threatening to spill over and embarrass me. "It sure doesn't look very big," I hedged, hoping he'd take the hint and just blindfold me or something.

"Sure it is. Look, I fit in it just fine." He turned to me with a dashing smile and slid in with one leg, then another, curling up on the inside of the trunk in a demonstration. "If I can fit, you certainly shouldn't have a problem—"

I didn't think, didn't even blink before my hands were slamming the trunk hood down on the car. His shouts and demands to be freed were muffled as I sat on the top of it, his hammering fists thumping threateningly against my ass through the metal.

Had I really just locked a mobster in his own fucking trunk?

Yes, yes I had.

I hopped down and scrambled for the driver's door, slamming it shut behind me. He had the key fob in his pocket, but the car was push start, so as long as the key was inside all the doors, you could start it and run just about anywhere you needed to go.

And I was counting on it to get me far enough away that I could dump his car and get out of there.

As I started the car, his demeanor changed drastically, and instead of hammering away on the hood, he was now banging on the back of the backseat. I had no idea how long it'd take him to break free, but I hoped it was long enough that I could get away. Or at least get somewhere I was safe.

My fingers fumbled over the visors, finding no sign of a garage door opener, and decided on the course of action I'd only seen successfully executed in movies.

Time to bust through the door.

It didn't occur to me that these doors might be made of something more robust than regular garage doors, not until I was jamming the car into reverse to move as far back in the stall as I could get it to go. When I threw the gearstick in first and slammed down on the gas, wheels spun, smoke flew, and my whole life flashed before my eyes as I was propelled into the seat, and we rocketed forward like the car had been fired from a damn gun.

The screaming in the trunk stopped momentarily, and then we slammed into the garage door—and through it, thank *gods*—and into the daylight.

Freedom.

I spun out a little as the tires hit the pavement and gripped it like glue. Getting control of the car was easier than I thought it would be, and I stopped the fishtail just in time to avoid oncoming traffic. Some part of the back of my brain recognized the wharf district immediately, warehouse after warehouse lining the street on either side of me, mingling with the seagulls that flew overhead and picked scraps off the sidewalk as I flew by. In a matter of blocks, I managed to get better bearings and took a turn that would lead me home—if I made it that far without my captive breaking out of the trunk.

I tilted the rearview mirror to focus on the backseat just in case and stepped on the gas, propelling us into the morning traffic.

The banging in the trunk returned with gusto, and now it sounded like he'd turned around to use his boots for more leverage. As I sped along, counting the blocks to my apartment, to safety, the hammering sound quieted, and I breathed a sigh of relief.

Maybe he'd given up.

Yeah, and maybe pigs would sprout fucking wings and fly, too.

I drifted around the next corner in my haste to get as far away from that warehouse compound as possible and nearly took out a cop coming the other way. As if a divine light shone on me from above, his lights came on as he spun around in the intersection and came racing after us, though the car I drove was far too fast for him to catch up to unless I slowed down.

Which I started to do until an arm snaked around me, and a cold, deadly sharp blade pressed into the skin right beneath my chin.

How had he gotten free without me hearing?

"If you slow down to let the pigs catch up, I'll slit your throat and end it before you can hit the brakes. When he gets to you, only a lifeless, broken body will be left, sweetheart, and I won't feel an ounce of remorse about it." His blade pressed into my skin, nicking me until a drop of blood trickled down the hollow of my neck. "Now, I want you to step on it and do exactly as I say. Do you understand me?"

I nodded frantically, already regretting my decision to try something this stupid. He'd take me back to their compound, and Ace would string me up and beat the shit out of me, making me regret every life choice I'd made up til now. Or maybe they'd have him slit my throat now and dump my body somewhere nobody would find it.

All manner of murderous scenarios traveled through my mind as I followed his orders to the letter, turning when he demanded it, staying just a few steps ahead of the cops. When we came up on the bridge that led into my neighborhood, his hand tensed, and the blade pressed even deeper into the skin of my neck, my eyes going wide as I wondered if this was the end.

"Grip that wheel and gun it. Twenty feet before the bridge, cut hard to the left, and you're gonna slip into the service tunnel. You'll have an inch or three on either side of the car, so you'd better hope your aim is as pretty as your ass in that skirt, or we're both dead."

"I'm not a skilled getaway driver," I balked, knowing damn well I operated like shit under pressure. "You can't mean for me to—"

"You're the one in the driver's seat, and there's no time for a switch, so you're it. Now buck up and hold on tight. Things might get a little bumpy until we get through to the other side."

I blinked back tears of panic at what might be my last minutes on earth and sent up a silent plea to get me out of this alive, then braced for impact as the service tunnel came into view.

"Slow down and let the cop think he's got you."

My foot automatically lifted slightly from the gas pedal, and sure enough, the cop behind us sped up, jetting like a rocket to get in range. My eyes flicked from his car to the road in front of me and back again, my stomach in my throat and my heart hammering a pattern of intense panic against the inside of my ribcage as the window of opportunity neared.

"Now! Gun it!" He leaned over the seat, and the blade fell away from my throat for a second, letting me breathe as I crushed the pedal to the floor and let out a battle cry, barely resisting the urge to close my eyes as I prepared for the end. With not a second to spare, I jerked the wheel to the left and slipped away from the cop before he had enough time to blink.

The wall of the concrete barrier came into my line of sight, with just enough space on either side to slip the car past. My whole body seized up as I measured the distance as best I could and committed to a side.

"Fuck! Fuck fuck fuck fuck fuck—"

My hands probably could have snapped the steering wheel with how tightly I clung to it as I slipped by the barrier and down the service tunnel, a solid six inches on either side of me as I held speed and curved the damn thing around the turns beneath the city streets, wincing as the scrape of paint warned me I'd gotten too close to the edge.

I didn't breathe again until we popped out underneath the bridge, safely concealed under the concrete and steel wire contraption that handled the vast majority of inter-city traffic. My breath left me in a whoosh, and I slammed on the brakes, the car coming to a screeching halt in the shadows of an overpass.

I didn't even think, didn't hesitate; I just flung my door open and fell bodily out of the car, my knees scraping the concrete as I landed with a thud, my legs too weak to support me. My lungs worked overtime, sucking in air like every breath was my last, and I wouldn't get another. With shaking hands, I shoved off the ground and stood up, leaning against the car for support.

Holy shit, I'm alive.

JOKER

CHAPTER SIXTEEN
SPADE

I *think I'm in fucking love.*

Day one of her kidnapping, and she'd already taken the bait I laid out for her, shoving me into a trunk and kidnapping *me,* moments before making a daring attempt at escape and nearly getting herself killed for the effort. I had my doubts about whether she could pull off the maneuver, but I was ready to lean over and take the wheel if I had to.

This girl was full of surprises, though. She didn't even blink, she just went for it. And when she fell out of the car, I didn't hear her lose her lunch, so that was more points in her favor.

I'd never done that with anyone else behind the wheel. It was always me driving, making the daredevil move when I knew I could do it. What took me months of wrecked cars and quite a few secret payoffs of traffic cops to perfect, she'd managed at the drop of a hat, proving once again she was perfect for me.

First, she stabbed me, then she kidnapped me and stole my car.

I got out of the car and stumbled a little, thanks to my lack of a working second arm, gripping the roof of the Mercedes as I rounded the front of the metal beast. The hood was hot to the touch, but I didn't care. I had only one goal in mind.

Getting to her.

Her eyes were huge, pupils dilated from the rush of adrenaline coursing through her hot blood. When she turned those doe eyes on me, and she smiled that megawatt smile, I felt it go straight to my heart—and then, straight to my dick.

"Fucking hell, sweetheart, you were amazing," I panted, leaning my hip against the car as I used my good arm to crowd her in. "Marry me."

My lips crashed against hers without preamble, without giving her a second to respond to my proposal, and it was like heaven itself exploded behind my eyes. With a groan borne of pure, unadulterated lust, I claimed her for myself, uncaring that she didn't immediately respond to my affections.

It didn't take long, though. Being in a near-death situation with someone tended to blur the lines of propriety.

Her hands moved up to tangle in my thick hair, pulling it free of the loose bun I kept it in, though the time in the trunk had done most of the work for her. Those claws at the end of her slender fingers worked against my scalp, drawing a moan from the depths of my soul as I plundered her mouth, my one good hand braced against the car as I pressed up against her, letting her feel the thick arousal she caused in me.

"Fucking Christ, sweetheart," I panted, our lips moving against each other between words as she responded to me, to the lust between us, her back arching even as she dragged my lips against hers again. I felt one of her legs throw itself over my hip, lining up her core against my stiff cock, rubbing against it like a fucking cat in heat, and it was all too much to bear.

She didn't speak words—not intelligible ones, at least—as her body rolled seductively against mine and she whined in frustration, aching for something more that she didn't want to admit to herself. Her hands moved from my hair to my neck, and she gripped my collar, holding me in place as her tongue slipped inside my willing mouth, tracing the line of my teeth, the arch of my tongue, mapping me out for her own pleasure.

Fuck, why was this so hot? Why couldn't I keep my hands off her? Why didn't I want to stop?

I kept my lips fused to hers as I inched her toward the hood of the car. When her ass was right where I wanted her, I lifted that other leg of hers and grabbed her ass, hoisting her with ease onto the car. She gave a yelp but no further protest, the sound muffled against my lips as I positioned her just right and leaned forward, bending her back.

She went without so much as a peep, her arms wrapped around me still, dragging me to the pits of hell with her.

My one good hand was in her hair in an instant, thumb brushing the side of her ear, tracing the strong column of her throat, drawing teasing circles as it went lower, until I cupped the back of her neck in my palm, fingers spread wide to feel as much of her as I could. Her encouraging moans as I broke off the kiss and trailed kisses down her throat were all the permission I needed, nipping and licking my way to the dip in the junction where it met her shoulder. She arched into my solid form as I nipped the sensitive skin at her collarbone, and the needy whine that graced my ears had my cock jumping behind my jeans in eager appreciation.

I wanted to be balls deep in her, and soon, so I didn't waste time. She wouldn't fight me. Not if I played this right.

"You taste like heaven and sweat, girl. My favorite blend." I whispered filthy things to her as my lips trailed the curve of her collar, the see-through top taunting me with the treasure I was so close to but so far away from still. "Fuck, I want you."

Her answering moan as she lifted those legs higher and wrapped them around my waist was fucking torture of the highest order. I mercilessly ground my hips against her center, now bared to me, hiding that honey hole behind nothing more than a pair of panties and some fishnets.

I couldn't take it anymore. It was torture, but not, and I needed to have both my hands on her before I fucked her senseless, riding this high we were both on together. With a grunt of pain at the brief twinge in my shoulder, I reached up and yanked off my sling, feeling the tug in the stitches but unable to give a damn. If they ripped, they ripped; I didn't care.

"You're mine, sweetheart," I growled, mindless with want as I pitched forward and ran a hand up her thigh, following the curve of her hip, pleased when I found her fishnets were thigh-highs, attached to a very smooth garter belt that her skirt hid from view. Or had, before I used my body to force it up those pretty legs of hers. "I'm gonna ruin you for any other man, you hear me?"

She mumbled some sort of affirmative against the top of my head as I reached into my pocket for the blade I'd slipped away when I wasn't sure if she'd pull it off, flipping it open with an ominous *click*. With a steady hand, I reached between us and slipped the knife up the front of her shirt, ripping it clean in two in my haste to get to her. Her protests were weak and didn't last long as my lips moved to the lacy bra covering her perky tits, and I drew the first peaked nipple into my mouth.

Her groan nearly had me coming in my pants.

"Fuck me," she breathed, arching her spine, pressing that nipple into my waiting mouth, her hands splayed behind her to support her weight.

"With pleasure," I groaned in response, letting my teeth do the work to pull the cup of her bra down and expose that hot pink flesh. I flicked my tongue against her tight peak, pleased when she responded by rolling her eyes into the back of her head and moaning loudly. I doubled my efforts before switching sides, teeth dragging across the sensitive skin for added measure.

My injured arm wouldn't support my weight, so I set it on other adventures instead, diving between our melded bodies to find the swatch of fabric that barred entrance to my favorite part of a woman. Another time, I might have fallen to my knees and eaten her out like she was dessert on the dinner menu, but there was no time for that now.

Another time, perhaps, I thought to myself as my fingers dragged up the expanse of fabric, pleased when she responded with a little yelp, followed by the most sinful of sounds I'd heard her make yet. Her hips canted into my touch, seeking the invasion of my fingers, something I was loath to deny her for long.

"Easy, killer, I'll give you what you need," I panted against her breasts, leaving those peaked nipples glistening with moisture as I moved back up to her mouth to worship her as I slid a finger under her panties and into her dripping, achingly tight core. "Fuuuuck," I moaned, cock twitching, breath catching in my lungs as her tight little cunt gripped me like a vice, squeezing onto that single digit like it was life or death. Her body sang to me, pleasing little whimpers as she slid her hands out from beneath her back and laid down on the hood of the car, legs spread, begging me to finger her out in the open beneath the bridge after running from the cops and nearly dying. "You better behave, or there won't be anything left for me to fill you up with."

"Oh my god, are we really doing this?" she whispered, her eyes closed against the assault on her body. She didn't shove me away, though, and that was consent enough for me as I added a finger to her tight channel, ramming them into her with a ferocity that amazed me.

She gave as good as she got, lifting her hips as she sought out the pleasure I brought to her with nothing more than a few digits on my hand. Her mewling cries morphed into panting pleas, and before long, she was tightening around me, her orgasm so close I bet she could taste it on her tongue.

But I wasn't about to let her have it, not like this.

With no warning, I yanked my fingers out of her pussy and brought them to my lips, waiting until she opened those beautiful, expressive eyes and looked at me before I slipped them into my mouth and groaned at the taste of her. I rolled my tongue around each digit, careful to get every drop of her essence off my skin before I removed them with a pop.

"One day soon, I'm going to taste you straight from the source, sweetheart, and you're gonna beg me for it."

"Never," she breathed, but there was no bravado behind her words, no actual denial, just arousal, pure and simple.

I opened my mouth to ask her if she was on the pill and then shut it just as fast, realizing I didn't much give a damn. I wanted to paint the inside of her with my seed, wanted to make sure she knew exactly whose bitch she was now. I wasn't going to let her go, not now, not ever, and to hell with Ace and anyone who thought they could say otherwise.

Mallory Stanton was mine, and I'd die before I let anyone take her from me.

"I'm going to bury myself inside you and fuck you senseless until you forget your own name."

My hand jerked down to my waistband, and with little effort, I jerked my cock free and lined the head of it up with her slippery cunt, wetting myself with her juices before I rammed the fuck home, her tight heat swallowing me down so well I almost came right then and there.

"Shit," she breathed, her hands fisted in her hair as I slid all the way in, taking my time so I didn't blow like a fucking teenager. My balls ached, but I wasn't about to go down as the quickest lay she'd ever had. I was a professional, and dammit, I'd act like one.

My dick might not be on the same page, but I didn't give a damn. He wasn't calling the shots.

I gripped her hips and fucked into her, my thrusts jostling the whole car as animalistic snarls left my throat and filled the air around us. She whimpered but didn't move, except to tilt her hips so I rubbed against the upper wall of her pussy with each ram of my cock inside her.

Mallory Fucking Stanton took my dick like a champ, and when she reached down to play with her clit while I fucked her, I nearly came apart. She was gasoline on my fire, the flames between us burning hotter than the fucking sun as I leaned over her and captured her lips with my own again, needing to swallow her moans like she swallowed me. When her hands wound around my neck in response, I leaned back up, pulling her with me, our mouths fused as I rocked up into her, bringing her ass off the hood just an inch with each pump into her sopping core.

"Fucking hell, girl."

She smiled against my lips, a teasing little lift of the corner of her mouth that drove me insane. I was so close, *so fucking close,* and I wanted nothing more than to fill her with my cum and take her home.

Let the others think what they wanted. I'd leave her dripping my cum from her cunt all day, every day, to hell with the ramifications. Mallory was mine.

All mine.

"That's right, sweetheart, take it, take all of me; that's a good girl." I was delirious with the need to come, the need to brand her, and my lips slipped from hers and traveled to her shoulder as she snaked a tiny hand between us and caressed the spot where we joined. Her finger brushed against my cock as it slipped inside her, and I came with a roar, unable to hold back any longer. Her fingers made quick work of her clit, and she was screaming right along with me, that delicious cunt clenching my length as I jerked and filled her until it leaked out and dripped over my fucking balls.

She went limp in my arms, boneless and sated with a smile of satisfaction on her pretty red lips. I didn't bother to pull out of her as I laid her down on the car again, tugging the cups of her bra up over those heaving tits as she gasped for air.

Fuck, I didn't like that I couldn't see those creamy globes and nearly uncovered them again before realizing she couldn't just walk around with her tits out unless I was ready to go on the most wanted list for a string of murders of every man who caught sight of them.

Her legs fell on either side of my hips, and with one last groan, I pulled free of her damnably intoxicating heat, growling as her panties slipped back into place and hid the evidence of our coupling from sight.

Not that it'd stay a secret for long. Those panties were already soaked when we started, and by the time we got back to the warehouse, she'd be dripping on the floor.

"Take these fucking things off," I demanded, running a finger along the wet material as she shuddered and twitched at the contact. "I want you to soak the seat of my car."

She bit her bottom lip but complied, slipping them down her hips a few inches before I got impatient and yanked them the rest of the way. I popped the garters on the way down, but she didn't seem to mind too much, her fingers working to refasten the snaps while I was distracted.

She moved to close her legs, but I stopped her with a hand on each knee, spreading her wide again to admire my handiwork one last time.

"I wanna see how wrecked you are for me," I ground out, my eyelids at half-mast as I reached down and smeared two fingers in her folds, collecting the mingled fluids there before I shoved those fingers deep inside her, forcing my cum and her arousal back inside, claiming her.

I leaned in, my face between her legs now, and licked a stripe right up the slit of her pussy with a low growl.

"Mine."

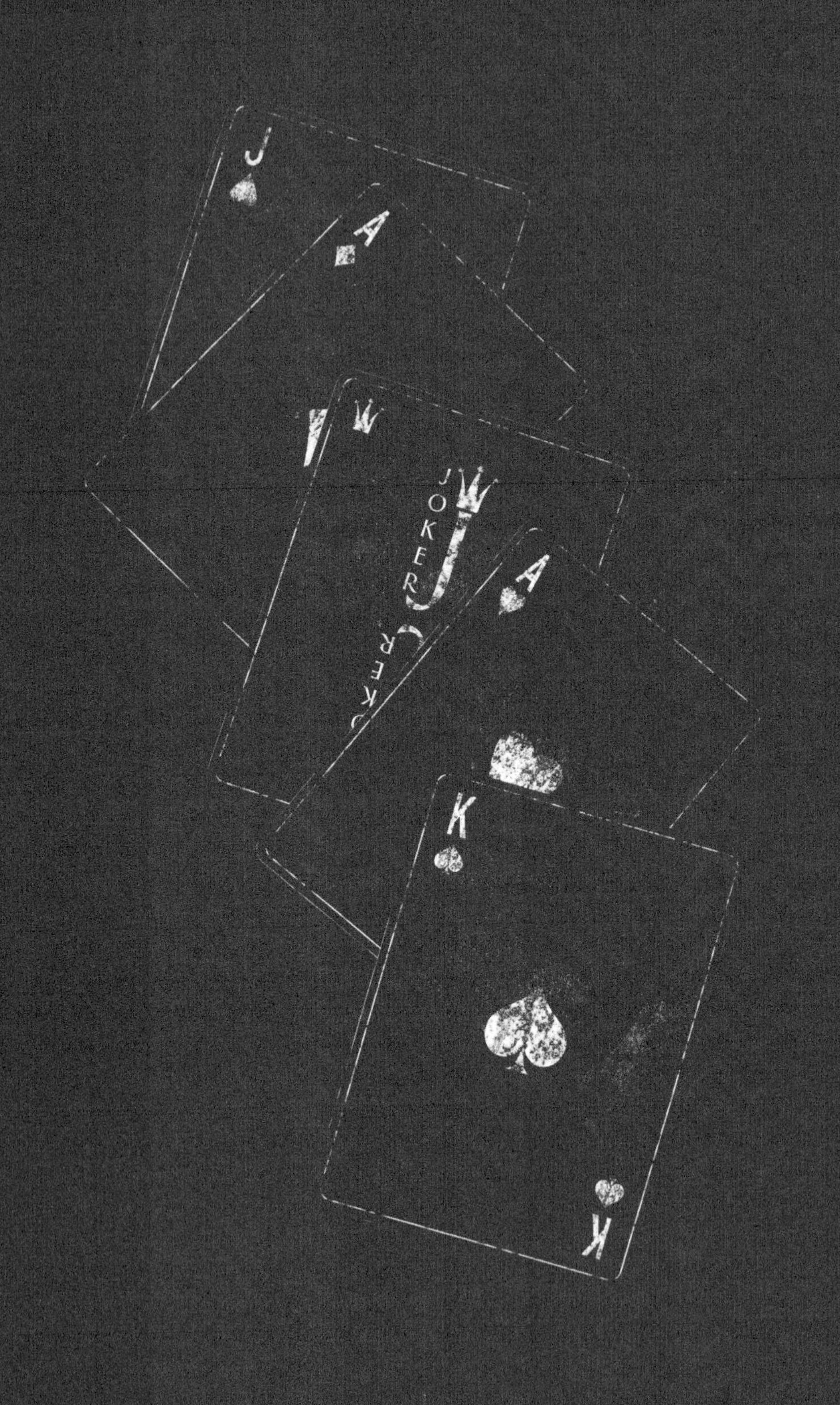
JOKER

CHAPTER SEVENTEEN
MALLORY

After I let myself be thoroughly fucked on top of a stolen car after outrunning the police, there really was nowhere to go but up. It was the single-most risque thing I'd ever done, sex with a stranger I'd stabbed the night before—and unprotected, no less.

Fuck.

Was he clean?

What even was my life now? One night with a band of criminals as their captive and I had already turned into a brazen whore slash getaway driver, a kidnapper, and was now guilty of grand theft auto.

I was no better than my old man.

Spade didn't let me wallow in my self-pity long.

He lumbered around the car with a hand around the base of my neck, guiding me into place on the passenger side of the vehicle before he released me with a grunt. "Get in and buckle up."

I stared at the door to the car, and something inside me recoiled at the idea of going back to being a prisoner. His prisoner. Their prisoner. "No."

He stared slack-jawed at me as if I'd sprouted another head. "I said, get in the car, sweetheart." His thumb brushed against the arch of my spine at my hairline, sending a shiver through me at the implied threat. "Don't make me ask again."

Sensing a fight wouldn't be the smartest option, I opted to listen to directions, pulling the door open with a shaking hand. When he saw me in the car and was satisfied with my secured belt, he marched back around the front and slid into the driver's seat, a grimace on his lips.

"Alright. Off we go."

His hands ran along the steering wheel as he navigated us down the dirt road we'd ended up on and plenty far away from where we'd come in before chancing a trip back to the main roads. I didn't pay attention to where we were headed, only what he was doing, and I noticed with a start that a fresh blossom of blood was steadily staining his shirt, just about where I'd stabbed him with my blade last night.

"Spade," I hesitantly whispered, a hand stretched toward him.

His eyes cut sideways to meet mine briefly as he kept driving. "What's cooking, good-looking?"

"Your wound," I mumbled, a blush working over my cheeks despite myself. "You're bleeding again. I think you tore your stitches."

His gaze flicked down to his shirt, and a slow smile spread on his lips. "It was worth it."

That was it. No concern, no interest, just amusement. Hell, I'd even go so far as to say he enjoyed it.

"You're not afraid you'll bleed out?"

He shook his head. "Nah. I'm not Joker."

I cocked my head, and something in my confused expression must have given him pause because he clammed up, saying nothing more on the subject.

I no sooner blinked than we were sitting in front of my fucking apartment.

"Why are we here?" I asked stupidly, staring blankly at the nondescript building with apprehension. My top was torn straight down the middle, and he was covered in blood, but the first thought that sprang to my mind was the hope that he was letting me go.

That he'd gotten what he wanted, so now I was free.

But my face fell as he stepped out of the car and onto the sidewalk, dusting himself off with another grimace of pain.

He peeked back into the car with a little twitch of his brow. "You coming, or do I have to come over there and get you?"

I scrambled from the car and followed him to the door, where he waited patiently for me to enter my code. I had to lead the way up, though, as it appeared he knew what building mine was, but nothing about where on the inside I made my home.

"This is where you live?"

The unspoken disappointment and surprise were plain to hear in his tone, and I rolled my eyes at his loss of touch with reality for those of us with a full-time job and an everyday life. "We can't all afford a tricked-out warehouse crib, asshole," I muttered, irate over his judgment. "This is what my measly salary pays for. It's home, and it's all I have."

I opened my apartment door and let him in first, watching as he crossed the room in just a few strides. The apartment seemed much smaller with a large man like Spade occupying the small space; it seemed much larger when my cats and I were the only inhabitants.

"So," he said, plunking down on the couch with an audible groan, "how's about you pack yourself a couple of days' worth of clothes, and I will feed these cats that you've told me so little about?"

"Sure," I muttered as I made my way back to the hall to my bedroom. "I'll get right on that."

"Do you have anything to drink in this place?" He stood back up and marched into my kitchen, the relatively small space almost comically so with his bulky frame hanging over the counter.

"There might be a beer or two left in the fridge, but I'm not sure how old they are. I don't drink very often—drinking alone is not *quite* as fun as drinking with friends." I left him to it and grabbed an overnight bag out of the hall closet, determined not to break down in front of him.

I couldn't deny how strange this whole situation felt, almost domestic in its simplicity. Here I was, freshly sexed up by a criminal who was now in my kitchen, feeding what amounted to my children. The two furballs in question had no loyalty, instead opting to meow loudly at their new master, who they'd already adopted thanks to his possession of their cat food.

They didn't seem interested in my return, only in the one who patiently waited for them to settle to feed them. Spade took to my cats like they were his own. As the familiar tinkling sound of small brown rocks hitting the bottom of a metal pan echoed through the hallway, I reached blindly into my dresser. I began to pull out handfuls of clothes, not even bothering to concern myself with the color or type. My only goal was to fill the bag and get moving again. If I stopped to think about it all, if I *really* stopped to analyze the situation, I might find things out about myself that I wasn't ready to admit.

For instance, my absolute abandon of all rational thought as I was getting railed absolutely senseless against the hood of a car in broad daylight.

I knew that once we left my apartment, we'd be heading back to their place, and I wasn't sure I was ready for the questions they'd ask when Spade told them what we'd been up to. *If* he told him. I still wasn't sure if he planned to tell them anything at all. Maybe he planned to throw me under the bus; I expected nothing less, to be honest.

Time passes slower when you're deep in thought, and it must have flown past me while I mulled over my uncertain future because the next thing I knew, two hands had grabbed me by the waist, and Spade's long, red hair was slowly sliding over my shoulder as he leaned in to see what held my attention.

It was a pair of skimpy red panties, because *of course it was.*

"Those are cute," he breathed against my ear, his body crowding me in like the heated wall of muscle that it was. I swallowed a yelp of surprise and stuffed the damn things back into my drawer, regretting the action as soon as I pulled my hand back out.

"Can I help you?" I snapped, aiming to defend myself as he encroached on my personal space some more.

My moment of weakness against his car was just that—a moment of weakness. It wasn't about to happen again. I needed to make sure this guy understood that.

His answering smirk hinted that he might not give a shit what my plans were. "We can't stay here long, sweetheart—"

I shoved at his chest, irritation rising. "Not your sweetheart, Spade. I'm your captive."

He leaned in and nuzzled my throat, sending a shiver down my spine and scattering my thoughts to the wind. "I don't recall forcing you to do a damn thing, Mallory. And last time I checked, most captives didn't marry their captors."

Now it was my turn to be confused. "We're not married."

He licked a line up the column of my throat and reached back into my drawer, retrieving the red panties I'd hidden away from his view. "Yet."

He was gone as suddenly as he'd appeared, calling for my fucking cats like this was his house and he belonged here. I stormed over to my closet and began yanking down all manner of clothes, not paying a lick of attention to what ended up where. A second bag joined the first, and I filled it with shoes of all kinds—sneakers, heels, sandals, slippers, you name it. If they were determined to make me uncomfortable in that damn place, if I was destined to be stuck in one spot, unable to do anything, see anyone, go anywhere, then dammit, I'd make it their problem what I was wearing.

I was half tempted to leave it all here and prance around in this ruined ensemble until they forced me into new clothes. But if I walked back outside in this ripped top and this leather skirt, I'd kick my own ass for it. And I could use a fucking shower, though I knew Spade wasn't about to let me take one, so I snuck to the bathroom and cleaned up with a wet washcloth as best as I could, whimpering a little at the sensation it stirred between my legs as I wiped his and my own sticky residue from between clenched thighs.

If being turned on was going to be a constant state of being around these men, though, I'd need a few other things to make it through my isolation in that fucking place. With a smile borne of pure contempt for men who thought they ran things simply because they had a dick between their legs, I wandered to my bedside stand and removed a little black velvet pouch, tugged it open to make sure all my supplies were safely stored inside, and slipped it into the bottom of my bag of shoes.

I'd be damned if I needed anything they had to offer. My only goal was to get out of this alive, and if I got to have a little fun along the way, so be it.

As almost an afterthought, I trotted into my bathroom and pulled the six months supply of birth control from the cabinet, adding it to the bag of shoes. I didn't plan to have any babies while I was a captive of criminals, not a chance in hell.

I'd die before I was saddled with these crazed, possessive, domineering, dangerous men for a life sentence.

THE CRIMINAL HAD A GENTLEMANLY SIDE, as he didn't let me carry any of my things to the car, even though I protested. I'd swapped the sliced-up sheer shirt for a ragged off-the-shoulder tee, some obscure eighties band plastered across the front, their tour schedule on the back. I kept the leather skirt because I didn't have much time, but Spade had me instantly regretting that as he used his injured arm to steer the car, and his perfectly healthy one migrated to my lap.

"Shouldn't you be driving?" I stuttered, eyes glued to the road ahead so I wouldn't look down and spot his hand in a very precarious place.

"I'm capable of multi-tasking, sweetheart," he shot back, his voice laced with amusement. "Why don't you sit back and enjoy the ride?"

I clamped my thighs together and scowled at his taunt. "I'm fine how I am, thank you."

His hand slipped between my knees, forcing them open just a fraction, and I bit back a whine at his nearness. I would *not* give in to him. I'd fight him the whole way. He might have had me once already, but that was a mistake. I blamed it on the adrenaline of being alive after such a daring escape.

"Open your legs for me."

His sinful voice was laced with an edge that could cut as surely as his knife, but still, I fought him, hoping my will was strong enough to hold him at bay.

His hand moved up a couple of inches, and he growled menacingly in the back of his throat. "I won't ask twice. You'd better learn that now, or we'll have some painful fun at home."

Home. He said it like he was determined that it should be mine, too. I still hadn't given up hope of being able to escape or them just letting me go.

I was delusional; sue me.

Grinding my teeth as I obeyed, my legs spread to allow his hand to grip my inner thigh possessively as he wove in and out of afternoon traffic, a stupid grin on his face. He didn't move to raise his hand to the juncture of my legs, a fact I was immensely grateful for when we pulled up to his compound and in through what *should* have been a wrecked garage door.

Instead, it had been replaced with a brand new one somehow, a feat that had to have cost a substantial amount of money to have occurred in such a short time.

My eyes flicked over to Spade, who still hadn't pulled his hand off my thigh. *Surely he hadn't had time—*

"Something you wanna say, sweetheart?"

His condescending tone set me on edge, and I huffed, crossing my arms over my chest with no small amount of childish petulance. "Nope."

His smile widened. "Okay then. Time to unload and get you situated."

I stepped out of the car when he did, my eyes cast around us quizzically. "You keep spare rooms for guests in here?"

"No," he deadpanned, pulling my bags out of the backseat. "But I've got two rooms, and you can use one of them. I'll even let you pick which one you wanna sleep in."

The two rooms, as it turned out, were his bedroom and his torture room, and there was no way I was staying in the latter. The smell of blood and sweat permeated the whole space, and I had to choke back a gag as I stepped back into the bedroom and shook my head.

"I'm sure as fuck not staying in there. It smells like you kill people in that fucking room."

His shoulders lifted in a half-assed shrug. "Maybe one or two, but like I told you, I prefer to leave them alive. Dead men tell no tales, but battered and broken ones squeal like fucking pigs."

I watched as he tossed my bags on his bed, their heavy weight mussing up the sheets where they landed. He flopped down into a nearby chair, wincing as it jarred his shoulder in the process. Before I could say another word, though, a knock sounded at his door, and the two of us froze.

"Spade? We need to talk."

JOKER

CHAPTER EIGHTEEN
BLACKJACK

I didn't want to read him the riot act. I didn't want to talk at all, not if I could avoid it. So when Ace delegated the shit job of reporting back to Spade for information on the man he used for street intel, I only did so because to fight him on it meant more words.

Words that were better spent elsewhere, or not at all.

When I pulled into the garage, I noted the new door, but though it confused me, I wasn't too worried. If there had been anything concerning that happened to damage the original, Spade would have told us.

Wouldn't he?

Surely the reckless fool wasn't as stupid as Joker was around this girl. I marched out of the garage and up the hall to the living quarters, betting I'd find his ass in his torture room, probably stringing the new girl up for his amusement.

I couldn't tell why that had me concerned for her safety, but it did.

She was no meek and wilting flower, not after she'd put up such a fight in the alley to get away from us, but every person had their breaking point, and perhaps he was hers. Spade certainly did have a way with people that usually sparked a bit of innate fear in them, even before he got close enough to put his hands on you.

So when she opened his bedroom door in a new top and that same skirt, her hair mussed like someone had run their hands through it repeatedly, it didn't take much in the way of mental gymnastics to tell what he'd been up to.

Spade fucked the captive.

She took one look at the expression on my face and backed up, swinging the door open to admit me into his room. "He's over there in the recliner thing," she muttered, her hand curled around the frame of the door, fingers gripping it like a lifeline. "I think he popped his stitches."

Sure enough, the smug but bleeding asshole was propped up in the nearby chair, trademark shit-eating grin spread across his face. "He looks fine to me," I muttered, pursing my lips at his lack of concern for my handiwork. "I'm not fixing him."

She inched around the door and put her hand on my arm, her fingers digging into the flesh there. "You have to! He'll bleed out—"

I ripped my arm from her grip and twisted her hand behind her back, shoving her face-first into the nearby wall. Spade clenched the armrests of his chair but didn't move, though I could tell he wanted to.

Her whimpers were like music to my ears, or they should have been, considering the error she'd committed against me. Nobody touched me, *nobody,* and I didn't take the violation lightly.

But her soft pleas and the tears that choked her now, they grated against my skin, made me ashamed for what I was doing to her.

Not that I could stop. At this point, punishing someone was necessary.

Better it be before she did worse.

"Don't ever put your hands on me uninvited again. Are we clear?" I leaned in to growl the warning in her ear, and she flexed against my pinning armlock, groaning at the stretch of her tender flesh as it neared its breaking point. She mumbled a muted *yes* and went back to her pitiful whimpers, turning her nose to the wall to escape me.

I shoved her harder into the wall and let her go, my hands tingling from the prolonged contact. A little thrill ran through me at the thought of her soft skin in my hold, just as a strange, empty feeling filled my black heart at the loss of her in my arms.

"Fuck you, BlackJack, she didn't know," Spade spat at me, and I decided right then and there that I *would* fix his stitches, just as soon as I ripped every single old one from his derelict body.

"She does now," I snapped back, marching over to where he kept a first aid kit hanging on the wall outside his torture room door. "Shirt."

He was quick to follow commands, peeling the bloodstained white tee over his head with no more than a slight wince of discomfort. I pulled a set of tweezers from the bag and prodded at the edge of his stitch string, tugging it until he hissed at my assault.

"If you're not gonna fix them, call someone who will," he growled at me, his hands gripping his thighs like a lifeline. "I'm not here to let you kick me when I'm down."

My lips twitched almost imperceptibly at his poor joke, and I abandoned the torment for actual work. I meticulously reversed the threads I'd put in him just last night and replaced it with a new strand of surgical line, doubling over the loops this time.

He wouldn't be popping these as effortlessly.

But just in case . . . I turned to the girl, eyes narrowed on her slight form hunched against the wall, rubbing her shoulder. "Stay off his dick until this has a chance to heal, you hear?"

"BlackJack," Spade growled in warning, but I was well past caring what he had to say about any of this. He was the reason I even had to redo my handiwork in the first place.

"I could just let Ace know what you're up to."

His lips slammed closed, defiance written in every line on his stoic features. "Fuck you."

"You're not my type."

He rolled his eyes and pointedly ignored me now, but that suited me just fine. The faster I could get this done, the faster I could have my answers and be out of the compound again. Away from the girl who—

Fuck, where'd she go?

I doubled my efforts on the stitches and tied off the last knot, tossing a square of gauze and some surgical tape at his bare chest in disgust. "Patch yourself up and wash the blood off. I'll find the girl."

I WAS NO SOONER out the door of his room than a sound down the hall drew my attention. It was coming from the commons, and since there were only three of us here, it had to be her. I followed the empty hall to her, confused when I found her sitting on the couch, knees drawn up to her chest, her arms around those fishnet-clad legs of hers. The boots she wore were muddy, and that mud was slowly seeping into the cushions, but I didn't give two shits.

What did give me pause was the fierce look of determination, of hatred and anger that left no room for a weak-willed woman.

Her father was Slim Jim, a known criminal in the mafia underworld. Perhaps he'd taught her from the start not to bend so easily, maybe even how to get the upper hand on a bunch of criminals like us. Or perhaps she was planning to use our weaknesses against us. She *was* a psychiatrist. Analyzing us and finding the chink in our armor wouldn't be hard.

"I'm not running away if that's what you think," she muttered coldly, her eyes on the blank television screen.

I took the seat across from her on the couch and frowned, hands in my lap. "You're not dumb."

She set her chin atop her knees, those strange little square patterns where her flesh peeked out drawing my eyes and keeping them there, transfixed. In a matter of a few minutes, with nothing more than a look and some exposed flesh, I was . . . curious. I wasn't immediately searching for a way to shorten this interaction.

I wanted her to talk to me.

Not because it was easy, but perhaps because like this, with her knees up and all the walls in place, she reminded me of myself, in a way. Back when living hadn't been just about surviving.

And a part of me was still curious how that felt.

"I'm not as smart as I'd like to think I am," she hedged, clearly uncomfortable with the assumption. "I mean, does a smart girl usually get kidnapped by the mafia? Does she let her father use her as a 'get out of jail free' card?" Her hands raked through those long brown tresses as a heavy sigh escaped her lips. I recognized the tactics for what they were, my heart hardening a little.

Make your kidnappers see you as a person. Humanize yourself.

"Those are not metrics by which intelligence can be measured," I pointed out, to my own confusion and irritation.

"Oh, so you're the number cruncher." Her gaze flicked to me momentarily, and she absently twirled a chunk of hair around one finger. "Tell me, big guy, what are the odds I get out of this alive?"

I knew she was looking for a solid answer, something to allay her fears, but I couldn't give her that, and I couldn't give her false hope. "Fifty-fifty."

Her soft lips turned to a pout, and I regretted putting them there, even if it was just the truth I gave her. "Well, that sucks."

I shrugged, my allotted words gone for the day. It had been a while, maybe even years, since I'd spoken so much, and ever since the good doctor slid into our lives, I was like a whole different person.

I refused to believe she was the cause. The complexity of the situation just dictated a shift in action. When Ace decided she'd be better off dead, that would be that, and we'd all move on as if Mallory fucking Stanton hadn't dropped into our lives and shaken things up.

Speaking of...

"You're supposed to be helping him, not stuffing him in a trunk, by the way," I remarked dryly, fighting the crease of my face as a smile spread. I had the feeling Spade intentionally set her up for that, but I had to hand it to her, it took balls to shove an armed and dangerous man in his own trunk and steal his car. "I still don't understand how you got it started without his key."

Her brown tresses bobbed around her head as she sighed. "You know, for intelligent criminals, you're pretty dim. It's called a key fob, and as long as it's in the car, it'll work." Her eyes were filled with amusement when they met mine, and my fucking heart stopped in my chest as she smiled brighter than the sun. "Besides, he was injured and mostly unarmed, and he practically put himself in the trunk. It's really not that impressive. Hell, all I did was shut it."

"Oh," was all I could muster. I'd forgotten about the key fobs. Usually, I drove a nondescript older car, as technology-free as possible, to stay under the radar while working. No key fobs, no fancy alarm systems, and no chance someone would break in and steal the stock radio sitting in the dash. It was a good thing I was learning now, that way, we could prevent the same mistake from being made in the future.

We sat there in awkward silence for a few more minutes before Spade came to find us, shrugging on a new shirt carefully and quite slowly for a man who was used to doing everything at breakneck speed. He eyed the distance between her and I and plunked down right in the middle, reaching for the little lady with a salacious grin on his lips.

When she balked at his advance and leaned away, he growled at her, and I kicked him in the side, rewarded with a nice groan of pain.

"The fuck?" he shouted at me over his good shoulder, eyes narrowed in suspicion. "What was that for?"

"Leave her alone," I ordered him, eyeing her carefully as she curled in on herself at the end of the couch.

"I do what I want."

He leaned toward her again, and this time, I stood off the couch, walked around it, and lifted her straight up off the cushion. Without a second thought, I took her straight to my room, closed the door on Spade's quickly-moving form, and locked the bolt that would ensure he wouldn't get in.

And then, confused and suddenly repulsed by my actions, I dumped her unceremoniously on the floor, inched over to my bed, and sat down.

"Shit."

She stared at me like I'd grown horns from the heap I'd left her in; meanwhile, Spade hammered at the door, yelling about *kidnappers* and *no fair* and a lot of things that were quite ironic when you stopped to think about it.

"Go away," I shouted back at him, hoping he'd take the hint. Fuck, she might have let him touch her once before, but as someone with severe hang-ups on physical touch, I could tell when someone just really didn't want to be mauled.

And apparently, Spade could only see two inches in front of himself, if that.

I watched her from my comfortable seat on the bed as she rearranged herself on my floor, tugging that damnable leather skirt down to hide her legs—and failing miserably. Her face was screwed up in a determined scowl, and those expressive eyes of hers looked relieved.

I took a small comfort in the fact that I was part of the reason for that relaxed gaze.

"So," she started, moving to her knees like she was preparing to do yoga or something, "I guess I should thank you for getting me out of that."

For her benefit, I grunted in the affirmative, nodding my head once.

She wasn't impressed with my lack of words. "You don't talk much, do you?"

My, my, aren't you such an observant one? "No."

She cocked her head and inched closer to the bed, but her advance stopped when she watched my body physically recoil in on itself. We were closer now, only a few feet apart, but I relaxed a little. She was perceptive, Dr. Stanton, and the people-reading skills that came with her territory served her well.

"You also don't like touching people." She raised her hand, turning it this way and that in front of her eyes as she studied it. "But you picked me up, not once, but twice now. And you've helped Spade with his wounds twice. So you make exceptions for certain situations, I'm guessing."

"Not usually," I muttered before I could stop myself, hating that she'd somehow managed to break down another one of my walls without even trying.

She cocked her head and studied me for a long moment, her lips pursed, a finger trailing over the bottom one like she was committing it to memory. "You don't like surprises, either."

"That's Ace's schtick."

She shrugged, letting my denial roll off her shoulders. "Seems like it might be yours, too."

I didn't say another word; I just stretched out and got comfortable as the faint complaints of exclusion echoed beneath the door separating us from the world. I stifled a small grin when she leaned back and stretched out along the floor, getting as comfortable as possible.

For someone who didn't like surprises as she claimed me to be, I was starting to enjoy *this one.*

JOKER

CHAPTER NINETEEN
JOKER

The interior of this stuffy-ass car would be the death of me someday, especially if I had to spend another minute inside it with Ace. After I'd sent off BlackJack to harass Spade, he picked me up to berate me about our unsuccessful attempts to garner some respect around here. It seemed whether I was with or without BlackJack, these ruffians down here answered to one master and one alone—Spade.

And that crazy bastard was out of commission, at least for now.

Hopefully, BlackJack could get some helpful information from him to help us break the ice down here.

"So, the two of you couldn't get a single rat to squeal down here?" Ace drawled tiredly, his fingers still prodding at the more sensitive spots of his face. "Shame. I'd expected ex-street rats to do better among their own kind."

That insult stung, and it was so out of character for Ace that it had me reeling in shock. "Excuse me?"

He turned to look out the window, his voice thoughtful, posture giving nothing away. "Have you found out where the threat we received after your little stunt came from?"

Thoughts raced in my head, darkening my expression as I

remembered the first thing Spade said to me when he called to inform me I was about to be a free man.

"You fucked with the wrong people, bud, and now they're asking us to pay — with interest."

"No solid leads, but I have a few general tips to pan out, see if anything comes from the lines I've cast." I bristled under the assumption that I was incapable of fixing my own problems. "I expect some to be more fruitful than others."

Ace snorted. "You'd better hope something pans out; otherwise, we'll be left with our pants around our ankles because you had to prove something."

"Don't you think I get it? I fucked up." My shoulders already bowed under the weight of my mistakes, but none more so than the mistakes that cost my family, my crew. "I'll fix this," I stressed, the landscape of the city rushing by as our car wove in and out of rush hour traffic. "You hear back from BlackJack yet?"

"No phone. I broke mine the night you fucked up with the therapist."

I quirked my brows at his loss of control but said nothing. I assumed that was why he hadn't messaged me before he showed up to get me.

I tossed him my cell as we swerved around another grandma driver. "Use mine. Find out what's going on."

Ace grumbled about *giving orders* but flipped the damn thing over and sought out BlackJack's contact info. He let it ring for a while, on speaker, until it went to voicemail. "Nothing. That's odd for him."

Not really, when you thought about it. He always preferred texting since he wasn't much for words. "Text him; bet he answers then."

Sure enough, moments after Ace typed up his demands, a little ding alerted us to a return message.

Ace's forehead scrunched up as he read the message, then reread it for good measure. "What the fuck does he mean, 'I'm busy back at the compound'?"

"Beats me." Ace could figure it out for himself. After all, what was I but a fucking street rat? A worthless one, at that.

Man, I needed a shopping day.

Whenever I got in my feelings about something, only two things made it better—alcohol and retail therapy. Since I was too busy to shop properly, it was time to rustle around for another bottle and fuck up that streak of dry time I had going on.

Ace would pitch a fit, but I didn't much care what he thought about it right now.

"Let's call it a day, Joker. Head back to the compound." Ace stuck my phone back in my jacket pocket and patted it gingerly, moving his attention back to the short shopping list of informants he'd sketched out this morning over coffee. "Most of these fuckers will take a day or two to track down, and I'm not in the mood to pull an all-nighter.

With you was the part he didn't tack on, but it hung in the air between us nonetheless. Nobody in the crew liked being my stakeout partner overnight—I couldn't sit still to save my life, and when we did recon, being invisible to passers-by was the key to not being made.

So when your partner kept having to get out of the car to stretch or making late-night runs to the convenience store for snacks, you tended to get irritable real fast.

I turned the car off at the nearest exit and slowed to a stop as I took in the familiar route home. No matter how many times we passed the tic-tac cookie-cutter duplexes, it never failed to amaze me how they looked so damn alike, but a simple coat of paint or hanging plant could set them apart.

Similar, yet so different.

Like the four of us.

We pulled into the garage in no time, and I couldn't help but notice there was something different about the doors we passed under. I didn't have time to dwell on it before Ace hopped out of the damn thing and rushed off to god knew what. I meandered about, taking my time, not wanting to be anywhere near him for at least the next few hours.

"What do you mean he's keeping her holed up in his room?"

Great. No doubt Spade was being a right prick, trying to scare Mallory or molest her, more likely. The man didn't understand personal space, nor did he grasp the idea of consent, but I never thought he'd sink so low as to—

"I mean, he just took her right off the couch and locked them in. They've been in there for hours now. I tried calling you."

That was Spade. Which meant—

"Wait, BlackJack has her?"

I came around the corner and stumbled across a hilariously comical sight. Spade was sitting on the floor in front of BlackJack's room, his arms crossed, staring up at Ace, who was clearly irate at this new development. BlackJack's door was locked, but there was a light on inside that streamed out from the crack at the base of the door. My eyebrows must have disappeared into my hairline because Spade snorted at my expression.

Ace was not amused. "BlackJack, get out here," he yelled through the door, his hand slapping against the solid steel monstrosity.

The man on the other side gave no answer, but a deadbolt clicked along the seam of the door. Then another, and one more, until the door inched open a crack to admit BlackJack's face in the sliver of space.

"What?" he deadpanned, giving Ace a stare that chilled even me to the bone.

"You can't lock her up against her will, man, that's—"

BlackJack lifted a brow. "Kidnapping? I didn't know we were against that now."

Ace opened and shut his mouth like a landlocked fish, confusion and irony warring with each other on his face for first place. Confusion won out, but it was soon replaced with irateness.

"Let her out here if she wants to come out, dammit, BlackJack."

He shrugged and flung the door open wide, gesturing at the girl lying on the floor of his quarters, fiddling with her hands in front of her face with a bored expression.

Ace just watched her curiously, but Spade stood up and nearly launched himself into the room, making a beeline for the poor thing, who immediately squeaked and flung herself behind BlackJack. The solid wall of man stiffened as her hands curled around his biceps from behind, but he didn't flinch away, and I think that, more than anything else, contributed to the way Spade pulled up short with a tortured twist to his features.

"Hey now, I thought we were having fun, sweetheart," he whined, trying to edge around BlackJack to get to her.

Mallory was having none of it, and she directed the taller man in a circle to keep him between Spade and herself. If I wasn't so stunned by the display before me, I'd have laughed at it all.

BlackJack didn't let people touch him. Ever. And here he was, allowing this waif of a woman to use him as a shield, her hands all over him. He might not be complaining, but I could see the strain in his eyes.

"Give her to me, BlackJack; I'll keep the crazy bastard at bay."

BlackJack turned his back to Spade and grabbed the doc, then shoved her toward me with a little nod. I gathered from the way he looked at her that she'd managed to get under his skin, too, though how she was turning these men into melting little chocolates in less than a day was beyond me.

Especially BlackJack.

Ace gripped Spade's bicep as he tried to fling himself out the door in my direction, stopping him in his tracks once more with a warning growl. "You're not going anywhere. Your people won't talk to these fuckers, so you're going to have to put on a brave face and pretend not to be injured for a day or two, so you can flush some of them out. Start on it tonight." He glowered over Spade at BlackJack, who hadn't moved since he released the doc into my care. "And you—we need to talk."

He marched off without a word in my direction, and I took that to mean I was dismissed. BlackJack marched on after Ace, and Spade grumbled all the way to his room across the hall about *mistreatment*, which I wasn't really sure he understood the definition of.

I led the doc down the hall to my room and pointed her in the direction of my bed with a grin. "Make yourself comfortable while I go hunting for something to drink." I made it to the door before common decency made me turn around. "You want anything? Food, drink, alcohol?"

There was a solid minute of contemplation in her eyes as she stared at me, her lips parting just a fraction as she mulled her options over. "I, uh, yeah, I could eat something."

"Allergies?" She shook her head no, and I shot her a wink and a smile. "I'll be right back. Don't worry about Spade—he won't bother you in here."

I marched to the kitchen and stumbled in on Ace and BlackJack's conversation, which they seemed not to care I was a witness to now. So, being there was little entertainment here, I decided to spectate.

"—don't care if she's our prisoner, you can't just hole up with her—"

"Spade was molesting her. What was I supposed to do, break his other arm?"

BlackJack's face was covered in a murderous cloud I'd not seen grace his expression in a long time. Usually, he wore it when his emotions were close to the surface, and he felt like hurting something —or someone.

I was privy to a bit of his past the others didn't know about—his own father had sold him to the streets after years of torment. When his mother died, the old man had turned to beating the fuck out of him when he held custody—which wasn't often—and BlackJack's scars were a testament to that fact.

Some scars, though, went deeper than the skin, and those were the ones he'd been left with that hadn't ever healed. His aversion to touch and reclusive tendencies crippled him socially and mentally, turning him into a shell of a man, a mere shadow of the person he could have been. But BlackJack did know one thing very well—the way it felt to be violated. To be touched against your will.

It was the only thing that could have spurred him to such close contact with the doc.

Ace didn't seem to see the urgency in such an admission. "Spade wouldn't hurt her; the fool's half-mad for her already—"

"And he's so mad about her that he ignored her when she recoiled away from him and tried to coerce her into physical contact. Even if we are kidnappers, Ace, we're not fucking rapists."

Our fearless leader managed to school his features a bit as he cleared his throat. "You have a point. I'll deal with Spade." He turned to me with a frown, those dark eyes piercing straight through me. "And what the fuck are you doing?"

I pointed to the cabinet beside me and waggled my brows. "Waiting for you two lovers to finish so I can grab some snacks."

BlackJack snorted and beat feet out of the kitchen, the solid sound of his door slamming a heavy echo down the hall as I pushed a bag of popcorn into the microwave. Ace muttered something about needing some air and made for his office, which negated his whole comment on the air thing, but whatever.

The ding alerted me to the sustenance, and I added a pinch of salt to the bag before grabbing a bottle of tequila Spade had hidden under the kitchen sink, a bottle of water, and some grapes hanging out in the back of the fridge. Satisfied with my haul, I returned to my room to find the doc missing, of course, so I dropped my hoard on the bed and marched off in search of her.

Thankfully, I didn't have to go far.

I found her at Spade's door, her hand lifted just a fraction away from knocking. She caught sight of me out of the corner of her eyes and paled, her whole body sagging in relief.

"My bags are in his room. I, uh, can you?"

"Go back to my room. I'll get them."

When she disappeared, I picked the lock and slipped inside his dark bedroom, sussed out the two bags that clearly didn't belong to a man like Spade, and snuck right back out.

Once a thief, always a thief.

Nothing more than a street rat.

JOKER

CHAPTER TWENTY
MALLORY

It wasn't that I needed protection from Spade. I knew realistically if I put up a fight, he'd probably, eventually, back off. But the only way I could see surviving this situation was to get these men on my side, and while I knew I could reasonably put Spade in the category where I would have an armory at my back if Ace were to decide I'm better off dead, he was also unstable and wildly unpredictable. A man with a torture chamber twenty feet away from his bed wasn't someone I could count on to consistently choose the smart option.

BlackJack was an enigma. There was something about his past that was decidedly off, and his heart was blacker than a fucking piece of coal, but inside that chunk of rock was a soft, beating thing, and I could see it in the way he protected me from Spade's advances when I wasn't eager to entertain them.

It didn't matter how good that spur-of-the-moment, life-ending, panicked sex was. I wasn't very up for entertaining another round, not now that I was thinking clearly and not panicking that my life might still end at any moment.

Ace was off the table. He'd shown no interest in anything but keeping an iron grip on his group, and I had to respect that. Control was everything, that and power, and if I took even a little bit of it away from him, it threw a wrench in all his plans. All in all, he was the most dangerous to my survival, the biggest threat.

Joker was—well, he was troubled. Alcoholic, clearly a bit sexed up, he reminded me of a dog that had been kicked a few times too many and was now looking for a kick around every corner. You could see it in the way he flinched around Ace, though I doubted that had anything to do with physical abuse.

And now that I was in his room, and he was heading back to watch me for the night, I might be able to work some details about him out that I could use to my advantage.

Survive at all costs.

Joker hefted my bags over one shoulder as he slid sideways through the doorway, a shit-eating grin on his lips. "Spade's already out on errands for Ace, so I broke in and stole these. I can't wait to hear him bitching over coffee in the morning."

He was careful about my bags, though he didn't need to be, and once he'd finagled them into a nearby chair, he turned around to face me with an absolutely unhinged grin.

"So, you're stuck with me tonight." He leaped into the center of the bed like a flying squirrel and reached for the bottle of liquor, popping the top with a flourish. "Whaddya say we get this party started?"

I realized then I'd gone from the arms of a lion to the jaws of a tiger.

"Uh, I don't really feel like drinking," I tried, hedging my bets that he hadn't seen me pound several shots of this particular brand of tequila at the bar the night they kidnapped me. Fuck, I could use a drink right about now—my life was about as unstable as I'd ever seen it, and I needed something to take the edge off. But if I lost my edge, I lost control, and I needed to stay alert in case another opportunity to escape presented itself.

"Nonsense," he drawled easily, flashing me that smile he wore for our video chat.

And then that smile spurred a thought of the contents of said video chat, and I reached out to grip the neck of the bottle where his hand still wrapped around it, dragging him and the liquor toward my lips.

The tequila burned like a motherfucker on the way down, and I fought not to choke on the cloying taste of it as Joker watched on with those pretty lips parted, tongue sliding between them across the seam to wet their surface as I watched.

I took three long pulls off the bottle, wincing as it lit my insides up quite nicely before shaking my head like a rabid dog. "Whoo, that shit bites."

It took me another couple of seconds to realize I was still gripping his hand—and the bottle—and release them both with a nervous laugh.

He set the popcorn between us and flipped around to watch tv, flicking from channel to channel as if the tension in the air between kidnapper and captive wasn't charged. Electric.

Wrong.

So fucking wrong.

I blinked stupidly when I realized a few hours into the aimless television shows that his silence had been swapped for soft snoring.

This fucker thought so little of me that he was willing to sleep on the job. I toyed with the idea of sneaking out but realized pretty quickly that was *exactly* why he wasn't afraid to sleep on the job—I wasn't getting out of here undetected. They might not have some state-of-the-art super security system, but they had fail-safes that alerted them if something moved where it shouldn't, when it shouldn't.

I glanced at the clock on the bedside table.

1:44 AM

Surely the others would be asleep by now. It might be safest to explore the compound while they were resting, so I could get a feel for the environment. With that thought in mind, I slipped off the bed and over to my bags, rifling through them until I found a pair of fuzzy sleep shorts. I slipped them on under my skirt and shimmied out of the leather, grateful for the modesty such a move afforded me, even if the alcoholic criminal on the bed was too out cold to notice or appreciate my ass.

His loss.

My curiosity got the best of me, and I moved like a cat around the room, stealthy and silent as I rifled through drawer after drawer, finding nothing out of the ordinary. Clothing, most of it nondescript, tees and jeans and cargo pants lined drawer after drawer until I pulled out one drawer that seemed awfully shallow for the middle of the bureau. My fingers slipped around the edges until I felt the part that was made to lift the base, and I gave the fucking thing a little tug.

The compartment underneath was empty save for a manilla folder, which I promptly pulled out to investigate.

What in the hell?

It was filled with nothing but polaroids of two boys, one blonde, one raven-haired, both with shit-eating grins of youth on their lips. The dark-haired boy's clothes were worn and ripped in places, strange, uneven patches littering their jackets, but he looked happy. The blonde boy's attire was much more prominent, not a stitch out of place on the clearly designer clothes. The starched white collar and yellow sweater vest were so at odds with the other child, it made my heart hurt to think how different their lives must have been.

Hell, they almost looked like younger versions of Joker and BlackJack.

I screwed up my eyebrows and frowned at the image of innocent youth, these two street urchin kids without a care in the world. No curfew, no rules, no permanence—just each other. And then I dragged my eyes up to the bed, where I spotted the sleeping grown man, his usually tense body relaxed from the booze and unconsciousness, an arm curled around a single pillow, clutching it to his chest.

I could almost see it.

I flipped through several more photos of these boys, though as the images progressed, you could see their stations eventually evened out. The blonde boy's designer threads slowly faded into ragged hand-me-downs, nearly matching the other boy's attire in haggardness. His smile never dimmed, though, not until the second to last photo.

It was of the two of them; I was sure it was Joker and BlackJack now because it couldn't be more than a few years old. They looked fresh out of high school or around that age, their smiles of innocence traded for panty-dropping smolders that could have lit a fire under any skirt in town. BlackJack's seemed effortless, though he looked uncomfortable wearing it, but Joker's seemed like his was an integral piece of his persona, an extension of himself that he couldn't be bothered to turn off.

The man in question, worlds apart from the boy he used to be, murmured in his sleep and rolled over, facing me as he shuffled quietly. I stuffed the pictures into the envelope hastily and shoved it back in its hiding spot, carefully rearranging the clothing as if it had never been moved. Somehow, I managed to get the drawer back shut and sneak around so that his back was to me again, without waking him.

There was quite obviously nothing left in here for me to investigate, so I moved to the bathroom, surprised to find a pistol taped to the underside of the sink, a full clip stuck to the grip. Unloaded but not unprepared. I had to admire a man prepared for anything.

His closet yielded no surprises past a couple of less-than-sharp pocket knives and a plethora of fancy clothing I had no doubt he looked stunning in.

It was time to turn my snooping outward.

I stuffed one of the dull blades from the closet in my bra and moved to the door, flicking it unlocked with all the speed of a recalcitrant mule, cringing as I waited for it to make a loud click. When I was met with silence, it was the sign I needed to step out of the room and venture forth like this was some sort of prison and I was an inmate planning a break.

Which was kinda true, I guess.

The hall was dark and empty, and behind at least one of the doors, I could hear *someone* snoring softly. My money was on Spade, but I'd already learned by now not to assume things about these men.

Creeping down the hall was easy enough since the whole place was virtually a new build. Nothing creaked underfoot, no strange sirens went off from a laser alarm system, no motion sensors, no visible cameras.

There weren't many places to go, so I wandered aimlessly with no actual destination in mind. The kitchen was blissfully empty, the shadows cast by the appliances and a few glowing displays almost eerie. Slinking into the ample space was too tempting to pass up, so I did, rummaging through the fridge (strangely empty save for energy drinks), the cabinets (where I liberated a candy bar), and the pantry, which wasn't actually a pantry.

It was a fucking armory.

And it was unlocked. Unlocked and strangely open.

This has got to be some kind of fucking test.

My brain whirred through the guys, trying to decipher who might have intentionally left it open, and immediately went to Spade. That crazy fucker would probably find it hot if I tried to murder him in his sleep. I wouldn't put it past him to try this shit with me for kicks.

Joker was out. Not just asleep, but like out-out. Out of the running. He was reckless, but not this reckless. And he didn't seem the type to enjoy a bullet between the eyes while he was passed out cold.

BlackJack didn't play games—or at least, that was the vibe I got from him. He took things seriously and was probably the least likely to do some underhanded shit like this. He seemed like anything superfluous was wasted, and this was definitely a level of extra he probably wouldn't sink to.

And then there was Ace. While it was possible he could have done this to see what I'd do, I doubted he'd leave that much to chance. He had a soul-crushing need to be in control, as evidenced by this whole dog-and-pony show, and that kind of desperate grip on control wouldn't leave an unknown variable like me with access to weapons that could be used against them.

My fingers itched to grab something from the shelf, to load a gun and take my freedom, but there was no way I'd make it out of here alive, not even with a fully loaded gun. I was a shit shot, for one, and I'd never killed a man, and even though these four had stolen me off the street and were now keeping me captive here, I couldn't reconcile the idea of killing them with the benefit of having my freedom.

Which was hilarious when you stopped to think about it.

I had qualms and hesitations about killing men who wouldn't hesitate to kill me if it came down to it.

Who would have thought?

J
A
JOKER
A
K

CHAPTER TWENTY-ONE
ACE

Moment of truth.

The kitchen had been quiet when I strolled in, looking for another drink to alleviate the caffeine headache forming behind my eyes from the unchecked late hours I'd been keeping lately. But then I heard the lock click on a door down the hallway, and I knew without a doubt who would be coming down that hall.

So I laid a trap and moved around the island to wait.

It was genius, really—we never kept the ammo and guns together, though they were in the same room, and it wasn't likely she could break a fingerprint scanner to open the drawer with clips stored neatly in rows behind her as she approached the pantry armory. So, if she took a gun, I'd know we couldn't trust her. If she even so much as put a hand on the fucking things, I'd snap her neck before she got a chance to leave this room.

I wouldn't leave this loose end dangling. The guys could believe she'd snagged a gun and gotten the jump on me, if it helped them swallow the story of her escape I'd paint. After a while, they'd move on, the sexy therapist and her mind games gone for good.

And good riddance.

If I didn't get rid of her soon, I'd need bigger fucking pants.

Just because I wasn't willing to bend to her girlish charms, just because I wasn't cowed by her pleas and soft lips, didn't mean my cock didn't twitch at the delectable way her hip dipped before it flared out in that skirt she'd been wearing. Just because keeping her was dangerous, didn't mean my cock didn't fucking stand at attention when her hair brushed away from her throat and that creamy expanse bared itself in invitation, in submission. And when her eyes flicked up to meet mine, big and shocked, with tears clinging to her lashes even as a different kind of moisture soaked her fucking panties—

Fuck.

I foresaw a cold shower in my very near future.

I had to get ahold of myself before I lost control.

Before I did something I'd regret.

My attention turned back to the pantry armory as Miss Stanton shuffled in front of the gun display, her hands hesitant and shaking as she reached out to skim her fingertips along my personal weapon of choice—a .9mm with a jet black grip and *Ace* engraved into the metal barrel.

It had been a gift from Joker the last time he fucked something up and needed to make amends.

"So stunning," she muttered to herself, her fingers slowly curling around the damn thing as I watched from my vantage point. A few more inches, and she'd have it in her possession completely. If she so much as stepped a single inch away from the doors with that gun, she was done for.

I clenched my fists as my cock jumped in the soft satin of my sleep pants, the fabric doing not a damn thing to help the situation. I bit back a groan and rolled my eyes. The *one time* I splurged for comfort and luxury, and it came back to bite me in the ass. Because of course it did.

Her fingers clenched around the barrel as she turned the gun in her hands, studying it like it would bare secrets to her if she looked long enough, close enough. A muffled *hmmm* escaped her lips as she cocked a hip and quirked a brow. I had her side view now, could see the deliberation in her eyes as she contemplated the choice she was about to make.

I hadn't realized I was holding my breath until she turned back to the pantry with a sigh and set the gun back on the hook she'd found it nestled in.

You've gotta be fucking kidding me. I give this girl an out, and she refuses to take it. What kind of idiot—?

I rose like a silent predator, stalking over to her while managing to avoid notice. When I stood but a few inches behind her, I watched over her shoulder as she brushed her hand longingly over an AR-15 on the wall to her right. She tilted her head and took the soft matte metal in just as I reached around the expanse of her throat and gripped it in my hand, choking the life out of her.

Fight or flight kicked in as I dragged her back away from the armory, her hands clawing at mine desperately, her legs kicking out beneath her. My grip held her in place against my body, and I knew if I could feel myself hardening against her ass, she certainly could, and I growled at the implications of my body's reaction to her, taking a huge whiff of her scent as I did so.

She smelled like vanilla and fear. Fuck, it was a delicious blend. Heady, sensual, rubbing against the inside of my skull like a fucking siren call.

My back hit the counter of the island, and I let out a grunt, followed immediately by another when one of her flailing legs caught me in the shin. My instinct was to release her, but my free arm tightened around her middle instead, my other hand loosening so she could breathe again, though only enough to not pass out.

I only had a split second to read her move as she pulled her head forward, and I spun us around so her midsection pressed painfully into the island counter instead of my spine. A quick swerve to the left as she jerked her head back kept me from gaining a broken nose to go with my screaming shin, but the edge of her skull caught my jaw and hit harder than one of Spade's fists.

"Fuck!"

I released her throat and shoved the top half of her over the counter, fingers gripped in her hair tightly to keep her where I wanted her and keep my face safe. Her arms came out to her sides and she slapped those manicured nails down on the marble she was leaning on, trying desperately to shove me off. Still, she hadn't begged yet, and some part of me wished she would. A sick, twisted part of me was just like my uncles, just like my grandfather, taking pleasure in watching someone inferior beg for their lives, for mercy.

It was one of the reasons I never handled the hands-on shit. I didn't trust myself to respect limits. To have any at all.

I leaned over her back, letting my stiff cock press into her ass with *purpose.* "Trying to take one of our guns, there, sweetheart?" My hips rocked obscenely as I relished the feel of that soft yet somehow firm part of her, barely encased in the short bed shorts she wore. *Fuck, the damn skirt had covered more.*

"Spade?" she squeaked, trying to turn her head to spot her assailant.

I chuckled low, tossing my jet-black hair out of the way as I nuzzled her throat, letting my breath caress the shell of her ear. The smooth satin rubbing against my dick reminded me how useful a woman could be to relieve some of the tension coiled tightly in my gut, but I pushed that thought aside, refusing to stoop so low that I used her like a whore.

I had control over *that,* at least.

"Not quite, sweetheart, but that was a good guess."

I felt the tremor trail down her spine as she placed my rasp with its owner, a little whimper of fear escaping her pretty lips at the realization of how fucked she was. The way she arched into my grip, trying to cut herself some slack, was honestly adorable but futile nonetheless. I only tightened my grip and bent over her more, my chest against her spine, pressing her flat.

Fuck, it would probably feel amazing to take her just like this, from behind, while she gripped the edges of the kitchen island—

"Please, please, I swear I wasn't trying to take them, I-I—"

There it was. The begging I craved like fucking air.

I relished the sound, bathed in it as my cock grew impossibly harder against her ass. "I know no such thing, Miss Stanton. All I saw was a thief with her hands on my guns—"

"You set me up," she growled, her fire rising to the surface despite her intentions. The ones with that internal fire, the will to live and the will to fight, those ones always tried to fight their true nature the most but ended up slaves to it regardless of how hard they denied the monster inside.

I was one such monster, but I'd long since stopped denying it.

"I laid a trap, yes, and you fell right into it." My lips curled into a cunning smirk as she writhed against me, fighting the grip on her hair.

She was probably a fucking goddess in the sheets. Wildfire, burning everything she touched, flaming so hot she'd consume a man with her touch, her lips, her fucking cunt—

My mind had deserted me, abandoned all common sense, and was running on blue balls autopilot. Fuck, it had been so long since I'd gotten laid, and tonight, my body was sending me the signal it had been too long, loud and fucking clear.

"Are you going to kill me? Was this an excuse to get rid of your little problem?" she spat, going limp against the counter in defeat. "Fine then, fucking do it. Quit playing games with me, asshole. I hate waiting."

She spoke with a lot of bravado, but there wasn't a whole lot of conviction in her voice, as if she were hoping I'd renege, that I'd let her go and shove her off down the hall, back into one of the others' rooms, to an imagined safety.

A nasty thought crossed my mind, and before I could shove it down, the fucker crawled up my throat and out into the room around us, speaking itself into existence.

"I would rather make you suffer the fate of humiliation for daring to touch my fucking guns, for even letting the thought of escape cross your mind." I released her hair and gripped her throat again, tilting her against my chest as I leaned away from the counter. "You don't want to die, not really. If you did, you would have put one of those guns to your own head and pulled the fucking trigger."

Her sleep shorts were fuzzy and thick but blissfully short, and the undeniable form of my shaft pressed deliciously against the swell of her ass. As I ground it against her, a realization came over her, a sudden epiphany of what, exactly, her humiliation might entail.

"You—no. No, you wouldn't dare—"

She spun in my grip, and now our bodies lined up flush against each other, my cock painfully aware that it was mere inches from the delicious hole it so desperately ached to be inside of. The fucker even had the nerve to twitch, earning me a groan of approval from the girl before me, though her cheeks tinged pink at the betrayal of her own body. Her hands moved up to my chest, palms flat against my racing fucking heart.

She searched my eyes for damn near a full minute, neither of us breathing, let alone speaking, until she found whatever it was she was looking for and nodded to herself.

"You're no rapist," she muttered, her lashes fluttering like I was one of the other besotted fools. "You're an ass, but you're not this."

My face almost split in two from the force of my devilish smile, the sound escaping me more of a snarl than anything else. "You don't know a thing about me, sweetheart. Don't think for a second you can psychoanalyze me, figure me out."

My mind screamed at me to stop before I went too far, but the convenient little switch inside my head was flipped, and I was past the point of return. The dam had broken, and unfortunately for Miss Stanton, my iron grip on that thin thread of control had just snapped.

And now she'd get the monster I tried so hard to hide from the world.

I'm sorry.

My hand lifted to grab her throat again, fingers wrapped around her pale skin like a living necklace. The moment her eyes went wide brought me little enjoyment as she realized she'd misread her captor. A small whimper slipped through her gritted teeth as I dragged her against me, our noses touching, chests heaving from the exertion, the adrenaline coursing through both of us.

"It's not rape if you're willing, Miss Stanton, and from what I've already heard, you're more than willing to spread these pretty legs in the face of danger."

CHAPTER TWENTY-TWO
MALLORY

Of all the people in this fucking compound to set me up, Ace would have been my last bet, but now it all made sense. The man really wanted to kill me to save himself the trouble of waiting me out, and if there was any fleeting hope in my head that he didn't plan to kill me when this trial period was over, it was gone now.

I was a dead woman walking.

Unless . . .

The only thing I could think that might save me was to disarm him, mentally, not physically. His eyes swirled with hatred and anger, but beneath the typical, easy-to-read emotions, something else flickered in their depths, something he didn't want me to see, didn't want anyone to see.

Loneliness. Pain. Regret.

Emotions I was well-versed in.

He might think I couldn't analyze him, but he was wrong. I knew that look that slinked through the bottomless fathoms of his soul, knew that blackness like my own hand. The loneliness of isolating yourself from even those who stood next to you dug deep and often left you feeling adrift, touch-starved. But this man had no scruples with being touched—he wasn't like BlackJack, with a phobia of the act. He just wanted to pretend that it didn't affect him. That he was above it.

I knew better.

This man was a wound-up spring, coiled so tight he was an inch away from snapping. And the only thing on his mind was making me pay for perceived slights to mask his own reaction to me.

I wasn't dead. I could feel his hard dick against me.

I wasn't happy about it, and I wasn't about to fuck him, either.

His hot breath fanned out across my face, his beautiful, stunning jaw ticking in annoyance as I looked away, playing his game. If it was a submissive he wanted, that's what I'd give him. The end game here was survival, and if there was one thing I was good at, it was surviving. Even when I didn't want to.

Just ask my wrists and my ER doctor.

His hand moved from my throat to my hair again, yanking my head back as he ran his aquiline nose along the soft column of my throat until he came to the junction of my shoulder. I shivered in anticipation of what he'd do, a traitorous moan slipping from me as he let his teeth graze the sensitive flesh.

He bit me in retaliation for my enjoyment, drawing blood like some vampiric cannibal. Those teeth of his were coated in a faint sheen of red as he pulled back and shot me a knowing smirk, licking the lingering drop of my life essence from his bottom lip.

Fuck, why were my panties wet? I didn't want this. I didn't want this *at all.*

But my whore vagina did, fuck if she didn't want all this danger, all this pain, everything this man could give me that none other had yet to scratch the surface of. My old therapist might call this my mind's way of coping with my past, but I'd never really liked the strange kinks I developed after failing to take my own life years ago.

His smirk fell when I shot him a shit-eating grin right back and leaned into him, threading a hand in his hair this time as I yanked us together and licked my own blood from his lips, moaning my pleasure against him.

His hips ground into mine, shoving me painfully against the counter as he responded with all the enthusiasm of a drowning man thrown a life preserver. The hand in my hair tightened, sending little electric shocks straight to my core as I returned in kind, our tongues tangling dangerously, feral gasps and moans escaping our joined lips every time one of us split for a breath.

His grip tightened and he yanked my head back, tearing us apart with a groan of regret. "Stop that," he rasped, chest heaving, eyes wide.

I tried not to smile too hard when he shoved me to my knees in front of him, crowding me in with the cabinets and his hips. I knew before he did what his plans for me would be, and I'd done worse for less valid reasons.

Drowning myself in sex was a whole ass phase of my life before the suicide attempt.

His cock was at eye level, and even though I didn't plan on my night going this way, I was still human, and the idea of this very attractive, very dangerous man—and what lay beneath his satin bed pants—being exposed to me, well, let's just say it gave me a thrill, a power high.

A rush I hadn't had in a long while.

Ace might think he was in control here, but it was the stiff dick in front of my face, twitching as I licked my lips, that really had the power. And by extension, now *I* held that power.

His hand in my hair tilted my head back, and I went willingly, staring up at the dangerous flash in his eyes, his lips turned down in a scowl. "You answer to me, Miss Stanton. You're my property as long as you're in my custody, and you do what I say, *when* I say it, do we have an accord?"

The thrill that went through me at his low growl should have slammed the brakes on this whole affair, but I was far past caring if either of us was in control. I didn't ask to be his fucktoy, but this man before me was far past asking for what he could *take.*

The realization that a part of me was sickeningly turned on by the idea of him *forcing me* slammed home with a frightening lack of concern, and not for the first time, I wondered if I really was fixed. The therapist I saw who'd insisted I'd make a hell of one myself always said there *is* no such thing as being cured, but I thought I'd left all my self-destructive habits in my past with the rest of those horrid memories that didn't line up with my new image.

Apparently, I was wrong. Obviously, I hadn't.

"Fuck you and your *accord,"* I spat, making sure to rise up against his tight grip just enough to cause myself pain. The response from Ace was immediate—his cock twitched in front of me, his lips parted, and his eyes nearly rolled back in his head at the fight I put up, though it was quite transparent. His hand disappeared for a split second, as did the rest of him, and I almost believed I'd chased him away—

Until he came back with a snarl and sank to one knee beside me, his eyes lit with something less feral and more unhinged this time, the cold metal of a pistol barrel caressing the side of my cheek pointedly as he dragged it downward, following the line of my jaw.

That other hand sank back into my curls and I whimpered again, this time in genuine fear.

His answering smirk had me questioning all the decisions I'd ever made up to now.

"Ah, not so brave anymore, now are you?" His eyes flicked to the gun, then back to mine, that tongue trailing over his bottom lip as the barrel slipped down the column of my neck, heading for my collarbone. "You see, you might *think* you can read me, sweetheart, but something you don't know about me is that I'm not what I appear to be *at all."* His gun slipped between my tits, hindered by the low neckline of my top. His gaze lowered for a second, his hand moving the weapon to the outside of my shirt along my ribcage. "I've got a short fuse, and I walk a tight line, doc, but when you push too hard, the beast comes out to play, the beast I've tried for years to hide from the world."

The gun was at my hip now, and I whimpered as he pointedly trailed it up the inside of the leg of my shorts, caressing my thigh with it like it wasn't a weapon, but a toy. My pussy throbbed in time with my hammering heart, the adrenaline and the rush battling each other for dominance in my brain.

I should not be turned on.

I should be afraid for my fucking life.

I should be in full-blown panic, not fighting the wetness between my thighs.

That gun in his hand brushed against my panties, eliciting a gasp from my lips, and just as suddenly, he jerked it away, rising to his feet again, hand still buried tightly in my hair. I felt the pistol again as he pressed it to my temple and jerked my head back so I met his fiery gaze.

"Take me out of these pants and suck me dry like I know you want to."

I damn near came from the way he demanded things from me with a gun pressed to my head.

I really was broken.

My hands shook as I raised them to the hem of his sleep pants, tugging them down and over his stiff, bouncing cock, a drop of clear fluid clinging to the tip like a tease. My tongue nearly fell out of my mouth in my haste to lick it up, and he rewarded me with a sinful groan of approval as he thrust forward and slammed his cock straight down my throat with no warning.

Fuck, he was big.

His length ran down the flattened surface of my tongue as I struggled to breathe, the grip on my hair so tight it brought tears to my eyes from the sting alone. One of my palms lay flat against his thigh as I took him over and over, his forceful thrusts gagging me around his length several times with no reprieve.

The gun slipped away from my head for a moment, but I paid it no mind, swallowing a few times in an effort to make him make those noises in the back of his throat again.

He didn't disappoint.

Clearly, it'd been a while since the poor man had gotten a good blowie, because his balls were already tightening against his body in preparation for the load he was about to shoot down my throat.

Gods, a sick part of me *wanted* his load down my fucking throat.

I wanted him to feel it as I swallowed his fucking essence, as I licked my lips and smiled up at him to let him know I'd enjoyed what he'd freely given.

With a groan, he rammed himself all the way into my throat and came, hot ropes of his seed slipping down the back of my esophagus as I swallowed against him, enjoying the sinful squeak of shock and pleasure that was decidedly un-Ace. When he finished, his whole body jerked back in surprise, but I simply leaned my head back and met that steely gaze with one of my own.

No words were needed for either one of us to understand the shift that had just taken place. His hand still clung to that pistol like a lifeline, but it shook now, and a little part of me was saddened by the fact that he seemed to have forgotten he held it.

"Fuck," he muttered, mumbling incoherently to himself as his fists left my body and rose to his head, pounding his temples in exasperation. He thumped the butt of his gun's grip against the soft flesh there, growling to himself in a manic snap that had me on edge.

I'd had patients like him. Patients that scared me just a bit, walking a tightrope that threatened to snap at the first sign of difficulty in life. But Ace's tightrope was taut and unforgiving, made of steel. He didn't fall, he just chose to step off it, tired of balancing between good and evil. And now, I was seeing the unhinged side of him, a side I feared he hadn't explored in a long ass time.

Men like that, men who *feared* their dark side, they were dangerous.

And I liked danger.

His hand twitched as I watched, half expecting him to leave me on that floor and replace the gun in his cabinet, but the other half of me wondered if he was about to finish the job since he had the damn thing out and in his grip.

Instead, he turned, whirling on me with a searing heat emitting from those gorgeous, expressive, tortured eyes. His free hand gripped my throat and lifted me off the floor, the armed one pointed in my direction, but thankfully not against my temple.

"Get on the counter, sweetheart," he commanded in a whisper, his brows constricting above his eyes like he wasn't sure whether he meant to speak the words or not.

I hopped obediently backward, my ass resting on the low counter, feet dangling before him. With a practiced move, his pistol-filled grip trailed to my thighs and shoved against one knee quite roughly, spreading me for his perusal.

And peruse he did. The hand lingering around my throat like a necklace did little more than hold me in place as his gun's barrel blazed a trail up the leg of my shorts once more, brushing against my panties so roughly I couldn't bite back the gasp that rose in my throat. His smile tipped up, turning him from crazed armed man to sinfully handsome yet dangerous playboy, and I swallowed thickly as his gun shifted sideways so his fingers could brush against the spot he'd just had the metal pressed.

Ace let out a low hiss, dragging his fingers up and down as he watched me closely, relishing the way my eyelids fluttered and my fingers clenched around the edge of the counter. "You're soaked, Miss Stanton. Positively *dripping.*" He shifted his fingers again and tugged my panties to the side, and I whimpered like the needy bitch I was, both appalled that I was letting him touch me like this, with a gun in his hand, no less, and also needy and eager for whatever torture he planned to wreak on my body.

"Tell me, sweetheart, have you ever come around the barrel of a gun while the man who's threatened to kill you fucks you with it?"

I had a second and a half to process the words out of his mouth before he was sliding the fucking gun in question right up inside of me with no preamble and no more warning. My legs twitched instinctively, trying to close against the invasion, and I reached forward and gripped his shoulders roughly, tears in my eyes as I begged him incoherently—for what, I wasn't sure.

"P-please," I whimpered, hands clenched so tightly I knew it'd leave marks on his skin, but he seemed disinclined to care.

"Please *what,* Miss Stanton?" he growled, leaning in to run his nose along the pulse point in my throat. "What do you need?"

The gun wriggled just a twitch in the beginning of my tight channel, and I keened at the foreign sensation, spreading my legs and begging him without using words that had long since failed me.

I wanted to come.

I wanted him to make me.

And I wanted that gun deeper inside my needy cunt.

I leaned back just a hint, arching my spine as he sank that gun deeper into me, slowly dragging the metal in and out of my sopping pussy as he groaned. The wet sounds coming from between us were nothing short of obscene, and I felt myself climbing quickly toward a precipice that I *wanted* to be thrown bodily from. My whole being yearned to come, to explode around his weapon of death as he reminded me in the most primal of ways *exactly* why the French called it *'la petite mort'*.

Just as I felt myself clenching around the gun, Ace's hand tightened around my throat, and a shocked gasp echoed from the doorway, reminding us there were other residents in the warehouse.

"Jesus Christ, Ace, what the hell are you doing to her?"

His hand jerked back, and the barrel of the gun inside me was yanked firmly away, the edge of the sight nicking me on the way out. The unexpected and unwelcome pain returned me to my fucking senses, and I moaned with embarrassment, covering my face with both hands as BlackJack stared on at the scene before him, his eyes flicking to my spread legs and the treasure between them, then quickly to the gun in Ace's grip, covered with a slick sheen of my arousal that was unmistakeable in the moonlight.

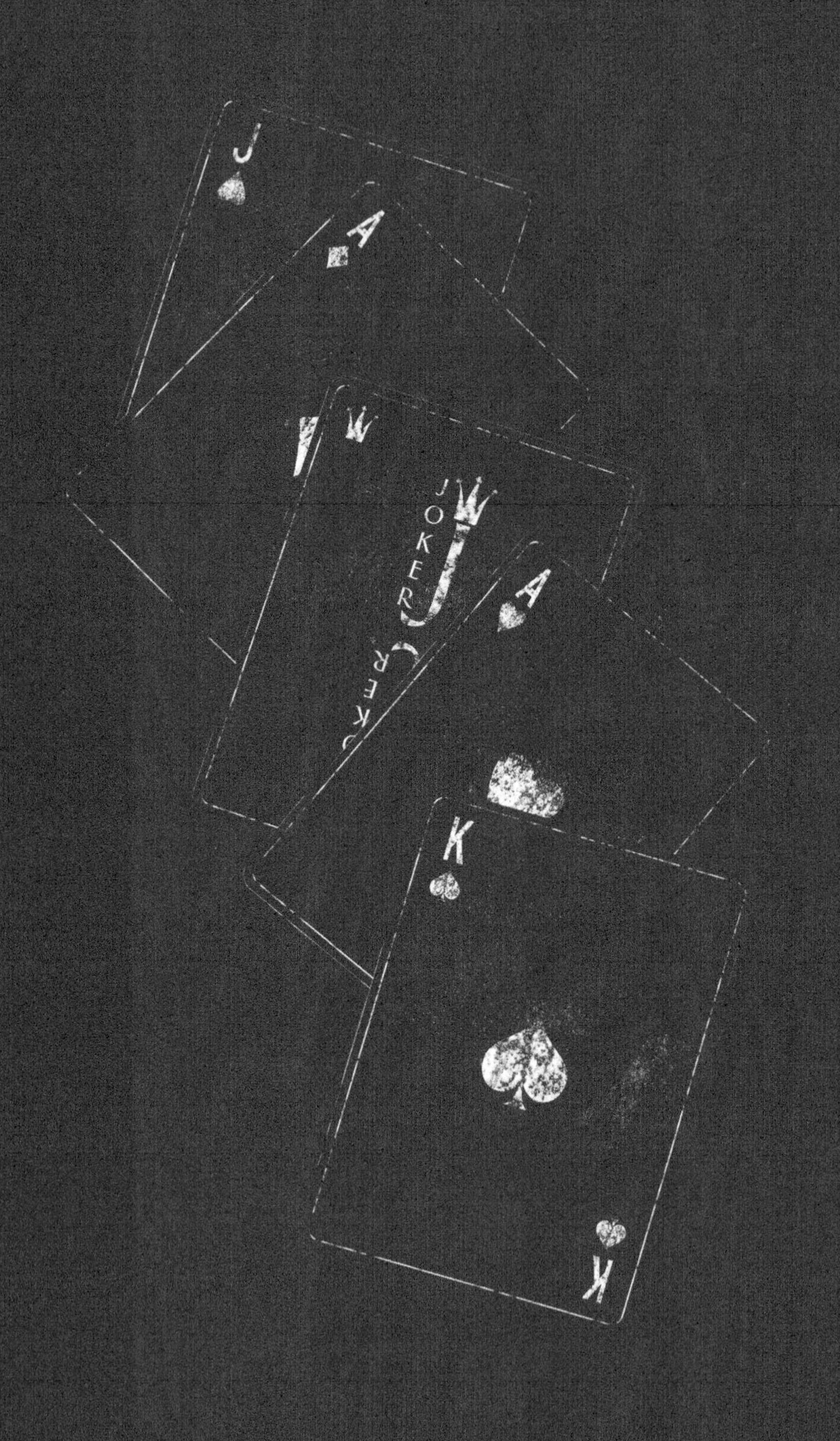
JOKER

CHAPTER TWENTY-THREE
BLACKJACK

"Jesus Christ, Ace, what the hell are you *doing* to her?"

Ace had his hand around her throat, the captive in front of him spread wide on the counter, and the barrel of that pistol had just come out from between her legs. Mallory moaned with embarrassment, covering her face with both hands as I stared at the scene before me. I couldn't help that my eyes flicked to her spread legs, *and the treasure between them,* then quickly to the gun in Ace's grip, covered with a slick, glossy sheen.

Ace yanked her off the counter and shoved her at me by the throat, a snarl of disgust ripping from his lips as he turned and shuffled off, gun still in hand. Instinctively, I reached out and broke Mallory's fall, gripping her by the shoulders as she stared at the floor between us. I didn't even think about it as I took in her frazzled state: hair tangled and tousled from being yanked around, shirt tipped over one shoulder, shorts askew as she tugged them back into place with shaking hands.

The only thing I could think of was the way he'd looked half-feral as he assaulted her on the fucking counter of the kitchen, with a gun, no less.

He'd snapped. And Ace, with no restraint, was dangerous under the best of circumstances.

I bent at the waist and fought the urge to take my hands off her, ignoring that general skin-crawling feeling whenever I touched someone else. "Are you okay?" I asked hesitantly.

Her head raised, and she tried but failed to meet my gaze. Recognizing embarrassment when I saw it, I let her hide herself from me, straightening as my hands dropped from her shoulders.

I was at a loss as to what to do with her, but I couldn't just turn tail and run out now. I couldn't leave her on her own out here with Ace wild like that. My gaze shot to the corner, where a faint light emitted from the slightly ajar door of the pantry armory, and the pieces clicked in my brain like a well-assembled puzzle.

"You broke into the armory?" I quirked a brow, but she just shook her head, fists balled at her side.

"I didn't," she sighed, exasperation oozing from her pores. "That asshole left it open as a test."

The other brow joined my first. "You failed."

"I fingered a gun or two, but I'm no idiot. What good is a gun when you're a bad shot?"

The shrug she gave me belied the regret in her that she couldn't properly defend herself even if she wanted to.

I remembered a time when I hadn't been worth shit with a gun. When someone took pity on me and taught me what to do with one. She was living with criminals, and we had enemies. The least we could do was make sure she could defend herself if something happened to us.

"Come here," I urged, offering her my hand. I hummed pleasantly when she took it, and I tugged her over to the armory in question, opening the door the rest of the way.

Her eyes went wide, and her gaze filled with apprehension for a split second as it met mine. No doubt she thought I meant her to pick out her method of assassination.

"Pick one," I urged, nodding toward the wall of pistols. "You're going to learn to shoot."

Mallory leaned back to stare up at me in bewilderment, cocking a hip out in that sassy way she had about her right before she picked a fight with you. "You're joking, right?"

I shook my head, gesturing to the weapons once again. "Tick tock, doc."

She reached for a Glock, but redirected at the last second, snagging a sleek silver piece from Joker's shelf. I shrugged at her choice—a .22 wouldn't kill, but it could maim in close distance. Apparently, my posture gave away the disappointment in her choice, because she put it back and moved along to Spade's shelf, perusing the pistols there.

"Here," I grunted, grabbing a small pair of matching green pistols from my own cache, "use one of these."

A small part of me itched at the thought of someone else using my guns. I didn't share, I didn't do touch, and I didn't like people encroaching on my privacy, but here in this little kitchen, none of that seemed to matter.

Her fingertips brushed against mine as she took the offered pistol from my hand, and I struggled to remember how to breathe as I spun to my left and slipped a finger over the hidden print pad built into the drawer on the end of the island. It popped open and slid out to reveal clips of all styles, loaded and ready to go. Selecting the two neon green ones that matched my guns, I took her hand again and led the way to the stairs leading down to the underground cellar we'd repurposed into a gun range.

Sometimes, using a warehouse as a home base came with added benefits.

The doctor's eyes blew wide when I flipped the light switch and revealed a whole row of shooting lanes, fancy white targets in the shape of humans at the end of each one, dangling from a string that ran the length of the run.

"What the hell is this?"

I quirked a brow and chuckled under my breath. "What's it look like?"

Those impenetrable eyes of hers locked onto me, giving me a

once-over that took far longer than it should have and lingered in places I'd rather not think of. "It *looks* like you're about to teach your captive to shoot. At an underground, personal shooting range."

I cracked a smile. "Perceptive."

"And they call Spade the crazy one."

I said nothing as she strode past me and picked out the lane furthest from the door—my favorite one to use, as well. I liked to put a wall to my back and keep an eye on the exit at all times, and the far wall was the best vantage point in the room.

Without a word, I lifted the gun from her grip, slipped a clip inside it, and handed it back to her. "Safety's on; flick it off to shoot, flick it back on as soon as you're done. Don't close your eyes, and don't tense up when you shoot." I grabbed her shoulders as she stared at the very loaded gun in her hands and spun her to face downrange. "Aim for the head or the heart. Two surefire death shots. Anything else, and you run the risk of missing vital organs."

She nodded resolutely and brought the gun up in both hands, arms slightly bent as she flinched prematurely and pulled the trigger.

Bang!

She rocked backward from the shot, falling against my chest with a little *oof* of surprise. My hands moved to steady her, and she pulled away, blushing from head to toe as she shot a look back over her shoulder at me.

I just smirked and signaled she should try again.

With a resolute nod this time, she squared up once more, her arms steadier in front of her, only a slight flinch this time. It was still enough to send her shot wild, and she winced as it nicked the edge of one corner, clearly way off-mark.

"Here," I sighed, setting my gun on the shelf beside me. My hands moved from her shoulders down her arms until they wrapped around hers, fingers twined over each other as I raised the gun in front of her and straightened her arms. "Arms extended, all the way this time. And don't flinch away."

"Easy for you to say," she huffed, rolling her shoulders pointedly. This time, when her fingers squeezed the trigger, the paper wasn't so lucky, and her shots landed at the base of the sheet, grazing where the target's kidneys might be, as long as he stood stock still and took the bullets.

The victory was a small one for her, but she smiled up at me like the fucking sun at midnight and lit a small fire inside me that blazed its way through the darkness I'd been hiding in for so long.

To watch her take such pleasure in such a small thing, something I'd consider a failure out of myself, was humbling. Here was this girl, who we'd kidnapped off the street over nothing more than a fucking unfortunate *wrong place, wrong time* thing, punishing her over Joker's fuck up. And she wasn't hiding from us.

No. Quite the opposite. This girl, this *woman,* she was worming her way under the skin of every guy here, and fast.

If we weren't careful, at least one of these fools would fall in love with her, and then where would that lead us if Ace decided she had to be disposed of?

The thought made me shudder.

"BlackJack?"

She muttered my name, not my *name,* but the only one I'd gone by in years, and a strange feeling roused in me, one I wasn't familiar with. To avoid dealing with it, I turned my attention back to her, lifting her arms once more, this time shuffling forward until her back was against my chest.

A position I regretted as soon as I realized what *else* that pressed together.

She fit against me like a fucking glove, dragging shame from the depths of my soul as I forced myself to remember she'd just been accosted by Ace. In a not-so-pretty way, too.

"Eyes forward," I muttered gruffly, nodding to the target. "Aim higher. Lean against me, and don't flinch unless I do. Match your breathing to me, and pull the trigger when you breathe out."

This time, I laid my hands on her waist, holding her in place, trying desperately to remind myself to be professional. Hell, it wasn't like I had any interest in taking her to bed with me. The aversion to touch that had plagued me since I was a street urchin wouldn't let her get that close. But I could ignore it for now, ignore the faint buzzing beneath my skin as I touched her tiny waist, my hands spanning around it like she was nothing but a wisp of air.

She took my orders and steadied herself, relaxing against me like a bar of melting chocolate, her arms steady and raised perfectly in front of her. With a slow breath in, she took aim, and on the release of that breath, she squeezed the trigger, putting a round neatly through the target's chest.

For a split second, neither of us moved. And then she was turning in my arms and squealing like she'd won the lottery, the gun abandoned on the shelf as she threw her arms around my neck and smiled.

"I did it! Did you *see* that shot? Oh my god, I hit the target, right in the chest! BlackJack—"

My eyes flicked to her lips, parted as she realized she was rubbing against me like a fucking cat in heat. I stood stock-still, holding onto my self-control, as well as the urge to panic, hoping neither burst through at the present time.

"Good shot," I whispered, locked up from head to foot, paralyzed by her embrace.

She read the room wrong and leaned in to kiss me, her lips brushing against mine softer than a feather for no longer than a second, but it still rocked my world, a heady rush filling me as panic fought against her warmth.

Unfortunately, panic won out, and I dropped my hands and jerked away from her, the air in the room suddenly too heavy, too stifling, too hot. I gasped, fighting the urge to vomit as the panic finally forced me to my knees.

Of course, she couldn't just leave well enough alone. Her knees hit the concrete in front of me as she lowered herself to my level, her hand extended in front of her, hesitating feet away from me as if she were afraid I'd break if she touched me. In all fairness, I just might.

"BlackJack?"

"Get out of here," I growled. "Go back to Joker, where you belong."

She recoiled as if I'd slapped her, but I didn't have time to focus on that. The sooner she left me to my own solitude, the sooner I could get a grip on myself and act like a human being again.

Slip on the cool mask of indifference.

She'd seen me vulnerable, something I never showed anyone else, and I couldn't have her think she had the upper hand on me, not with two guns sitting just feet from us.

Never mind the fact that she hadn't so much as moved to grab one since she set hers down.

"Go!" I barked out, standing again, towering over her with the height advantage I held, trying my damndest not to shake while I worked at intimidating her.

Whether or not it worked, I got my desired effect, and she turned on a heel and trotted back the way she'd come, her bare feet slapping noisily against the concrete steps until the door shut, silencing the sound.

I breathed a sigh of relief and leaned over against the wall, bile rising up my throat and splattering the floor at my feet as the panic wove through me, wave after wave of weakness showing me I wasn't good enough, would never be good enough.

How fucked up was it that even a touch I wanted, a touch as innocent as the one she'd instigated in her excitement, still had the ability to bring me to my knees, twist my gut, and remind me of all the times grown men had tried to put their lecherous hands on my body as a child on the streets?

I didn't want to taint her with that.

That was my personal hell, and nobody should have to suffer that weight but me.

I couldn't get that close to her again. Mallory Stanton was dangerous to my well-being and my mental health.

And yet some sick part of me wanted more.

JOKER

CHAPTER TWENTY-FOUR
MALLORY

I left that basement and didn't look back, rushing back to Joker's room and the safety it represented without a second thought. I slept on the floor next to his bed, curled in a ball beneath a flannel I found draped over his nearby doorknob. I couldn't bring myself to crawl into the bed, even though I didn't doubt he'd be asleep and in no shape to accost me when he woke.

I was more right than I cared to admit, pleased to see him stumble from the bed and flail around his room in a state of haphazard disarray as he sought the magical remedy to his hangover.

I woke when he tripped over me on his way to rifle through the nearby dresser.

"Fuck!" I yelped, flinching away from his body as he landed atop me, arms and legs akimbo, eyes squinted against the light filtering through the window.

"Shit, sorry," he muttered, scrambling to grip the drawer as he rolled off me, already focused on another thing. "Head is killing me. Wanna just do me in and save me the trouble?"

I giggled despite myself. "You did drink over half a bottle of liquor to yourself last night. What did you expect?"

He groaned, holding a hand to the side of his head as he slipped to the floor and crumpled in a heap. "Fuck, I didn't expect to get that wasted and pass out." He cocked his head pointedly. "I also didn't expect this to hurt so damn much, either."

I fought the smile that rose in me at his discomfort. "You know, if you just stopped drowning yourself in booze, you wouldn't wake up feeling like someone dragged you through the pits of hell."

He flashed me one of those award-winning smiles and bent his legs, his feet spread apart just a bit as he draped those long arms over the tops of his knees and stared at me through them, ringlets of blonde hair framing his face in a messy but endearing ball of bedhead. "And I suppose this is where you tell me I should deal with my issues head-on, doc?"

My foot darted out before I could make my brain process the logical thought behind it, kicking at his foot playfully. "I'm the mind reader here, not you, buddy."

He spread his arms wide and grinned, wincing as his hangover headache announced itself again. "Well, doc, do your worst."

I pretended to think about it for a second, but I wasn't really in the mood to entertain him. "Nah, not today," I hedged, hoping he'd drop it. "Can I borrow your shower?" I asked instead, hoping he'd say yes. After last night's debauchery in the kitchen, I wanted to wash the stickiness from my thighs, wash the memory of Ace's hands from my skin, the feel of his breath against my ear overwhelming me even in the daylight.

"Care for some company?"

I laughed at his half-assed attempt at flirting. "You couldn't stand up straight long enough to do anything."

"I don't need to stand for you to sit on my face," he pointed out, eyes flashing darker, more lustful than they'd been before.

I had to be careful with Joker. He was sinfully alluring, like that old saying, 'you catch more flies with honey than shit'. *And good god, was he all honey.* That boy had a tongue that curved around words as well as I assumed it'd curl around other parts of a woman's body. He was a playboy, a manwhore, a literal himbo, and I had no time for a shallow pretty boy.

I had to survive, but I didn't have to sell my body to do it.

Not yet, anyhow.

"You'd drown if you did that," I pointed out, crawling over to my bags to rifle through them for anything I could wear that didn't scream 'whoreing myself out at a punk rock concert'.

At the bottom of the bag was a pair of jean shorts, an oversized, off-the-shoulder tee, and some fresh undergarments. I yanked the paltry offering from the pack and sighed, wishing I'd paid more attention to what I'd shoved in this bag when I was at my apartment.

I would have picked more carefully if Spade hadn't been frazzling my last nerve.

Resigned, I rushed off, feeling much better once I'd rinsed the evidence of the night before from my body. I imagined all the bad and unsettling parts of the night before washing down the drain with the suds of my shampoo and closed my eyes as the hot water scalded my skin, taking the shame I felt and replacing it with contentment.

I wouldn't let myself feel bad about what I'd done.

Not this time.

Joker, thank god, had a hairbrush hanging out on his counter, along with some lovely hair products I didn't often get to splurge on, so once I'd slipped into my outfit, I cracked the door open to ask him if he minded me using them, only to find him gone.

And Spade was lying across his bed, eyes trained on the bathroom door, a slow smile spreading across his lips as we locked eyes.

Fuck.

"Hey there, sweetheart," he drawled, his eyes obviously eager to see what I wore for the day. "Sleep well?"

I inched the door closed and locked it, listening to his chuckle on the other side of the wood as I debated my choices. The likelihood of the others knowing he was in here was slim to none, especially since they'd had to rescue me from him last night. I could stay in Joker's bathroom indefinitely. Eventually, someone would come looking for me.

Right?

Or, I could own this shit and run roughshod over him, ignoring his obvious horndog attitude.

A third option ghosted through my skull, and I dismissed it as soon as it formed in my head.

There's a gun and clip under the sink. You could shoot him.

BlackJack's words echoed hollowly in my head, reminding me that not just last night, I couldn't shoot straight to save my life.

Only aim at something you're prepared to shoot.

I decided to be liberal with the hair products, taking my sweet time prepping myself for the day. When my locks were tamed into a high ponytail and my face fresh, I strode from the bathroom like I was invincible, untouchable, above the rest of the world, hoping it would dissuade Spade a bit.

It didn't.

He rose from the bed and was at my side in seconds, penning me in against the wall with his hands on either side of my head, his arms like a cage, preventing escape. "Well, don't you look like a breath of fresh air, doc," he taunted, his nose drawing a line from my shoulder to the spot just below my ear. "Smell abso-fucking-lutely divine."

He shoved off the wall when I refused to entertain his toying, like a petulant cat whose mouse had rolled over and played dead. I watched him go, confusion twisting the relief I felt at his absence.

Why did I want him to come back and cage me in again? Was I going insane?

"Get some sensibly sexy shoes on, sugar, and grab some coffee. The boys will be busy with other things today, so you're coming with me to a match."

I turned to face him, nothing making a lick of fucking sense. "Excuse me?"

Match?

What the fuck?

"Yeah," he sighed, absently picking his nails with a pocketknife. "I'm part of a sparring ring, boxers, you know, and we let off some steam with unofficial matches now and again. Good place to get information, too," he added, almost as an afterthought. "Especially if you've got a pussy between your legs."

He wanted to use me as an informant. Fucking fantastic.

"I'm nobody's plaything, Spade," I started, aiming for confident and demanding but missing the mark and hitting every rung on the way down. I landed somewhere close to scared and irritated, and he laughed at my bluster. "I'm not whoreing myself out for information."

He rose and strode past me, shoving the door open with a flourish. "I'd never whore out my girl for information I could just as easily get with my fists." His eyes met mine and contained nothing but seriousness. "Let's you and I go get some coffee, and I'll explain on the way to the ring."

I didn't have a choice, really, so I followed behind him, unsure what the day might bring but ready for anything.

I should have grabbed the gun.

HIS GYM, as it turned out, was a few boxing rings, an MMA sparring section, and some random punching bags and lifting equipment on the main floor. But on the basement level, where he led me with a little smirk and a pat on the ass, that's where the real business happened.

Wall to wall, the place was packed with men who clearly wouldn't think twice before cutting your tongue out for an insult. He assured me none of them would be armed—"house rules"—but I had severe misgivings over whether these criminals, here for what amounted to an underground fight club, gave two shits about the house rules.

"Spade, are you sure this is a good idea?" I whispered in his ear, still a stretch even in the heels he'd plucked from my bag with a smirk on his lips. "This looks like a dangerous crowd."

His grin grew wider as he leaned against me and used the need for privacy to yank me closer until I was damn near plastered against his front. "So, the doorman who frisked us is a homophobe. Never goes near a guy's front pockets if he can avoid it. I have a knife on my thigh strap. If shit goes bad, not that it will, but *if,* then you can reach down my pants and pull the blade out."

I blanched at the realization that he'd managed to find a surefire way to get my hand on his junk, then I decided to play ball.

If he could tease and taunt and be slick to get his way, well, then so could I.

"You'd better be careful, tough guy. If that blade moves just a bit too far, I could cut off a vital part of your anatomy. So hands better not wander while we're here, or I'll put on a show of a different kind as I gut you and take off."

His cock stiffened against my thigh, and he groaned against my temple. "Fuck, doc, you're gonna be the death of me." He shifted, his length brushing against my core this time, and now we were both a bit frazzled. "You can't say things like that to a man unless you're willing to follow through." I felt his lips ghost against my ear, and then his teeth nipped at the shell of it gently, eliciting an involuntary moan from me. "Just promise me you'll make it hurt when you break my heart, sweetheart."

I didn't have a witty retort, and his eyes wandered over to the ring as the next match came to a bloody and fist-pumping end, the crowd roaring like some wild thing, untamable, unhinged, just like the man at my side.

"Let's get closer to the action, princess," he quipped, tugging me along like a piece of arm candy as every man we passed stopped to stare.

At who, I wasn't sure.

We watched two more matches from the sidelines, his hand constantly wandering to tuck itself in my ass pockets or curl around my ribcage, his thumb brushing against the side of my breast whenever the mood struck him. On the third pass, I moved to swat at him, just as the announcer called out the victor and turned to us.

"And now, the fight you've all been waiting to see tonight—the nightly victor and his challenger!"

The crowd went wild, and Spade's arm banded tighter around me for a second as he locked eyes with the man entering the ring.

"Let's all welcome the newcomer from across the pond, the illusive and dangerous *Soldat!*"

"Soldier," Spade muttered against my temple, his lips curled in disgust. "What a joke."

The man in the ring didn't *look* like a joke, though whether or not he'd once been a soldier was up for debate. His body was lean yet muscled, a toned physique it took work to maintain—work this man didn't seem to shy from. He stalked around the ring, hands loose at his sides, eyes dark and hair hanging around his face in loose brown waves, painting a picture of an unconcerned killer that set me on edge.

Regardless of whether or not Spade got on my nerves or didn't respect the word no, I didn't want to see him killed, and I suddenly had the feeling that was exactly what would happen if he *ever* stepped in that ring with this man.

"Spade," I started, turning toward him with a hand on his chest, "I don't—"

My concerns were silenced as he leaned into me and initiated a heart-stopping kiss, his lips crawling over mine, needy, desperate, searching. I groaned and realized this was the time to reach for that knife he'd strapped up with and made a show of pretending to grope him for good luck. We were pressed so tightly together that there was no way anyone could see the small blade I slipped against my wrist as he pulled away, but there was no hiding the shiver that ran up my spine as his tongue slipped between my lips and coaxed me open like a fucking blooming flower.

Spade might have a code of honor, but damn if he couldn't kiss like a sinner. His hands twisted around me, refusing to let me go, and for the time being, I was completely okay if they didn't. In this room full of deadly men and dangerous, bloodthirsty criminals, Spade really was the lesser of all evils—the safest port in this storm.

He ended the kiss as the announcer cleared his throat pointedly. "And the runner-up for the night, *Demon!*"

With a last, softly affectionate kiss to the temple and a pat to the ass, he pulled away, and we faced the ring again, watching the two fighters circle one another as they sized each other up. I fought the urge to flee, every molecule in my body itching to be anywhere but here.

I should have grabbed that fucking gun.

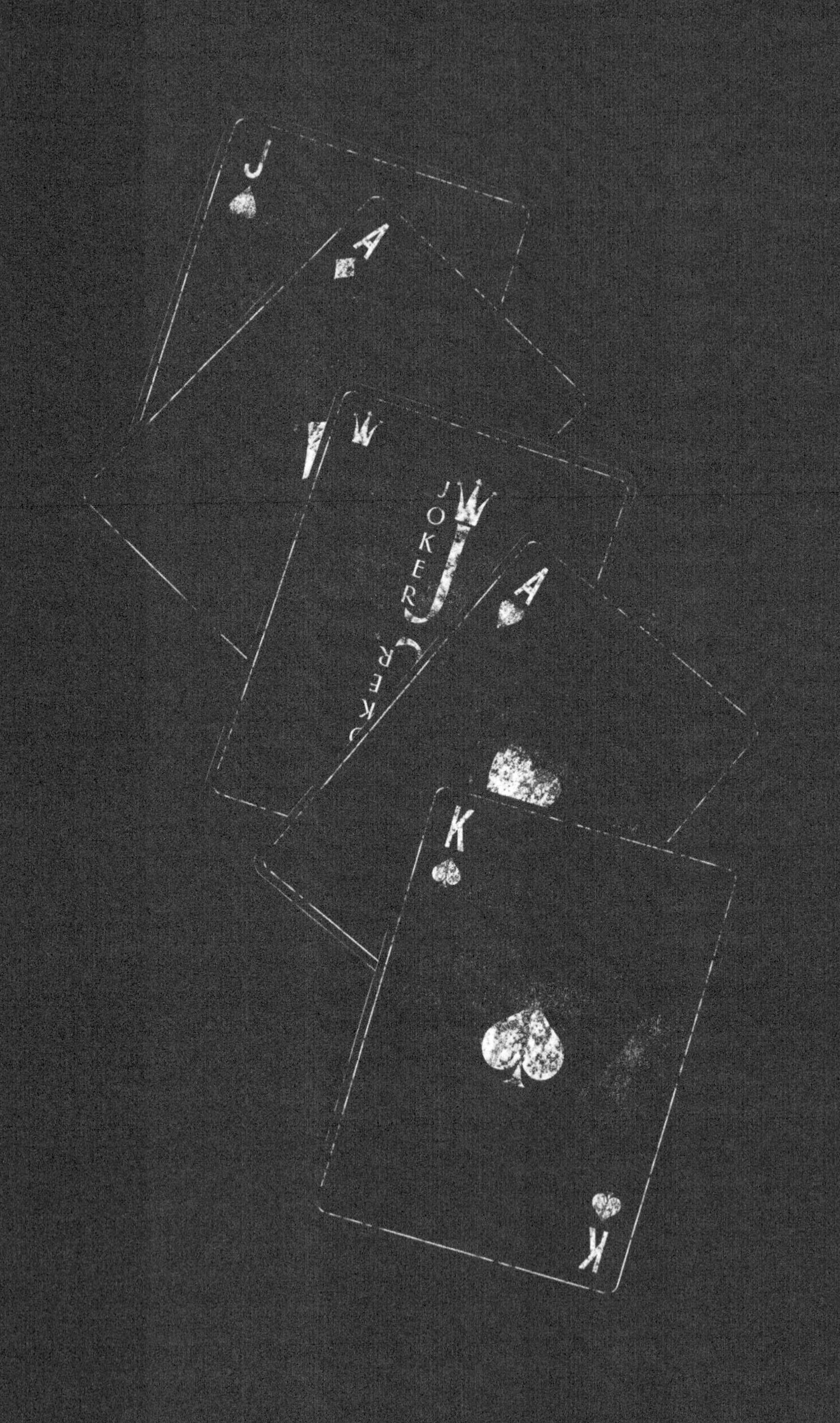
JOKER

CHAPTER TWENTY-FIVE
JOKER

I wasn't supposed to be here.

I was supposed to be out with Ace, watching his six while he interrogated some asshole with information on our new unknown enemy—an enemy we now had *only* due to my indiscretion and an unplanned heist.

When I got my hands on the asshole who gave us the bad info, I'd wring his damn neck until he choked on his tongue, friend of my father or not.

It wasn't a surprise when Spade announced he was going to the rings today. Even maimed like he was, he'd probably glean some solid info while he trolled and placed bets with the seedier of the underground crime lifers. But when I returned to my room and found the doc missing, I knew he had taken her with him, sneaky bastard that he was.

He probably convinced her she *had* to go.

So I was here to rescue her. Take her back to the compound, where she'd be safe.

I wove in and out of the crowd as the announcer called the match in progress to a halt, proclaiming the winner to a mixture of cheers and boos from the crowd, depending on where they'd placed their bets. Money exchanged hands, or tickets were distributed, and some men shifted to the side of the room to collect winnings and leave, their preferred match over for the day.

I was so focused on finding Spade and the doc that I almost missed the announcement of the next fight.

"—Soldat!"

Fucking Christ, it couldn't be.

The man they called *Soldat* strode into the ring like he owned it, his swagger muted and understated but no less deadly in its intent. He locked eyes with someone hidden in the glare of a spotlight on the ring, and from this side of the room, I couldn't possibly hear it, but I just knew the madman up there *growled* at whoever he'd just been staring at.

I knew this man.

In the underground, where I'd lived for most of my life as the son of a criminal, you heard stories of some of the fiercest men to walk the streets above. Men who no man was brave enough to tangle with. You learned very quickly there were some you didn't dare cross if you valued your life.

The Soldier was one of them.

They said he killed so many men in his service to the Kings he'd lost count. That men would rather kill themselves than face his ruthless fists. That he once tortured a fellow enforcer until the man swallowed his own tongue in an effort to escape the madness.

So the Soldier cut it out and kept going.

I shuddered at his mere presence, knowing what it meant for us.

If the Soldat was here, then the Kings were hunting for someone.

Their timing couldn't possibly be more ironic or damning, depending on their reasons for being present in what they considered the slums of Khula City.

As I shook off the heavy feeling in the air, my feet moved once more, shuffling along as I nodded to people I recognized, shook hands with a few old business partners, and stopped to chat here and there when it might help me get closer to the people who wanted my head. I'd almost convinced myself that Spade lied about his intended destination to throw us off his trail when a familiar tinkling laugh echoed to my left, and I turned to find the doc in Spade's arms, tossing her head back as he told jokes to one of his old sparring partners.

She didn't look like she was here unwillingly. She looked like she was having fun.

Maybe my decision to come had been a waste, after all.

I was conveniently hidden behind a group of bangers here for the festivities. As their attentions turned to the circling fighters in the ring, I inched closer, so I could use them as cover while eavesdropping on the conversation between my cohort and the men now surrounding him.

Three new men had sidled up to Spade, their eyes cool and cunning as they flicked between him, the doc, and the match in the ring. Other people on the floor made room for these three, and it set me on edge, the way they seemed to make the room move around them instead of the other way around.

The tallest one spoke, his voice like a sweet, proper British purr as it left his lips. "Ah, you must be Spade. We heard you fought here, but you're not on the list for the night." His eyes cut to the man in the ring currently pounding the life out of his opponent while cheers rose from the crowd on the other side of the ring. "Our *Soldat* was most excited to meet you in combat. He's heard you're undefeated here."

Spade's upper lip lifted in a sneer as he put two and two together. "I am undefeated, two years running. Your man is probably lucky I'm not here to fight tonight."

You fucking idiot.

As much confidence as I had in the man, I knew he wasn't a match for the crazed King in the ring. With every draw of his fist, blood slung behind him, splattering his close spectators in freckles of red. His lips were lifted in a snarl as his opponent pleaded for mercy, something the man above seemed disinclined to grant him.

But these rings weren't death matches. And even the Kings weren't above the rules.

"That's the match! Winner, by a landslide, *Soldat!*"

He stood in the center of the ring like a ghost of a man, a shell with nothing inside, and his eyes found Spade with unerring ease.

The King beside Spade gripped his forearm pointedly, tossing his head toward the ring. "If you're not going to be throwing punches, perhaps you'd like to trade a few words with my man there?"

Spade growled, but his hands released Mallory, and he shrugged off the King with a roll of his eyes. "I didn't know this was your territory, *thug.*" His eyes roved over the doc with slow purpose, hesitating on her face until she gave him a slight nod. "You lay a finger on her, I'll break every last one of them."

He tossed his head back and laughed maniacally. "As if I'd waste my time."

I rubbed absently at the gun tucked safely between my shoulder blades, hidden from view by my stance and from the prying eyes of the doorman by the fat fifty I'd been slipping him on occasion to look the other way when I walked in. I'd never caused any harm, and broken up more than one fight to help him out, so he really didn't need much in the way of persuasion to not pat me down.

The weight of the metal on my back, tucked neatly inside its holster, was a reassurance of an insurance policy for my life, should I need it.

Mallory watched Spade walk off with a tight jaw and hands balled into fists at her side. Determined to follow him, she swerved around a smirking King as he crossed his arms over his chest and tipped his nose up at her like she wasn't worth the dirt on the bottom of his shoe.

She no sooner got a foot beyond him than two other men appeared like shadow wraiths, slipping their arms through hers and tugging her back where she started as she fought their grasp.

"Hey, no, wait—*excuse you, asshole, I was going somewhere—*"

They set her back down in front of the Brit, and he practically leered at her, his lips quirked up in that smirk he'd worn since he first walked in, no doubt.

"You aren't going anywhere, pet. Let the two grown men have a chat, and then you and your keeper can slink off where you came from. We just want some information, that's all."

Mallory, god love her, cocked a brow and tilted her head to the side like she struggled to take him all in. "And what does that have to do with me? I'm not *your* property, ya fuckstick."

The two men on either side of her closed in, but she held her own, keeping them both at bay with a pointed look.

"That's far enough, bitch," one growled at her, his eyes narrowed as she stared him down though she was a whole head shorter than him.

"Look who's talking," she snapped back, a smirk on her face that had me harder than a steel beam in my pants.

Fuck, she could give as good as she got.

She was perfect.

Too bad Ace was determined to find a reason to kill her.

The second one put his hands on her shoulders, and the little yelp she let out when his hands constricted against her skin and dug into the flesh beneath her shirt had me seeing red.

I shoved through the crowd of gang bangers shielding me from view and stepped up behind the asshole manhandling the doc. Steeling myself for a fight, I tapped him on the shoulder, really ramming my finger into the skin there to vent some frustration.

He turned around and sneered down at me. "Who the fuck are you?"

"I think you're hurting the lady," I drawled politely, playing the role I'd been born for. "Perhaps you should let her go."

"Yeah? And maybe you should go fuck yourself."

Mallory winced as his one-handed hold on her tightened, the skin on her arm turning a mottled red beneath his grip. I wasn't about to let her be manhandled, and without thinking, I reached out and peeled his fingers back, then finished the move with a solid punch to the face for his troubles.

Aaaaand that's about where things went south.

Fast.

Mallory ducked as his arm swung right where her head had just been and lumbered past her on its way to me. I managed to lean back in time to miss the damn thing by an inch, maybe two, and ducked around him, wrapping my arms around his neck in a sleeper hold as we turned to face his boss.

The Brit had the nerve to laugh, fucking *laugh,* at my display of aggression, his eyes flicking to Mallory for a split second, then back to me. Those dark green orbs lit up with recognition, and his scowl deepened when I didn't return the look.

"I can't believe it. Fortune smiles upon us tonight, gents. Meet Cassian Fontaine, son of the sleaziest rat in lockup down south."

I flinched at his cavalier use of my full name. Nobody used my full name, not even my father now. That bastard had left me for dead and turned my mother over to his boss in an attempt to save his own thin skin. Ultimately, he took the fall for a crime he didn't commit, used as a scapegoat for the bigwig's son. Mom rotted in a hole in the wall, where she died alone and miserable, in pain to the end, her beauty and life ripped away like the wind.

And me, they gave to the streets, turned me out like a fucking dog, where I begged for scraps while my father wove his way in and out of jails, taking plea deals, rolling over on any criminal he thought wouldn't remember him when they got loose, anyone he thought could be spared to save him time inside.

The mark on his head grew so large, jail eventually became the only place he was somewhat safe.

"Mallory, get behind me," I growled, pleased that she didn't argue as I moved in a half-circle, keeping the asshole King in front of me at all times. "What the fuck are you scumbags doing on our turf? You've never shown any interest in this side of town before."

I felt the doc's hands on my shoulder blades, heard the quick intake of breath as she realized there was a pistol strapped to my spine. Her fingers traced the outline slowly, as if she were learning where to grab it if needed.

Good fucking girl. That's right.

I knew I'd seen something special in her, had known it ever since I heard her beautiful voice on that video call.

"Let Spectre go, Cassian, and we can talk like gentlemen."

The man in my arms looked like he was about to pass out, so I shoved him off my chest and into the man who'd demanded his release, my left hand moving backward to find Mallory. I grazed her hip, inches away from mine, and smiled. She'd stay put behind me, and that would keep her safe.

I hoped.

"What do you want, King? Spit it out and get on with shit, or get out of here. You haven't been welcome downtown in a long time, and that's unlikely to change any time soon."

Mallory slid off to my side, her hands on my arm, her eyes on the Kings who stood before us, eyes alight with something feral as they watched her. Their de facto leader growled a warning, and the other two backed down, content to cross their arms and watch on.

"What I want is information, Cassian, and you're just the man to get it for me."

J
A
JOKER
A
K

CHAPTER TWENTY-SIX
MALLORY

These men were trouble. Trouble I didn't want to be a part of.

When Spade was led off, and they drug me away from him, I thought I was about to have to pull a knife in what was clearly a gunfight, but Joker showing up was a godsend. A fucking miracle in its own right.

As was the pistol strapped to his back. I wasn't sure how I would get to it if I had to, but knowing it was there was a bit of assurance that if shit went south, I might stand a chance of surviving.

Joker stared down the man in front of him, uncaring that he was outnumbered three to one, or that his assailants had Spade god knew where. "What kind of information are you after?"

"Information on some criminal activity that pertains to a business associate of mine." His eyes narrowed, lips pursed as he considered his next words carefully. "A jeweler, as a matter of fact."

In the short time I had been at their compound, I hadn't heard any talk about jewels, and they didn't strike me as jewel thieves. What did this man mean, criminal activity involving a jeweler? And why would Joker have that information handy?

"Can't help you," he drawled, though his hands moved to his

pockets, a move I knew was designed to hide the tremor in them. I'd seen it a lot in my drunks and my guilty patients. They hid their hands because it was the easiest tell to spot. And Joker was a drunk *and* a guilty man, so he had doubly as much to hide. "I'm not really in the business of information anymore; sorry about that—"

The King leaned forward threateningly, grabbing Joker's shirt in his fist as he yanked them together. "Now, listen here, you little shit—"

"Hands off him, too. The offer to break all your fingers still stands."

Spade sauntered over just then, a scowl on his lips, the *Soldat* right behind him with a matching grim expression on his lips. The King released Joker but didn't back down. He turned to his soldier instead, a curious look in his eyes.

"Anything?"

The strange, withdrawn man shook his head. "Nothing."

"Hmph." King swirled his fingers in a loop above his head, and the other three men fell into place behind him. His eyes found Joker again, narrowed and menacing as they burned with danger. "Put your fucking nose to the ground, dog, and find out who took my friend's jewels, who put them up to it. I'll be back soon enough for your results—and you'd better have them, or I'll have me a new pet to play with." His gaze flicked to me, moving up and down my body in a slow perusal that left me feeling filthy and violated. "And I play rough and break pretty things."

Spade growled this time, stepping in front of me pointedly. I finally curled into Joker's arms, perfectly content to be between the wall of muscle and him. No more words were exchanged, but the intent was clear.

He most certainly meant me.

"I think it's high time you leave," my fierce protector ground out, eyes trained on the invaders as they stared each other down. Spade stood his ground, body tense and coiled, ready to strike should he need to.

The King scoffed at our little show and turned on a heel,

marching off with all the regality of an actual royal. Once he and his posse were out of sight, the three of us let out a collective breath, relieved the tense situation didn't come to a worse head.

Joker frowned over my head at Spade. "What did the ham-handed one want with you?"

Spade shrugged, gesturing toward the back of the room. "A match and answers."

"Answers?"

Another shrug. "He wanted to know who I worked for, what gang I represent in the ring. I told him nobody, gave him no answers. He threatened to beat it out of me next time if I didn't come up with something by then."

Joker's arms tightened around me, and I shivered at the touch. He didn't seem to notice, though, and kept on with Spade as they walked over to the backdoor leading to the parking lot where their vehicles no doubt sat, waiting.

Spade led us to the sleek black beast in the corner of the lot, his lovely two-seater, and grinned knowingly. "You brought your own car?"

"I'm not letting you wander off with the doc, Spade. You probably brought her against her will—"

Spade's laughter drowned out the rest of Joker's complaints as he opened the passenger side door and pointed at me. "Get in, doc."

I had a choice to make here. If I protested, I doubted he'd fight Joker over me, but there was a chance he might. On the other hand, I *was* sort of coerced here under the guise that I had to come.

I looked over at Joker, drumming up all the sad eye power I could muster. "I don't want to go with him. I'd rather ride with you, Cass."

Spade's brows climbed up his face, eyes blown wide at my cavalier use of Joker's real name. "Oh, you two are on a first-name basis?"

Joker's cheeks turned a shade of pink as he cleared his throat, eyes on anything but me. "I never asked her to call me jack shit, asshole—"

I spotted a chink in his armor and exploited it like a sonofabitch. "That's not true. I do remember your instructions to *say it again* very clearly, on our little video chat." My eyebrows wriggled as he turned a deeper shade of pink, his hand tousling those soft blonde curls atop his head. *"Cass."*

Spade chuckled and closed the passenger door of his car, swinging the keys around at the end of one finger as his smile widened. "You heard the lady, *Cass; she's* riding with you." His gaze trailed over my body, stopping at my eyes, his own flashing with mirth. "Go easy on him, sweetheart; he's got a soft soul inside that ruffian's body."

"Noted," I shot back, suddenly feeling like three kinds of a fool for toying with these men when they were far better armed than I.

Joker's car was much more understated, silver instead of black, with a very pointed pinstripe down the sides that added a touch of flair to its sleekness.

My brow lifted as I stared at it. "Sweet ride, buddy."

He clicked his key fob and hid a soft smile behind his curtain of hair, still redder than a sunburn. "Thanks."

I tugged my door open and slid in, relishing the feel of the butter-smooth leather against my thighs as I got comfortable. The fucking heels Spade had insisted I wear were uncomfortable, and I wasted no time lifting one leg to my lap so I could tug the buckles free.

Suddenly, Joker was at my side, kneeling on the ground, shielded by the door from view. His eyes fell to my legs, his hands hovering above his knee, lips parted slightly. "Why don't you let me help you with those? They look awful uncomfortable, doc."

I bit my lip but nodded my assent, twisting my body in the seat to let my legs dangle in the open doorway. His soft hands set to immediate work, slipping the band free of its buckles and fastenings with a practiced move before sliding them down the length of my calf, long fingers brushing my ankle as he freed me from the wretchedly uncomfortable torture devices. I sucked in a quick, shocked breath when he moved to the second leg, feeling very exposed even though I was wearing shorts this time instead of a skirt.

I still felt bare, like I might as well be wearing next to nothing where he was concerned.

Especially when his hands tenderly cupped the arch of my foot and set it inside the car, then trailed up the inside of my calf, over my knee, and swirled little patterns into the skin of my thigh like a brand.

"You know, my name *does* sound rather sexy when *you* say it."

His fingers brushed the sensitive strip of my inner thigh that sent shivers through me, his eyes lifted to mine for a brief second, and a knowing smile brushed over his lips.

I couldn't resist tucking a stray hair behind my ear while he watched, feeling very much like an ordinary girl at that moment, out on a date with a considerate man, about to share a tender kiss.

Except I wasn't an ordinary girl, he wasn't a considerate, ordinary man, this wasn't a date, and this wasn't about to turn into a kiss—

"Mallory," he breathed, inching closer, his hand frozen on my thigh as our faces neared, the whole process achingly slow as his fucking gorgeous blue eyes smoldered me into a pile of ash. If he was a flame, I was a phoenix, and all I wanted to do was fucking burn, to be reborn right the fuck now.

"Cass," I whispered, reaching out to take his sharp jaw between my palms and yank him closer, our lips barely touching, the final barrier before I did something I would surely regret later.

But he'd come to my rescue, and like Spade well knew, I was an adrenaline junkie, and the whole ordeal left me hot and bothered and totally off-kilter. I felt wild and untamed, like I should do something I wouldn't do under normal circumstances.

So I kissed him.

And fuck all if he didn't kiss me right the hell back, so damn good I forgot my name.

The sinful moan he let out as our lips parted nearly had me coming undone as his hands planted on the seat beside my hip and against the dash, and his whole body crowded me into my seat now, his hips between my knees, like he'd crawled a thousand miles to taste my lips and found me sweeter than the headiest nectar.

I itched to run my fingers along his throat, to the back of his neck, where those golden locks met his skin and teased the tip of his spine, so I let them, opening myself to him as his knee found purchase on the edge of the seat, his head tilting down now to keep us connected as he struggled not to climb on top of me in the fucking front seat. His other foot stayed connected to the ground outside, and thank god one of us was still thinking clearly, because my senses had all left me as his tongue delved into my mouth, running across the side of mine and sliding around it in a circle like he'd been born to kiss.

"Fuck," I panted against him, my lips shifting to get a better angle as he plundered away, stealing my breath, my sanity, my whole fucking lot of dignity—or what was left of it. That hand frozen on my thigh hadn't moved, either, and I marveled at his decorum and control, even as I arched against the feelings he inspired in me.

Headiness. Need. Urgency. Attraction. Lust.

Fuck, I was toast. Did I say I wanted to get in his car and ride home with him?

Was it too late to call the forward-but-not-as-tender Spade?

"Such eloquent speech, sugar," he breathed against my lips, touching but not, our noses tip to tip, lashes fluttering as we tried and failed not to make direct eye contact. "Do you kiss your mother with that mouth?"

I pushed back the familiar ache at the reminder of the woman who'd given everything in her efforts to raise me right and dragged out a quip to match his.

"No, but I kiss bad men with it."

His groan was fucking downright feral as the words hit home, but instead of pushing forward like I expected him to, he pulled back and yanked himself out of the car, waiting patiently for me to drag my other leg in before he closed the door between us.

I could see the fucking stiffy he was sporting against the seam of his jeans, but he didn't press, didn't push me like Spade did, and for some reason, that was even hotter than the rush I'd gotten when Spade took me, urgent and desperate, on the hood of his car.

I'd set out to bring these men to their knees, to land somewhere in the safe pile of people they wouldn't kill, and instead, I was out here losing my heart to these criminal bastards, their devil-may-care lifestyle rubbing off on me the longer I remained their captive.

Who knew; maybe soon, I wouldn't even want to leave.

JOKER

CHAPTER TWENTY-SEVEN
SPADE

The compound was abandoned and silent when I pulled into the garage, grinning like a loon at the new door and the latest sign BlackJack had stuck to the middle of it on the inside.

Please, At Least Open The Door If You're Going To Steal A Car

He had a funny bone or three in his body and could be quite the jokester when he felt like it, and I had to applaud his sarcastic humor.

Joker and the good doc would take their time, or so I expected, so I sat down in the kitchen and started eating the leftovers he'd left in the fridge while I waited. Imagine my surprise when they pulled in mere minutes after me.

He must have been bursting at the seams to fuck her if it only took—I glanced at my phone screen—*seven minutes.*

I pointedly ignored them as they entered the kitchen through the garage door, shoveling the pasta more urgently in my mouth as Joker's eyes found me and then traveled down to the inconspicuous container I was busy emptying and rolled his eyes with a sigh.

Mallory danced across the kitchen like the hounds of hell were on her heels, and from the way Joker longingly stared after her as she busied herself in the fridge, rooting around for food, no doubt.

A thought occurred to me, and I blinked, stunned our stupid asses hadn't thought of it already. "Sweetheart, when was the last time you ate?"

It had been a few days since we'd kidnapped her, and I wasn't sure if any of us were used to thinking of anyone else as far as nutrition, in a pattern of takeout when and where we had time to grab it. And I certainly hadn't gotten her anything recently.

There was no hiding the flush of embarrassment on her face as she peeked over the rim of the door, then ducked back down. "Uhhh, Joker brought some food back to his room last night, so—"

"I mean a real meal, sweetheart, not snack food."

She didn't answer me, so I slid off the stool I occupied, dumped the now-empty container in the trash, and stalked over to her, crowding her with my body. "Doc."

She froze like a deer in headlights, turned to face me, and blushed deeper. "A few days."

Fuck, we had been starving the poor thing.

We had a no-delivery policy to keep our location anonymous, so ordering something was out. I let my mind stumble through different ideas, settling on the most obvious one. "We'll go out to eat, then. On me." I shot a look at the poor fool who was too busy being lovesick over a girl he'd doomed to possible death to notice I'd eaten his meal for the night. "Joker can come, too, since I sort of ate his dinner."

Her eyes flicked from the lovesick puppy to me, weighing her options. Food, I would imagine, was quite the temptation, considering she had to be starving for something good, and I happened to have an in at just the perfect spot. Hell, I could even have Ace and BlackJack meet us there, so we could all replenish our energy stores.

Finally, she sagged against the fridge door, shutting it slowly. "Fine, I'll let you take me to dinner. But what do I wear? My choices are . . . *limited.*"

I had plans for her that didn't involve pants, and I would be damned if she thwarted them. She'd come to appreciate and enjoy my particular brand of foreplay, of that I was sure.

"Put on a dress."

Jesus, Mary, and Joseph, kill me now.

It turned out that the good doc hadn't packed any dresses, but Joker's closet of castoffs from one-night stands was rife with choices, so he invited her to peruse it. Unfortunately, he'd been through a recent phase of girls so skinny you could snap them in half, so the options were not quite the perfect fit.

In fact, the dress she wore now had been the only one that would fit over her hips, and she fucking *spilled* out of it like Niagara Falls over the fucking cliffs.

She stood at the bottom of the stairs, running her hands down her sides in an effort to smooth the bodice that clung to her like a second skin. It took every ounce of control for me not to turn her around, bend her over the stairs, and rail the dogshit out of her where she stood.

Her eyes were hesitant as she searched mine, futilely tugging at the bottom hem of her skirt. "Is it okay? Clearly, I'm not his usual type," she growled as an afterthought, shooting a glare that could melt steel over her shoulder at Joker.

He had the good sense to look embarrassed, but I just howled with laughter. "Sweetheart, his type is two-legged with a pussy. Don't worry about it." I reached out and took her hand, spinning her around while she struggled to stay *in* the damn thing.

The shelf built for her bust was a size or two too small, the waist a teensy tight, and the skirt too short, but fuck all if I cared. She could have dressed in nothing at all, and I'd have had no hesitation about showing her off naked as the day she was born in the middle of any of these uptight five-star restaurants.

Her legs went on forever, and thank heavens she fit the shoes that went with the dress. Whoever had left this ensemble behind in Joker's room had obviously not wanted any reminders of the man she'd tangled with the night before.

Either that or Ace had seen to her dismissal.

Hard to tell.

Joker's strangled whimper of defeat when she tossed her hair and accepted my arm was damn near a victory bell at ringside, sending a jolt of pride at my obvious victory through these thick veins. I smiled all the way to his car and took the backseat with Mallory as Joker resignedly slid into the driver's seat.

He knew where we were going. He didn't need my instructions to get there.

I laid a palm on the doc's leg, my eyes straight ahead as I felt her tense below my fingertips. I wouldn't push her too far, not yet. I'd wait til I had her someplace she couldn't run away, then have my way with her. She'd come around once I was knuckle-deep in that pussy.

KAZ'S KITCHEN was a hole-in-the-wall fine dining spot owned by a man who'd lost one too many fights to me in the past. I also happened to throw a fight against him to help pay for it, so now I had a standing invitation to stop in for food any time on the house. I didn't take advantage of it often, but today was special.

She was special.

I hadn't told Mallory yet that I'd decided to keep her, come hell or high water. She didn't deserve to die, we all knew it, but Ace was still on the fence, and I wasn't the only one who'd noticed how fast she seemed to worm her way into our routine, our minds, our fucking hearts. Hell, three days in, and I caught myself fantasizing about her clothes on a hanger next to mine. Sharing my bed.

Things I knew Ace would have my ass for even dreaming about.

And yet, I didn't care. Mallory was fun, she was a fighter, and she didn't give in to me out of ease or comfort. I liked a girl who struggled against the very fabric of human need in an effort to keep herself on some imagined moral high ground.

We both knew she was no saint.

Not the way she wielded that butterfly knife.

I held out my hand to help her from the car, earning myself the briefest flash of bright red panties beneath that too-short skirt. She tugged up on the top and sighed when her thighs snuck out of the bottom, taunting me with their creamy sight.

I reached down again and tugged on the hem for her, pleased when she shot me a grateful grin instead of a scowl, and even let her hand linger on my cheek with a soft pat of appreciation.

Who's the little puppy now?

Joker offered her an arm to escort her in the doors, but she smugly refused any help, choosing instead to strut her stuff and give us both a look of what she thought was hers to deny as we followed dutifully behind.

The host stopped her with a frown, taking in her dress, no doubt assuming she was a paid floozie, an escort for two wealthy patrons who were themselves underdressed a little by his standards. "Excuse me, miss, but we have a strict dress code here—"

I shoved in front of her and crowded the little shit who dared to look down on her, staring his lanky ass down like he'd insulted my mother. "You'd best hold your tongue, bud, or I'll rip it out for you." My eyes roamed the room over his shaking shoulder, and I frowned when I didn't spot the familiar face of my old nemesis, the Candlestick. "Where's your boss?"

"Uhhhh, h-he's not here, si-sir," he sputtered, his eyes locking in on a well-dressed floor manager across the room. The woman he'd sought out started a quick path to us, desperate to diffuse the obviously tense situation.

She was a new face.

That wasn't something I'd anticipated.

"What seems to be the problem, sirs?" she queried, tipping her head to the side as if a shot of her at an angle, her tits on full display, might placate us. "Anything I can help with?"

"Yeah," I growled, already at my limit of stupidity. "Your little host here insulted my date and held us up—where's Can—Lumiere?"

She batted her eyelashes at me and then turned to Joker, offering him the same flirtatious smile she had thrown at me a second ago. "Ah, the owner is out with his wife tonight—reservations at another wonderful establishment. If you have some arrangement with him, might I suggest coming back at a later—"

I had stopped listening at *out with his wife* and had already pulled my phone from the pocket of my pants, dialing Kaz herself from memory. When she picked up, I recognized the familiar growl of her husband, an ex-MMA legend, in the background of what I knew to be the hardest place in town to get reservations at.

Cinco.

"Tyson, how nice to hear from you. We were beginning to wonder if you'd ever come up for air."

In the distance of the call, Candlestick made his displeasure at their interrupted date known. "We were not worried; she was. I know you're sturdy like a roach—no getting rid of you, eh, old friend?"

I smiled at their banter, something that made their brand of love an appealing future for myself. "I stopped in with the crew and my date for dinner, but your regular employees are all out, it appears."

Kaz sighed. "Ah, yes, the flu's going around. We lost six servers this week on the schedule, and things are tight. Lenny's from the kitchen, he's not a good host, but he's all we had in a pinch."

"Your floor manager's standing right here. Perhaps you'd like to talk to her instead?"

Her husband wrangled the phone from her, his frown evident in the tone of his rumbling baritone. "Give the phone to Janet; I'll talk to her."

I shrugged, a slow smile spreading over my lips. "Sure, I'll hand you to Janet."

As I held the phone out in her direction, Mallory's eyes followed the way she pressed her arms together outside her bosom to push those puppies into my face. Her snort of derision was laughable and cute.

"You might tell your manager to put her tits away and stop flirting with customers, too," she quipped, low enough for only Janet to hear —or so she thought.

I heard Candlestick's knowing laugh over the line as he cleared his throat and waited for Janet's meek *'yes, sir?'*.

Two minutes later, we had the best seat in the house, in my opinion—right by the kitchen, in the corner, where we could put our backs to the room or against that wall, high-backed booths giving us some cover, which was ideal for the things I planned to do to this fiery, jealous little vixen the second I had her penned in next to me. There was a bottle of the house wine chilling in an ice bath in the center of the mahogany surface, a basket of fresh bread next to it, and five wine glasses as I'd demanded.

Janet was nowhere to be seen; our waiter was a younger man with a soft smile and a scar that told of a past that didn't match his sweet personality. Just Kaz's type she liked to hire—men with a sordid past and a need for retribution and a second chance.

Men like Candlestick and myself.

"What can I get started for you three while you wait on your other guests to arrive?"

Mallory slid into the booth, and I hustled to slip in after her, shoving her to the end to keep Joker from taking her other side. I wanted her totally at my mercy, though I didn't think she'd turn to him for help with how she felt about him right now.

"Waters all around, my good man. We're going to need them."

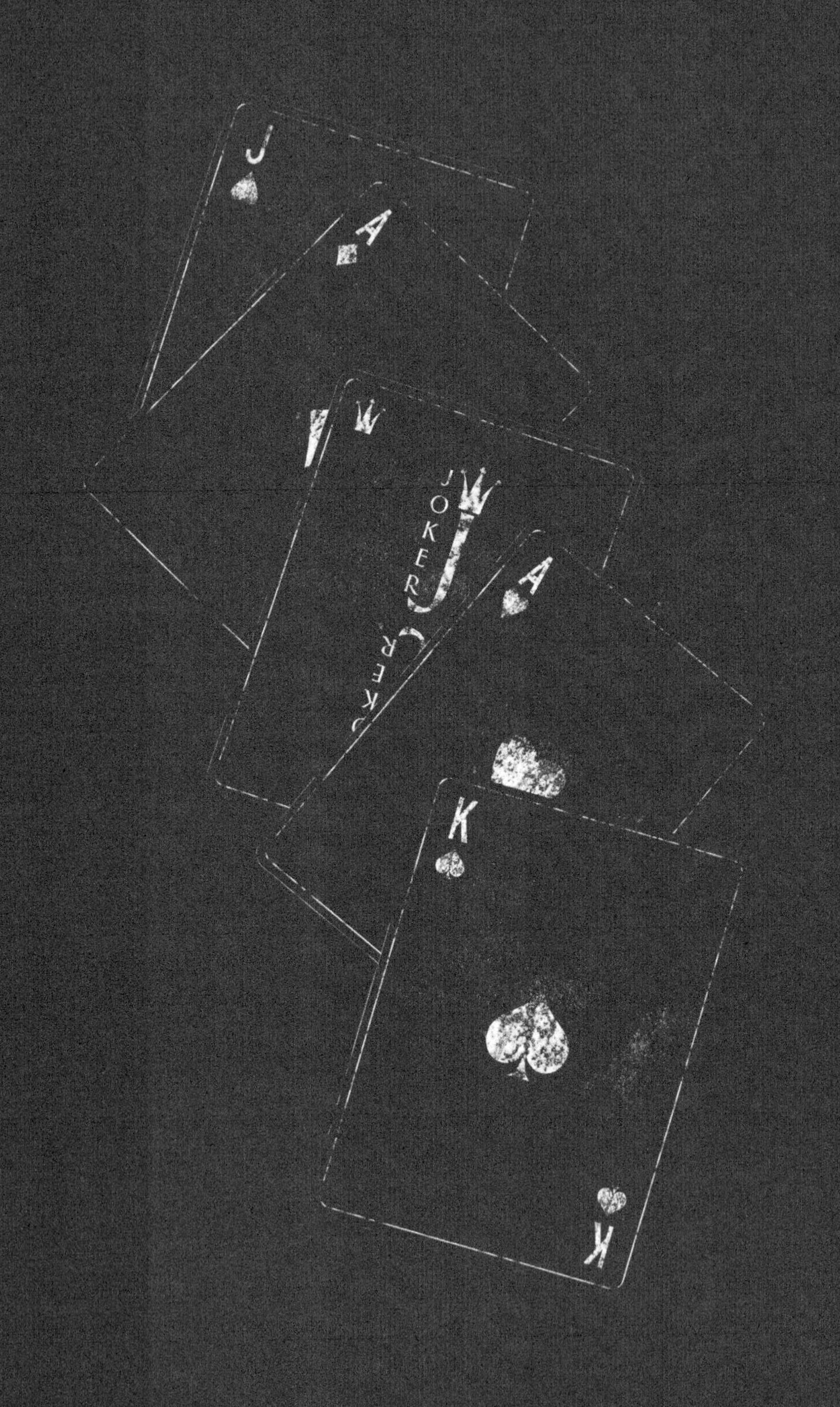
JOKER

CHAPTER TWENTY-EIGHT
BLACKJACK

"So, where to?"

Ace slid into the front seat with a groan, his sleek form settling into the chair with a slight flinch. He'd taken a good hit from the asshole who'd gotten the jump on us at Johnny's, and a bat to the spine was enough to knock most men out for quite a while.

Ace wasn't like most men. Beatings were a regular training exercise for men destined for the Yakuza.

"Kaz's, according to Spade. Claims he's got a surprise."

Ace rolled his eyes and leaned against the cool glass of the window as I pulled out of park. "I hope it's fucking alcohol, for once. I could use a good bottle of Kaz's house chianti."

Knowing Spade, I doubted it had anything to do with alcohol and everything to do with the pretty little therapist I was currently trying to avoid.

TURNED OUT, we were both pleasantly—or not—surprised. There *was,* in fact, a chilled bottle of the house chianti sitting front and center of the table, and two empty glasses waiting for us. Joker sat at the table with a grim look on his face, like he might be sick, and I chuckled at the desperation on his face, taking note of the missing members of the party.

Looked like Miss Stanton had picked a favorite for the night, and Joker had lost out.

Ace slid in next to Joker, and I stayed standing, surveying the scene like usual as I waited for the missing two to rejoin us.

I had a thing about sitting on the edge of the booth, and I wasn't in the mood to do a lot of sitting-standing fire drill shit, so I would wait.

Why that turned out to be a mistake surprised me, I'll never know. I seemed to have the worst luck lately where this woman was concerned.

These goons had dressed her in a fucking whore's dress, and one that was far too small for her to boot. Her legs went on for miles beneath the high-rising hem, and the top was so small her tits nearly fell out of the shelf they balanced precariously on. And if I wasn't mistaken, she was *not* wearing a bra.

On the outside, I was silently fuming. On the inside, I wanted to take off my coat, throw it around her, and whisk her out of there. Everyone stared at her as she teetered past them in those skyline-tall stilettos wrapped around her feet, a hand or two darting out almost as if to cop a feel, until I met their gazes and conveyed the likelihood of their death should they complete the thought.

I distinctly remembered the girl who'd worn that dress to Joker's bedroom two months ago. She'd been wasted, whiny, and a complete druggie, high off her ass when she walked in, high off her ass when she stumbled out in a pair of sweats and a tee that had seen better days. She abandoned her dress and shoes in her haste to get the fuck out of our compound after Ace made it clear she'd be lucky to keep her life if she muttered a word about her time there.

She wouldn't last long on the streets, anyhow.

Mallory gave me a hesitant peek out from beneath her lashes, and I felt like twenty kinds of a heel as I gestured to the booth instead of meeting her gaze.

She stepped aside, closer to me, and waited for Spade to take his seat first. The look she shot Joker, her back ramrod straight, arms tight against her sides, neck stiff, told me whatever he'd done, he would suffer for it for quite a while yet.

Women. These idiots should have learned by now not to cross one.

Apparently, I put too much faith in them.

She slipped into the seat and made sure to leave me a wide berth, which I appreciated more than I could say. Her fingers curled around the half-filled glass of wine Spade handed her, and she downed it like a champ, handing it back with a nervous glint in her eye.

Spade leaned into her, his voice a low growl, but I'd long since learned to pick up on his lip movement and read his words even when I couldn't hear them.

"I've got some real fun planned for you, sweetheart."

Her rumbling denial managed to choke a chuckle up my throat, though I managed to stop it in its tracks.

"Not happening, buddy. Keep it in your pants."

I watched his arm shift as his hand snaked over to her lap as if he weren't even trying to hide it from a soul at the table. Ace was too busy pouring himself another glass of wine to notice, and when the waiter arrived with two fresh glasses of water and a smile, Mallory looked very much unsettled.

"So, have we decided what we'd like to eat?"

Mallory squeaked from her seat beside me, though she was a foot or two away. Her palms slammed onto the table top as she bit her lip and smiled haltingly up at the young man. "Oh, sorry, I'd like the . . . mmm, the alfredo special, please. And perhaps a shot of tequila?"

Ace frowned at her choices. "Leave off the margarita, Miss Stanton. We already have one drunk to live with, might as well not make it two."

She flushed in embarrassment, as did Joker, and curled in on herself as she nodded to the waiter, refusing to meet his eyes. "The alfredo special will do, thank you."

He jotted down her order and moved around the table with practiced ease. When he shuffled off, I frowned across the table at our leader.

"Was that necessary?"

He smirked and refused to meet my eyes. "Worry about yourself, BlackJack." His gaze slid over to the woman in question, a sneer lifting his lips. "Who the hell thought dressing her like an escort was a good plan?"

His eyes widened as a distinct and audible *thud* echoed under the table, and his eyes dropped to where his lap would be, were there not a piece of wood blocking his gaze.

Hers was all venom, the slight lift to her brow only accenting the tilt of her lips as she stared him down for his asshole comments. "Well, if I had my own clothes, I wouldn't have had to dive into Joker's Narnia of Whores and squeeze into something made for a child-sized bitch, but you're going to off me anyhow, so who cares how these assholes dress me up?"

The cunning, brave woman must have slammed her stiletto into the gap between his legs to drive the point home.

She was growing on me, and from the smile on his face, she was growing on Ace, too, despite himself.

His hand dipped beneath the table, and from the looks of it and the sound of her sharp inhale and look of pure shock, he must have wrapped a hand around her ankle, trapping her foot in his lap.

His eyes met Spade's across the table. "Wreck her before the main course comes, or I will."

"Now, wait just a second," she started, but clearly, the two of them weren't listening anymore. Ace held her in his grip with a conniving grin smeared on those lips of his, and Spade's hand was now quite plainly in her lap, though she didn't seem to be eager to be so splayed out in a public place.

Add *not an exhibitionist* to the list of things I now knew about the doc that I never expected to.

Spade got to work beneath that too-short skirt, and I sat back in the booth, my head falling against the top of the cushion as my eyes drifted closed, trying to resist the urge to watch her face as they did who knew what filthy things beneath this table to her.

It didn't stop the noises she made, however, and I was painfully aware of the booth moving with every little shift of her hips. When I took a chance and peeked out from beneath one eyelid, I spotted Spade's nose against her throat, his lips barely moving, probably filling her ears with all manner of filthy promises I had no business overhearing.

"Oh," she whispered, her eyes flicking to Ace, whose grin had grown exponentially and morphed into one of obsessive possession. The beast inside him had risen to the surface and come out to play with his new toy, leaving the tame, rational, in-control Kohei locked away in some far-off land to watch the spectacle before him.

Mallory writhed in place as Spade snarled against the soft skin below her ear, and a soft gasp left her lips as she bit down on the bottom one, trying her damndest not to cry out at the sensations the man to her left was causing her. I shifted in my seat as the full weight of the situation fell on me, making my pants uncomfortably tight, and realized her right leg was practically against my knee, with the way Ace still held it in his grip. My mental calculations took a left turn, and I realized there was no way that skirt wasn't around her waist by now, as hard as she struggled to keep it down as she walked.

Fuck, I bet she was leaving a wet spot on the damn seat beneath her.

Not now, fucker.

Spade eased up on her, though he left one hand between her legs as the waiter approached again with a pitcher of water to refill our glasses and a basket of bread, which Ace set his sights on one-handedly. I swallowed every last drop of my new glass of water and absently shoved it toward the edge of the table, eager for more, when I nudged it a little too far, and it fell off and tumbled to the floor.

Every set of eyes turned to me at once, and I realized my mistake the second the poor lad started to kneel to retrieve it.

If he knelt too far down, he'd get a face full of the activities beneath the booth, and then three of these men, if not all four of us, would likely have to beat the memory out of him.

I stretched out my arm and stopped him from making the biggest mistake of his career. "I'll get that."

He chuckled and tried to brush off my offer. "Thanks, man, but it's kinda my job—"

Ace leaned forward and gave the boy a dangerous snarl. "Let the man get the cup for you. You work hard enough, and it's his fault he's so damn impatient." His eyes turned to me, feral and lit with a cunning glint. "Go on, BlackJack, pick it up."

I slid from the booth and did as he bid, my eyes flicking up against my will as my fingers clasped the cool glass in their grip. It was a small miracle I didn't shatter the damn thing in my hand.

Spade had his hand between her legs, several fingers inside her knuckle-deep as he ran a thumb along her slick folds. She twitched as her legs attempted to snap closed, but Ace's hand still circled her ankle, and his thumb ran along the swell of her arch as he held her in place.

I knew I was twenty shades of red when I rose, though it had been a two-second affair, and I felt like a total skeeze, a peeping tom as her eyes met mine and then turned away in shame.

I made her ashamed of herself. I pushed her away. And now she couldn't bear to look me in the eyes.

Fantastic.

"Here," I growled at our server, handing him the cup without a second thought, pleased when he removed it from my grip.

I almost couldn't bring myself to sit back down next to her.

But needs must. So I did, albeit a bit tenser than before.

Spade's grin widened as he twisted his wrist under the table, his arm shifting forward as his angle changed, and two petite, slender hands gripped the edge of the table as her head fell back and her eyes drifted closed, her lips parted in a perfect *'O'* of absolute bliss. She whimpered quietly, and I felt her leg twitch against mine as Ace released her foot. It fell from his lap, and her legs spread wantonly as she arched her back in the booth and rocked her hips, seeking release, too far gone now to care that Spade's hand was under her skirt in a fucking restaurant where people could see and hear her.

She was on the verge of an orgasm, and Spade would no doubt see she got it.

Just as her eyes fluttered open and she turned to him to beg, his hand slipped all the way out from under the table, and he licked them off like it was a show, denying her that peak while taunting her with her near-release.

And then his eyes met mine, and a haughty smirk turned his lips up that also turned my gut.

Was this . . . *jealousy?*

Was I really jealous of this obscene display? Was I jealous that Spade had the wherewithal to finger-fuck a woman in public, that he *could,* because he didn't have some stupid issue with physical touch as I did?

Hell, I hadn't even thought about doing those things with Miss Stanton—until now.

Now, it was *all* I could think about, all my fucking brain could conjure up as she groaned impatiently, grinding down into the chair as she sought some relief from the precipice he'd abandoned her on. I almost felt bad for her, nearly bad enough to reach down there and finish her off myself, but I wouldn't know the first thing about pleasing her like *he* did, like they *all* did. And I wouldn't be able to bring myself to touch her like that if hell itself threatened to rise up and swallow me.

I'd burn instead, through no choice of my own.

Her soft whine of resignation killed me, crushed my insides, but all I could do was watch as the bastards who'd tormented her chuckled between themselves while Joker and I watched on, shame and regret on both our faces.

The main course couldn't come fast enough.

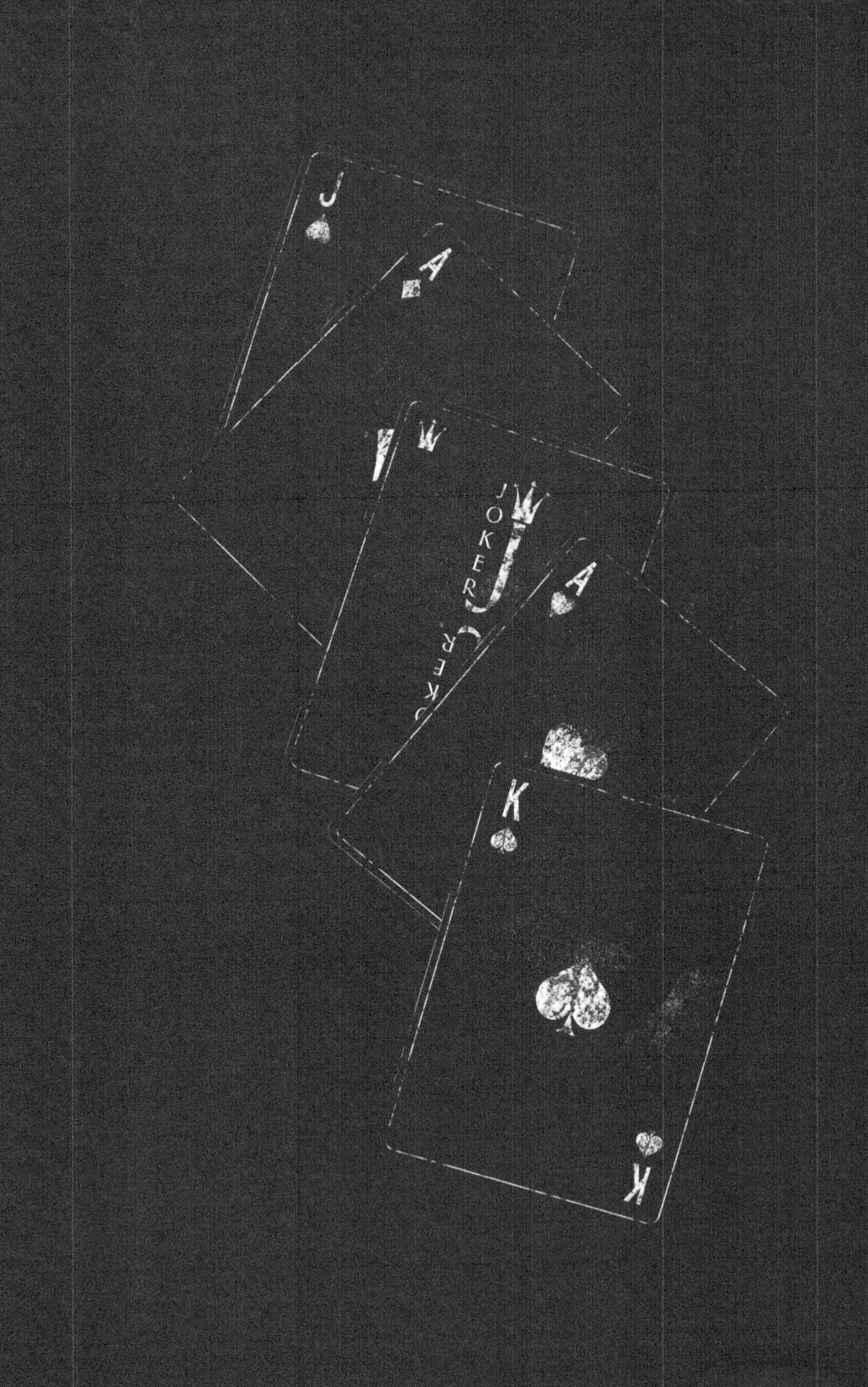
JOKER

CHAPTER TWENTY-NINE
MALLORY

The trip back from the fucking nightmare that was dinner was too long. Too fucking long by half.

Spade had promised me a surprise, but somewhere along the line, the psychopath's brain rewired itself, and instead of completely debasing me in a fucking booth, he only just barely gave me a taste of bliss before yanking his sinfully coated fingers from my greedy core. He was a fucking tease, and if he expected me to bow to him the second we walked in the door, he was mistaken.

I'd shove one of these stilettos through his black heart before I spread my legs for him again after that little performance.

I was pretty sure BlackJack got an eyeful of what was going on underneath the table, too.

Talk about embarrassing. The poor man couldn't get out of that restaurant fast enough, but bless the fact that he was a man of few words because that meant things were only *silently* awkward between us.

Joker and Spade sat in the front seat of the car, much to Spade's chagrin, because I lifted my heel and promised to grind it into his dick if he so much as tried to sit next to me in this car. And he'd be otherwise occupied with Ace when they delivered me back to the compound, so I wouldn't have to fight his dumb ass off after this car ride. I did not doubt that BlackJack would do his damndest to avoid the fuck out of me after this debacle, so he was out.

That left my jailer, Joker, who was currently carrying a massive tally in the 'asshole' column, thanks to his fucking closet full of random women's clothing.

Who the fuck keeps shit like that as a trophy from one-night stands, anyhow?

I was all too eager to rip this fucking torture device from my body so I could fucking breathe again, and the minute Joker put it in park, I was on my feet and click-clacking all the way up the stairs, down the hall, and into his room, where I fell to the floor at my bag and rapidly rummaged around for *anything else* to wear.

Fuck, the girl who owned this black ensemble must've starved on a regular basis. *Poor thing.*

The seams practically split apart as I peeled the fucker off, not even caring that the door was wide open and anyone could just walk by and see me naked as the day I was born, save for this red thong that was soaked and about worthless now.

I peeled it off, too, flinging it to the nether regions of Joker's cluttered room. *If he found it later, he could sniff it and jerk off, for all I cared.*

I briefly debated taking a shower but passed on the opportunity, realizing I wanted to do something far more than I wanted to do *that.*

I wanted to fucking get off, scratch the itch Spade put underneath my skin.

The only problem was, I wasn't eager to be walked in on.

I closed the door almost all the way and peered into the corridor, trying to crane my ears for any sign of the men I staunchly avoided. The whole hall was silent, so I closed the door and cautiously padded over to the opposite side of the room and climbed onto Joker's bed. A frown crossed my face when I realized there was something square and hard beneath the mattress itself.

Of course I investigated that shit. You can't expect a bitch *not* to. And the fruit of my labors?

A fucking laptop.

A connection to the outside world.

I was nearly giddy with excitement. I could contact the police; I could get ahold of Gem, maybe see if someone had filed a missing persons report.

It was sheer luck, then, that when I powered the thing on and clicked on Joker's icon, there was no prompt for a password.

Almost too good to be true.

Almost.

I quickly opened the internet, pleased to find it was connected to a wireless router with a signal. Fingers flying across the keys, I went to the search bar and entered my name, ready to see scores of articles about me, missing persons, or what have you.

So imagine my surprise when I found *nothing.*

The national database for missing and exploited persons returned no results for my name or social, and neither did the local precinct's search engine. My social media was dead in the water, but there were no comments about 'hey, where'd you go' or 'sure has been a while since you posted last', and it was like someone had poked a hole in my sails, deflating the wind and leaving me still, empty, sad and pathetic.

Nobody was looking for me.

I didn't even want to see my phone now, sure that I'd find Gemma had sent me some generic apology about ditching me at the club, and she'd assume my failure to respond meant I was mad at her. She, too, would move on if I simply failed to ever speak to her again. And my boss, my landlord—they only saw me as a dollar sign, one in the red, one in the black. When I stopped showing up to work, the calls would still be accepted. We weren't on any sort of contract. If the bills kept being paid, my landlord wouldn't have shit to say about the apartment being a glorified cat kennel.

I was nothing, nobody, in the grand scheme of things. By isolating myself, I'd made it damn easy for them to steal me and get away with it.

And something in me clicked.

Someone moved down the hallway, heading for the stairs, and I held my breath, certain I'd be found out, but I listened for the sound of his footsteps going down the metal stairs, and then, I pulled the laptop into my lap and logged into the therapy site.

I'd be damned if I sat here and suffered while the world went on around me—lost and forgotten, but still a woman with needs.

Needs that were the only thing I had to hold onto at this point. The only thing I could control the outcome of.

With one click, I was in the archives—the place where all my appointments were stored, where all the calls and videos went, just in case we ever needed to look one up again. They stayed there for six months to a year—usually, the only people who ever needed the recordings were a future therapist or the cops.

What I was about to do . . . well, I don't think it was something that had ever happened or would ever happen again.

I didn't bother to go hunting for the toys I knew were somewhere in my bag. I didn't want to move, and I was already comfortable in the center of his bed, leaning propped up against his headboard, a stack of pillows at my back.

I clicked 'open' and held my breath, waiting for the video to start.

The moment his voice echoed from the speakers, my face flushed, and I started second-guessing everything. But my conscience and my body were two separate entities, and I watched as the mouse crept over to the 'loop' button and turned it on.

My eyes were glued to the screen as he flashed up in the recording, staring at me with that disheveled head of blonde hair, those 'fuck me' eyes, and the upturned lips that beckoned me to forget why this was twenty kinds of wrong.

"Say my name," he moaned, and I knew in the part of his video I couldn't see his hand was on that cock of his, tugging to the sound of his legal name on my lips.

"Cass," I echoed along with recording me, my hand slipping to my lap, between my thighs, probing the wetness I found there. I could lie to his face for days, weeks, months, and tell him I wasn't attracted to him, that I didn't get wet every time he fucking touched me, but something about that devil-may-care attitude and those kissable lips, and the long, slender fingers that caressed so gently when he wanted to taunt me with the truth I denied, held me in thrall.

My head fell back as I rubbed along my slick folds, up and down, his lips against my throat burned into the memories I'd never tell a soul about. I slipped a finger, then two, inside myself, hips arching, soft moans matching the wet squelching noise filling the air.

"Cass," I whispered as the video looped again, as I spread my legs apart, as I added a third finger and the laptop fell between my parted knees, as Joker stared straight at me while I finger-fucked myself into oblivion. "Cass, *yes—*"

My free hand gripped the headboard behind me, and I bit back a plea for that bastard as my orgasm washed over me, hard, fast, and unforgiving, ripping me apart and refusing to let me piece myself back together until I accepted defeat.

As the peak hit me and took me over the edge completely, I choked on my scream of pleasure and nearly cracked the wood beneath my fingers. My hips lifted off the bed, my back arched like a bowstring, and my legs tremored.

My lips parted on a gasp just as the door swung open and Joker himself walked in with a dangerous glint in his eyes and a knowing, victorious smirk on those kissable lips, swinging his keys from an outstretched finger.

"My, my, my, someone's been a naughty girl." I scrambled to grab the laptop, but I couldn't get to it fast enough, and his brows rose as our conversation looped again and his voice played back to him.

"Is this what I think it is, beautiful? Are you fucking yourself to my voice as I jerked off to yours all those days ago?" He shoved my laptop off the bed and crawled between my legs before I could even bother to close them, gripping my ankles to keep me from running away. "You know, if you wanted the real thing, all you had to do was ask."

I'd taken the edge off the need Spade left me with, but it was still there, simmering just beneath the surface, a violent, writhing thing that demanded I take my pleasure from this eager man, even though I was still salty over the fucking clothes.

Jealous of women who'd spent far less time in his bed. A man who possessed me only because he stole me from myself. And now, broken and disheartened, still desperately horny, and feeling a little like discarded trash thanks to the quick internet search for myself, I gave in.

I gave the fuck up and let him hold my ankles in his long-fingered grip, let him stare longingly at my very bare body, vulnerable and exposed and weak and—

"Fuck me, Cass," I whispered, needing to feel *something. Anything.*

His eyes met mine, curiosity and confusion in their depths, but thankfully he didn't voice those emotions, those questions I could see roiling in their depths. He simply did as I demanded, like the golden retriever he was at heart, and I let go as his fingers trailed up my calves, drawing little teasing circles against my skin.

My eyes drifted closed as the sensation of his hands on my body lulled me into a false sense of calm, everything else fading away, disappearing down into the pit where I threw all the things I didn't want to think about, where I locked away things I couldn't bring myself to deal with. His fingers were all I could feel as they rounded the back of my knees, barely brushing against that sensitive part of me that rarely saw daylight.

Fuck, if he just kept touching me all night, I could probably drift off into ignorant bliss.

But then he trailed those fingers back down and lifted my left leg at the ankle, resting it on his shoulder as his head turned, curls brushing softly against me while his lips pressed against the skin there. They moved up the inside of my leg, kiss after kiss, sometimes gentle, like a feather, sometimes more insistent, like he struggled to contain his desire to taste me.

Before I knew what had hit me, his hands were on my thighs, and his lips had left me as he settled in for a fucking feast between my spread legs.

"Fuck, beautiful, if you were the fruit of that forbidden tree, I would have been cast out of Eden on day one."

My lips parted with a gasp as his aquiline nose brushed against the smattering of hair covering the target of his affections. My hands still gripped the headboard, but one loosed itself and tangled willingly in those golden tresses that hid his face from view. When I pushed the hair from his face and knotted it atop his head, his eyes flicked up to meet mine, those questions stirring in their depths again.

"Tell me you want this, gorgeous," he breathed, the hot words fanning over my mound and sending tingles down my spine. "Tell me you want *me.*"

And there it was, the connection I wasn't looking for. The need that stirred inside me also rose unbidden in him. Not only a need to fuck away our feelings, but a need to *belong*. To be *wanted*. To be *missed*.

He wanted to be worth something, and so did I, and the fact that I found a kindred soul in him when I should be running in the other direction scared me more than I cared to admit—more than I wanted to even *think* about.

I took a deep breath while this gorgeous Adonis of a man lay between my spread legs and admired me from his vantage point at eye level with my pussy and jumped in headfirst, knowing this was the pivoting point, the beginning of the fucking end.

There was no going back from here.

"I want you, Cass."

JOKER

CHAPTER THIRTY
JOKER

"I *want you, Cass."*

Four words eternally sealed my fate with hers.

To hell with Ace and his plans to kill her. *I'd die first.*

I hadn't heard my name on the lips of such a fucking angel in all the years I'd been alive, and nothing had ever sounded more like heaven. No other voice that had emanated from a woman lying naked in my bed stirred such intense feelings inside me.

None of them had ever known my name, though. Mallory did, and she wasn't afraid to use it.

"Hold on tight, doc," I muttered, diving into her wet cunt with vigor and a whole lot of excitement.

Fuck, she tasted better than the sweetest wine.

My cock was harder than a rock from the wanton display she'd presented me, atop *my own bed, no less,* and fuck it all, when I first stumbled in, I thought she'd used my laptop to contact the authorities, and who knew, maybe she had, but I couldn't think about that now.

I couldn't think *at all* right now. All I was, all I knew, was her and the feast that lay before me.

My tongue trailed down the seam of her slick folds, swirling around the entrance to her sweetest of holes. I groaned as I slipped that organ inside, tasting her all around me, her arousal a heady, sweet thing that would have stiffened me on the spot were I not already sporting a steel rod from between my legs.

"Oh god, Cass," she moaned, her fingers tightening in my hair, tugging me closer as she arched her back and gripped that headboard even tighter. "Fuck, yes, right there—"

I put my hands under her thighs and cupped her ass, tugging her even closer, tighter against my mouth as I plundered her like a fucking pirate, tongue darting in and out, tasting and teasing and stoking her fire as her moans met with mine. All I wanted to do was make her come, show her how good the real thing was compared to the recording she'd made.

Oh, fuck, just wait, sweetheart, I've got so much to show you—

Her thighs tightened around my head, and gods have mercy, but I would gladly wear these glorious pillows as ear muffs for the rest of my life, never hearing another thing again, if I could stay right the fuck here between her legs and sup on her arousal like a man dying of thirst.

"Jesus, Cass, where'd you learn—*fuck!*"

Her whole body bowed as I slid two fingers inside her, right alongside my probing tongue, twisting them to caress that spot inside her that some women thought was naught but a legend. Most men hadn't even heard of it, let alone cared to find it, but with the right pressure and movements, I could have her singing soprano in seconds, squirting like a fucking porn star, soaking my bed just how I liked.

I didn't bother with other women, but for her, I'd fucking bend over backward to make her feel good.

And I could make her feel *very good.*

My lips pulled away from her as I panted, sucking in a breath as my two fingers crooked against her from the inside and my thumb grazed over her clit. "Yeah? You like that, beautiful?"

"Fucking Christ, don't stop," she growled, her eyes lit with a fire that spoke of lust and desire that could scorch a man to ashes as it burned. I wanted her to turn me to ash, fuck, I wanted to burn in her flame for eternity—

When the fuck I had turned into a poet, I had no idea.

My fingers increased their speed, ramming insistently against that special spot inside her, demanding something her body wasn't accustomed to giving. She writhed on the bed, fighting it, and a smile crossed my lips as I placed them against her clit and sucked, flicking my tongue out to taunt her sensitive bud as she keened, clawed at my sheets, and shuddered around my fingers.

Her incoherent mumbles and twitching limbs melted into the bed with her, and though she didn't get that whole experience, I'd left her a satisfactory boneless puddle, just how I wanted her before I moved on to other activities.

Before things went too far, though, perhaps it was time we had a little conversation, came to an understanding.

Like recognized like, and she and I might have come from different circumstances, but there was something in her that called out to something in me, something it recognized. But before we could have a *real* talk, there was something we needed to get out of the way first.

I trailed a finger up her leg, over the curve of her hip, pleased when she let out a little moan of approval at the touch. My head lay against one of her thighs, hair fanned out beneath me, tickling the soft skin I'd just peppered with kisses moments ago.

"How did you find my laptop, Mallory?"

I hadn't taken to calling her by her name, and I could tell the change of pace set her on edge, like she'd been given something she didn't expect, and it left a bad taste in her mouth.

She sighed, closing her eyes again as I watched her. Hiding from me. "I laid on the bed and felt a lump, so I went snooping."

"And you just—"

"What kind of criminal mastermind leaves his computer unlocked?"

I smiled against her skin, my fingers moving over the soft swell of her stomach, dipping as her abs did in the center. "One who's trying to catch a nosy doctor in the act."

Her body tensed. "You planted it to see what I'd do."

I held up my hands as she shoved off the pile of pillows, her face screwed up in a vengeful rage. "Now, wait a minute, I didn't plan—"

She was already withdrawing, closing herself off again, shutting down, putting up the walls I'd just worked to shatter. "You left it unlocked for me so you could see if I'd call the cops, is that it?" Her backpedaling had ended in her running into the headboard, and there was nothing nearby for her to save her dignity with, so she crossed her arms over her chest and narrowed her eyes, knees bent to hide her gorgeous, enticing core from my view. "Well, good news, Cassanova—you don't have to worry. When your boss kills me, there will be no missing person report, no need to worry about anyone missing me. I've been MIA for days, and not a single person I know cares enough to notice!"

I sat up while she sobbed into her hands, the grief she'd been hiding behind the lust taking center stage, ripping her iron self-control and bending it until she was a mess of a human. I reached out to touch her, but she launched herself from the bed and into my bathroom before I could get a grip on her, and the slamming door, followed by the *click* of the lock, was like a door in my heart closing, a nail in my proverbial coffin.

Fucking great.

Without even trying to, I'd broken the good doc, and now all I had to show for it was the taste of her lingering on my lips, the smell of her cunt on my fingers, and the sadness and guilt roiling in my gut, fighting for dominance.

My feet carried me to the door without another thought, the urge to comfort her rising from a place I hadn't visited in a long time.

Water ran on the other side, but there was no telling if she was actually *in* the shower or not. And unfortunately for me, I didn't have a key to the bathroom.

I didn't think she'd try anything drastic, like killing herself, so the only thing left to do was wait her out. I could handle that, no problem.

AFTER AN HOUR of the water running nonstop, I decided maybe I could use some help and some fresh air. Which is how I ended up in front of BlackJack's room, my hand raised to knock on the damn barrier between me and the mysterious, quiet one.

Three knocks was all it took, and then three locks turned on the other side of the wall, telling me to back up. I retreated two feet and waited patiently, a sheepish smile on my face as BlackJack's grim countenance peered out of the dark abyss beyond.

"What?"

I bounced on the balls of my feet. "I, uh, need you to pick a lock?"

"Is that a question or a statement?"

My frown deepened as his words rolled over me. "Listen, asswipe, I need some fucking air. I've been waiting for Mallory to come out of my bathroom for an hour, and the water's still running, so—"

His door yanked open, and he nearly ran me over in his haste to cover the short distance to my room. I could barely keep up, and when I rounded the corner to my room, his shoulder was bent, and he was two steps away from my door, using himself as a battering ram.

"Jesus, BlackJack, I said pick the lock, not break the door down—"

The wood splintered as his big body slammed into it, but he didn't even stop, and it buckled around his form as he plowed right through it and into the large bathroom. He flung the wood away as he spun in a circle, wild eyes looking for her, the urgency in his movements starting to concern me.

"BlackJack?"

He darted off in the direction of the shower as I neared the door, and much to my utter horror, he yanked the glass door off the fucking hinges and stepped into what had to be frigid water pouring from the overhead fixture, crowding overtop a figure curled up on the floor, her skin deathly pale, soaked to the fucking bone.

"Fuck," I whispered, hands carding through my hair nervously as I just stood by and watched the man with the immobilizing dislike of physical touch lift her from the tile floor and check for any signs of life. His lips brushed hers briefly, and a relieved sigh left his lips when he found air escaping between them.

"What the fuck did you do?"

He didn't wait for an answer, his posture stiff as he rushed from the bathroom and through my bedroom, out into the hallway, where he dripped all over the carpet with reckless abandon. He turned on his heel and headed straight for his own room, laying her atop his bed with no regard for her soaked state or his own. My hands shook, but I was unable to do more than watch as he tended to her, throwing his blankets atop her, checking her pulse, pulling her hair away from her body, and wringing it out over the side of his bed.

Each drop of water that splashed against his carpet sank in like the feeling of helplessness that rooted into my chest and took hold.

"Don't just stand there, you idiot; get some towels!"

His snarled commands were strange; they felt foreign as they tore from his lips and assaulted my ears, fighting through the fog of helplessness I was blanketed in. I rushed to his bathroom and yanked the first stack of towels I could find down off their shelf, running like a madman back into his room.

He stared at my paltry offering and shook his head as I stood there with my arms extended, shoving the towels at him like I was brain dead. "You think this is enough? What can I do to help?"

He took the towels and cringed as my hands crowded him in my efforts to touch her, make sure she was still okay, still breathing.

What would have happened if she'd stayed in that shower any longer?

She could have died, and it would have been my fault, all because I left my laptop unlocked, trying to catch her, at Ace's orders.

Ace and I were going to have a nice chat when he came back.

"Get her something that *fits* that she can wear. Something from her bags, maybe." BlackJack lifted her head and wrapped a towel around her head, dabbing at the soaked curls matted together as the girl they clung to shivered beneath the blankets he'd piled atop her.

I ran off, a goal in mind, anger building in my gut at myself and the whole situation I'd caused.

Perhaps it was time I paid my father's old friend a visit and got to the bottom of things.

JOKER

CHAPTER THIRTY-ONE
BLACKJACK

She was too fucking cold.

There was a brief moment where I debated ignoring Joker's insistent knocking at my door, but I was eternally glad I didn't. Had he ignored the situation for a moment longer, there was no telling what would have happened to her.

All aversion to touch fled my brain when I found her curled on that bathroom tile, soaking up the frigid water spewing from the shower, sluicing down her body like the fingers of death. She was so cold, had been cold for so long, she'd stopped shivering—and that meant her body had begun to shut down. She'd started to give up.

"Who hurt you, princess?" I wondered aloud, brushing my hand back and forth over the towel wrapped around her head. She'd begun to shiver in earnest now, her body waking up now that it had been relieved of the constant assault of freezing water.

Joker came in with a handful of articles of clothing, panting like he'd run a mile, a worried frown marring his otherwise pretty face. It was almost comical how oblivious and yet how smart he was, his concern only outshined by the flighty absent-mindedness that seemed to always plague him. I had a soft spot for him, being that he'd always been there for me, had pulled me off the streets a long time ago. He was the closest thing to a brother I had, and I hated to see him so distraught.

"I grabbed what I could find, man. I hope it's enough."

He looked like shit, and if he didn't get some air, he was going to set me on edge right there with him. "Get out of here, Cass. Go down to the store and pick up tea bags, some chicken soup, and while you're at it, maybe a *fucking Xanax* out of the cabinet for yourself, pal."

It was the longest grouping of words I'd strung together since we left the streets and joined the WildCards, and Joker's slack-jawed awe tuned me in to the strangeness of the situation.

"Feeling talkative, are we?"

I rolled my eyes into the back of my head and sighed. "Someone has to keep their head. Now go."

He turned on his heel and skipped the Xanax, and I didn't breathe a sigh of relief until he was out of the compound and the sound of his car starting registered on the sensors connected to the monitor across the room from my bed.

I turned back to the girl in my bed, perching on the edge of the mattress as I sorted through the pile of clothes Joker brought.

Underwear—fucking insane, how little fabric women's underwear consisted of these days—sat atop a pair of jeans, which looked like they'd be uncomfortable and quite hard to put on her without her assistance. A shirt sat beneath them, some tank top contraption with six straps—what the fuck went where?

I couldn't put her in any of this. There was no fucking way. I mean, aside from the panties, which sent a shiver of apprehension down my spine.

I'd never touched a woman, not in any way that counted, not since I was very young, and the thought of sliding panties over her naked nethers had me twisted into knots. But someone had to do it, and I had a feeling that she'd be eternally upset if Joker so much as laid a finger on her right now. I knew he hadn't forced her into bed, whatever it was they'd gotten up to in there, but he'd hurt her somehow, and the pain ran deep—deeper than the skin.

So I'd buck up and handle it, like a fucking adult. I wasn't some blushing boy who'd never seen a vagina.

"Just because you've never stuck your dick in it, doesn't mean you can't handle one maturely."

I knew the room wouldn't echo back reassurance, but saying it out loud somehow drove home how stupid my reluctance was. With a sigh, I heaved myself up off the bed and crossed over to my dresser, rifling through my shirt drawer until my hand closed around a soft cotton tee, several sizes too large for her feminine frame, but that was okay—it would cover her quite well, and the extra fabric meant extra warmth.

I didn't stop to linger on the strange pang of pride I felt at the idea of her wearing my shirt.

Nope.

Not even a little.

JOKER HAD BEEN GONE AWHILE, but he'd sent a text to let me know the air was doing him good, which was the goal. I advised him to take his time, sat at the head of my bed, and pulled the blankets over Mallory's sleeping form, the sound of her breathing and the return of color to her cheeks a relief to my edgy mood. The strange crawling sensation was back, making me itch to shed my skin and maybe take a shower, but I ignored it again, focusing instead on the woman whose presence in my bed set me on a tilt.

Her breathing was deep and even, reassuring as it reached my ears, and something in me ached to brush my hand along the span of her jaw, to feel her, remind myself she was warm to the touch and alive and would be fine.

I didn't.

I couldn't.

Being this close to her was already a challenge, and I only hoped that when she awoke, she'd resist her uncanny urge to touch me.

As if summoned by my thoughts, she stirred against my pillow, a pillow that would no doubt forever smell like her from here on out. That thought shouldn't make my cock twitch, but it did, and it made something in my heart squeeze painfully, as well.

Fuck, these feelings were difficult to handle. I could only imagine what adding touch to the mix might do.

Her stunning amber eyes opened, lashes fluttering softly as she tried to get her bearings, looking around the dark room in confusion before they settled on my own.

"BlackJack?"

She didn't move, thankfully, nor did she pull away, and I held my breath and nodded, waiting for her to continue her line of thought.

Her fingers stretched out against the blankets, and she shuddered as a remnant chill passed through her. Her lips turned down in a frown, and she peeked beneath the blankets, searching out my eyes again after she noticed her clothed state.

"What happened?"

Only hours ago, I'd been steadfastly ignoring her, avoiding her presence, eager to hide away and never be near her again, but now, fuck if I wouldn't kill anyone who tried to take her from me. I wasn't used to such a visceral reaction, but it somehow felt natural, right, like I *should* feel like this about her.

"You and Joker got into it, and you locked yourself in his bathroom. For an hour."

She glanced away, perhaps remembering how things escalated from there. We didn't know what she'd done after that door closed, and I actually wanted to. I wanted to know why she'd nearly killed herself, why she'd been shoved into such a catatonic state.

I echoed her earlier statement, though with less urgency. "What happened?"

She shook her head and refused to look in my direction; instead, her eyes bored a hole into my wall. "I don't want to talk about it."

Her hands moved together and she rubbed absently at one of her wrists, teeth working her lower lip as tears formed in the corner of her eye. And then, as her hand pulled away from the wrist it rubbed, I spotted them, plain as day.

Scars.

Suicide scars.

My hand shot out and gripped her wrist, pulling it toward me insistently as her eyes widened and she fought me. Uncaring of her half-dressed state, she rolled to her knees as I tugged her hand up for my perusal, holding her steady even as she threw all her weight behind an attempt to free herself.

"H-hey, don't—"

I brought the old wound to my lips and placed a tender kiss there, pouring out all the things I couldn't put into words into that one small gesture of comfort.

When my eyes rose and met hers, they, too, were full of tears. Tears for the beautiful creature who'd been so deeply scarred she'd tried to bleed herself dry to escape the pain.

"Who hurt you?" I whispered, refusing to release her hand as I hovered just above her skin, my hot breath still dancing across her skin.

She refused to answer, shaking her head again, her wavy tresses free of the towel that had fallen by the wayside as we struggled against each other.

My answering growl stilled her as she stared up into my eyes once more.

"Who hurt you, Mallory?"

I almost didn't think she'd answer me, she hesitated for so long. And then, just as I was about to release her from my hold—

"I hurt myself, BlackJack, but then again, you already knew that."

"Jonah Hale."

I leaned in, our hands falling to my lap between us, and stared deep into her eyes, searching for her soul, seeking the understanding I knew hid within their depths as she stared back at me in confusion.

"What?"

"My name wasn't always BlackJack. My mother called me Jonah."

She melted into a fucking puddle at the soul-bearing admission, and I watched as her hand lifted, then fell before it had a chance to touch me, then lifted again against her better judgment before settling in her lap atop the other one as confusion and consternation flickered across her features.

"Jonah," she muttered, testing it out on her tongue, rolling it around between her lips like a sinful plea. I felt parts of me come alive at the sound of that name in her voice, parts of me I thought I'd lost long ago to the streets.

I wanted to wrap that sound around me like a blanket and fucking drown in the depths it held.

I almost didn't want to speak again, afraid she might clam up and all of this would be for naught. I also was loath to break up the peaceful calm that settled over us in the silence.

She made the choice for me.

"My father wasn't the best person to be around. When he *was* around, anyhow. He took his anger out on my mom whenever he came home, and when he left, things weren't great. He never left her enough to pay the bills, but he expected us to always be there when he returned. Like obedient fucking dogs."

She stared down at her lap, twisting her hand in my grip so she could see the scars, forcing herself to remember.

"When momma died, he'd been gone for so long, I thought he was gone for good. Things got really hard, but I was grown by then, an adult, so I just moved on with life, until one day I just woke up and didn't want to keep surviving. Life was desolate, lonely, and not worth shit to me. I'd given up.

"I was hungry, starving, there was no power, and I hadn't spoken to a human being in days. Momma's body hadn't even rotted in the ground yet, and I was ready to join her." Her laugh was hollow and weak. "I wasn't even legal drinking age, for fuck's sake."

She turned her free hand over and bared a second set of scars to match her first, and my other hand curled protectively around this set, too, shielding her from the painful reminder.

"The doctors say it's a miracle I survived, but my therapist thinks there was a part of me too stubborn to die. Probably got that from my father, the fucking prick."

Every single nerve ending in my body was on high alert, tingling with her nearness, but instead of pulling away, I tugged her forward into a hug, albeit one that made my skin crawl. She let me hold her there for a few seconds, then pulled back, knowing the touch itself probably made me feel like tearing my hair out.

"You don't have to make yourself uncomfortable, BlackJa—*Jonah.*" Her smile was brittle and soft, but it still managed to make me feel like I was staring into the sun. "You don't have to touch me to comfort me. Your presence here is a comfort already."

I shook my head at her insistence. "What if I . . . "

I wasn't sure if I wanted to, if I was ready for this step, but I wanted to see if I could, if it were possible to change the things life had beaten into me.

"What if I want to?"

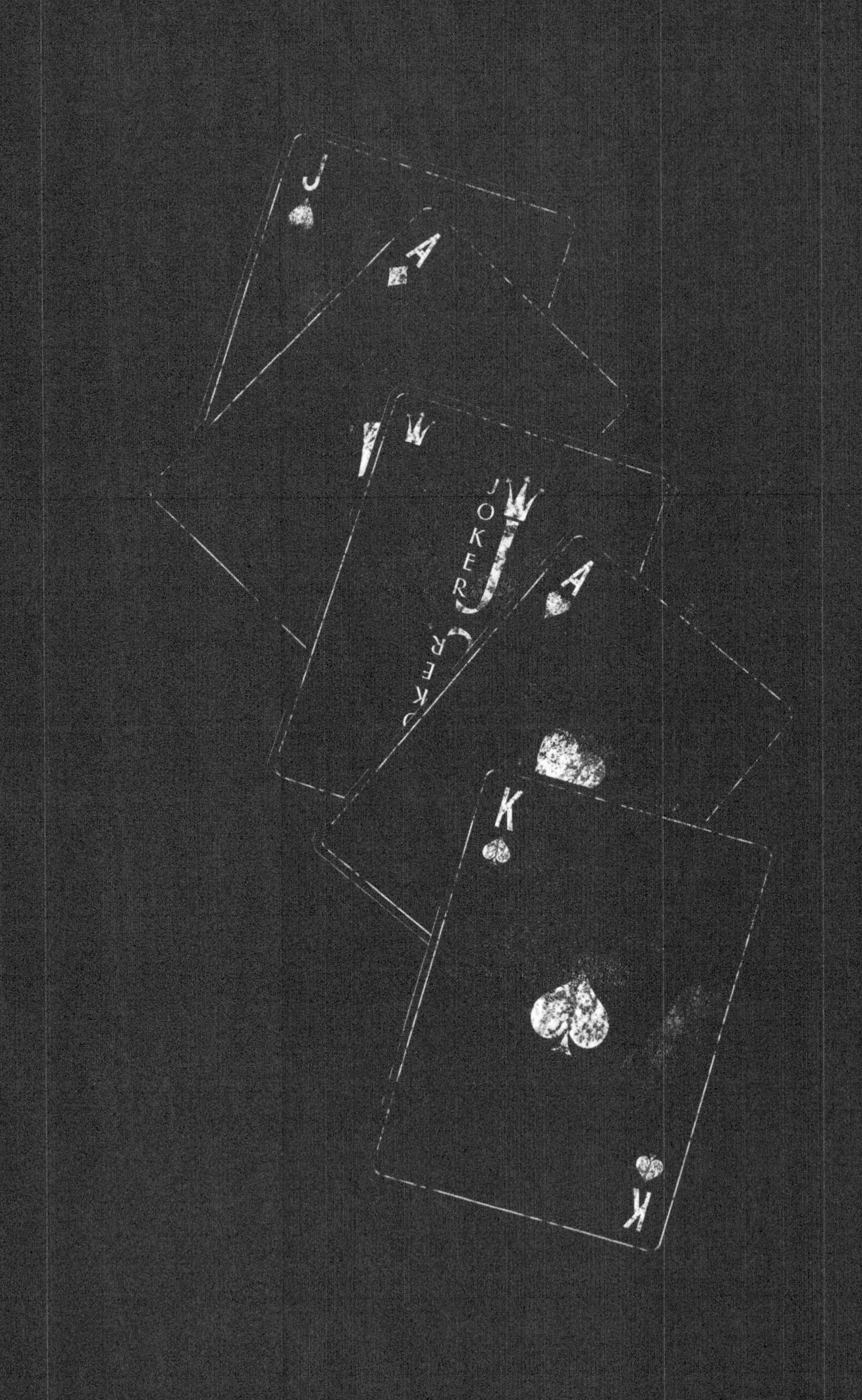
JOKER

CHAPTER THIRTY-TWO
MALLORY

There was no way I heard him right.

"Come again?"

Here I was, so fucking close to BlackJack—

Jonah. His fucking name was Jonah.

He shook his head, withdrawing already. "Just forget about it; it was a stupid idea—"

"No!" I damn near shouted, my hands falling atop his in his lap. I clutched them tightly, demanding he meet my gaze, holding tight until he did. The therapist in me cringed at this forced contact, but sometimes you couldn't put on the kid gloves, and he was a fucking criminal; not like he wasn't used to being uncomfortable. "No, I-I . . . I want to help. I'm just—I guess I just don't understand why."

He blinked slowly, his gaze never wavering as those full lips that graced his stubbled face parted, his tongue darting out between them to wet their surface.

Fuck I wanted to kiss those lips again.

I knew how they felt against my own, but I wanted more. I was greedy, and maybe it was because he was the only one who didn't openly rile me up, covet me, or treat me like an object, but *this man* I could see myself with. Maybe in another world, on another planet, we could have been normal together, he and I.

"It's not a pretty story," he hedged, running a hand through his short black hair. There wasn't much there to tousle, but his long fingers drew noticeable lines through the mop of unruly strands present and made me ache to do the same.

I smiled at his attempt to avoid the door he'd opened himself. "And I'm a therapist. An anonymous, online therapist who people turn to when they can't bring themselves to face one in person. You'd be surprised by the grizzly stories I've heard."

I pulled back my hands to make things a little easier, and his eyes noted its absence with a raised brow. "You might wanna get comfortable, then, doc. It's a long story."

I stretched out on his bed, belatedly realizing I was wearing a shirt that wasn't my own, and no pants. My fingers picked at the soft cotton, my hair falling over my shoulder as I stared down at it, unable to let go of the confusion. "Not to get sidetracked, but whose shirt is this?"

"Mine," he growled, his eyes flashing with a familiar emotion that I was well-versed in.

Fuck, why was that so hot?

"We'll revisit that later," I nearly whimpered, feeling much more exposed as I grabbed a pillow from behind him and got comfortable at the foot of his bed, my back against the wall, legs stretched across the bed, tangled in damp sheets I didn't want to ask him about right now.

I was pretty sure he brought me here and put me in his bed, soaking wet, with no regard for anything but taking care of me, and that thought made me feel immensely fucking vulnerable.

I waved my arm, signaling that he should proceed, and smiled when he let out a little chuckle and settled into the pillows at the head of the bed.

"Well, I guess to start, I'm a foster kid. Or rather, I was." His hands twisted in the sheets at his side, but he gave no other indication that the topic aggravated him. "My father had a heavy hand, and it found my face quite often, so the state would swoop in every now and then and take me away, give him some bullshit anger management courses, and send me back. Until I started running away from the foster homes. Then, he had to track me down when he needed me.

"I say needed like it's a good thing, but it wasn't. It never was."

There it was again, that urge to reach out and grab his hand, the simple touch reassuring for most people, but not him. My fingers twitched, and my lips twisted in a scowl—but of course he fucking noticed, and his own lips curled in a small half-smile, his brow quirked at the funny jerking my fingers were doing.

And then he got serious again, the momentary humor in his gaze turning hard.

"When I hit a certain age, he tried to sell me into the sex trade. I —" He stumbled over his words, his memories, and I physically ached to comfort him, but touch was my love language, not his. I didn't know what to do, how to help. So I just waited.

"I was thirteen."

I couldn't bite back the gasp of shock that escaped me. *"Fuck,* Jonah. Thirteen?"

His nod was slow and solemn. "Yeah. But I managed to get out of there before anything bad happened."

I wasn't sure whether it was appropriate to be relieved yet or not.

"You escaped?"

Another subdued nod. "For a little while, at least. Then my father tracked me down on the streets again, and his heavy-handedness turned into something far more sinister than a beating." He shuddered, remembering something he didn't want to vocalize, perhaps couldn't. "I would have preferred the beatings."

His gaze turned to the window, where thick, dark curtains hid much of the room away, blocking out the sun like he feared it might burn him. When he turned back, some of the shadows of his past had been subdued, but not all of them.

A few of them still lingered in his hazel eyes.

"Touch was kind of a sore spot for me after that period of my life, and when I managed to go back on the run, I ran into someone I knew from the streets—Joker. He kept me alive, nursed me back to health, made sure I was safe. And then he taught me to survive on the streets. By sixteen, we were thicker than thieves—and we were that, too. But though he mended my body, nobody could mend my soul, erase the trauma. I couldn't seem to shove the memories back long enough to say two words, so I just stopped talking somewhere along the road."

He leaned forward and lifted one of his hands, hesitating to the left of my ear. "Watching the guys interact like normal humans makes me ache to feel the same, but nothing's ever made the idea of physical touch appealing to me. Until now," he breathed, his fingers hesitantly tucking a stray strand of my hair behind my ear.

"What made you change your mind?" I whispered, afraid to speak too loud, lest I spook him, like a skittish horse.

"Who," he corrected, his smile softening. "And it was you."

His fingers lifted to parted lips, and I nearly whined as I watched them ghost over them, then move outward and ghost over mine. "When you kissed me, those memories tainted a moment that was otherwise arrestingly beautiful. I don't want anything from my past to taint you. That's why I pushed you away."

I nodded at his explanation, so many things falling into place now that I knew the context. "I was never mad at you for that. I just figured you were busy."

"I was, but not so busy you never saw me. That was entirely by design."

I wanted to steer this conversation away from the harsh reality he'd revealed to me. Sure, I'd heard things that ranked up there from plenty of clients, but it felt different when you were sitting in front of a man who'd just bared his soul to you, who you achingly wanted to comfort but couldn't.

"Sometimes, I can shove the itch down when I touch you; I can ignore the crawling under my skin at the action of touching someone. But it always claws itself free eventually."

PTSD was a fickle bitch, and there were many techniques out there that people used to manage it, but there was no cure-all. Every person was different. So there was no guarantee anything we tried would work. It was like shooting blanks in the dark unless he wanted to medicate, and something told me the closest these assholes got to medicating themselves was an illegally procured bag of hydros when someone got shot.

"There are some things we can try if you're up for it, but I can't promise they'll work—"

He grabbed my hands and squeezed them damn near to breaking in his eagerness. "I'll try it all. Where do we start?"

WE SPENT the next few hours testing different techniques, alternating between pressure points and a gentle brush against his arm or disassociation and a hand-hold, but nothing seemed to work. I would have long since given up if it weren't for the distraught look in his eyes every time his skin started to crawl with the familiar feeling of irritation and anxiety when I touched him or he touched me.

Hell, I was beginning to think maybe this was outside of my purview. That I wasn't the therapist I thought I was—one more thing to add to my growing list of insecurities.

But then, the bastard had a breakthrough and surprised the hell out of me.

He had his phone in his hand and was staring intently at the screen, his lips curled in a tentative smile. "Says here we can try combining exposure therapy with cognitive re-training therapy. That the combination of therapies might help work through my triggers."

I loved that he was being open and responsive to this, to me. That he was talking more in these last few hours than the entire time I'd been stuck with them. Hell, I'd try anything he wanted to at this point. "Hit me with it, pal."

"So it says here, you can retrain your brain to recognize the negative things you associate with the trigger action, aka touch, and teach yourself to become desensitized to the actual act through repetitive exposure."

I arched a brow ironically. "So you want to get naked? Repeatedly?"

The first hint of that devil-may-care smile on a much younger Jonah in one of Joker's pictures flitted across his lips and nearly had me swooning like a woman in one of those period movies. "Something tells me getting naked with my therapist is sort of taboo, Mal."

Mal. Two hours in, and this man already had a nickname for me.

I was a goner, if I wasn't already—completely, wholly, utterly.

I reached out and swatted his chest playfully. "You're the one who said you needed to desensitize yourself with repeated exposure. I was just clarifying." I pretended to pick my nails, looking away from him for a moment. "Besides, I'm not *really* your therapist. So it wouldn't be taboo, per se."

He was suddenly crowding me against the wall, his arms caging me in, his hands pressed against the drywall, his face looming over mine from above as he stared down into my eyes. "Shame, that. I find I'm rather fond of the idea of an illicit yet taboo relationship with my not-therapist."

My smiles came easier around him, as did my laughter now. Being around the enigma that was BlackJack had always been easy, but now, instead of the silence he provided, it was the half smiles and pleased laughter that wrapped around me.

A man willing to be healed was always one of my greatest weaknesses, after all.

I CRASHED in his room that night, though halfway through the night, he abandoned the bed to wander around the warehouse. After a ten-minute absence, I decided to wander out to the couch, still wearing nothing but his shirt and a pair of underwear that proudly proclaimed I was *the queen.*

I passed out there and didn't wake back up until he came searching for me, picked me up, and wandered back to his room.

Almost like he didn't want to be alone in there.

I was honestly glad for it. If I'd been sprawled on that couch in the morning, wearing his clothes, there was no doubt the others would never let him live it down, and their mocking would no doubt set him back.

I had to face down Joker, though, when we woke again because I was in sore need of a bra to go under my strappy tank. And he was in possession of all my clothing in his room.

I snuck in while he snored, oblivious to my comings and goings—or so I thought. When I made it to my bags on the far side of the room, his snoring stopped, and I heard the telltale groan of a man stretching, the accompanying noises a universal code for *fuck mornings.*

His eyes found mine as I turned to face him, on edge about the way I'd acted last night, everything from my fit about the clothes to the wanton use of his bed, to how I nearly tried to die in his bathroom.

Good man that he was, he broke the silence first.

"Sleep well?" he muttered, rubbing the back of his head as he took in the clothes on my body and my now decidedly less-pale skin.

I shrugged, reaching down to rifle through my bag. "I slept okay." Maybe if he didn't ask me to talk about it, we could pretend it never happened.

"So, about last night—"

Of course he'd want to talk about it.

I was saved from the awkward conversation by the fact that none of my clothes were where they should be. I frowned at the now-empty bag, lifting the one that had contained my shoes and finding it, too, empty.

I frowned at his sheepish expression. "Not to get sidetracked, but where are my clothes?"

His frown turned into a little bit of a sheepish smile. "Check Whore Narnia."

No. He wouldn't.

"Cassian, I swear to god if you put my clothes side by side with—"

I yanked the closet door open and was about to go full-on murderous when the bluster melted away.

This man, this beautiful fucking man, had removed all the whore clothes from his closet and replaced them with mine, or what little bit I brought with me. I wasn't sure where all the other clothes had gone, but he'd filled this closet with my things, even going so far as to line my shoes up on the floor nice and neatly.

I turned back to him, stunned nearly speechless.

"You did this?"

His nod was barely perceptible, but I caught it as he blushed a pretty shade of red. "You were safe with him, and I needed something to keep me busy." He ruffled his hair absently, still not meeting my gaze. "Couldn't sleep."

I turned away, ashamed I'd sunk right back to that lowest of lows so easily. I wanted to tell him everything—wanted to make him understand how fucked up I was, but I was ashamed that he'd gone out of his way to do something nice for me, and all I'd done to him last night was use him for some fucking—literally.

Just as I pulled a bra from the hanger, someone knocked at the door, and Joker scrambled to open it before they pounded right through it.

"Keep your pants on, asshole; I'm coming—"

He opened the door to an irate Ace, whose face was now sporting a hell of a shiner on the left side. "Get your ass to the kitchen. There's been a complication."

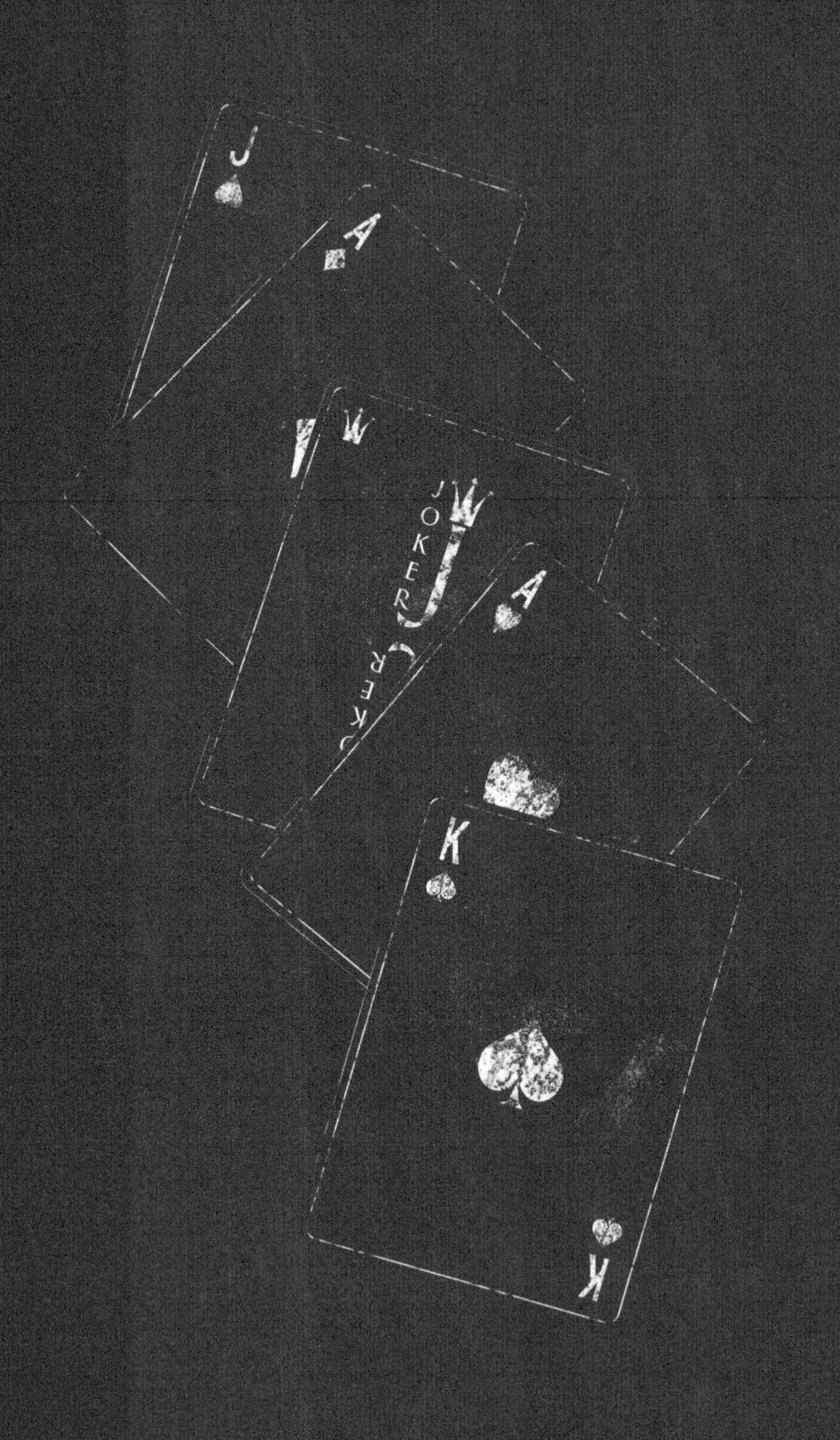
JOKER

CHAPTER THIRTY-THREE
ACE

Trouble, as it turned out, was more than brewing. While we'd been worried about one lone woman, while my men fell at her feet like horny lovesick fools in a matter of days, the enemy had snuck closer and sunk his talons into my turf—*our turf.*

And that couldn't be ignored.

I sat at the head of the table, BlackJack on my left, Spade at my right, and Joker directly in front of me.

"There was a lovely development last night at the racetrack," I started, noting Spade's grimace of frustration and pain as he nursed the stitches he damn near pulled to keep me from taking the butt of a shotgun barrel to the face. "I ended up on the business end of a pump action twelve gauge, reputation be damned. Turns out someone's going around town, telling people we've lost our touch, and that we're jewel sharks now, thieving from our own kind to fill our pockets."

Joker sank lower into his seat, shame marring his sleep-tousled features. "I've had no luck pinning my contact down, and they've moved locations." He shook the last dregs of exhaustion from his face and lifted the nearby coffee to his lips, basking in its warmth and the caffeine boost it gave him. "If he's still around, though, I'll fucking find him, don't worry."

I steepled my fingers on the table. "See that you do."

Spade grumbled from his seat, leaning it back on two legs to stretch for the pot of coffee on the counter. Just as his fingers nearly curled around it, a manicured set of nails tapped against the glass and lifted it out of reach, the girl it belonged to clucking in the back of her throat at his antics.

"You're going to snap those legs and end up on the floor one day, you fuckstick. Here, let me help, lazy ass."

She bent over the table and refilled his cup, moving around in a circle to hit Joker's mug next, a soft smile on her face as she looked each one of them in the eyes. Some sort of understanding passed between her and BlackJack when she stopped to fill his cup, and my eyes widened as she laid her hand on his shoulder, and he covered it with his own.

Matter of fact, every face in the room wore matching expressions of shock, except for the two of them.

Before anyone could comment on the strange moment that passed between the two of them, she spoke up again. "What about those assholes you two ran into at the fights, Spade?"

My eyes slowly swiveled in his direction. He hadn't even mentioned running into anyone, let alone attending the fights. "Did you get in the ring?"

Spade shot her a scowl, and she smiled saucily and moved behind me like that would afford her some level of protection from the maniac at the table.

His growl froze her like a deer in headlights. "I didn't get in the ring, and there's nothing to tell. The Kings just happened to pay our rings a visit, that's all. They're looking for information and throwing their fighter in our face."

BlackJack's jaw ticked as he frowned. "Who?"

Joker set his cup down and sighed. *"Soldat."*

I swore under my breath. "Fuck me, Spade, you better hope he doesn't come back, or you'll be looking for a new side gig."

The Soldier and the Kings were notorious in the criminal underbelly, both having a hell of a track record attached to their names.

The gang as a whole was a bunch of ex-mafia brats who'd made their own crime syndicate, built it from the ground up as they sniped their competition's men and their contracts. Their leader, Arthur, was a ruthless sonofabitch, a twisted British bastard with the uncanny ability to get under your skin with a look, and the brains of a genius.

He was also BlackJack's distant cousin.

And the Soldier? Well, the rumors about him that circulated were more a body count and less actual rumors. He was ex-Soviet scum, a hired assassin who made no distinctions of right or wrong when it came to hired hits. He was also a man who'd found creative ways to *'accidentally'* kill men in the ring for a perceived slight, and he'd never lost a match. Until now, he stayed on the upper echelon's circuit, private matches held for affluent clientele paying far more than he'd make in the slums.

He had to be here for a damn good reason. No doubt he was slinging his arm wide to scare someone who knew something into coming to the surface.

"What are they looking for?"

Joker sank lower in his chair, hiding from me, and I had a feeling what the answer would be, but it wasn't the man of the hour who spoke up.

"From what I understood, they're looking for a jewel thief."

I craned my neck up to put Miss Stanton directly in my line of sight. "And what, pray tell, would lead you to that assumption?"

She frowned and leaned over my shoulder absently, filling my coffee with more of the rich black life-giving liquid we were all addicted to. I absently noted the swell of her chest in the tight tank top as she pulled back again, a finger to her chin as she dwelled on it.

"So, the one in charge—they called him King, all lined up really nice when he snapped his fingers, too—he said a business associate of his had been robbed of his jewels, told Joker he'd best put his nose to the ground to find out who did it and who put them up to it." She sauntered to the sink, dumping the last dregs of the coffee down the drain as she rinsed the pot and set it back where it belonged. "He was a bit of a prick; all of them were, really. I'm glad those assholes didn't kidnap me instead of you."

BlackJack snorted coffee out his fucking nose at that, Spade choked on his, and Joker's lips curled in a smile over the rim of his cup as I blinked stupidly, waiting for them to recover.

I may have cracked a smile, albeit a small one.

"Well, look at that, I still have the ole 'shock and awe' down." She poked me in the shoulder, staring down like the cat that ate the canary, all victorious ferocity with her little grin and the glee dancing in her eyes. "And is that a smile I see? Gosh, Ace, there's hope for you yet."

Her demeanor and the cavalier mood at the table had me all out of sorts, like there was a private club assembled, and I was the only one *not* a member. An old, familiar part of me ached to be included, but then the ugly creature that demanded order and a lock on the chaos and unknown reared its head and snapped me back to my senses.

"Do I *look* like I'm in the mood to joke around, girl?"

Before she could shoot back a witty retort, I shoved my chair back and grabbed her by the wrist, yanking her into my lap. She struggled for a brief second, but she went willingly enough, freezing when I had her right where I wanted her.

Spade's little escapades worked me up the other day, and I was reluctant to keep denying myself the pleasure of her flesh when she seemed quite willing to give it up to the others when they demanded it.

If Spade and Joker could reap the benefits, then dammit, so could I.

I glared at the men in the room who suddenly looked like they were two seconds from bolting to give us privacy.

That was the *last* thing I wanted. I wanted them to watch me debase her, watch me wreck her; I wanted witnesses to her shame.

I hated the way she made me feel. How she got under my skin like no other could, set me on edge and consumed my spare thoughts like a fucking plague. Perhaps if I marked her for the others to see, the beast inside of me would calm down.

"None of you best fucking move an inch," I growled, spreading my legs to force Miss Stanton to straddle one of my thighs. Her hands darted out, and slightly faded nail polish caught the light of the overhead bar as she clenched the edge of the table and ceased protesting, her eyes flitting to each of the others, seeking help.

She'd get no help from them, not against me.

"Joker," I groused as I grabbed her around the throat from behind, smiling sadistically when her pulse skittered out of control beneath my hand. "You're the whole reason Miss Stanton is here, and she's a distraction that's causing you to lose your touch. King asked you for information, but so did I, and you've not brought me anything of use yet." My other hand tugged a knife from my pocket, and I brought it up to Miss Stanton's neck, pointedly pressing the flat of the blade against her creamy white skin, pleased when he reacted like I hoped —nearly jumping out of his chair.

"I'll get you what you need, Ace, but this isn't how we do things—"

I stood with Miss Stanton still attached to my thigh, leaning slightly over the table right back at him, my anger rolling off in waves, her throat still tightly gripped in my hand behind the sharp edge of my blade.

"You don't tell *me* how to run things. That's *my* job around here. You are the informant and the thief. And you're the sole reason this situation is even *on* our doorstep, so solve it, or I'll make sure her headstone says *'If Only Joker Had Done His Job'.*"

No sooner than the words were out of my mouth, I regretted every single one.

The table went deathly silent as the ramifications of the sentence sunk in. Miss Stanton was the first to react, her whole body going slack in my grip, all the fight drained from her. As much as I wanted to be sorry, I couldn't afford it. She'd been slowly undermining me with her seductive body and long lashes, turning the guys into veritable mush. Spade was injured, Joker was lovesick and foolish, and

BlackJack—well, something was always off about him, but I was never sure what was constant and what wasn't, so it was hard to tell.

And there was me. She'd done things to me, too. Things I wasn't proud of.

Joker kicked his chair backward and scowled at me as he stalked around the table, his hand closing around the blade of my knife with deadly intent. I waited patiently to see what he'd do and was not disappointed. *Or perhaps I was.*

He snarled at me, eyes narrowed to near slits as the other hand began to peel my fingers off the blade's handle. I could feel blood trickling down his hand and over our tangled fingers, but he seemed not to care, more concerned with removing the dagger from her throat.

Perhaps he'd then try to shove it in mine.

Spade's good arm tugged a very quiet Miss Stanton from my lap once Joker'd freed her, and he shuffled her out of the way and into the next room as I had a standoff with the first man to ever join my little crew. The man I'd trusted through all his ups and downs over the past six or so years. The man now palming my dagger and staring at me like he wanted to rip my heart out of my chest with his bare hands.

"If you've got something to say, fucker, then say it already," I spat out, stepping away from him, careful not to drip any of his blood from my hand onto the tile. Ceramic was a bitch to clean.

"I'll do my job, Ace, but you keep your hands off the doc—"

"I don't make deals, Joker. You get that information, and maybe we can talk."

He stormed off with a huff, slinging blood everywhere, uncaring of the mess I'd now have to clean up. With his departure, it left only myself and BlackJack in the kitchen, and the silence was pleasant after the little episode.

They only further proved my point—the woman was a liability, and she affected their daily performance whether they cared to admit it or not.

BlackJack had moved to the fridge, where he stood with his hand in the freezer, slowly packing a baggie with ice. He didn't speak, but when he closed the door and approached me where I stood, I had the strangest feeling that he *wanted to* say something to me, and that it wasn't pretty.

But unless he spoke up, I'd never know what it was.

"Go ahead," I grumbled. "Get it off your chest."

His eyes held mine as he searched for something I'd lost a long time ago, it felt like—my humanity. My compassion. "We don't do things like this, Ace. Get yourself together, or I will."

His back was the last thing I saw as he dropped the bag of ice in my hand and marched off after the others.

JOKER

CHAPTER THIRTY-FOUR
SPADE

The following two weeks went by in a blur. I spent plenty of time on the circuit, making the rounds and checking to ensure my contacts stayed intact while I was inactive, for the most part. Joker filled his days with information seeking, hopping from one high-roller to the next, seeking side jobs under the guise of money, but exploiting every hired hand position to get closer to the truth.

Ace spent the first week shooting Mallory confusing looks over the morning breakfast table, but she still fed us all daily since I was stocking the fridge.

I wouldn't have blamed her for poisoning it all. Especially his.

She didn't, though, and her return glances were cordial and all smiles, none of the apprehension I expected her to hold around him.

After a week of this, Ace caved, and he'd been back in Japan with his uncle on 'business', or so he claimed. Only one person could get ahold of him, and BlackJack wasn't inclined to do so, not after the knife debacle.

It was going on the third week when Ace finally called to let us know he'd be back before the end of the month, and he didn't sound any more pleased than when he left.

In fact, if it were even possible, he sounded more haggard and rough than ever.

We were all sequestered in the commons where we'd first brought Mallory when we kidnapped her, and though she hadn't admitted it yet, we all knew she was here to stay. She hadn't said as much, but her actions spoke for themselves.

She'd been flitting from one bed to the next in Ace's absence, though we were all pretty low-key about things. I'd had her next to me last night, but she'd been so worn out after a brisk swim with BlackJack that she'd been asleep before her head actually hit the pillow.

I might be borderline insane, but I wasn't a prick. I let her sleep, content to breathe her in and watch her as the peaceful content washed over her and relaxed away all the stress from the day, washed it away and left behind only a calm that smoothed the wrinkles of her forehead from a perpetual frown, loosened all the muscles in her body so I could tug her against me. She always curved like a cat against the expanse of my body, and I relished the contact.

When she wandered from my bed to another, the damned thing felt empty in a way it never had before.

I didn't mind sharing, really. Some guys might have an issue with a woman who wasn't satisfied by just his cock, but I knew better. She wasn't banging BlackJack—I'd hear it, seeing as how our rooms were right on top of each other. And she might be sleeping with Joker, but he wasn't home much to take advantage of it, and her daily interactions with him hadn't changed.

It felt like everyone was out of sorts. Busy, bored, or off-kilter.

She was currently in my shower, the scent of her perfumed, mint shampoo invading my room, filling it and my nostrils with the teasing scent that followed her everywhere. My cock was hard as a rock, and I sat atop the blankets and tugged down my sweats, trying to remember the last time I'd tugged one out.

It had been a while.

My cock bounced eagerly in my lap as I took myself in hand, fisting my length with a groan as the water shut off in the shower. I had three choices—stop before she came out, race her to the finish and see if I could come before she left the bathroom, or tease myself and wait for her to join me.

Ideas two and three sounded like fun. What kind of man would I be if I didn't warm up the car for her while she got ready?

And if I busted a nut before she walked out of that bathroom? Well, there was always the next round.

I got five slow pumps in before I was aching for something far more appealing than my hand. My feet were on the floor, sweats kicked off and discarded in my haste as I stormed over to the bathroom and yanked the door open, pleased at the slight blush that covered her towel-clad body as she spotted me, and then my cock.

Her eyes went wide at the monster between my legs. Of course, she'd never seen it in the daylight. I could hardly fault her for staring.

"Jesus, that thing is huge," she breathed, like she hadn't had the fucker three ways to Sunday, stuffed in all three of her willing holes at least once.

"I assure you, even in the daylight, it fits, sweetheart."

She rolled her eyes at my bravado and moaned as I took it in hand again, closing the distance between us in two steps. She blatantly turned away from me to stare into the mirror, smearing whatever lotion Joker bought her recently across her nose, rubbing it into her cheeks, shooting me a smile in the reflective surface as my hands moved up to rake through her damp tresses.

Mallory fresh out of the shower was my favorite thing in the world lately, followed closely by Mallory spread naked in my bed, face flushed from orgasm.

It was a sight to behold, for sure.

I braced against the counter and rubbed my cock against her pretty little ass, easily slipping right up under that towel of hers to fit nicely between her cheeks as I groaned into her neck. She had a way about her that made a man wild, made him want things he had no business wanting.

"Spade," she half-ass protested, even as she shifted against me and spread her legs just an inch, "I have to get ready. Cass promised to take me to replace the clothes you ruined today, and he's supposed to be here any minute."

I bit at the juncture of her throat and her shoulder, dragging a breathless sigh from her. "I'll have to make it good and fast, then," I growled, more than able to rise to the challenge. "You work on your face, I'll work on this pussy."

She whimpered, nodded, and bit her lip, returning her eyes to the mirror as my left hand snaked to her front and loosed the towel from her body, letting it fall to the floor in a puddle.

"So soft," I uttered against the nape of her neck, using my other hand to brush away the stray hairs there as I laved open-mouth kisses along the ridge of her spine as my other hand found her taut nipple, working it with practiced pinches and strokes, rolling it between my thumb and forefinger as she moaned and slapped a hand against the counter, fumbling for a little green bottle of oil she used on her roots every day.

"Fuck yes," she hissed when my hand trailed lower, brushing against her greedy cunt in a teasing move that had her arching and rubbing that ass against me like a cat in heat.

Tight, hot, and wet were all the easiest words to describe where I buried my fingers as she whimpered and rocked against them, her attempts at beautification forgotten as I hiked one of her knees up on the counter and slid in beside my own finger, the fit so fucking tight my balls nearly burst right then and there.

Gods, she was so fucking tight.

A man could die happy, buried to the balls in her. I wouldn't want to go any other way.

"Jesus, Spade," she moaned, her hand reaching up to slap against the mirror as her eyes met mine in the reflection and nearly rolled back into her head. I rocked into her, my hand reaching up to join hers on the mirror, our fingers laced together as she moaned and I grunted, our bodies slapping together obscenely, my countertop completely wrecked.

And that was precisely how Joker would find us, me mid-stroke, my fingers curled around her hip to toy with her neat little bud, making her scream for me, if I didn't hurry this party along and get her where she needed to be.

"Fuck, sweetheart, need to feel you around me, coming for me—"

She arched her back, reached a single hand up into my hair, and ripped it free of the bun I'd piled atop my head. Mallory had an obsession with my long hair, and who was I to deny her the things that made her happy while I was railing the fuck out of her in my bathroom at eight in the morning?

"Harder, Spade," she groaned, chest heaving as I doubled my efforts and nearly rocked her up into the reflection of us in front of her. "Yes, god, just like that—"

My balls were fit to fucking explode, my calves were screaming, but there was no way I was about to stop now. You'd have to take a taser to my taint to drag me out of her wet, willing hole, and even then, I'd probably fill her with my seed before I slipped out and twitched on the floor. The sweet feel of her wrapped around my length as I dragged in and out of her, gasping for air, was almost too much, and yet somehow not enough.

"Come for me, Mallory," I groaned in her ear, feeling my balls tighten against the base of my shaft as they prepared to give her what her greedy cunt needed, what she begged me for all the damn time. "Clench around that big cock for me, beautiful, that's right—"

"Lucyyyyy, I'm home!"

Just as the generic-ass greeting carried up the stairs in Joker's annoying lilt, Mallory's core tightened around me, and she let out a scream worthy of a porno flick, both hands on the mirror now, hips twitching as I bit the back of her neck like an animal and groaned into her, my cock twitching, filling her to the brim with hot ropes of cum that shot from its tip.

"Fuck!"

She slumped against the counter for a second while I pulled away and tugged a clean washcloth from the shelf and cleaned her up, then set to work on myself, loath to wipe away the evidence of her arousal on my cock, but knowing damn well it would be a sticky mess I didn't want to deal with when I went to work out today.

She wrapped the towel back around her body and slipped out into the hallway, peeking down the stairs at the landing where Joker still stood, a slow smile spreading over his lips at the sight of her, recently ravished and very much sated.

"I'm coming, I'm coming," she insisted, her answering smile teasing at the corners of her mouth as he chuckled to himself.

"Sounds like you just did that, beautiful," he teased, cocking a brow playfully as she turned even redder and scampered off in search of some clothing to cover herself.

I sauntered out of my room a few minutes later, shirtless, hair down, but a bit more presentable, a gym bag thrown over my shoulder, filled with my usual equipment, and met his gaze head-on as he stared down the hall, waiting for her.

"Have fun shopping," I offered as he shot me a mock salute.

"About as much fun as you had redecorating your bathroom," he shot back, all teasing grins now. "Maybe even more."

I had to laugh at the challenge in his voice. If there was one thing I knew, it was that he wasn't about to outdo the performance I put on this morning. Not while he was shopping for dresses, jeans, and whatever else women needed in a new wardrobe.

"Put a new lingerie set on my card, and maybe a nice dress. I want to take her out and finger her under a fancy tablecloth again."

Joker nodded and calmly took the card from my outstretched fingers, pocketing it just in time for Mallory to slip out into the hallway in a pair of nondescript shorts and a tee that was decidedly not hers. It wasn't one of mine, and I didn't even recognize the band on it—or the writing.

Come to think of it . . . the writing looked distinctly Asian in origin.

"Hey, doc, where'd you get that shirt?"

She fingered the edge of the hem, staring down at the band in question like that was a stupid question, perhaps the dumbest one I'd ever asked her. "Where the fuck do you think I got it from?" She shrugged and looked back at the now-open door behind her. "It's Ace's. Though I didn't think the man owned anything that wasn't black."

Good heavens, she was going to be the death of us all. "You'd better put that back where you found it when you got home, or the boss will have a fit."

Joker took her hand and nodded in agreement. "He's right. If he catches you in his shirt, Ace will have your ass on a platter and your head on a spike."

She flipped her hair over a shoulder and led the way down the stairs with a little girlish giggle laced with what I assumed was a hint of unhinged, menacing glee. "Well, he'll have to catch me first, and I'm done letting him push all of us around. He just needs a firm hand, is all."

Maybe around his cock, but I had a sinking feeling she was about to bite off more than she could chew.

JOKER

CHAPTER THIRTY-FIVE
MALLORY

He called on a Monday, and finally, on a Friday morning, the door to the garage opened, and a frazzled, jet-lagged Ace stumbled into the warehouse like the sunrise had chewed him up and spit him out. Twice.

He was so focused on his mindless drive to find coffee, he didn't even notice me in the kitchen until I crossed in front of him and slid a hand into the fridge to fetch the eggs.

Even his eyes were slow to track as they followed the line of my arm up to my face, which was all smiles and calm, even though on the inside, I wanted to strangle him still for what he'd done to me last time we shared this kitchen.

For the knife.

For the blood.

For everything.

"There's coffee on the counter, and a fresh mug in the sink, if you want some," I offered hesitantly, afraid he might lash out and bite me like a rabid dog if I wasn't careful. "I was just about to make breakfast. You look like you could use a plate."

He eyed me hesitantly as he took a seat at the table, perhaps too tired to argue. I wouldn't look a gift horse in the mouth, but it might be nice to know what brought about the sudden change in demeanor, and if it was temporary or more permanent.

He stared off into the distance, like he wasn't even there, sitting at the table but miles away. Sensing something was off was easy–it was figuring out what to do about it that proved the more delicate task.

Ever since the incident in the kitchen three weeks ago, there'd been no love lost for Ace in their hearts. Even Jonah, who on some level understood Ace's monsters, his darkness, still couldn't stand to be around, had refused to pick him up from his flight.

It looked like dealing with things was up to me today.

"So," I muttered, wandering to the far side of the kitchen for another mug to fill with coffee, "Spade's healing nicely. He thinks he'll be able to hop back into the ring in another couple of weeks or so. Stitches will probably come out next week if he's lucky."

Ace didn't acknowledge my commentary, not even with a nod or a twitch of a single muscle of his face.

Fine. If that was how he wanted to play it, we'd play it that way.

"BlackJack is down at the racetrack with Joker, said something about making sure they were respecting the rules, though I have a feeling they won't need the extra firepower they took with them. Not after Spade called around and politely offered to put a bullet between the eyes of any asshole willing to take their chances."

The pitch-black coffee swirled lazily in the pot as I lifted it and filled Ace's mug, remembering to add the single scoop of sugar he insisted made the liquid tolerable, before setting the pot back on the burner and moving back to the table.

I took a seat a few feet from the man who'd almost taken my life a few weeks ago, the man who'd fucked my mouth ten feet from where he stood now, the same one who'd put a gun inside my lady bits and threatened to shoot me while I came.

I mean, that was kinda hot, not gonna lie–but clearly, I had issues, so make of that what you will.

I settled into my seat, folded a single leg in half, brought my knee to the edge of my chin, and scooted his drink with my free hand.

"You know, you can drink it. It's not poisoned or nothing."

His eyes flicked over to the mug of steaming brew, and I felt a sense of relief flood me as the corner of his mouth twitched just the slightest, and he picked up the mug. Steam curled around his jawline, partially obscuring his face as he closed those piercing eyes and inhaled the scent of familiarity, routine, and the mundaneness of coffee in the morning. He brought the cup to his lips, downing half of it in one go.

It was always a miracle to me how these men managed to suck down their coffee so damn fast. It was scalding, hotter than satan's ballsacks in the Georgia sun. I could hardly sip the cup I had, and I'd added creamer to mine.

When he set the cup down, his eyes flicked to the other end of the table, where my new cellphone sat, black screen, forgotten but for the faint sound of music emanating from it.

I hated silence, hated when it was just me in this colossal ass compound, especially while I made breakfast. So I'd turned on some faint dregs of classical music to keep me company. I assumed by the look on Ace's face he hadn't been made aware the boys had cloned me a burner phone, so they could always reach me.

In fact, I knew they wouldn't have. Ace would have said something along the lines of *no fucking way in hell.*

My hand darted out and palmed the little electronic, tucking it safely away in my pocket after silencing the music with a flick of a finger. Meeting Ace's gaze again held no appeal, so I stared into the swirling pit of my coffee and sighed, wishing more than anything that one of the others had been here for his arrival again.

He had me on edge. His silence was unnerving, but his whole person was giving off strange vibes that left me feeling like I'd been thrust into a boat and shoved off the shore, no paddle, no life vest, in crocodile-infested waters.

Shit.

I realized a little belatedly that I'd started pulling ingredients for breakfast but never got that far, and I was out of my seat in seconds, bustling about the kitchen like a fucking bee on crack, unable to stand still for a moment or more. In no time at all, there was a veritable smorgasbord of delicious offerings on the counter, from eggs to bacon, french toast, and even fresh sliced fruit offerings. Ace's face was still trained on the table, so I just piled a little of everything on a plate for him and nodded to myself, determined to break through the icy demeanor. I didn't plan to sit in silence for the rest of eternity, and food was one surefire way to get through to him–one of my first lessons while under the tutelage of Joker himself.

I knew all their little weaknesses, thanks to him.

Well, almost all of them.

He stared at the plate as I slid it in front of him like he hadn't had food in the three weeks he'd been gone, and without a word, he lifted the fork from the ceramic dish and started shoveling food into his mouth, somehow still managing to make it look proper and somewhat elegant. I wasn't convinced he wouldn't choke, he was going so fast.

I made myself a plate and joined him, pleased he was at least eating something. He might not be talking to me right now, but he accepted food, which was a big step for him.

His silence lasted all the way through his plate of food until we were both staring at empty dishes sitting in front of us, neither one eager to break the silence.

It probably would have gone on like that forever if not for the sound of my phone's vibration going off in my back pocket. Ace's eyes snapped up at the faint buzzing, and it was as if he'd snapped out of the trance with a code word, like he'd suddenly awoken from a dream.

"Who the fuck let you have a phone?"

I shrugged and silently willed it to stop vibrating, but if it was one of the boys–and who else would it be at this point?--they wouldn't stop calling til I picked up. With a heavy sigh, I pulled it from my pocket and flipped the screen up to see who'd be talking to Ace.

What a surprise. "Spade, actually, though it was Joker's idea."

His brows quirked up as his scowl deepened–*great, he's back to normal.* "Hand it the fuck over."

I laid down the fancy android and slid it across the table, wincing as he slammed his fingers into it and lifted the receiver to his ear.

"Why the fuck does the captive have a phone?"

I winced at his tone, already hating the fact that he was back and I was here alone. There was no running from this one, oh no. If he decided he wanted to do something to me, he'd do it, and I wouldn't stand a chance of escaping him.

"So you trust her? How adorable. And also stupid."

"I *did* choose to stay here, you know," I interjected, but one look from the side of Ace's eyes had me clamming up again.

He turned his attention back to the phone, grumbling as he listened to the man on the other end. When he'd heard what he needed to, he ended the call without a word to the other party and pocketed my phone. My sputtered protests met that impassive, dead gaze again, and after a minute of them falling on deaf ears, I simply gave up.

Talking to this man would do me no good. Might as well save my breath.

"Whether you chose to stay or not, you only did so to save your own life; therefore, it's loyalty bought, not loyalty given. I don't trust you as far as I can throw you." His gaze slithered up and down my body pointedly, pretending he saw something there that disgusted him. "And that's not far to begin with, mind you."

Stupid fucking liar. I knew damn well I wasn't a pound over one-fifty, and he could suck my asshole if he thought otherwise. Plus, I knew my body turned him on no matter what he said. His escapades in the kitchen proved as much.

"Yeah, well, you'll have to start trusting me eventually, ya chuckle-fuck, or you'll be wasting a ton of your time chasing around a woman you pretend you don't want."

His growl permeated the air almost as well as the thick, sharp *thud* of his fist against the tabletop. "I don't want my crewmates' sloppy seconds, bitch."

"Sloppy?" *How fucking rude.* I was the complete *opposite* of sloppy, and I was nobody's seconds. "How come when a man sees four chicks at once, he's a player, but when a woman does it, she's a whore?"

He didn't answer me, and I didn't want him to. I wanted to shove his smug fucking smirk down that arrogant mouth, right past his too-straight, too-white teeth, wearing nothing but a grin of victory.

But that wouldn't do anything for me now. And he'd likely just put that gun back to my head and end me if I pushed any more.

"Fine, be that way. Clearly, whatever you did and wherever you went did absolutely nothing for your *sunny fucking disposition,* you prick." I tossed my hair over one shoulder and wandered to the sink, dumping my coffee cup with a bit more flourish than was necessary. I was fuming, absolutely *livid,* and I wasn't about to let him see how his bullshit affected me.

No way, no how.

"Where are you going?" he asked in a dry monotone as I marched for the kitchen door, dirty dishes forgotten until later.

I didn't bother to turn around, choosing instead to flip him off behind my head as I strolled on out and into the hallway.

If he wanted to pursue me, that was on him. I wasn't spending any more time in his presence than I had to, and now that he'd taken my phone, there wasn't much to do but sit around and read or tidy up the guys' rooms.

So I started in Joker's.

TWO HOURS and two loads of laundry later, I'd finally managed to make his room look less like a tornado had blown through and more like an adult man lived here, so I rewarded myself with a random book from his bookshelf, stretched out across the bed, a smile on my lips as I devoured every word, waiting on one of the boys to come home.

Home.

It was strange how I'd begun to think of this place as home now. Hell, I'd been here over a month, and it wasn't looking like I'd ever go back to my old life. Like a part of me was already ensconced in this fucking place, in this crew.

Like I'd become their de facto queen while the boss was away.

The guys bent to me whenever I needed something; with Ace out of the way, not here to tell them how to treat me, I felt less like a forced captive and more like a part of their little sect, their family. Now that he was back, would that change?

This was honestly one of the only places I'd ever felt safe, as fucked up as that was–safe with my kidnappers, go figure.

But after three weeks missing from my everyday life, and not even a single text or call from the people I expected to miss me, I realized there was nothing left to go back to but two cats who'd love whoever fed them nightly, and some house plants I killed more often than nurtured.

What the fuck did I stand to gain by running away?

Still, I wasn't about to sit around this place while mister stick-up-his-ass marched around and put knives to my throat to motivate the other guys. I wasn't anybody's fucking toy. Or bargaining chip, for that matter.

The garage door lifted, and in rolled one of the guys' vehicles. It was getting easier to determine who was who, but so far, I hadn't managed to separate the cars from each other. Usually, I relied on a text to tell me who to expect, but–

Couldn't get a text if your phone wasn't in your possession.

And Ace had mine.

Fucker.

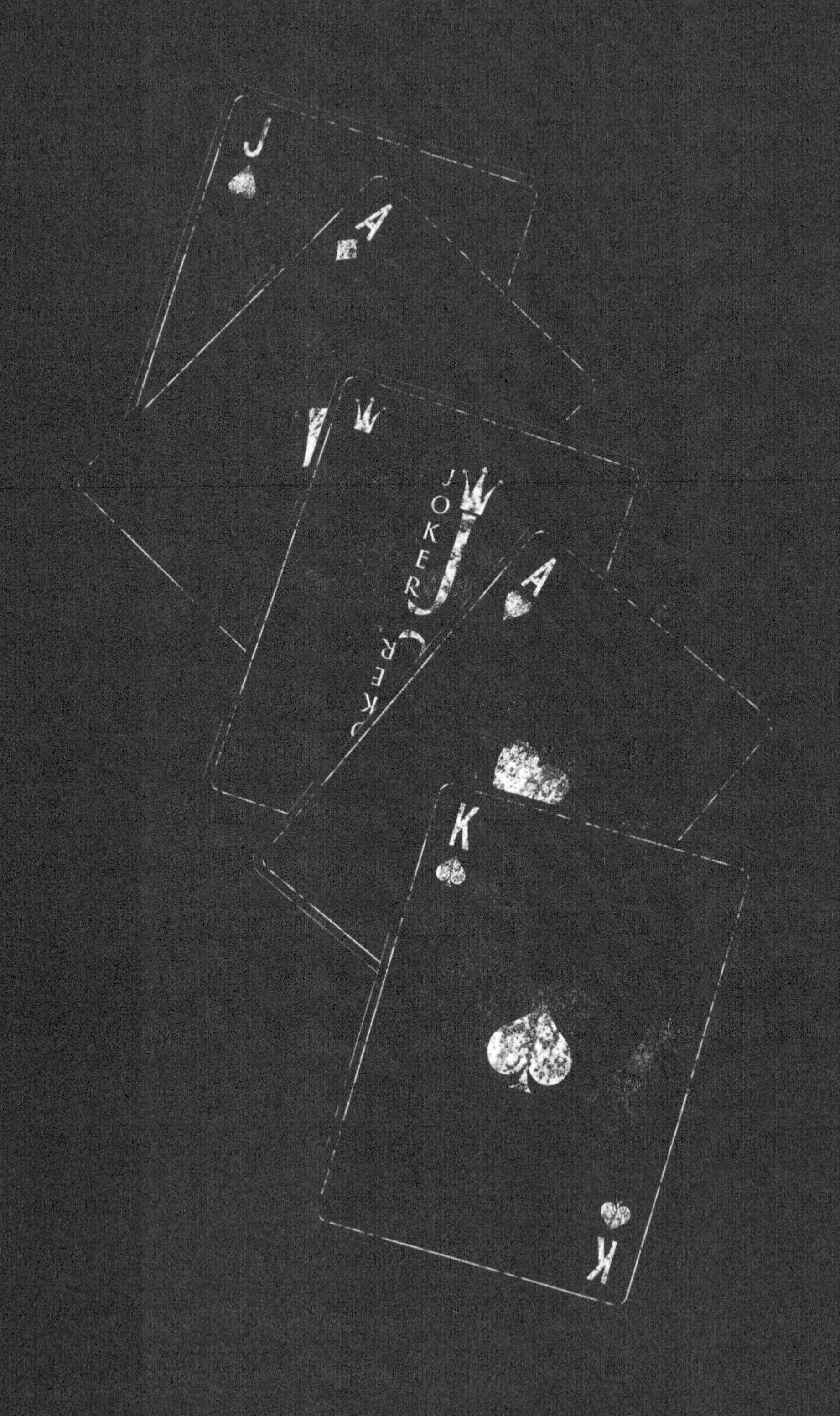

CHAPTER THIRTY-SIX

JOKER

If I had to suffer through one more fucking interrogation today, I was going to go through the roof. I needed a break. I needed air.

What I really needed was a tall, cool glass of Mallory, naked, in my bed, spread eagle and ready to be brought to the heights of pleasure.

What could I say? I had a thing for the doc.

She had managed to weasel her way into my fucking soul, and in the week Ace had been gone, I'd been doing everything I could to make her happy. I wanted to see her smile every fucking day of my life, regardless of what put the smile on her gorgeous cheeks.

I wasn't still making amends for letting her nearly die in my shower.

I wasn't.

Maybe if I told myself that enough, it would start to be true. I could believe it for a change. Trick my mind out of the constant guilt and anguish.

I slammed the door of Ace's fancy car and growled under my breath at the fucking luck of it all today.

Dealing with the scum of the earth always left me with a sour taste in my mouth, but I pulled just enough street urchins out of the alleys today to get what I needed–a lead. And if it panned out–and I was sure it would–BlackJack would be able to tell us who the fuck threw that info in the lap of our contacts and why.

Someone had known who we'd be hitting. They knew the fucking jewels belonged to the Kings. And they knew the ensuing battle between them and us would be a hell of a bloodbath if it came to it. My only guess was they'd planted the info so they could wipe two players off the board for the price of none.

Someone else wanted to take the top spot in our city, and they'd pitted the Wildcards against the Kings for sport.

I almost marched right past the kitchen until I spotted Ace, of all people, washing fucking dishes, a towel thrown over his expensive button-down as he hummed to himself.

My hand curled around the door frame as I danced backward and peered in, surveying the scene.

"You're back," I muttered, too stunned to come up with something witty to say. "How was the flight?"

He didn't turn around to answer me, but his stiff shoulders and the little roll of his head he did to pop his neck said it all. "Fucking miserable."

I moved slowly into the room and took a seat at the table, flipping through the intel and notes I'd jotted down during the little bit of investigative work I'd managed to finish today. "They always are."

Ace peered in my direction out of the corner of his eye, his hands still busy scrubbing at several plates and a skillet half-submerged in the dishwater he'd run. "Anything eventful happen while I was out?"

I shrugged pointedly, lazily tipping my chair back on two legs. "Not a whole lot. Got Mallory a cellphone, did some recon, stuck my nose to the ground–and I did manage to get a lead today, but I don't think we're going to like where it goes."

Ace shut off the water and tugged the towel off his shoulder, wiping his hands dry as he turned to face me. "And where exactly does that lead point to?"

"I don't know yet, but it's not good."

I filled him in on what I'd dragged out of my younger informants, the ones who listened well and managed to make themselves invisible in the sneakiest of places, pausing to throw in some suspicions here and there that really got me wondering.

Ace's sigh permeated the air, like heavy creme in a soup that doesn't quite want to blend with the base stock. "So what you're telling me is they may not even be *our* enemy, they most likely are after the Kings, and they assumed we'd wipe them off the board for them."

"It's a working theory," I drawled, rising from my seat with a groan. "But I could use a shower unless you wanna talk more about it. Not much we can do until BlackJack gets back and can run his magic online."

"He's on his way, ironically enough," Ace grumbled, "shouldn't be long."

"Fantastic, when he gets here, page my ass."

I marched out of the room and up the stairs, prepared to flop face-first on my bed with a flourish until I flipped open the door and spotted a very adorable doc with a very adorable smile waiting for me with a book open in her lap and one of my shirts draped over her shoulders.

"You look like you're enjoying yourself," I remarked dryly, peeling off my shirt as I moved toward the bed. It started a new pile on the floor by the bathroom door, which made me realize she'd cleaned my room. "Oh, shit, doc, you didn't have to tidy up for me."

Her lithe shoulders lifted, wrinkling the band logo on the front of her shirt. "I was bored. Ace took my phone, something about '*I can't be trusted*' or some shit."

I frowned at the door, determined to march back out there and retrieve it for her. He had no right to take it, especially since this was allegedly an equal playing field here. Ace might be the brains, the organizer, but he was outnumbered, and in his absence, our democracy had worked quite well.

I'd be damned if I'd go back to a dictatorship.

"We'll see about that–"

She shot off the bed and had my arm in a death grip before I could reach the door. "Now, now, let's not be hasty. I don't want you to start anything with Ace on my behalf the second he returns." She eyed my naked chest with a fair amount of appreciation and a little bit of lust. "You planning to take a shower?"

I smiled down at her, Ace and the phone forgotten–just like she wanted, I assumed. "I was."

Her lashes fluttered low. "Maybe I could . . ." Her fingers trailed down my pecs, over a taut nipple, tracing the lines of my abs, until she reached my waistband. "Maybe I could join you."

"Baby, all you have to do is ask, and you shall receive." Her hands went around my neck as I hoisted her in my arms like she weighed nothing, her legs wrapped around my waist as she rocked against me. "You dirty, too?"

Mallory tossed her head back and laughed, and fuck all if it wasn't the most amazing thing I'd ever seen in my life. She hadn't laughed like that since she joined us, and I would take the feel of it crawling over my skin like a lover's caress to my fucking eternal grave in hell.

"I'm always dirty when you're around, Cass."

Fuck.

This girl was the only one on the planet who could bring me to heel with nothing more than my name, and I hoped she never realized how much power she held over me or I'd be done for.

"Well, let's go be dirty together."

Exactly one shower and two rounds of amazing shower sex later, I'd managed to roust up a clean outfit and get the both of us presentable. By the time we wandered out of my room, the others had rounded up and returned to the home base. Ace and Spade stood in the kitchen, chatting about an upcoming fight he thought he was well enough to enter, and BlackJack was predictably sprawled on a nearby couch, soaking up all the chatter without contributing in the least.

Some things never changed.

I tugged Mallory into the commons by her arm and slingshotted her in BlackJack's direction, knowing damn well she'd make herself comfortable on the couch, curled up against him.

She'd been working her hoodoo therapist magic on the big lug, and though he still wasn't handing out hugs around the room like an old granny at family dinners, he let her touch him, and he touched her back. I wasn't sure how far they'd gone, but BlackJack had always liked his privacy, so we didn't pry.

And Mallory wasn't the type to kiss and tell unless she was trying to play me and Spade against each other.

Which she did whenever the mood struck her.

"Go play nice with tall, dark, and brooding, doc," I teased, shooting the man in question a wink when he rolled his eyes and growled under his breath like an angry bear. The second Mallory was within reach, though, he reached out and tugged her into his lap, one of his legs stretched along the back of the couch, caging her in as she put her back against his chest and curled her head on his shoulder. His chin rested gently atop her thick mane of chestnut tresses, and with a jealous sigh, I moved into the kitchen and cleared my throat.

"Hey, assholes, if you two are done arguing about paid brawls, we should probably get the whole gang up to speed and make a plan of action."

I knew the moment Ace realized things had truly changed around here. It was the second his eyes found BlackJack and Mallory tangled on the couch, his hand gently trailing through her hair as she scrolled through his phone.

"You follow some of the weirdest accounts on Twitter, you know that?" she teased him, holding up what looked like a deep fake of a prolific government hacker's account. Little did she know, that probably was the real deal. They'd gotten good at hiding in plain sight. And BlackJack never followed anyone without reason.

Ace had frozen pretty much in place as he walked into the room, his jaw nearly unhinged from the rest of his face as he stared in disbelief at the scene in front of him.

Spade nudged him in the back, trying to get past. "Hello, this isn't a parking lot; move yer ass, man."

Ace's attention was successfully diverted as he smarted from Spade's belligerent mouthiness.

"I would scroll my own," Mallory whined, "but Ace took it. Says I can't be trusted."

BlackJack's eyes drifted over to where his boss stood, a whole plethora of confusing emotions whipping around on Ace's face as he struggled to regain his self-control. "Give her the phone back, Ace. She's not hurting anyone with it."

That worked to snap him out of his daze. "She could be in cahoots with the cops, working as an informant to bring us down in return for some reward–"

"Bullshit," I joined in, growing more irate by the second. "We'd know. BlackJack cloned her phone; we see anything going in and out–"

"You did what?"

Mallory's eyes were wide, and I realized belatedly I fucked up. Me and my big, fat mouth.

"Fuck."

BlackJack grabbed her arms before she could lunge at me over the couch, tugging her against himself. "Hey, now, it was necessary. Just a precaution."

"You didn't tell me about this precaution why?"

He shrugged, shutting down on her in the face of her anger. "You didn't need to know."

Ace looked smug as fuck, sitting in his wingback chair, his lips curled in a feral grin as he stared at Mallory with an unshielded look of conquest. "See? Even those lovesick fools know better than to trust you completely."

"Fuck you," she spat, throwing BlackJack's phone at his head. She was out of her seat and on the move in seconds, and so was Ace, after narrowly missing the projectile aimed at his head.

"Well, that went well," I muttered, flopping down in Ace's place as their shouting match trailed down the hallway and up the stairs. "Should we go after them?"

"Leave them go," Spade muttered. "It's about time their bullshit come to a head, anyhow."

JOKER

CHAPTER THIRTY-SEVEN
ACE

If this woman got any more irritating, I'd fucking fling myself from the roof of this building to spare myself the trouble of dealing with her.

Miss Stanton would do well to learn her fucking place around here.

I'd tell her as much the second I caught hold of her.

I watched her duck into Joker's room and slam the door behind her, but she had to know I'd get through that flimsy ass paneling. No tiny chunk of wood was going to stop me this time.

A few weeks away from this place was supposed to remind me of my roots. Remind me where I came from, help me control the beast inside myself. Instead, all it had done was remind me why I left my fucking country to begin with.

My family had always been Yakuza, as long as I'd been alive, as long as they'd been recording their history. But they hadn't always been dishonorable men. The newer leaders ushered in a world of violence and bullshit that went against the code established generations before, when samurais and seppuku were popular and gunning down innocents to make a statement was not.

These new men cared only for the power and wealth that came

with it. They didn't care about their neighborhoods, the places their families grew up, lived, thrived. They ruled with fear and took from those weaker than them, offering no protection, helping none on their way to riches and glory.

Fuck anyone in their way.

I remembered that I'd abandoned those practices because I had always wanted to be an honorable man.

And here I was, chasing a woman against her will down my own fucking hallway, planning all manner of unmentionable, unthinkable acts against her person to punish her.

Hell, if I had my way, I'd drag her right back into the commons and shove her to her knees, fuck her raw, and leave her there with my seed splattered against her ass for the others to see.

She was ours, but she wouldn't control us. She needed to learn, even though she chose to stay here, she wasn't one of us. She might be a little jaded by life, but she wasn't a Wildcard and never would be.

"Oh, Miss Stanton, you might as well unlock that door and give yourself over. If I have to break it down to get to you, it won't be pretty."

I put my hand against the door and waited. Surely she'd be smart enough to see the error of her ways.

When the sound of a lock being disengaged wasn't forthcoming, I slammed my hand against the wood, growling under my breath at her stubbornness.

"I'll give you one more chance, Miss Stanton. Then, I'll drag you out by your hair and show you what I do to bitches who think they're in control here."

I hardly recognized the man I was becoming. I'd always had such a firm grip on this nasty side of myself, but around the doc, I lost all grasp on my sanity. She made me feel things I'd long since stopped feeling, made me half out of my mind with frustration and anger and rage and–

Fuck, I wanted things I had no business wanting, felt things I had no business feeling. She twisted my whole fucking existence and set it on its head, and she'd been doing so since she first sprayed me in the fucking face with that watered-down bullshit excuse for mace she carried in her purse.

"Fuck off, Ace, I'm not coming out," she yelled through the door, fanning the flames of my ire even higher.

I reared back and slammed a booted foot right in the middle of the door, just missing the lock and handle. The satisfying sound of splintering wood beneath my heel made my cock hard in my pants, and with another heft of my foot, the door was left swinging from its hinges, a little worse for wear but still somewhat solid. It gaped open to reveal a very pissed-off Mallory Stanton, standing dead center of the room, in one of my tees, no less, and a short pair of shorts, her arms folded over her chest, her hair in a convenient ponytail, staring me down like I was the one in the wrong here.

Fuck that. This was my compound, my crew, my fucking castle, and if anyone was in the wrong here, it was the bitch playing at queen without permission. She was nothing more than a little girl putting on her mother's shoes, makeup, and fancy pearls, dancing around the room pretending to be a grown-up.

"You're playing with a dangerous man, Miss Stanton," I purred, stalking her like a big cat stalks its prey. I circled her as I stepped into the room, and she turned with me, keeping her eyes on mine, never backing down.

Good. I hated when they backed down. I *hated* a fucking coward.

This one had spunk. Maybe not a lot of brains, but she had spunk.

She lifted a brow and smiled that lopsided grin Spade wore half the time. "What makes you think I'm not used to playing with dangerous men, huh?"

I snorted. "Just because you're flinging pussy around and using it to mind control my fucking men doesn't mean it'll work on me, sweetheart."

Her other brow joined the first as her lips twitched. "Not your sweetheart, asshole."

"You are whatever I say you are, Miss Stanton. You're *mine,* and as such, I'll call you however I please."

"You can call me anything you want, I guess," she sassed when my back was to the far wall and hers was to the door, "but I won't come when you call just because you demand it. Even dogs have their limit."

"Good thing you're not a dog, eh?"

"The only bitch I see here is you."

With that parting shot, she took off, slamming the door in my face as she fled the safety of Joker's room. Broken though it was from my earlier assault, it still hung me up, and I growled and snarled with frustration as my hands clawed at the broken wood, flinging it from my path.

"When I catch you, bitch, it's game over. You're not going to like your consolation prize."

My taunt echoed down the hall, but she gave no indication of where she was.

Forced to hunt. I suppose there are worse homecoming gifts.

And once I had my hands around her pretty little throat, I'd choke the fucking life from her for leading me around by my damned nose. I didn't like the lack of control she made me feel, the absolute unmooring of my iron-fisted lead over this crew. At this point, if I gave an order the bitch didn't like, I had no doubt they'd mutiny to make her happy.

Dammit! This wasn't supposed to happen.

She was supposed to be a pretty little distraction, not something they fell head over heels in lust with. Spade had been gone from the moment she drove a knife into his shoulder, and I'd been too blind to see it. Joker followed not long after, but he and his drunken bullshit having got us in the situation in the first place had nothing on the fact that the man was so starved for affection and attention that he'd take it however he could get it.

And BlackJack. Cuddling on the couch with her like he hadn't cringed away from any sort of physical touch for the last ten years of his life.

What the fuck had happened to my men?

Was I the last sane one of the bunch?

"Come out, come out, wherever you are, little bitch," I growled, sliding around the corner at the end of the hall to peer into Spade's room.

Nothing.

But his torture room door was cracked open.

Interesting.

If she went in there, perhaps she was braver than I gave her credit for.

My footsteps were silent as I crossed the pin-neat room in darkness, half-crouched as every step brought me nearer to my target. I was so convinced she was behind that door I didn't bother with preamble; I simply thrust it open and strode in like a confident fuck, knowing damn well there was no possible way she could overpower me.

"Okay, the game's over, Miss Stanton, time to pay up." I spread my hands wide and pretended that every nerve ending in my body wasn't alight with lust, the same desire to rut and dominate her that no doubt flowed through my men's veins now raced through mine.

Not that I'd ever admit that to her or anyone. Hell, if it were between me and my gods, I still wouldn't utter that out loud.

Yeah, so what, she got my cock hard. Most pretty women could do that. She was a nuisance, a distraction, one my men and I couldn't afford anymore.

So I'd do what was needed. I'd dominate her, break her, and take away their little plaything so they could focus on the task at hand–sussing out our enemy and eliminating the threat on our lives.

Like they should have been doing all along, not playing house with a fucking captive.

I was so ensconced in the trenches of my own victory, so distracted by my guaranteed win, that I didn't notice the sound of the door swinging closed behind me until the latch and slam home of a bolt echoed in the empty room around me.

And then the lights went out, and fuck all if I wasn't left in the damn darkness, silence surrounding me, no chance of escape, no hint as to where the little minx was hiding, nothing.

"I don't know what you think you're going to do, but you can't overpower me, Miss Stanton," I chuckled darkly, closing my eyes, listening for anything–a telltale footstep, the drag of a heel, the sound of a breath, even a rustling fabric. She gave nothing away, damn her, and there were any number of weapons on the walls in here that I had no idea if Spade even locked up.

"You're right," sounded her voice to the left of me, and I spun, only to realize it had moved with her next words. "I can't overpower you. But I can make you feel helpless. Weak. Afraid." I spun once more, but she shifted again, and now the words were behind me. "Like you did with me."

The feel of cold steel pressed against the base of my neck had my blood running cold, the heat from our little game of cat and mouse replaced by something more visceral, more dangerous.

She had a fucking gun.

How?

Even in here, Spade didn't keep firearms, and I didn't think any of the guys were stupid enough to have given her one, so that meant she'd found one stashed around here somewhere.

I didn't feel comfortable assuming that she also hadn't found ammo.

Whatever idiot left an unlocked weapon lying around would get an earful when I got out of here.

"Okay, Miss Stanton," I muttered, calmly taking a deep breath. I refused to let her think she'd won somehow. But I also wasn't an idiot, so I simply stayed calm and held my position. "What do you think you're going to do with that gun?"

She shoved it harder into my spine, and I winced at the bite of the steel, the way my skin curled around its' invasion. "You're going to do what I say with no argument; you got that, boss man?"

My lips twitched, anger building in my gut, but I nodded slowly.

"Good," she twittered, the metal moving away from my skin. "Now, go ahead and walk forward until you feel the chair, and take a seat, Ace," she commanded.

I wasn't sure what would come from this foray into her little game, but my whole body was alive with the promise of a fight. Adrenaline pounded through my veins as my knee bumped into the metal chair Spade tied all his victims to before ripping off fingernails, beating them to a pulp, or whatever vile manner of torture he inflicted on them. It amazed me to no end he hadn't brought this minx in here to suffer at his hand. It'd probably get him the fuck off.

"I'm waiting, Miss Stanton," I taunted, my voice like butter in the thick air as she shuffled forward.

I felt the gun at my temple again and swore under my breath as she straddled my lap and jerked the light on above us, bathing us in a dim yellow glow.

"So, you like to be in control, huh?" The cool metal slid down the side of my jaw, much like I'd done to her all those nights ago on the counter, before forcing her to her knees and feeding her my cock to prove a point.

I swore that night I'd never again touch her, that she'd never get my cock. I'd be the only one who wouldn't bend to her feminine charms.

But with her straddling my lap, a gun to my head, a sick, broken smile on her lips, something in me stirred against my will, racing to my cock to force it to attention for her. Something I didn't like. Something I wasn't altogether comfortable with.

"I won't fuck you," I insisted, biting my tongue when she rolled her hips with a little giggle that sounded slightly unhinged. "I'm not like the others. You can't pussy whip me."

"I don't want you whipped, Ace," she insisted, the gun under my chin now. "I want you to feel the way you make me feel every time you come near me." Her hands ran through my chin-length hair and yanked back, forcing my head to follow, baring my throat to her. "I want you to hate yourself for the way you feel when I touch you." Those pretty lips of hers brushed against my throat, the barrel of the gun right next to them, clashing with one another–cold and hot, hard and soft.

"I want you to admit you want this."

My breathing grew labored as she palmed the half-hard cock in my pants, growling at my ear as the barrel of that gun cut into my skin, a twinge of pain following the twist of her wrist as the little red raised sight at the end roughed up my Adam's apple.

"I don't want anything from you, bitch," I spat, hoping she'd back off if I asserted my absolute refusal of her. If I denied myself the pleasure she offered, maybe I could look myself in the mirror tomorrow. "I won't fuck you."

"So you've said," she drawled, and I realized perhaps something else had changed about her while I was gone. She'd spent weeks as Spade's little plaything; perhaps he twisted a small part of her while I wasn't here to watch him. "But I don't think you mean it."

I felt her weight leave my lap and breathed a tiny sigh of relief, one that stuck in my throat as she let the gun trail down my chest and stomach until the fucker was pointed right in my lap.

Her laugh was almost feral. "How's it feel to have a gun between *your* legs, Ace? Feel good?"

So it was an eye for an eye she was playing, was it? Despite my usual desire to control all aspects of my life, I felt myself rise to her challenge, the beast within me getting off a little on the danger.

"Well, I don't know, personally, it would probably feel better if I had a hole to fuck down there, but you wouldn't know about that, would you, sweetheart?"

I could just make out her wide eyes and parted lips as she let out a shocked gasp, reared back, and scowled at my pertinent mouth. "Fuck you, Ace," she growled, and that's when that pistol came down on the corner of my temple and knocked me right the fuck out.

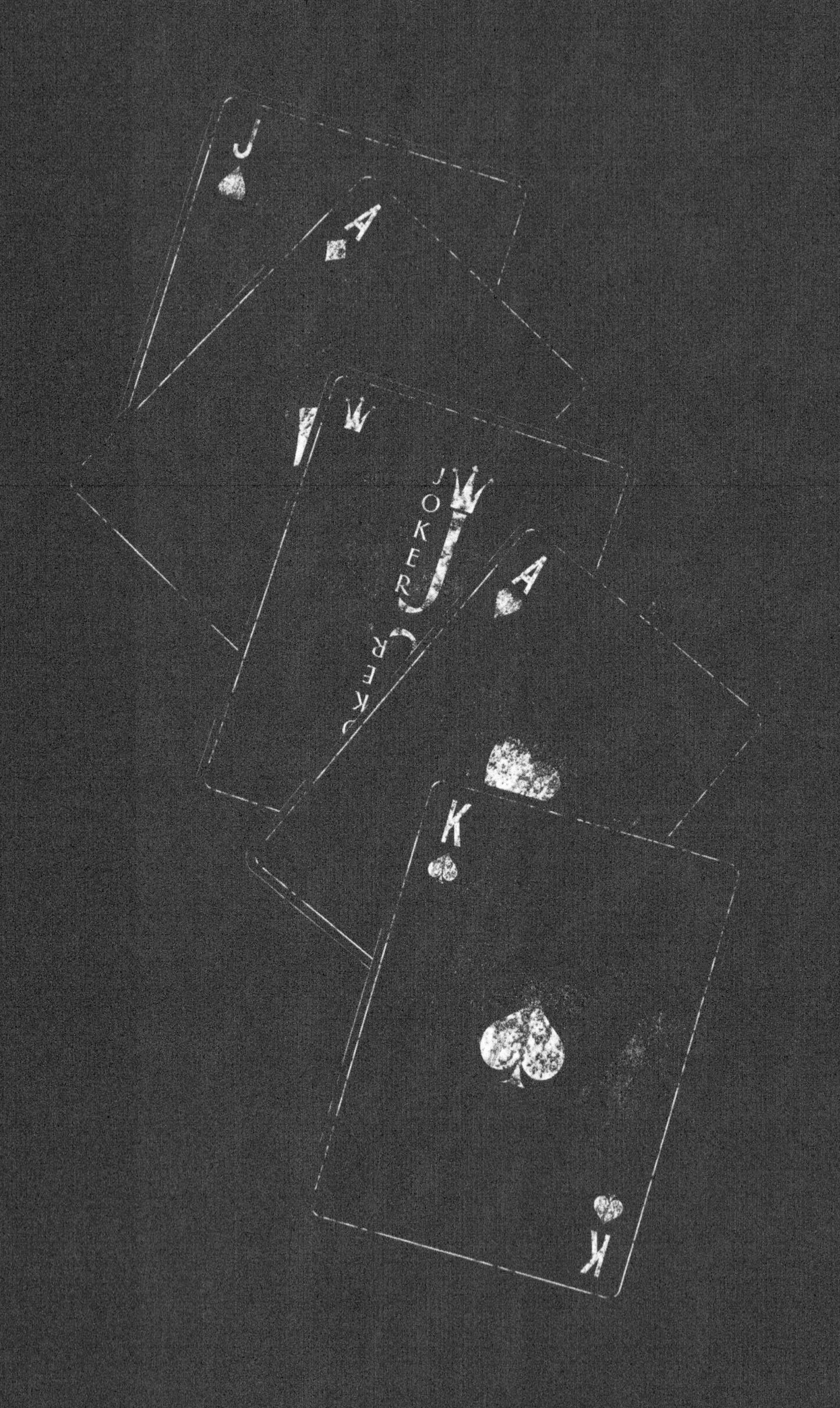
JOKER

CHAPTER THIRTY-EIGHT
MALLORY

"Oh, fuck, I killed him," I muttered, watching as he slumped in the chair and his eyes rolled back into his head. "Fuck."

Fuck fuck fuck.

I rushed over to the door and hesitated on the threshold, weighing my options.

Option one: bring one of the guys in on this as security.

Option two: handle it like a big girl and deal with the fallout.

It had been my decision to instigate him. My decision to talk back. I knew he wasn't in the right mindset to taunt, but I did it anyhow.

When I fled him on foot and holed up in Joker's room, the walk to the bathroom had been completely automatic, as had the feel of my hand wrapping around the grip of that gun as I ripped it and the ammo from beneath the counter and loaded it up.

I wouldn't shoot him; that was a given. I didn't have the stomach to do it, but maybe if I waved it in his face a little, it might save my ass.

Ace was dangerous at times, and I'd poked a bear for fun. Therapist though I was, a sick part of me enjoyed being threatened—hurt, even. I wanted the power struggle between me and their fearless leader. So much, in fact, it seemed that that enjoyment and thrill overrode the common sense in my brain and blocked out all rational thought.

I circled him in the room and led him on a hell of a chase right into Spade's torture room. I wouldn't question why he left it unlocked, and I'd been in here a time or two in the week Ace had been gone, mainly to find creative new uses for the chains that hung from his ceiling.

But this time, something new unfurled in my stomach as I ran, as Ace chased me and growled into the darkness like some fucking panther, coiled, ready to strike.

I was horny as fuck.

I wanted this man, and it did no good to deny it. I'd wanted him since he put me on my knees in the kitchen and demanded I suck him off. I'd never been one for submitting, but something about him made me want to. It stirred a desire in me to fight, to rail against the rules and order imposed on me by this man who most certainly thought he owned me, but did not.

And after his antics in the kitchen, both times, I was about done with his bullshit. He took my phone, made me uncomfortable in the one place I always felt happy these days, and held me against my will with the threat of death.

And I was so sick of being his toy.

His little prize.

I had no idea what he'd initially planned for me, whether it was to be the guys' plaything, to keep them occupied and help relieve some stress, or if this was all a power flex for him. But I did know one thing for sure.

Ace wanted me as much as I had started to want him, and now that I'd had a taste, and so had he, things were at a standstill until one or both of us gave in.

My whole body sang with the familiar hum of adrenaline, and I slipped the clip out of the bottom of the pistol grip before I shut off the light in Spade's torture room and waited. The only light in here to guide me was the sliver of fluorescence coming from the hall and through his room.

And then Ace walked right into my trap, and suddenly, I didn't want to play coy anymore. I watched as his cockiness and swagger shored up the image he'd built of himself, secure in the knowledge that he could overpower me once I showed myself.

Taking the gun had been a split-second decision, but it now felt like a very good one.

I tugged his shirt off, carefully tossing his clothing over a nearby table so it didn't get dirty, and then used the belt around his waist to strap his hands behind his back. I didn't know how long he'd be out, but a man like him probably had a high pain tolerance, as well as a good rebound time. It came with the territory of his chosen profession, right?

When he finally started to stir, I crouched on my haunches at his feet, smiling up into his face as those gorgeous, deep eyes opened and met mine with hatred and spite and something else, something fiery that even he fought inside himself.

Lust.

I knew you wanted me, fucker.

"Wakey wakey," I sang, nudging his knee with the tip of the gun, careful not to reveal its' ammo-less state. I might not be willing to shoot a man, but that didn't mean I wanted him to know I wasn't actually capable of it. "Nice to see you're back with us, bud."

My whole body felt like a rubber band stretched taut, near to snapping with the anxious energy that rebounded inside me. I smiled as he watched me stretch out first one leg, then the other, side to side, bouncing on the balls of my feet as his eyes were irrefutably drawn to them one by one.

He was no less affected by me than I was by him.

And then he tried to move his arms and the realization of what I'd done washed over him all at once.

Rage, betrayal, frustration, defeat, confusion, and arousal all played over his features like the most subtle of symphonies, warring with his brain to make sense of the situation.

"You fucking tied me up," he whispered, awe and anger intertwined in his tone. "You've got to be fucking kidding me."

"Not as much of a weak bitch as you assumed I'd be, now, am I, Ace?" I reached for his pants and smirked wider when he tried to angle his hips away from me, as if he could possibly get away. "Now, now, let's not do that. You're pretty heavy for a skinny Asian guy, and picking you up off the floor isn't on my list of things to do tonight."

No, what *was* on the schedule tonight was much more fun, now that I was allowing myself some free liberty here.

I was going to take away his power by fucking his brains out, and when he finally broke and breathed my name, I'd walk away and leave him here, wanting, like he'd done to me in the kitchen when he set me up and threatened to kill me.

Maybe if he were a good boy, I'd even let him bust a nut inside me. After all, I had a thing for that, apparently. Or at least *Spade* seemed to think so.

Who knew?

He stopped struggling, and as a reward, I let my fingers trail over the prominent bulge in his pants, one he stared down at like it had betrayed him in the worst of ways. And I guess, in a way, it had.

He'd tried to demean me with it, tried to deny the way he felt toward me, but in the end, his dick couldn't hide the truth–the thought of fucking me left him weak.

I wanted him weak. As weak as he made me feel with that knife to my throat. Or the gun in my pussy.

"Now here's what's going to happen, Ace," I drawled, the gun waving around to punctuate the words spilling from my mouth. "You're going to sit still and take it like the good dog you are, and I'm going to show you what it feels like to have your choice taken from you. To be held at literal gunpoint while your body betrays you. I'll make you desperate for a reprieve while your body rushes headlong toward a release you don't want." I tapped his cheek with the barrel of my gun when he looked away and grumbled under his breath, bringing his eyes back to me. "If you behave, maybe I'll even let you get off."

His eyes were blown, pupils dilated, and his breathing erratic as he leered at me, jaw tight and body rigid. "So you're going to rape me, is that it, Miss Stanton?"

I smiled at him and slipped my shorts down my legs, letting them pool on the floor, not a care in the world to whether or not they'd be wearable when I got done here. "You can't rape the willing, Ace. You taught me that."

I saw the defeat and resignation slide into his eyes the second his own words slammed into his head. Like a boomerang coming home, those words hit different when you weren't the one saying them.

"Fuck you," he spat, his eyes drawn to my legs even as his shirt fell over my thighs and hid everything from view.

"You will, soon enough," I returned, a smile on my lips and a laugh bubbling in my throat. "And you'll love every fucking minute of it."

His pants were tight across his obvious erection, and I took pity on him, freeing the fucker from the confines of his slacks with a flick of my wrist. That cock sprang free, and he hissed as the cool air hit it, my eyes widening as it throbbed against my hand.

His lips thinned as he stared me down, much like a cobra preparing to strike, whose fangs had already been removed. He held no bite, and I wasn't afraid of him anymore. Temporary bravery, but bravery nonetheless.

His shoulders tightened as my free hand caressed his thigh through the soft fabric of his pants, earning a responsive, eager jerk from his member and a moan between pursed lips. He was fighting this, but we both knew he wouldn't win.

And I deserved every fucking minute of his eventual surrender.

My body fell flush against his as I straddled his waist and sat down, lips curling upward as his cock brushed against my folds, still twitching and eager, though he pretended he wasn't. But this wasn't about to be over that easily–he hadn't made it easy on me, so I wasn't about to make it easy on him.

"Doesn't feel like you're fighting me, Ace," I whispered, lips at his earlobe as I nipped at the cartilage there, rocking my hips against him as he bit back a groan. Pride swelled in me–I was about to bring the leader of this group to his knees for me, and all it was going to take was one good ride. "Go ahead, fight me. I want you to resist."

His eyes never left mine any time they were within view, and the fire burning in his steely gaze had my pussy clenching on air, desperate for his particular kind of beast to break free and ravage me.

The others were fun, no doubt about it, but Joker was sweet, Spade was fast and rough, BlackJack–well, I wasn't sure what he was, but I had the feeling he'd be the soft one. Ace struck me as a man whose body could bend you until you broke, pleading for the privilege and thanking him for the abuse. He had a sinful mouth and a rabid stare that reminded me of being chased by a dangerous animal, and I wanted to be caught.

I needed to be caught. Something in me, something broken, needed to know that even the beast could lose control. That I had some semblance of power.

We both knew any imagined power was nothing more than an illusion, but it was an illusion that would serve my psyche well.

"You want this, don't you, Ace?" I taunted, arching my back as my tits pressed against his chest and my hair cascaded over my shoulders and down my back. "Too stubborn to admit it."

His answering growl had me wetter than a fucking water hose. "I don't want you," he snapped, eyes narrowed near to slits, lips curled in a snarl. "When I get free–"

I trailed a finger down the side of his neck, the gun barrel mirroring the move on the opposite side. "When you get free, I'm sure there will be hell to pay, but for now, I'll have some fun, and who knows? Maybe when I'm done, you'll forget all about punishing me and stop denying what we both know to be true."

"You shrinks are all alike," he groaned, his hips rocking up into mine despite him. "Thinking you know what's in my head just because you've got a fancy license."

I moaned wantonly as his thick cock slipped between my folds and teased at the juncture of my thighs beneath the shield of his tee.

"Fuck, Ace, if fucking me isn't what's on your mind now, you're a terrible liar."

He didn't answer that one, too busy fighting the obvious truths that played out across his face–his eyelids drifted shut as his head fell back, and he groaned at the feeling, the deep rumble doing things to my insides I wasn't even prepared for. His shoulders strained the belt's leather as he fought to put his hands on me, and a tiny part of me reveled in his state of constraint.

It was a fitting comparison for the way he'd held me in contempt, in check, since I first arrived here.

I rocked forward and lifted my hips just so, letting his cock notch against my opening, teasing myself as I let just the head of him slip inside my eager, waiting channel.

"F-f-fuck," he whispered as I took another blissful inch, then pulled back, leaving him dangling right there, a mere hair's breadth away from heaven.

"Admit you want this," I panted, needing him inside me like yesterday. I was torturing both of us now, there was no avoiding it, but it didn't mean I liked it. "Give in and tell me you want me, and it'll all be over."

"Go to hell," he spat in reply, though when I repeated the motion, some very broken and confusing sounds ripped from his throat. Somewhere between a moan and a laugh, the musical timbre skated across my nerve endings and had me wanting nothing more than to make him make it again.

"Already there," I ground out, taking another inch of him, pleased when the vein on his neck popped out as he struggled against his bonds. "And I'm taking you down with me."

When my hips rolled once more, his groan ended with a gasp. Sweat beaded on his forehead as he struggled to maintain his image of self-control, but his hips told another story as they damn near lifted the chair from the ground in his search to bury himself in me.

His body had given up the fight; I just needed to hear him say it.

"Come on, Ace, admit it." I nipped at his lower lip, my tongue smoothing over the surface as I teased his mouth with my own. "Tell me you want this. You want *me.*"

I squealed as he grinned in my face and tipped the chair backward, toppling us both to the floor with a maniacal laugh.

JOKER

CHAPTER THIRTY-NINE
ACE

The idea was a solid ten. Tipping us over to get the upper hand on her was the only way I knew I'd be able to dislodge her and possibly loosen my bindings. What I hadn't counted on was the absolute agony of landing on shoulders stretched too far, adding extra pressure on already tortured limbs.

And my cock, the smug fuck, hadn't bothered to free himself from the confines of her tight, willing hole. In fact, as her full weight fell atop me, she inadvertently sank down on the whole of my length and ripped a fucking feral, animalistic groan from my lips as I filled her to the fucking brim and she clung to my shaft like a second skin.

I'd fought this desire for so long, and now it was all in vain. She'd managed to get what she wanted, which was my cock inside her.

But I'd never give her my complete submission, my surrender. She wouldn't get that. Never that.

"Why do you have to make everything so damn hard?" she complained, her legs still straddling me, though the feeling of being filled to the brim must have been a bit of a consolation prize, if her languid smile was any indication.

"Untie me and find out how hard I can make things," I snarled, teeth clicking as they snapped together like a croc's.

Her answering smile was addicting. It spread over her face slowly, like a color-changing mood ring, one great wave of alteration that left me breathless, though I'd never admit it.

"You'd like that, wouldn't you?" Her hands splayed over my chest, and I struggled to breathe as the full implications of her skin on mine struggled to the surface of my addled mind. "I won't be untying you anytime soon, mister. You'll take what I give you with a fucking smile on those pretty lips of yours."

"When I get free–"

She didn't give me a chance to finish the threat. Instead of listening to my verbal abuse, she rose up on her knees and fell back down on my waiting cock, bouncing eagerly atop me as she wrecked my whole fucking existence.

Denying I wanted her wasn't an option anymore. I might not have admitted it out loud, but my body told her what I refused to–she could read it in every rise of my hips as she pulled herself up off my length, in every shallow breath as her body swallowed me whole again, relentless, desperate, needy.

I lay there, in pain and irritated beyond belief, with a beautiful woman bouncing on my very eager cock, dragging my soul from my body with every little salacious moan that fled her lips like a bird regaining its wings. I felt parts of me tear apart, rended limb from limb as her nails scored little red trails down my chest, her eyes rolled back in her head like an overwhelmed goddess taking her pittance.

My shoulders flexed once more as she let the gun drift away from my head, my wrists twisting in the slightly less tight leather. My fall had done more than just upset our balance–it worked to partially free me. And if I managed to get all the way free–and I would–I'd show her how big of a mistake she'd made here.

Fuck the gun. Fuck my life. I needed to take back my control.

"Jesus, Ace, you feel so fucking fantastic inside me."

Her hips rose and fell in a serpentine fashion, much like a cobra in the hands of a snake charmer, but instead of me luring the movements out of her, she lured matching ones out of me, my hips rolling in time with hers, the dance between our bodies like the most beautiful, perfectly choreographed duet. Hell, it was like watching an artist paint the finest art, each thrust like a brush stroke, each moan a dip in the paint.

The urge to take over grew with every second I lay there beneath her, buried inside her, and now I couldn't remember why I'd fought her in the first place. Surely there wasn't a good enough reason on the planet to deny myself the pleasure of fucking this absolutely divine pussy.

Hell, no wonder my men were so gone for her.

My left wrist slipped from the grip of the belt, and soon, my right followed, and before Miss Stanton had a second to process what was happening, I'd rolled us so she was under me, the chair abandoned, my arms braced on either side of her head as she pointed that gun right between my eyes and stilled with my cock still inside her.

"How'd you get out?" she gasped, her hips canted as that delectable body sought out my touch, the movement she'd been in charge of until moments ago.

I quirked a brow and looked past the muzzle of the pistol, our eyes locked in a battle of wills as my lips spread in a feral grin. Sweat dripped off the end of my nose and onto her cheek, but she didn't seem to care. Her hands stayed steady, and her eyes never wavered.

"You don't use a man's belt as a restraint, Miss Stanton," I growled, thrusting against her pointedly. She rewarded me with a little squeak, and my smile only grew wider. "I'm well-versed in the finer uses of that strap of leather, and you did it wrong. Perhaps someday soon, I'll teach you how to really restrain someone with it."

I rolled my hips again and she moaned this time, her cunt fluttering prettily around me as she rocked against me and wrapped those long, supple legs around my waist, riding me from below. Soon, it was all I could do to hold onto my sanity as she shuddered around me and her eyes fluttered closed, that gun wavering just enough–

It wasn't an opportunity I planned to miss. With a flick of the wrist, I'd disarmed her without even stopping my thrusts, still rutting into her like a beast on the filthy concrete floor as her eyes flew wide and followed the trajectory of the pistol.

Her eyes weren't so brave anymore, now that she didn't have anything to defend herself against the beast above, but I wasn't going to hurt her.

Not anymore.

No, now all I wanted to do was imprint myself on the inside of her soul and leave a piece of each other buried there for the other to carry with them. I wanted to worm up inside of her, curl up, and die a happy man.

I wanted Miss Mallory Stanton, and the last little wall in my head finally crumbled as I admitted it to myself.

"Hold on, Miss Stanton," I growled, wrapping her legs around me a bit tighter before I rose from the floor, bringing her with me, my cock never leaving her sweet, sweet hole.

One of the only times being blessed with a big dick was utterly beneficial, I supposed.

Once she was in my arms, her hands wrapped around my neck, all bets were off. I slammed her back into the hard metal wall and fucked up into her willing pussy, snarling expletives in her ear as she shuddered around me; I moved across the room and stopped against the door, my back to it this time as she rocked against *me,* fucking herself on my shaft while I groaned and shoved the door open. If it weren't for the fact that I had no idea how often Spade changed his sheets, I'd have stopped right there and fucked her in his bed before moving on.

I managed to get her into the hall before I stopped to rut like a beast again, pinning her hands above her head, her ass sitting just on the edge of a stand smack in the middle of the walkway. She arched against me, her keening mewls of pleasure only building the pressure behind my balls.

I couldn't get enough of her, and I'd already had too much, and now I'd never fucking let her go.

But first . . .

"You have been a bad fucking girl tonight, sweetheart," I whispered in her ear, my teeth grazing the sensitive flesh just below her dainty lobe at the juncture of her throat. "I'm going to have to teach you who's boss."

My teeth bit down into her skin, my cock twitching at her surprised yelp of pain, even as she tightened around me and canted her hips.

My little bird liked pain.

How intriguing.

Those glorious tresses cascaded down her back as she panted with need, thrusting those perfect tits out for my perusal as she tossed her head back on a moan. "Fuck, you gonna put that pistol in my pussy again?"

So it appeared she liked that, too.

"Would you like that?" I asked genuinely, my voice raspy, my whole equilibrium wrecked. At her nod, I chuckled, taking a peaked nipple in my mouth as it enticingly bounced in front of me. "Well," I muttered around the stiff peak, "it wouldn't be much of a punishment if you enjoyed it, sweetheart."

"I won't tell."

God, even when she was being a brat, she was fucking phenomenal.

I lifted her in my arms again, hands splayed over her firm ass, fingers spreading her open to take me deeper as I strode quickly to my office–my room was too far, and I was losing patience quickly. I didn't even bother to shut the door–if one of those fuckers came along and had something to say about the show she was putting on, I'd throw my fist through their face with a smile on mine as I filled Miss Stanton with my future children.

Children.

Pregnancy.

"You're on birth control?" I growled as I set her ass on the edge of my desk and leaned over her with one arm, shoving *everything* off the top of the ostentatious mahogany monstrosity so I could lay her back against it.

"Yeah," she muttered, her cheeks stained a faint shade of pink. "I'm safe."

"Oh, you're far from safe, but that's not what I asked, Miss Stanton." I thrust into her again and gripped her thighs, tugging her fully against me as I threw her ankles over my shoulders and folded my new favorite bitch in half. "You're mine, and I don't like unexpected surprises, remember?"

She bit her lip but nodded her understanding as I brought a hand between us and swirled the pad of my thumb around her clit, picking up the pace with a groan. I was so fucking close to blowing my load inside her it was criminal, but I wanted to draw this out. Really enjoy the moment.

She was too intoxicating, too dangerous. Too alluring.

I'd drown in her fucking pussy all day, every day if I had my way, and that wasn't conducive to my work.

"I want you to come on my cock," I commanded, a growl in my voice that had her panting faster, her eyelids drifting shut, lip fastened securely between her perfectly even teeth. "Come on, Miss Stanton, you know you want to."

The feisty little minx shook her head at me, tossing that wavy mane of hair side to side as she fought the urge to let go and shatter around me. "Not until you admit it," she panted, her hands twisting in my hair, curling around my bicep, those sharp nails digging in like an inescapable vice. "Admit you want this."

"I'm not admitting to shit," I ground out, my finger on her clit intensifying. "Now you've got two choices—you can come with my cock buried in you, or I can pull it out right now and make you wish you'd taken the easier option."

I saw the flash of fire in her eyes a second too late, and her feline smile spread languidly over that gorgeous, alluring face. "If you can't admit you want me, then I can't be bothered to come on command, asshole."

Fuck.

She always had to do things the hard way.

"Suit yourself, sweetheart," I growled, yanking my dick out of her tight heat with a groan of pure, unadulterated loss. My cock nearly wept with the desire to be back inside her, my balls ached with the need to come inside her, but if denial was what she wanted, denial was what she'd get.

A small part of myself was under the illusion that if I ignored the urge to fill her with my seed, I could pretend she didn't have control over me, that my body was still mine to control.

Even though we both knew it wasn't.

I fisted myself and put my other hand in her hair, dragging her to the end o the desk and down to the floor, where she eagerly fell to her knees. A flash of hesitation and frustration washed over me as I realized there was nothing sexual I could do to her that would feel like I was winning. It was as if she had no limits, as if any sort of interaction with her was reward enough. She was eager and willing no matter what I did.

But then I shook it off and returned to the task at hand.

"Open your mouth and stick out your tongue, Miss Stanton. I'm going to come all over your tongue, and you're going to swallow it down like a good girl. Then, you'll climb right up here on my desk and let me finish you off."

She scrambled to acquiesce, even going so far as to reach out and take me in hand herself, shooing me off my own cock as she worked her talented fingers up and down my length, swallowing me whole instead of waiting for me to give her the load she so desperately wanted. Her left hand palmed my balls, and a lone finger teased my puckered hole, drawing a very embarrassing squeak from me as my cock stiffened and I came down her throat, her muscles tightening around me as she swallowed every last fucking drop.

And then she licked her lips and gave me one last parting pump before she climbed atop my desk and waited patiently for me, her legs bent, knees spread, pussy fucking dripping with arousal.

I held her gaze until I could no longer meet it, and turned my focus to her siren slit, licking and sucking and biting like a madman who'd lost his way and believed he'd find it again in her cavern of womanly wonders. My tongue delved deep into her hole, swirling around as I added two thick fingers and fucking rammed into her at breakneck speed, needing to feel her thighs tighten around my ears as she shook from pleasure.

"Let me hear you say my name, Miss Stanton. I want them all to know who has you screaming to the rafters."

"Oh, Ace," she complied, her orgasm building with every breath we took in tandem. *"Ace—"*

I stood up lightning fast, my hand moving to wrap around her throat and strangle the breath from her lungs. I didn't like my code name on her lips. It didn't feel right. Some twisted part of me had given in to her, and now, she'd have proof, but I was well past caring.

Tonight, she could bask in the knowledge that she'd bested me. Tomorrow, we'd go back to how it was, and that was that.

"Call me Kohei, sweetheart."

She didn't get a chance to reply as I leaned over, a hand still buried in her cunt between those creamy thighs, working her to a frenzy as she came around it, shaking like a leaf, my lips tangling with hers and swallowing my name even as the whisper of it caressed my ears like a long-lost lover.

I came again, my load shooting from me against the side of my desk as I groaned and stroked her through the wave of pleasure I'd wrung from her body.

And then the high came crashing down around me, and I realized what I'd done.

Miss Stanton owned a part of me now, one I could never reclaim.

And I didn't feel a bit of shame about it.

JOKER

CHAPTER FORTY
JOKER

The smug fucker kept her as his own little plaything for a whole fucking week. She laid up in his bed, in his room, playing dutiful fucktoy to the boss as we sat around and suffered from her loss. BlackJack was back to being withdrawn, Spade was broody and almost killed a guy he'd been roughing up to get information, and me?

Well, let's just say I wasn't at my highest moment.

I currently sat in my bedroom, with a pair of her panties wrapped around my cock as I jerked off to the memory of her swallowing said appendage with a smile on her lips and a groan in her throat.

Even blowing a load into those silky fuckers didn't assuage the ache in my balls anymore.

I was two steps away from marching right into his office today and demanding her back, but Ace was still at odds with me, and until the Kings were dealt with, it might be wise to avoid any altercations with him.

The familiar buzz of my phone vibrated in my abandoned pants, and I yanked it angrily from its' hiding place and brought the fucker to my ear, growling in whoever's ear was pressed to the other side.

"What the fuck do you want?"

Spade's chuckle greeted me, and what little hardness I still had in my cock went flaccid at his tone.

"Jerking one out, were you?" I didn't grace him with a reply, so he continued. "I'm fighting tonight. The Kings are supposed to be in attendance, and if I don't get back in that ring, I'll lose my cred. Last thing any of us needs is for my good name to shrivel up like your cock."

I rolled my eyes but pulled my sweats on nevertheless. "And this concerns me why?"

"Because you're coming to the match, and you're bringing Mallory with you, dipshit." He huffed, covering the receiver to muffle the sounds around him. "You're all coming, but one of you needs to stay at her side, and maybe if you volunteer for the position, Ace might let her out of his death grip and we can play with her again."

I had to admit, I very much liked the sound of that. "Fine. What do I tell her to wear?"

He growled in my ear, both our minds already on the same track. "Something sexy."

"Why does that not surprise me?"

THE FIGHTS WERE in full swing when the five of us strode into the gym, Spade dressed to the nines in his gear, bouncing around like a fucking fool, his arms windmilling around in a circle as he worked out the kinks of two months out of the ring.

I never once in my life doubted the man, but I had severe misgivings about his capabilities tonight.

Spade at top form was a beast. Spade out of shape and out of practice?

The truest Wildcard of the bunch.

Ace clearly held no such doubt, as he was already off to the bookies to place bets in the man's favor. BlackJack was glued to Mallory's back, his eyes sharper than usual after hearing the Kings were in the building—at least one of them.

Spade was bopping along to her left, like a kid hyped up on candy, teasing her as she blushed prettily and threw fake punches in his direction. I'd never seen him happier to be in his element than he was when she was with him. Until she came on the scene, his pregame routine was to take off to the locker room and brood until they called his name to bash in the skull of some poor sap.

Mallory Stanton might have been a complete accident, but she was a happy accident, and I wouldn't trade her for the world. Being without her felt incomplete, and now that I could put a name to the feeling of constant drift we'd suffered before she was in our lives, I didn't ever want to live that way again.

With the understanding that we'd meet back up when Spade's match started, the four of us split up, Mallory arm in arm with me as I trailed around the ring and eyed every poor sap in the crowd about to lose his weekly winnings, trying desperately to spot the Kings before they spotted us.

Of course, I couldn't get that lucky.

"Hey, Cass, I've gotta hit the bathrooms."

I sneaked a look over at her and pulled her tight against my front, languishing in the feel of our bodies molded together as they should be. We fit like two pieces of the puzzle, and I couldn't deny how good it felt to have her in my arms again.

"You have to hurry, and stay in sight, okay?" I reaffirmed, knowing damn well I'd be in sight the whole time. Still, there were actual pieces of work in the crowd, and I wasn't about to take any chances with her.

"Yes, yes, I know, Cass, I'll be careful." She waved off my concern and trotted off after leaving me with a chaste kiss on the cheek.

If I had my way later, she'd be kissing another part of my body, a lot less chastely.

My eyes stayed glued to her backside as she trotted over to the far wall, unmolested by any of the leering men who dared to look at her. My eyes locked with BlackJack's across the room, and I shook my head.

We didn't need any casualties tonight, not here in the open.

These men might be utter shit, but they were not the target tonight.

The Kings were.

We'd managed to suss out most of the leads we found, and the results weren't pretty. All signs pointed to the old Rizzoli Mafia, trying desperately to stir something up to move in on two of the largest territories in the city. I hadn't managed to pin it on them for sure yet, but it was only a matter of time, and BlackJack was the best intel guy I knew. If anyone could link the bastards to the bad intel, it was him.

We just needed to buy some time.

I waited around for another few minutes before an apprehensive shiver ran down my spine, and I started a slow saunter over to the bathrooms lining the far wall. I'd only turned away for a second, maybe two, to look in BlackJack's direction; there was no way she'd disappeared in that amount of time.

But she wasn't one to take long when she knew we were watching for her.

Mallory knew the risks.

I flipped open my phone and shot off a text to her, hoping she'd respond immediately. As the seconds ticked by, the feeling of dread in my stomach only grew until I pulled the next woman aside who wandered in and back out of that same bathroom, my eyes wild and my hair frazzled from the repeated motion of my hands running through it nervously.

"Hey, what gives, asshole?" she nearly shouted, trying to yank her hand out of my grip as I tugged her out of the main line of sight of the room. "Lay off, prick!"

"Shut yer trap; I just need to know if another woman was in there when you went in."

She stopped fighting and cast her eyes around, perhaps trying to determine if this was some sort of trap. "Place was empty. Nobody in there but me."

I released her and shoved my way into a women's restroom for the first time in years, rabid and panicked, when I found what the other woman had promised to be true—the place was empty.

Mallory was gone.

We combed the whole fucking floor, BlackJack and I, before finally dragging Ace into it. I'd hoped to avoid his involvement, knowing damn well I'd get an earful about how incompetent I was if I couldn't look after a single little woman, but he surprised me.

"We'll find her, one way or another," he growled, his hands balled into fists. "Either she was snatched, or she finally decided to run."

I shook my head at his declaration, refusing to believe after all this time, she'd decided to leave us. "She wouldn't run. Where the fuck would she go?"

He shrugged, his eyes darting over to a quickly-approaching Spade. "Fuck. We need him at the top of his game; not a word until we figure out what's going on, you hear me?"

I swallowed the sick feeling that fell to the pit of my stomach and nodded in agreement. "Sure."

Spade danced to the left and right, bouncing on the balls of his feet as he grinned like a loon and made his way over to us. When the bastard realized Mallory wasn't present, his face fell, and I realized we didn't need to speak it into existence for him to know what was going on.

Spade always knew.

"Where is she?" he asked, his prancing turning to a powerful stalking, shoulders straight and tense, arms at his sides but ready to swing. "Hello, are you all dense? Where's our girl?"

Ace shook his head, a heavy sigh escaping him. "She went to the bathrooms and never came back. We're trying to work out where she ran off to now."

Spade fucking scowled at the other man, his lips curled in disbelief. "She wouldn't run off. She loves us."

BlackJack rolled his eyes, choosing to remain silent rather than go up against the madman in our group. I was on the same level as him, honestly, and I didn't need her to say it to my face to know the doc was falling for us all hard. Hell, she'd put a gun to Ace's head and fucked his brains out, for heaven's sake. If that wasn't love, I wasn't sure what was.

And let's not forget how she handled BlackJack's stoic ass with kid gloves, slowly turning him into a semi-functioning person again.

"She didn't run off, Ace," he doubled down, seeing the hesitation in our leader's eyes. "Ace, fucking say something—"

"If she didn't run off, someone managed to pick her off in less than two seconds, and I find that hard to believe, Spade."

He was saved from a lengthy argument by the sound of Spade's name being called to climb into the ring to await his nightly challengers. Spade was hesitant and no doubt would have dropped out in a heartbeat if he didn't think us capable of finding her. And then there was the hefty bet Ace placed on him. If he walked off, he'd be paying that back out of his own pockets, and there was no way he had coffers that deep, not after such a long stagnant period out of the ring.

"You'd better find her," he growled before he turned on a heel and marched off, rage and anxiousness hunching his shoulders, filling his frame with a dangerous blend of energy that spelled trouble for any man dumb enough to go against him.

I had no doubt if we didn't find her before Spade walked back out of that ring, there'd be hell to pay. Friends or not, crew or not, when it came to Mallory, Spade was a wild animal, and without her?

Well, I didn't want to know what he'd do without her.

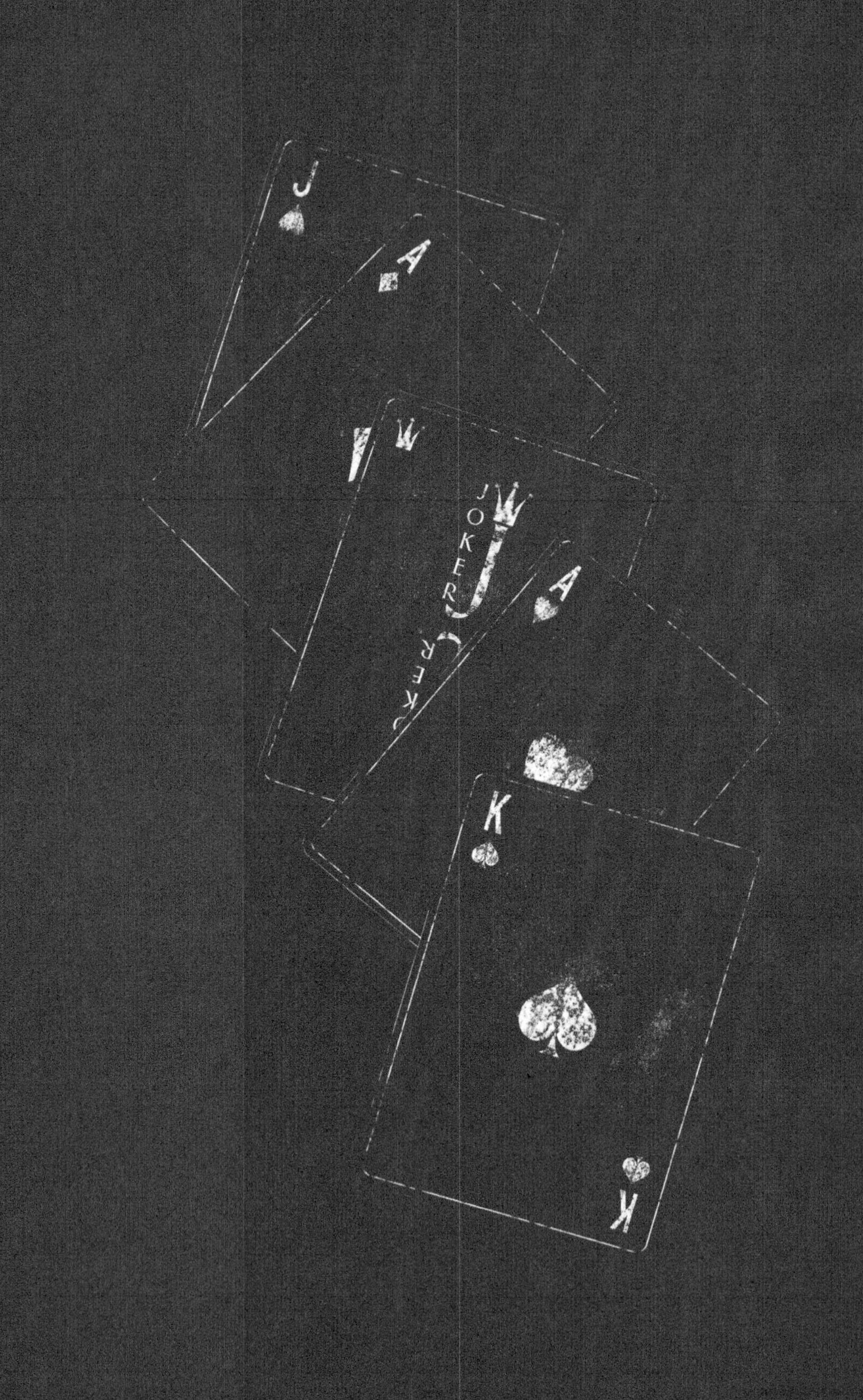
JOKER

CHAPTER FORTY-ONE
MALLORY

"For fuck's sake, can't a girl just go to the bathroom without being accosted?"

The King who'd come to snatch me up was the same one who'd grabbed onto me the last time we'd had a little run-in, and he was no less threatening now than he was then. The only difference now was that none of my men were around to save me. I was well and truly on my own; the Kings made sure of that.

"Shut your mouth and follow me," he grumbled, his raspy voice setting me on edge.

No doubt this man swallowed rocks for breakfast without batting an eye.

Grouch.

"You're a fucking pleasant one, aren't you?" I shuffled alongside him, struggling to keep up with his brisk pace.

When he didn't answer me anymore, I pouted like a petulant child, irritated that these assholes saw me as no more than a fucking pawn in their game.

And of course, their leader was the foulest of them all.

Tall, moody, and rough nearly threw me in the lap of the other man, and a sick feeling trailed down my spine as he rearranged me so

I could see the ring, his hand at the base of my neck, gripping tightly, like he was afraid I'd do something stupid, like bolt.

I was dumb, shacking up with criminals, but I wasn't death-wish stupid. Not anymore, at least.

"So, we meet again, Miss Stanton," he purred in a voice that no doubt had other women dropping their panties like whores desperate for a dick, but all it did to me was set me on edge, made me grind my teeth as I was made to feel like a toy. "Tell me, what brings all the Wildcards out in force tonight? Was it because they're planning something against the Kings?"

I scowled at him and let out a low growl, hoping to imitate that dangerous glint Spade always had in his eye before he laid into an informant who crossed him. I probably fell short, but what the hell. It was worth a try.

"Fuck you, asshole, we're here for the fights," I spat as he laughed at my piss-poor attempt to intimidate him. Out of the shadows emerged the other two who'd been with him the last time we had the misfortune to run into each other, and my eyes blew wide when I realized the dangerous one who didn't talk much wore clothes very similar to Spade's ring gear.

Fuck, was he planning to fight him?

Spade didn't stand a chance if they came to blows, as much as it pained me to admit it, even just to myself.

"What's the big idea, fuckwads?" I complained loudly, hoping the others would hear me and swoop in for the save. At my little outburst, the leader tightened his grip on my throat and yanked me back against his chest, my neck bared to his gaze, submissive and pliant against my will.

"If you enjoy being able to speak, Miss Stanton, I strongly suggest you keep your pretty mouth shut unless you're asked a question," he growled, his eyes narrowed in on my pulse point. "Yours wouldn't be the first throat I've ripped open with my teeth."

From the way his eyes gleamed in the dim lighting reflected off the ring, I had no doubt he'd do it without a second of hesitation, so I clammed up, self-preservation kicking in for a change.

That deadly smile curled upwards like a slithering snake at my obedience. "What a well-trained bitch the Wildcards have. Smart, too. Perhaps I should get myself one."

Their fighter stepped forward with a warning growl, and the King who had me in his grip growled back, much like two alpha males fighting for dominance in a dog ring. Whatever happened between the two of them was over before it even began, and I was being turned on the asshole's lap to face the ring, hand still firmly at the base of my throat.

"Watch your man in the ring. It'll be the last time he wins before my soldier gets to him and rips his head from his shoulders to prove a point."

Spade was always an enigma, and I couldn't help but be enthralled by the way he danced around the ring today, the vibrancy in his step only outweighed by the almost-childlike excitement of being back in his element again. He delivered two heavy-handed swings to the side of his opponent's face and was quickly declared the winner of that bout and the next. It appeared the challengers today were of a weak caliber, and he'd barely broken a sweat as he plowed through them, one by one, his confidence building with every swing.

The announcer boomed over the shouts of men placing new bets or collecting on old ones, throwing the whole room into a strange, pregnant silence at his announcement.

"We have a new challenger for the reigning champion—*Soldat,* undefeated in his own territory, versus Spade, two-year reigning champion and house favorite. Two minutes to place bets, folks; get them in while you can!"

Every nerve ending in my body was on fire at the thought of Spade going toe to toe with one of the most dangerous men I'd ever met. Still, I couldn't do more than sit still and watch as their brawler stalked over to the cage and stared my fighter down, his dead stare more intimidating than any bluster he could have put on.

Spade's eyes flickered from the Soldier to his leader, and when those gorgeous, expressive eyes fell on me, he simultaneously let out a breath of relief and sucked in one of fresh panic.

I watched his eyes lock on mine, and his whispered promise fell from lips that were split but still readable, their intent clear as day.

Behave while I beat this prick's ass.

I could practically hear the maniacal laughter accompanying the declaration in my ear, and a little giggle escaped me before I could rein it in, angering the man whose hand tightened in response.

Too bad for him that Ace and Spade choked me harder when they were fucking me raw.

The sick fuck was getting hard beneath my ass as he watched the two opponents size each other up like slabs of beef at the butcher shop, and it took everything in me not to gag at the feel of him. Joker had wanted to see me dressed up, but for the first time in a long while, I regretted my choice of clothing.

If this piece of literal garbage put his hands any more on me, I'd castrate him and damn the consequences.

I spotted BlackJack across the room, finally, but his eyes didn't drift to mine, no matter how hard I willed it to happen. My bluster deflated and my head fell, but a rough yank of a hand in my hair had my eyes returning right back to the ring as the bell rang and both men circled like cats toying with a mouse.

The way they mirrored each others' moves was eerie, as if they'd both trained under the same ruthless teacher, but if they'd had ties of some sort, Spade would have said something.

Right?

He hadn't given me any reason to think he'd lie to me—not like Ace had on several occasions.

So it must be a coincidence that Spade's opponent seemed to know exactly what he was going to do, when he was going to do it, and managed to counter every single move with practiced ease.

Soldat landed a hit straight in the center of Spade's nose, the sickening crunch of it breaking loud enough to echo over to where I sat, wincing at the secondhand pain. From there, it was all downhill.

Spade was fast, but he was out of practice, and whereas once I'd suspected he might be able to hold his own against this man, today, there was no lingering doubt that he was going to lose.

I had a fleeting thought that, had I had my own money, I could stand to make a ton more right now if I put it on the King in the ring, but it was gone as soon as it arrived, a traitorous thought that had no business in my head.

"Do you enjoy watching my man tear yours to shreds?" the asshole had the gall to ask, his low-timbered voice whispering across my ear as his lips pressed dangerously into my hairline just an inch back. "His blood littering the ring, dropping every time he turns around, like a wounded dog: lost, disoriented, still convinced he stands a chance."

He turned my head to the left, and I spotted the asshole who'd dragged me over and put me at this man's mercy, a gun in his hand, visible at just the right angle. He rocked it back and pointed it, and when I followed his line of sight, I realized he was aiming right for Cass.

Fuck.

"What's your game, asshole?"

His soft chuckle sent shivers down my spine. "Well, Miss Stanton, it's quite simple. Their time is running out, and I need information. I want to know who pulled the heist on my jeweler, and I am tired of asking nicely and waiting for results." His buddy cocked the gun in his grip, a malicious grin spreading over his face as he locked eyes with his boss.

The same boss who ran a hand up my leg, stopping for only a second on my upper thigh before teasing the hem of my skirt with a calloused finger.

It made me fucking sick.

"I could give the nod and have all your men killed in less than a second, and before the club got their wits about them, we'd be gone like a fly in the wind." He turned my chin now to BlackJack, where another of his men stood off to the side, the familiar glint of brass knuckles flashing on his hand as he gripped the lapels of his out-of-place coat. "So, the choice is yours, pretty thing. You gonna convince them to give up their secrets?" His nose was an inch from my cheek now, and I swallowed the bile rising in my throat as I tried desperately to lean as far away from him as possible. "Or should I just keep you and use you as collateral?"

Even as the words echoed around us, I realized it wouldn't work. Ace might be fucking me now, but that didn't mean he'd risk his whole crew for my insignificant ass. "Joke's on you, buddy. I'm not worth spit to them. I'm just their little plaything, and when Ace gets tired of me, I'll be back where I started, in a shitty life, with my two cats and a rundown apartment that has a water leak when it rains."

"You're a bigger fool than those men of yours if you think I'll believe that." Spade's eyes locked in on me, and a vicious snarl fell from his lips as he took a right hook to the face for his momentary distraction. "Your fighter can't stop himself from looking over to make sure I'm not hurting you, and every time he does, my man lands another punch."

My eyes fell to the floor in shame. He had me there, but what was I supposed to do? It wasn't like Ace went around leaving guns unlocked after our little chase incident. And though Spade gave me back my butterfly knife, it was securely tucked in my drawer at home, safe from the wandering hands of the club staff. I could no more defend myself right now than change the direction of the wind with my mind, and he and I both knew it.

So did my Wildcards.

"These fools have let you rise in their ranks until they put your safety above their own, pet, which makes you a dangerous asset." He dragged that hand of his up the inside of my skirt another inch or two, and I tried to escape his poisonous touch, to no avail, as the only place I could go was further into his lap, his obvious erection pressing pointedly into the curve of my ass as a reminder that while the men I slept with now did so voluntarily, he might not be as forgiving if I chose not to give up what he wanted. "Perhaps if I take out their queen, they'll be more than eager to bend to my will."

The familiar sound of a pistol bullet clicking into place behind his head had me smiling viciously.

"Looks like you'll never know, now, will you?"

His angry snarl in my ear was punctuated by a short laugh, and my eyes trailed along his line of sight as Spade fell to his knees, blood pouring from a gash on his forehead, his chest heaving with the exertion his body suffered with each breath he took. *Soldat* stood behind him, hands cradling his head, ready to snap a neck at the first sign of trouble.

"Looks like we're at an impasse, eh, Watanabe?"

Ace's answering growl was all the confirmation he got, and then I found myself being released and tipped off his filthy lap into the waiting arms of my dark knight, my black-souled savior, as the King watched on and laughed maniacally.

"You can fuck right off, asshole," he growled, "you and your information. Someone's playing you, and you're too blind to see it."

"Best be careful, Wildcard," he echoed, taunting Ace with a wink and a smirk as he tugged me away from the madman. "Loyalty is hard to come by in this part of town, and I've got enough money to buy it all."

JOKER

CHAPTER FORTY-TWO
BLACKJACK

That did it. The fucking Kings were as unstable as Spade on his worst days.

It had been two days since the incident at the ring, and we were all still on edge about it. Ace couldn't walk outside without panicking that a new homeless person had taken up residence on our block. And heaven forbid a strange car happened to ride by us more than once.

We were all on edge, each for our own reasons.

Joker knew if they found out he was the one who'd done the heist, his life would be forfeit. Spade was still seething over his loss at the hands of their brawler. I'd hacked into the gym's security system and made it a point to watch their every move, and still, somehow, their ghost had outwitted me, looping useless footage under my watchful eye.

Ace was just . . . well, Ace. I think he took it as a personal affront that his prize had been snatched up right beneath his nose.

Right now, we were scattered in the house—Spade in his torture room, beating the fuck out of a Kings informant he picked up on the docks; Joker in his room, washing off the dirt from a day of working amongst the trash heap of the underworld; Ace was holed up in his office, perusing who knew what.

That left me and Mallory. And I had a hankering for more of her touches.

The retraining therapy she had me on was great—I held her longer and longer each time, and her touch no longer made me recoil in disgust. It was slow going for a while, but the way she looked at me when I pushed past my discomfort and got out of my own head long enough to touch her, well, it was worth all the mental agony I worked up.

Fuck.

The semi I sported behind my sweats was becoming a common occurrence, not that she seemed to mind, always with that little smirk and a wink as she sashayed away from me in shorts too obscene for her to wear out of this place, or the so-called innocent caresses of her own body when she knew I was watching.

She could make a killing as a torturer if she could make all her victims fall in love with her first.

Love.

I stopped in my tracks, unable to move a step further as the realization jolted through me at breakneck speed. At some point in all of this, baring our souls to each other, saving her from near death, her steadfast determination to return the capabilities of a normal man to me, she'd managed to worm her way into my soul, and damned if scraping her out would be more like torture than a rescue at this point.

"Mal," I called out, seeking her like a sunflower seeks the sun each day, aching to have her light shine on me, cleansing me and making me whole again. "Mal?"

I searched every fucking room in the damn place—bedrooms, kitchen, bathrooms, even the fucking office, but found nothing. Still, I knew she was here; it was just a matter of figuring out where she could possibly be hiding—

"Mal?"

I poked my head in the garage and peered around, pleased when my eyes fell on her shapely backside bent over a car's open hood, earbuds in her ears, her hips wiggling to the music only she could hear. I ached to wander over and put my hands on her while she was unaware, so I gave into my baser urges and snuck up on her, moving like a shadow, the distance between us closing with every step.

The second my hands slid around her hips, she yelped and jumped a good foot in the air, her fucking adorable crop top riding higher on that flat expanse of skin. I let my thumbs graze it as she spun in my arms, and her shock turned to a playful scowl.

"Jonah!"

Her swat at my chest was like a fucking fly landing on me, and I laughed at the tickle, my eyes sparkling with a lightness I hadn't felt in years. My lips drifted forward and danced across hers, just for a second, but it was enough to trigger her usual response—first, she froze, then she melted into it, letting me lead this dance as our lower halves melded against each other.

I broke away first, as usual, my eyes blown wide, pupils dilated, no doubt, panting with need.

"You know, with that music so loud, anyone could have snuck in and kidnapped you, and you wouldn't have a chance to even scream."

She twined those oil-stained fingers behind my neck and leaned her ass against the edge of the car. "Well, I guess it's a good thing I'm keeping my current kidnappers close," she quipped, letting one of her hands trail down my chest, smearing us both with oil and grease. "Do any of you men believe in basic car maintenance? Ace hasn't changed his oil in years, it looks like."

I lifted a shoulder in a half-assed response, my mind elsewhere. "Joker keeps his bike maintained, at least."

She scowled at me as if I was somehow less of a man for never bothering to take my car in for an oil change.

I had more important things on my mind usually. Like now, for existence.

I was painfully aware of how close to her I was, and I'd stake my life on it she could feel the hardness in my sweats, aching for her.

Not that I knew how to use that on her.

"Jonah," she whispered, her head cocked to the side, eyes at half-mast, those long lashes drawing me in like the sweetest taste of an addicting drug. "You're all dirty now." Her eyes trailed over the grease spots she'd left on my skin, a faint worry line forming on her brow.

I wanted to open my mouth and taunt her with suggestive innuendos, like Joker and Spade. I wanted to roll my hips like Ace did to her when she got too close, showing her the things I planned to do to her body. Hell, I'd settle for half-cocked honesty at this point. But I wasn't any of them, and I wasn't sure I could work up the words building in my chest.

The urge to not speak had risen again in me, and I took a deep breath, fighting it back as I forced myself to articulate, to communicate something, anything.

Words, idiot. Use your words.

"You're dirty, too," I muttered, my tongue feeling quite like someone had coated it with a layer of fur and glued it to the roof of my mouth. "Wanna conserve water?"

Fuck, that was less than sexy, but whatever. It felt natural, though dorky, and if her answering smile was any indication, she didn't mind my less-than-suave approach one bit.

"I'd like that a lot."

WE RACED up the stairs like two kids trying to outrun the boogeyman, laughing and clambering over each other to be the first to my bathroom. When we made it to the safety of my room, for the first time in a very long time, I didn't bother to lock all my deadbolts and shit, choosing instead to keep my eyes—and my hands—firmly attached to the stunning woman in front of me.

Her top hung loosely off one shoulder now, the familiar band on the front giving me pause for a second.

"Is that one of mine?" I asked hesitantly, fingering one of the sleeves as she tried to hide a smile.

"Maybe," she teased, "but it's mine now."

I bit my bottom lip, debating how far to take this. I had all but invited her to take a shower with me. Could I bring myself to take her clothes off, too?

Did she even want me to?

Her soft fingers covered mine briefly, tugging them away as the indecision bled from my body, the choice thankfully taken from me as she tugged her arm out of one sleeve and yanked the thing over her chest and head, tossing it to the floor with a shy grin up at me.

Fuck, even her underthings were absolutely salivating.

She wore a sexy little black bra, the cups only halfway covering her gorgeous tits, the tops breaking over the tiny thing like a damned waterfall of skin.

My palms itched to cup them, but I held back. Surely women liked it when men took their time. She got enough of the super-speed, no holding back from the other guys. I wanted what we had to be different.

I was a patient man, and that would bleed over into my love life if I were actually about to start having one.

"Fuck," I whispered, my eyes wide, mouth agape. I couldn't bother to fucking care that I must look like a damned fish on the docks. She was beautiful. "I . . . *fuck, Mal.*"

Her giggle ran over my skin like a live jolt of electricity, raising the hairs on my arms, making my cock twitch in my pants, saliva filling my mouth. I wanted to roll in it, bathe in the sound, fuck, I wanted to hear it in my dreams when I lay down to sleep.

"That part comes after we get you cleaned up, stud," she whispered, her fingers dancing through the hair scattered over my chest beneath my shirt.

My brain short-circuited, then stopped working altogether as the implications in her words set in and processed.

Fuck me, this was really happening.

I've gotta tell her I'm a fucking virgin.

I opened my mouth to utter the words, but they didn't come out. All I could manage was a brief squeak, then I snapped that puppy shut to avoid any further embarrassing sounds from leaving me as she lifted my shirt and tore it from my torso, her eyes glued to the expanse of me directly in front of her.

"Shit, you look good without a shirt on," she sighed, her lashes fluttering. My eyes tracked her lips as she sucked one between her teeth and gnawed on it, abusing the soft thing for a moment as her eyes flicked back and forth over me, studying, contemplating, planning. "You've been holding out on me, Jonah. I could stare at you for hours."

I felt a blush creep up my skin at her raw admission, the desire radiating from her in waves too powerful to ignore. The familiar itch tried to rear its ugly head, and I made a split-second decision, my hands tugging her against me as I fell back on my bed, dragging her with me, my fingers finding purchase in her hair as I brought our lips to each other and relished in the feel of her pinning me, holding me down, by my choice.

I let her drown me with her essence until the feeling subsided, and moved to break away, but my tongue darted out with a mind of its own and teased the crease of her lips, and she parted them for me, her own grazing against mine like a taunt, a dare.

Come get me.

I might be a fucking virgin, but I'd kissed her plenty of times. And I wasn't about to back down from a challenge, even if it did threaten to be my undoing.

"We've got all night, princess," I heard myself whisper, my lips trapping hers for more, tongue mapping out the inside of her mouth like it was uncharted, virgin territory.

Her hips straddled my lap, and I groaned into her kiss as she rocked against me, her own moans blending with mine. I lay flat on my back, legs dangling over the side of my bed, dry-humping this fucking veritable angel like a horny teenager, and suddenly, I was filled with shame.

How the hell could I treat her like this? She deserved much better than this fumbling bullshit.

Maybe this was a mistake.

I shoved myself into a sitting position and wrapped my arms

around her waist, crushing her against me as my eyes drifted shut and I just focused on holding on to her, clinging to the hope that I wasn't as out of control as I feared.

Her soft hands found my hair and ran through the silky strands, nails raking gently over my scalp soothingly. "Hey, we don't have to take things fast—"

Fast?

"Mal, if we go any slower, I might die," I breathed in exasperation. "I don't know what way's up, I can't sort my brain to save my life, and my whole body feels like it's on fire." I nuzzled against her collarbone, staring into her gorgeous eyes like she somehow had the answers I sought. "What the fuck is all this? Is this normal? Do you go through this every time?"

Her lips parted in a slow grin, one that felt very predatory in nature as it nearly split her face in two. Girlish laughter with a hint of chaos rippled from her lips, and she leaned down and placed a few gentle pecks against my open mouth, refusing to take it any further as I struggled through all this emotion and feeling and confusion.

"Oh, you poor thing," she teased, her hips slowly rocking against me. "You're new to all this, of *course* you are."

I suddenly felt like six kinds of a fool and set her gently on the bed before marching straight for the bathroom, shutting the door behind me.

What a fucking idiot I'd been, thinking she'd want someone like me.

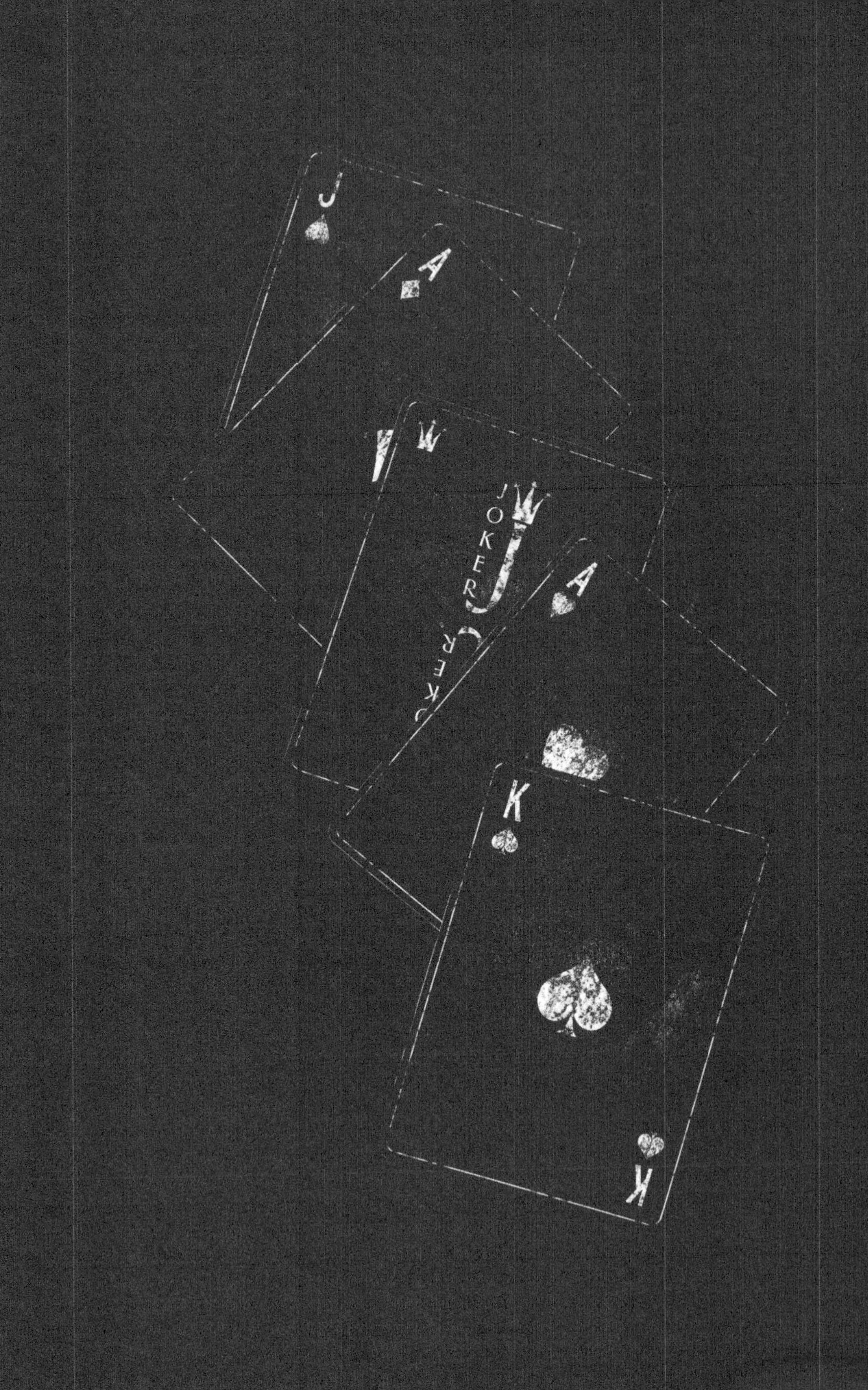
JOKER

CHAPTER FORTY-THREE
MALLORY

I fucked up.

I fucked up badly, and the only way I knew to make it better was separated from me by a thick bathroom door. And of course, the emotional distance I'd managed to wedge between us.

"Jonah, open the door and let me explain—"

I raised my hand to start pounding, but my hand kept going and knocked on a bare, hairy chest instead, stunning me to near silence.

"I'm sorry—"

He didn't give me a chance to finish that line of thought before his hands wrapped around my wrists and jerked me into the bathroom with him, kicking the door closed behind us. I didn't have more than a second to breathe before he had backed me against the same door I'd just come through and slammed his lips against mine, demanding entrance now, his tongue eager, probing, instead of hesitant and gentle.

I didn't mind either version of him, but this one was taking what he wanted, and I secretly rejoiced at his progress.

When his lips left mine, they trailed down my neck, over my shoulder, and down one arm, until he came to my knuckles and kissed each one, feather-light, while he made eye contact and slaughtered my vagina with those gorgeous hazel depths.

"I want you, but, fuck, Mal, I'm not sure I'm enough."

My heart constricted at his raw admission. Here was this gorgeous man, working past his huge aversion to touch, taking what he wanted, yet somehow he managed to second-guess himself still.

Maybe it was time I showed him how much I wanted him right back.

"Are you worried I won't like it?"

His eyes averted, he nodded slowly, even as I took his hands in mine and brought them to my hips. "You don't hear women bragging bout bedding a virgin, Mal."

I set his hands on my hips and cupped his jaw in both of mine, dragging his face to mine with no small amount of determination. "You are a fucking miracle on legs, walking sin, and damn it all if I give a flying fuck whether you've had sex before or not, you dumbass." Slowly, I leaned forward and brushed my lips against his again, teasing him, taunting him with short breaths, a quick flick of my tongue against the edge of his mouth. "So what if you don't know what to do with me? It only means I get to teach you exactly what I like." I nipped at his lower lip with my teeth, pleased when I drew a tiny drop of blood. "And you've always been such a fast learner, Jonah."

"Mmm," he agreed, his eyes fluttering closed. "And you're such an amazing teacher." A groan ripped from his throat as I reached down with one hand and cupped him through these gods-blessed grey sweats. "So fucking hands-on."

Our lips stayed molded against each other, his back bowed to accommodate the difference in our height as I dragged my nails down his spine. "We're not going to get clean out here, Jonah," I muttered against his mouth, gasping for air. "Take my bra off."

His hands fumbled at the clasp at first, but he took a deep breath and calmed himself, finally freeing my breasts from that stupid-ass shelf bra. Before it could fall from my ribcage and my breasts swing free, his hands were cupping them reverently, like he'd just won the fucking lottery.

"Jesus, Mal, you're so fucking soft," he breathed, cock jumping in his pants against my thigh as he leaned further down and flicked his talented tongue out and grazed the tip, a gasp ripping from my throat at the feel of it.

So fucking electric.

"Try what feels right, Jonah. Explore. My body is your wonderland."

His answering growl was enough to have me shivering where I stood, my panties wet between my legs, aching for him to make his way there and discover how he affected me.

I'd never been touched by a virgin before, but if I had to compare it to anything, I'd say it felt like being worshipped at an altar, like I was some physical manifestation of a god, and he was my loyal follower. His fingers grazed over every inch of my skin, dancing across the indentations of my ribcage, curling around the peaked tip of my nipple as he rolled it between two fingers, experimenting with his movements as his inexperienced touches pulled various vocal sounds of enjoyment from the depths of my soul.

But fuck, if he didn't speed things up, not only would we not be taking that shower, but we'd both likely die from blue balls.

"Not to be rude, but we can revisit this slow exploration later. I want to climb in that shower with you and wash up, and maybe put your hands on me in some ways you haven't thought of yet."

His answering gasp was all the agreement I needed.

His fingers were at my shorts in seconds, tugging them down so fast they nearly ripped in two. He hit the floor on his knees and shoved his face into the juncture of my legs, inhaling like a fucking starved man at a buffet through the rough lace of my thong.

"Jesus fucking Christ, Mal, do you taste as good as you smell?"

I shrugged, suddenly more self-conscious than I'd ever been in my life. When Spade went down on me, it was like another Saturday morning, but when Jonah put his face there and worshipped me before he'd even had the chance to know a woman in such an intimate way, it did funny things to my insides I wasn't sure fit in the carefully-constructed image I had of this whole thing.

"I've never had the pleasure to put my face there, so your guess is as good as mine."

He didn't hesitate to drag those lacy wonders down my legs and find out, his tongue leading the charge like he'd gone to fucking school for this. When the tip of that talented organ grazed a circle around my clit and dipped lower, just the right amount of pressure on the sensitive nub, I threw a leg over his shoulder and let his hands move to cup my ass, supporting my weight for me.

"Are you sure you've never eaten pussy before, babe? Cause fuck me, you do an outstanding job at it."

I felt the bastard's grin against my sensitive folds. He didn't answer me, choosing instead to growl in agreement against my clit as I gripped his hair and ground against his face. There was no room for shame in my actions, only pleasure, and the only regret in my body was I couldn't touch his cock while he so eagerly devoured my arousal and begged for more.

"God, I'm so fucking hard it hurts," he groaned, palming his erection as I watched on, my traitorous vagina fluttering, clenching around air, needing what he had.

"Why don't you get off those knees and get in the shower with me, and we'll take care of that little issue," I gasped, sliding my leg back to the floor, eager for his cock inside me. I didn't even care if I managed to drown in the shower while I took it, I wanted him, hard, soft, fast, however he wanted to take this.

"Mal, I might be a virgin, but even I know that's not a *little* issue."

I couldn't help the chuckle that ripped from my chest at his tease. "Okay, big guy, you got me there."

There was no time for him to react when my hands gripped his waistband and yanked his sweats to his knees, and nearly gave myself a black eye with the fucking anaconda he'd been hiding away in those sinfully seductive pants.

"Holy mother of god, where do you put this thing?"

I'd seen a fair bit of dicks in my life, but I'd be damned if I'd seen one like this before.

All guys liked to pretend they were god's gift to women and ended up sporting a below-average cock despite all their claims. However, if you'd told me the quiet, reserved, virgin BlackJack was hiding an easy ten or more inches of length in his pants, I wouldn't have immediately believed you.

Even staring at it, I was having a hard time believing it. And ten inches might not even be giving him enough credit. The fucking thing looked like it could impale me and brush the back of my teeth from the right angle. And fuck me, it was so thick.

I'd never been much of a size queen, but that was a monster.

"I don't even know if it's gonna fit," he stammered, blushing at my sudden reticence. My pussy, however, didn't have the same hesitation, and I felt the moisture slip down my thighs as a whimper quickly followed.

I jerked him into the shower stall and turned the water on, needing something to distract myself from the absolutely mouth-watering dick behind me. Not that it worked, but I made every good-faith effort not to let my mind wander.

There wasn't a doubt in my mind I was about to be very sore in the morning, especially if we went more than one round, but you know what?

Worth it.

Totally worth it.

The fucking disco stick of the century nestled between my asscheeks as I adjusted the temperature of the water, Jonah's hands sliding around my torso again to return to fondling my breasts like a man on a mission. And while I was thrilled his aversion to touch seemed to be buried deep, way down deep for the time being, I wanted those eager hands elsewhere.

The decision to spin in his arms wasn't a conscious one, nor was the slight shifting I pulled to put my back against the cool tile to one side. Water droplets cascaded over his shoulders and down his pecs, rivulets forming between the dip and curve of his abs, following that vee at his hips, and making a very poignant picture as it sluiced around his cock and dripped from the damn thing.

Jesus hell, it looked like a battering ram.

And I was about to let it rearrange my insides.

Spectacular.

"Jonah, take one of those hands south and explore some uncharted territory," I whispered, reaching down to wrap both my hands around his cock, squeezing, tugging, rubbing my thumb over the sensitive tip as he moaned at the sensations.

And then his long fingers probed the slick folds at the juncture of my thighs, and I damn near passed out. He sank two fingers inside me with a groan, licking his lips as those long digits flexed and curled inside me and wrecked my world. Spade's fingers were wide, but they were short, not like Jonah's. Jonah's fingers easily reached up inside me and hit that spot that promised to have women seeing stars when they came.

"Fuck," I squeaked, slamming my hands against the wall for support. "Oh, fuck, *yes."*

Jonah looked pretty pleased with himself, a slow grin curling his lips as his other hand twisted in my hair and dragged my face closer until our foreheads touched. His breathing was erratic, and between the two of us, I wasn't sure who was more in awe of the other.

"You . . . you like that?" he practically purred, his fingers sliding in and out, dragging against my inner walls so sinfully it nearly had me coming apart at the seams. Fuck, his fingers weren't harsh and calloused, like Spades, nor were they thin and feminine, like Cass's. They weren't demanding, like Ace's. No, they were slow and methodical and patient and *fucking christ on a cracker—*

"Ohmigoddontstop—"

I screamed, like those feral porno screams you think *have to be fake*, and my legs shuddered as I nearly collapsed from shock, gushing between my legs, his fingers still buried inside me. My eyes rolled back in my head, and I scrambled to grip anything that might hold me up, locking on his shoulders at the last second.

"Fuck, Mal, I killed you—"

He tugged me against his body and slid over to sit on a convenient divot in the wall, obviously designed for shampoo, but that doubled as a nice bench.

Fuck, we should have started on the bench.

"Oh, no, loverboy, I'm nowhere near dead," I panted, a limp fucking noodle in his arms. "Just wait til you're all clean and I get you out of this shower."

His cock jumped eagerly against my back, and I managed to find the energy to paste a silly, sated smile on my face. His arms were like a safe harbor, a port in a storm, and I let him hold onto me as I half-ass-washed us both up, cleaning the random specks of grease from our skin.

When we finally finished in the shower, he was still hard as a rock, and my legs were finally functioning again. The fastest drying-off in the history of the world commenced as we raced to see who could finish first—the only time we'd be doing that tonight, I suspected.

And then, the moment of truth, as I wrapped my towel around my torso and turned to him, realizing I was the only one still wearing one.

So I dropped it around my ankles with a raised brow, a squeal of excitement escaping me as he bent at the waist and hoisted me over one shoulder like a fucking caveman, carrying me off into his room, where he dumped me unceremoniously on his bed and grinned down at me like a loon.

I raised my arms and invited him down to join me.

JOKER

CHAPTER FORTY-FOUR
BLACKJACK

I never wanted to leave her fucking arms again.

Mallory pulled me down on top of her, and it was like all the instincts I didn't know I possessed rose to the surface, demanding to be let loose. I wanted to bury myself inside her, even though I had no idea what it would feel like. I just knew it would be good.

Fuck, as often as the others tied her up, it had to be the most amazing feeling in the fucking world, being stuffed inside Mal's miraculous muff.

Ha. Ha ha.

Not the time for jokes.

My eyes didn't know where to look first. Sure, I'd already seen her naked once before, but this was a much different situation, and here she was, laying herself out for me to taste, touch, feel, whatever struck my fancy.

"I don't even know where to start, Mal," I admitted, the familiar heat rising in my cheeks.

In true Mallory fashion, she reached out and shoved me on my back, her palms smoothing over my chest as she devoured me with her eyes this time. Tables turned, I still had a delicious view of all of her, but I nearly swallowed my tongue when she slithered down the length of me and put her lips around my cock, no hesitation in her movements, her lips stretching almost comically around it as she worked to go as deep as possible.

Fuck, I could feel her damn throat constricting around my head.

"Mal, uh, *huuuungh,* Mal—"

I struggled to keep my thoughts coherent, but she seemed not to have the same issue, her free hand fondling my damn balls as she used me like a gargle stick, swabbing the back of her throat with the tip of my dick over and over, my eyes going crossed from the feel of her mouth—

"Mallory, fuck, I don't—*please!"*

I wasn't even sure what I was begging for, but as she hummed around my length, my back bowed, and I arched off the bed, coming down her throat with a roar.

I wasn't sure how long it took me to return to fucking earth. My heart was slamming against the inside of my chest, fighting to get free; good lord, kill me now, but my whole body was practically vibrating with a low, pleasant buzz just beneath my skin.

"Wow," I whispered, my lungs working double time to bring oxygen back into my body. "That was something else."

"Mmm, if you liked that, you'll love what comes next," she murmured, her lips moving up my skin, setting off new shockwaves everywhere she touched.

I lifted my arms, though they felt like concrete, and wrapped them around her as she slinked up my body and straddled my waist. "And what might that be, princess?"

She giggled girlishly and rocked her hips, and damn me if I wasn't stiffening again beneath her like a horndog on steroids. "Oh, you know, the actual sex." She quirked a brow at me and smiled. "I assume you've got an idea of how that part works, right?"

"I know what porn is, Mal; I'm a grown-ass man, for fuck's sake," I grouched, rolling my eyes. Fuck, just because I'd never stuck it in a woman before, didn't mean I had no idea what the mechanics behind the act were. "Im sure whatever I don't know, you can fill in the blanks for."

She lifted her hips just an inch and rocked them back and forth, her folds parting around my quickly-hardening manhood, slicking me with her own arousal. The moan that ripped from her throat matched my own, and I threw my head back, riding out the wave of bliss.

The ends of her hair tickled my chest as she leaned over and nuzzled my neck, her lips leaving a hot trail down the side of my throat. "You know, I think you might be the biggest I've ever had," she remarked as if commenting on the color of the sky or the direction of the wind.

"That a good thing?"

Her energetic nod reassured me slightly, tits bobbing in the air before me. "A very good thing. But you're going to have to hold still while I get used to this monster, deal? No funny business."

I had no idea what funny business she spoke of, but whatever she wanted, I'd give her, hands down, no question asked. Her knees pressed into the bed as her palms flattened against my stomach, and she rose carefully above me, her core hovering just above my stiff prick. She reached a hand down and pointed me right at the entrance to her slick hole, and I whined needily when she let my tip brush against her opening, coating me with that heady arousal.

Fuck, I just wanted her to make it fast. If this were what it was like to face down death, I'd gladly do it, but for fuck's sake, don't torture a man—

"Jesusmaryandjoseph—"

She sank down onto my dick, taking inch by glorious inch inside herself, and it was like fucking nirvana, the way her body swallowed my girth and length with eager, pulsating waves. She moaned, her hand still at the base of me, and I dared to look down as she took it inside her, still not even halfway down my length.

"Fuck, so big," she panted, her breasts heaving, lip caught between her teeth as she sank a tad lower, breaths coming in short, rapid pants now. She looked halfway murdered, and I almost told her to stop—

surely that couldn't be healthy. Maybe there was such a thing as too big—

"Mal, if it's too much—"

She covered my mouth with the hand she'd been balancing with and accidentally slid down the remaining few inches of my cock in the process. A ghastly moan slipped from between her pursed lips, mingling with a dry laugh, and fuck if this wasn't the most fantastic feeling in my short life.

She sucked me in like a starving woman, her core tight and wet and fucking so, so warm—

"My god, I feel like I'm being split in two, Jonah." Her neck rolled, and I grinned as she cracked it audibly, sighing at the feeling.

"So . . ."

"So," she breathed, "now the real fun starts. Jesus, you fill me up so well I think I can feel you in my ribcage."

She rose on my cock, letting me slide all the way out save for the tip, and then sank down on me again, taking the whole thing in one smooth glide, only a whimper slipping from her.

"Fuck's sake, princess, I think I'm dying." My eyes were squeezed shut at the almost criminal way her tight hole sucked me up again, clenching around me harder than her mouth, begging me to blow my load inside her, consequences be damned. "I've died and gone to heaven, and you're my personal angel."

"Mmm, I like the compliment, but I'm hardly an angel." She rose and fell several more times, her body settling into a rhythm she was clearly familiar with. The pace was slow, but I was a barely-broken in stud, and my balls ached to fill her, repeatedly, over and over tonight until there was nothing left to give and I'd dehydrated myself from the sheer volume of fluids I lost in the process.

"Tell me how to please you," I begged, my hands on her hips, lifting her when she rose, dragging her down when she fell. "I want to make you feel as good as you make me feel."

She brought a single hand down and tugged mine off her hip and around to the front, spreading herself for my exploring fingers. "Touch that part of me you were so enamored with earlier," she commanded, "use your thumb, fuck, yes, oh my god you're a natural—"

Her back arched as she sped up her pace, the added stimulation to her clit sending her into a desperate spiral. I watched, enraptured, as she shattered with a moan atop my cock, squeezing me so tight I feared I'd pop out.

"Fuck, Jonah, fuck, fuck fuck *fuck!*"

She fell to my chest, her hair fanning out atop me, my cock still buried tight in her little hole. She'd stopped moving, but I didn't want to, and I wasn't sure where to go from here. It almost felt impolite to ask her—

"Put me on my back and fuck me. Drive that dick into me until you split me apart."

Her soft hand on my jaw was at strange odds with the way she was asking me to treat her, but who was I to deny the woman? She told me she'd teach me, and here was the perfect opportunity to see how much I could lead with instinct alone.

In a blink of an eye, I flipped us so I stretched out above her, nestled between her legs, my hips still melded to hers. She lifted those perfect, long legs and wrapped them around my waist, canting her hips to take me deeper.

I rocked my hips hesitantly, testing out the motion, and fuck if it wasn't the sweetest feeling in the world. God, if this was fucking, I never wanted to stop.

I'd fuck her like it was my job for the rest of eternity. To hell with leaving this bed. Mallory was mine, and I wasn't about to relinquish her anytime soon. I wanted to die with her cunt wrapped around my dick like some crazed worshipper of Medusa.

Instinct took over, and soon the only sounds that punctuated the air were the steady slap of skin on skin and our commingled moans of rapture. My balls ached to release their load, and I was too far gone to ask the right questions. Later, I might look back and regret it, but now, all I could think was spilling myself inside her, marking her so the whole house knew I'd had her, and she was mine now.

"Jesus, Mal, I—"

She bit my bottom lip and thrust her tongue inside my mouth, both of us warring for dominance in a kiss that stole my breath away with how desperate and filled with emotion it was. She gave me more than pleasure in that action, told me stories without words, made promises of pleasure and pain that had me nearly feral, and with one last thrust, I lost all control, slamming to the hilt inside her as rope after rope of hot seed shot out of me and painted the inside of her.

It just kept coming, an endless deluge that made my spine fucking ache, but the way her eyes rolled back in her head and she moaned my name made it all worth it.

J
A
JOKER
A
K

CHAPTER FORTY-FIVE

SPADE

If I had to listen to those two one more time, I'd stab myself in the ear for some relief.

Ace and I sat in the kitchen, listening to the sound of Mallory screaming BlackJack's name as he railed her for the fifth time this morning. The corner of my mouth had been turned down in a permanent scowl for the past hour, and I brought my third cup of coffee to my lips, sipping on the only thing keeping me sane right now.

"He's going to ruin her for the rest of us," Ace grumbled, very out of character for him. He wasn't the pouting type, but now that Mallory had gotten under his skin, too, he'd changed subtly, getting more possessive, more protective, and a lot warier. I caught him watching her sleep a few times when he thought he was the only one awake. It was sorta creepy, but I could understand.

If anyone understood the obsessive need that came with dating Mallory Stanton, it was me, the man who'd been obsessed since the jump.

I heard Joker's door open and slam down the hall, followed by a few loud bangs and his very irate voice at a near shout.

"If you two can find time in your schedule between sexcapade marathons, perhaps you could calm the fuck down and join us for breakfast."

I don't think he waited for a response, and the corner of my mouth twitched upward in a grin for the first time this morning.

I handed the poor sap some coffee when he finally found his way to the kitchen, and he dropped into a seat next to me, looking worse for wear. We all were. Not like anyone could get any decent sleep with the world's loudest screamer repeatedly finding her peak from sundown to sunrise.

"How did you two sleep?" Joker muttered, his eyes sinking into their sockets, purple rings under his eyes from a lack of sleep.

If Joker didn't get eight solid hours, he looked like shit the next day.

"Sleep? What's that?" Ace joked, his lips pressed so tight together the damn things had nearly disappeared. "Fuck if I know. I didn't even bother trying. Probably would have had to drive to the end of the block not to hear those two."

"Mmm," he agreed, sipping the life juice between his hands. "Good coffee."

"Thanks, it's the third pot," I complained, rising to refill myself yet again. "I'm on cup four."

"Ouch. That's a bit rough," he pointed out. "Hope you're not planning anything strenuous today."

"Only plans on my docket are to collect my winnings at the gym." I pulled out my pocket knife and began picking out the dirt from beneath my nail bed. "You?"

Joker shrugged. "I'm supposed to follow some dirtbag who owes the Kings his life—only because he owed them thousands, which has conveniently been wiped from his ledger."

We turned to Ace next. He met our gazes and shrugged. "I'm staying here. Someone put in a call to Mallory's phone last night and never said a word, so BlackJack and I are planning to find out who—"

"Won't take long. All I have to do is hook it up to the laptop and run a reverse search. Maybe ping some towers."

BlackJack strode proudly into the kitchen, wearing nothing but a pair of low-slung sweats and his smirk, Mallory trotting along like a dickmatized fool behind him. I resisted the urge to slam my fist into his smug ass face and growled instead, taking a huge drink of my coffee to singe the anger from my throat before I said something stupid.

Ace seemed to not have the same hesitation.

"You should be walking like a fucking penguin from all that noise you made all night."

Mallory raised a brow but took a seat with a slight wince of discomfort, one she tried desperately to hide from BlackJack. I had some guesses as to why that was, but odds were they were all wrong, so I didn't bother entertaining them. I passed her a little wink and returned to my coffee when she smiled at me, hoping she'd enjoyed herself.

I didn't mind sharing, but fucking hell, I was now seriously considering installing soundproofing myself next time I had a spare minute to myself.

Joker huffed in annoyance when we were all finally sitting around the table, running a hand down his face as a groan rumbled out of him. As if summoned by the sound, Mallory's eyes finally found their way to him, and she nearly dropped her coffee as she gasped, noticing the black rings beneath his eyes, the drawn look, and the sickly pallor of his skin.

"Oh my god, Cass, who the fuck hurt you?" Her hand stretched across the table, like she could soothe away his pain with a touch. "You look terrible."

"Thanks, doc, really helpful," he complained, rolling his eyes at her observation. "I didn't sleep last night. Would you have any ideas what kept me up?"

She blushed prettily and averted her eyes. "Um."

BlackJack punched Joker in the arm, perhaps a bit rougher than necessary, but hey, when you're getting laid for the first time in your life and some asshole knocks on the wall, you get what you deserve for that dick move. "Fuck off, prick. Don't make her feel bad about it."

"Oh, if it isn't the man of more words in one month than he's spoken in ten years. Please, tell me more about myself."

I tuned out their taunting and watched Mallory as she turned to Ace with a nearly audible eye roll and asked him what the day held for everyone. When he'd filled her in, she tipped her head and smiled at him, momentarily blinding everyone in the path of that stunning display.

"Would you take me out today? I, uh, need to grab a few things, and I don't want to go alone."

Ace shrugged but said nothing, his eyes sparkling with those unsaid words I knew we were all so close to spilling to her.

Every fucking one of us was irreversibly in love with her, and it was only a matter of time before one of us spilled the fucking beans and told her to her face. Hell, if I weren't entirely sure her pussy was practically murdered after last night, I'd pull her over the table and fuck her into the wood while I screamed it at all of these fuckers, claiming a piece of her before anyone else had the chance.

Though, it could be said I'd claimed most of her firsts with us. I kissed her first, I had my dick in her first—

"Sure, I'll take you wherever you need to go. BlackJack can run your phone while we're gone."

She turned to BlackJack with a grateful smile, and he leaned over her and planted a lingering kiss on her upturned lips as she drank him in. When he pulled back, her breathless giggle nearly gagged me.

"Thanks, babe," she crooned to him, and he gave her a little nod, his proud smile back in place for us as if to say *eat shit and die, motherfuckers, she likes me best.*

She gave him a nickname first.

Maybe we weren't the only fools here head over heels.

I let that thought simmer as we slowly slipped out of the kitchen one by one, leaving Ace and Mallory alone to discuss their travel plans for the day.

THREE HOURS LATER, I was elbow-deep in a bloody beatdown with a man who spilled far more than he'd ever planned to, my fists aching from the number of times I'd slammed them into his perfectly aligned veneers.

Well, once perfectly aligned. They were quite a mess now. Would probably be thousands in work to straighten them and reset his jaw, but that wasn't my problem.

"So, you wanna come clean and tell me who the fuck paid you off and why?"

The pussy of a man in my chair winced and spat a glob of blood and one more tooth from his mouth onto my no longer clean floor. "I told you, crazy fuck, I don't know anything."

Boy, I bet it *hurt* to move that broken jaw of his. "How's the face, fuckwad? Does it hurt? Looks like it hurts."

A little meow dragged my attention away, and I groaned as I realized one of the furry fucks I'd relocated from Mallory's apartment had wandered into my torture chamber and was now tracking bloody pawprints all over the room.

The counters.

The floor.

Hell, they were even on the walls.

Cats.

Innocent lives, Spade. Don't kill innocents.

I was reminded of a conversation we'd had not long ago, Mallory and I, about how innocent a house cat really was, and I stifled the laugh that bubbled up inside me.

"Come on, kitty crusader, you're gonna need a bath before I can take you back to your mother, and I don't have the time now, so it's into cat jail for you."

I lifted the smug little shit by the scruff of his neck and carted him off to the plastic kennel I'd used to transport him and his sibling to their new home. Hell, I'd even cat-proofed the doors into the garage, making damn sure none of her little fur babies could escape. I hadn't told Mallory yet that I brought her things back for a more permanent stay, hoping to surprise her when she returned, earning some of that sweet, sweet attention and love she was busy laving all over BlackJack.

Once the cat king had been securely trapped, I wandered back into the torture room, smiling like a loon when my return elicited a whimpering moan of fear from my little plaything.

I waggled a brow at him and grabbed a hammer from the nearby table, waving it back and forth in the air in a perfect arc.

"Now, where were we, Tommy? Ah, yes—you were trying to convince me the Kings don't own your loyalty and silence. Now tell me why I should believe you, buddy boy, and maybe I won't hit you too hard when you lie the first time."

He groaned through his mouth pain, drool slipping from the corner of his mouth, pooling on his knee as he slumped forward and passed out. I leaned forward and sniffed, wrinkling my nose at the horrid smell.

"Fucking animals, the lot of you. Weak little animals. My woman's cat has more balls."

The chucklefuck had gone and pissed all over himself and my chair, on my floor, and didn't have the decency to even be honest with me.

Maybe I was slipping. Maybe my time out of the game had seen me go a little soft.

I planted a booted foot at the edge of his seat, right between his legs, and tipped him backward, knocking him over. When his pathetic head hit the floor, soaking him in his own piss, he groaned, and those beady little eyes opened wide again, whirling on me in abject horror.

"Last chance, you spineless pustule on the asscrack of society. What are you doing for the Kings?"

His lips split into a slight grimace, and he coughed up blood, wincing at the few broken ribs I'd graced him with when he'd tried to run. "I didn't do shit for them. She did."

My brows furrowed and I puzzled over the confusing seed of doubt he'd managed to plant in my brain with that single sentence.

There was no way.

Not possible.

"What the fuck are you on about?"

His grimace turned into a grin of satisfaction, perhaps pleased that his death wouldn't be in vain, that he'd gotten one up on me before bleeding to death in the torture room of his worst nightmare.

"By the end of the day, they'll have gunned you all down. And she's going to lead them right to you."

I yanked out my phone and dialed Ace's number, scowling when it went straight to voicemail. "You'd better not be lying, you fuckwit, or I'll feed you to the fishes tonight." I redialed him, and again, straight to voicemail.

Of all the times to be unreachable.

I locked him in my room and tossed the key on my bed, running full tilt to the garage, just barely managing to skirt the cat in the hallway that still roamed free for the time being. In a minute flat, I was peeling out of the drive, the garage door closing behind me, rubber peeling off on the street as I raced toward the coffee shop where BlackJack and Joker were supposed to meet them for lunch.

I just hoped I'd get there in time.

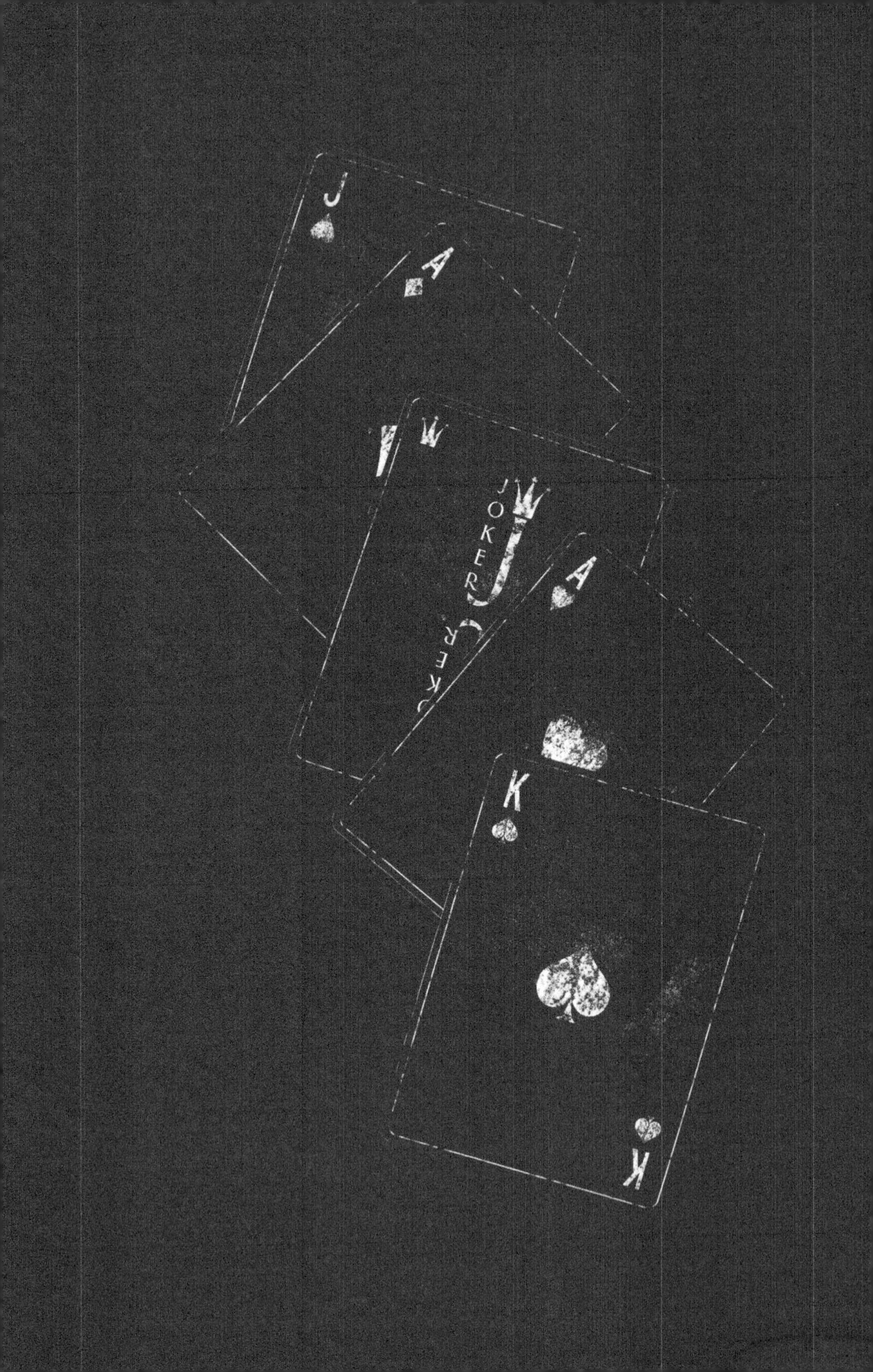
JOKER

CHAPTER FORTY-SIX
MALLORY

It was hot. Abnormally hot today. Ace and I grabbed a table outside on the patio at the nearby coffee shop and bakery, my eyes trailing after Cass as he grabbed our order at the counter. BlackJack was late—held up in traffic, he'd said. And Spade had insisted he was otherwise occupied with a far less sanitary activity, so he was out.

The air just before the moment everything went sideways was tense, charged, and so fucking thick it was nearly suffocating. I felt the wrongness of it deep in my bones, but having never faced such a situation before, I didn't recognize it for what it was until it was too late.

And then the first bullet flew, a woman screamed, and pandemonium erupted around us.

Plates, cups, and people went flying in all different directions as a gun peeked out of a nearby car with blackout windows, and the barrel flashed in our direction, bullet after bullet tearing into the crowd, some striking the wall, some the tables that were upturned in the madness, some finding purchase in passers-by. Innocents.

I swallowed my scream and dove under the table just as a bullet whizzed past my ear, the sound sending chills down my spine and jarring me into action. I crawled on hands and knees, hiding behind anything and everything, slowly working my way to the door that led into the building to safety.

I had to get to Joker. I had to find Ace. I had to make sure they were alright, and then we had to get the fuck out of here before we were killed.

I had no doubt this was a targeted hit, and unless another criminal organization was sitting here enjoying their midday coffee and fresh muffins, the Wildcards were the target.

"Cass!" I screamed, my voice drowned out in the cacophony around us. "Kohei!"

Neither one called back, and the sinking feeling in my stomach sank even lower, making me near sick with fear. The bile rose in my throat, and I swallowed it down, determined to hold it together until I could find the others.

Just as I peeked out from behind a table that had fallen on its side, another round of bullets rattled off in my direction, and this time, I wasn't even ashamed at the fear-tinted scream of panic that left my mouth. I'd never been brought up at the sound of gunfire. Threats and waved fists, sure, but my father, for all his faults, had never brought home the gunfights.

This shit . . . was insane.

If I didn't die here, I'd fucking roll over dead of shock.

My knees were bleeding, dragged through shards of glass and splintered wood, but I powered on, waiting until the bullets ceased for a reload before I scrambled to the open door and slipped inside the building, my back against the cool tile wall.

Fuck, I was screwed.

We were all screwed.

A cold, clammy hand circled my wrist, and I nearly screamed again before a second hand slapped over my lips, cutting off the shrill sound. I was shaking like a leaf, but it couldn't be helped. I knew the signs of shock, of a panic attack, and if one or the other didn't do me in soon, it would be a damned miracle.

It took me a minute to recognize the hand over my mouth as Kohei's and the hand on my arm as Cass's. When I did, it abated some of the panic, but not much, and I swallowed the lump of fear lodged in my throat. When they turned me loose, I took a deep breath and tried to breathe like a normal human, not that it worked well.

Just when I thought things couldn't get any more hectic, tires squealed into the parking lot, and a gunfight ensued, the sound of two pistols returning fire against the semi-auto rifle that had taken aim at us. The sound of air leaking from a tire preceded the sound of more tires squealing, and then everything was quiet again.

Dead silent, in fact.

No screams, no crying, no panicked calls for loved ones. Just an eerie silence.

I realized belatedly it was because my brain was shutting off, and I'd been tuning out the sound of Joker talking to me on my left.

With a shake of my head, I cleared my ears, and it was like a needle punctured the bubble in my head, letting in all the frantic sounds, pressing in like a cloud of death and agony.

And then Spade and BlackJack were pulling us from the rubble, and I was too shaken to say a word. I let them herd us into waiting cars and peel away from the building, curled into the side of the backseat of Spade's road beast, confused, angry, and more than a little scared for my life.

FROM WHAT ACE managed to put together, the Kings had ordered a hit on us, in broad daylight, with no concern for innocents who got in the way. The death contract the perps had conveniently dropped on the ground as they fled the scene had the men's names on it, but not mine, and ever since Ace linked the strange phone call I'd gotten on my cell to a King's informant, he'd been staring daggers at me across the table.

He hadn't said it aloud, but I knew he thought I'd betrayed them. That I had something to do with this bullshit hit.

I didn't, but that didn't stop him from thinking it.

As my last lifeline left the table to jump in the shower, I debated taking the coward's way out and begging off to shower with him, but Ace's eyes and his dangerous aura had me pinned to the spot, and I sat there like a good girl, refusing to leave until I'd been told to leave.

When the sound of running water had begun to drown him out, Ace turned his attention fully on me, and a dangerous smirk twisted his features into something unrecognizable.

Something dangerous.

"So, how long have you been in cahoots with the Kings?"

I stiffened and faced the window, my arms still curled protectively around my middle, like I might fall apart if I let go. "I don't know what the fuck you're talking about, Ace."

His answering snarl said more than words ever could.

And then he was jerking me from my chair and yanking me down the hall to the garage, too fast to even form a retort or yell for assistance.

Ace threw me in the front seat of his car and slammed the door, waving a gun pointedly at me with the real threat that should I run, he'd shoot me. I sat stock-still in that front seat and hated myself for the tears that flooded my eyes, fighting them back, praying to whatever god was listening that they wouldn't fall in front of him.

I'd never forgive myself if I broke down in front of a man who thought me capable of sleeping with him, giving him everything short of a declaration of love, and then turning around and having him killed.

He sped away from the compound and raced down main roads, every building and skyscraper we passed blurring into one another, nothing but a continuous hodgepodge of shapes and squares, glass and metal and concrete that were indistinguishable from each other. His anger radiated off him in waves, but even I knew better than to try and make a run for it. At the speeds he was clocking, if I bailed now, I'd die before I stopped rolling.

We both knew I had nowhere to go.

We'd traveled a few miles and left the familiar part of the city behind when I finally worked up the courage to speak to my twice-kidnapper.

"Where are you taking me?"

He didn't take his eyes off the road, but his hands tightened around the wheel, his mouth drawn taut. "To the men you betrayed us for. Only fitting you should shack up with them now. I'm sure you've promised them something worthwhile to get them involved with our daring yet foolish escape attempt."

"So we went from betrayal to escape, that it? You give me fucking whiplash."

His hand darted out and wrapped itself around my throat, just like good times, but this time, instead of choking me while I rocketed toward orgasm, he threatened to kill me with it and end me for good. The look in his eyes was one of deep betrayal, and I realized even while he was balls deep in me, he'd still refused to believe I could be choosing this—choosing them--for any reason other than pure survival.

And nothing I said now would ever change that.

But I had to try.

"Ace—"

He shook me by the throat, cutting off my words like a knife through butter. "I don't want to hear your lies."

"Not lies," I squeaked, but he wasn't listening. He whipped his car into the drive of a lavish house, slamming straight through their decorative iron fence like he had not a care in the world.

I clawed at his hand as I realized what he planned to do, fear and panic and bile rising in my throat as my fucking heart broke.

Here I was, once a captive, realizing belatedly, too late, that I was in love with my fucking captors, each and every one of them, and I'd never bothered to let them know they meant something to me. And now, I'd never get the chance.

If I was ever allowed to walk out of this house alive, they'd probably think everything Ace said was true, and they'd hate me, too. He'd make sure of it.

Kohei.

Cassian.

Jonah.

Tyson.

My kidnappers. My captors. My jailers.

My whole fucking reason for existence now.

And the four men who held my heart forever in their palms.

Who would grow to think of me as an enemy.

A betrayer.

I gripped Ace's wrist in my hands as he leaned over me and shoved open the door at my back, and as several armed men approached the car, I made one last plea to him, those traitorous tears finally slipping free of their moorings, spilling over and trailing down my cheeks in the ultimate betrayal of the way his actions were tearing me apart.

"Kohei, *please—*"

He shoved me off of his arm and screeched to a stop, throwing me bodily on my ass from the open door before he threw it in reverse and turned to look over his shoulder.

"Kohei!" I screamed after him, struggling to find my feet and get my legs beneath me, but it was no use—the guards had caught up to me now. As their cold hands clamped over my biceps, a keening, heart-wrenching wail ripped free of my chest and echoed around the courtyard of the estate he'd dropped me at, trailing after his fast-disappearing car as it drifted around the next turn and out of sight.

I folded in on myself, limp and over life at this point, and waited for my end to come at the end of one of their guns.

Of course, it wouldn't be that simple, and as I was dragged into the house, a strange feeling washed over me, a feeling I hadn't had to worry about in years.

Surrender.

More than anything, right now, I wanted to curl up and just die, his betrayal hurt so bad.

A piece of me was gone; without it, it was like I'd forgotten how to breathe. Like life itself held no meaning but just to exist. And suddenly, I didn't want to anymore.

I was dead, and it was all his fault.

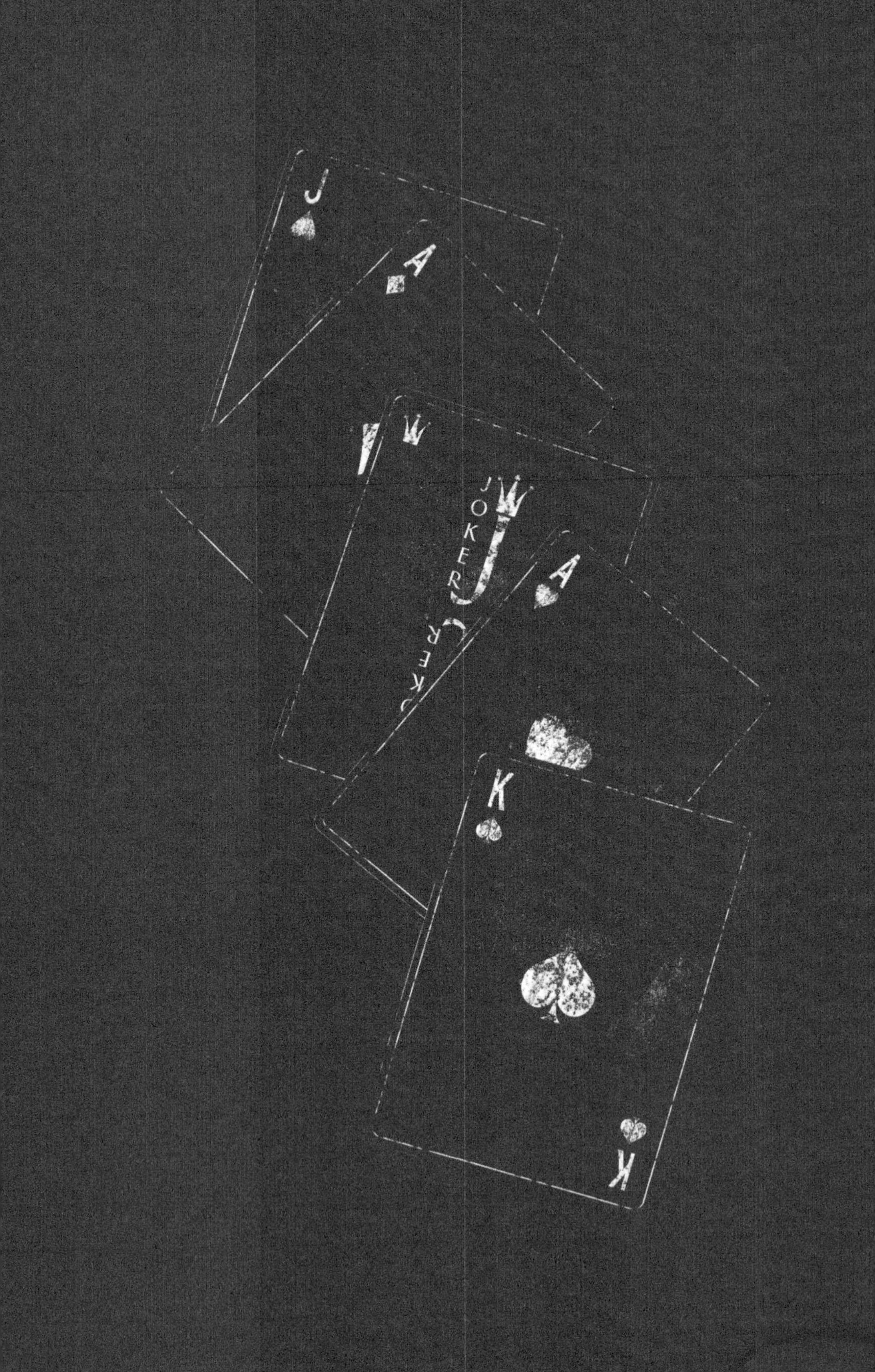
JOKER

CHAPTER FORTY-SEVEN
JOKER

"You're a fucking idiot, man, but I never thought you'd be capable of this kind of traitorous, crazed bullshit!"

Spade was busy shoving Ace into the wall repeatedly, and the fucking moron just let him, standing there like he hadn't just thrown our girl to the wolves. He'd been inconsolable ever since Ace pulled back in with an empty, half-wrecked car and a look of shame on his face.

It took all of a half hour to get the asshole in Spade's torture room to turn over the details of the people who'd hired him, the ones who'd put a tracker in our girl's jacket when we weren't looking. Turned out, there was more than one mad dash for power, and our earlier lead was right—the Rizolli Mafia had hired squads to take a hit at both us and the Kings—but the Kings played it smart, and intelligent men with a hit on their heads never left home.

We were so busy playing hide the sausage that we'd forgotten to watch our own backs.

Maybe a part of Ace had been right—Mallory was a pretty distraction that we'd all let ourselves get caught up in—but damn it all, we fucking loved her, and this wasn't how decisions were made in our crew.

CHAPTER FORTY-SEVEN

Ace had gone rogue for the last time.

"If they kill her, Ace, I'll fucking make sure you suffer every single punishment they dole out to her just for breathing." Spade slammed his fist through the drywall beside his leader's face, a grimace on his lips. "I fucking swear to you, Ace, if I never hear my name spill from her lips again, I'll hurt you until I break my own rules and leave your corpse on the doorstep of the fucking Yakuza as a warning."

Ace turned away, his eyes filled with regret. "I'll make a call, Tyson, okay?" He'd stopped calling us by our code names when BlackJack slammed his fist into Ace's gut and declared the Wildcards no more until Mallory was back with us, safe and whole.

If Ace wanted to stay alive, he'd fucking have to grovel at our queen's feet and beg her forgiveness.

And even then, I wasn't convinced he'd be fit to lick the soles of her shoes.

Spade's howl of fury reverberated off the walls as he yanked open the door to the armory and began ripping guns off his shelves, strapping a number of knives to his person like he was preparing for guerrilla warfare on his home turf.

"Spade," I muttered, side-eyeing the man like he was going crazy.

Which he was.

We all were.

We were certifiable and breaking apart without her, just as we had been before she showed up.

His eyes whirled on me, and the look in them made me feel uneasy. It was the look of a broken man, cracking apart and relishing the pain as he did whatever he could to feel useful.

"Spade, do you really think charging into their stronghold armed to the teeth is a smart idea?"

BlackJack strolled in with a frown on his lips, his hair combed back and slicked down, a suit and tie gracing his lean frame as he tucked a gun into a shoulder holster beneath his coat. "It's better than nothing, which is what you're doing sitting there like she's going to magically fall back into our laps."

I frowned, hating that he was right but knowing damn well we could get killed pulling this shit. "Do you think they hurt her?"

Spade's shoulders hunched, and I swore I heard him clench his jaw so tight a tooth cracked beneath the pressure. "If they did, I'll make them hurt a thousand times worse."

Ace had left the room but returned now, a bit worse for wear but mostly cleaned up, his polished three-piece business suit pissing me off the longer I stared at it.

He huffed in annoyance as Spade crowded him out of the room, not letting him further than the doorway. "I'm going to help, Tyce, get out of the fucking way."

Spade sneered at him, and the look could have turned a lesser man to stone. "Don't you think you helped enough already?"

Ace flinched, but he held his ground. "I just got off the phone with an old friend—"

BlackJack stepped up, his hand falling on Spade's shoulder before the man could do something reckless, like shoot his friend. "We don't need your help, Ace. I'll get us in there. We'll extract her and bring her home, where she belongs."

"Let him come," I spoke up, not backing down as all three men stared blankly at me. "We could use another set of hands, and let's be realistic; he's not going to do anything to get himself killed. It was a mistake. Let's let our queen decide if he's worth saving or not. She's the one he betrayed."

Ace looked like he might wither away and die at the suggestion that Mallory dish out his fate, but there was no choice but to go with it if he wanted to leave this house alive.

THE ESTATE that for all intents and purposes should have been in an upheaval was startlingly quiet when we approached. The guards that should be stationed in front of the house were missing, and the cars in the drive had all been gifted flat tires, courtesy of someone who knew how to incapacitate a vehicle, no less.

"This doesn't look good, guys," I muttered, spotting two inert forms by a guard building. "Looks like two downed guards by the entrance gate. We aren't the first ones here."

Spade let out a fucking whine at the news, his already frayed mental state breaking more under the knowledge that there could be two factions to fight our way through to get to her. "Fuck, I'll kill them all, man, if they hurt a hair on her head, shit—"

BlackJack slapped him on the back of his head, rolling his eyes. "Shut it, moron. Silence equals an element of surprise."

We snuck around to the front door, and the evidence of an attack was more evident here—not that the dead guards weren't already a huge indication. The door had been rammed in, most likely by pros, the screws holding the latch in place ripped straight from the wood and left to cover the floor, bits and pieces of wood scattered around them. The door lay on the ground beyond its frame, scores in the wood surface, most likely from the ram and several pairs of boots.

"They breached the front pretty easily, no casualties," Ace muttered, his brain kicking into analysis mode like it did when he was formulating a plan that left no room for error. His need for control was slipping back in, taking over again, and I winced as my boot came down on shattered glass, the sound echoing abnormally loudly around us.

"Fuck."

We all stopped and listened for the sound of another group of people, but the air was unnaturally still, like there was nothing living in this house. Not anymore.

Had there been a shootout? Had they fought to the last man, taking every single attacker down with them?

We pressed on, sweeping the house, finding not a single soul in the building before we came to the back door and found the sight of the bloodbath.

At least twenty men lay in a backyard garden, some draped over bushes, some laying on the cold ground, their bodies all sitting in pools of their own blood, riddled with holes and slashes that told a gruesome story. Not a single body stirred as we walked by, not a single one held a pulse. But they all wore the same uniform, and that alone told me they were the same bastards who'd attacked our group at the coffee shop, and just like there, they'd failed here, too.

The guards out front all wore a very conspicuous uniform, and none of these bodies had the same clothing.

Spade spat on one as we walked through the yard, his disdain rising to the surface. "Fucking worthless scum, attacking people while their backs are turned. You get what you deserve."

We rounded the building, coming face to face with an ongoing standoff, the four of us managing to drag ourselves out of the line of sight before being spotted.

BlackJack moved around the area and took the high ground, mapping out the road ahead before returning to us with a frown on his lips.

"Four men along the far wall, all armed, looks like some of the Kings we've encountered at the gym. They're pinned down, six men to the left of the poolhouse, all hunkered down, reloading, regrouping."

Spade growled, his eyes wild again. "Any sign of our girl?"

He shook his head, a deep sadness in his eyes that speared me to my core. "Not that I saw."

Just then, a shout rang out, followed by a bellowing, rage-filled cry that could belong to only one person.

Arthur Hale, leader of the Kings.

BlackJack's estranged cousin.

"You can take this place over my dead body, you scumbags!"

I just vaguely registered the sound of a grenade pin falling to the ground before the men hiding from their targets screamed, and a loud boom echoed out over the courtyard.

Two men got hit in the fallout, and the other four scattered, taking cover around the yard. I slid my clip into the handle of my pistol and inched forward, ready to help take the assholes out, when the sound of heaven opening up and angels falling to earth reached my ears, and I nearly fainted with relief.

"Give me the fucking gun, Arthur; I want to shoot the bastards myself."

I watched as a man popped up to the left, and without batting an eye, Mallory brought her hand up and unloaded two shots right into his chest, dropping him like a lead weight. She swiveled as I stared on in awe, gunning down a second man stupid enough to reveal his hiding spot in an attempt to take her down.

He got a bullet between the eyes for his trouble.

Ace and Spade were creeping around the yard, and they were only a few feet from our girl when one of the men on the ground lifted his gun and took aim while his comrades distracted her.

Neither of them noticed the gun aiming for her head.

Not fast enough.

"Mallory, move!"

Her eyes jerked to mine and she froze, *fuck, why did you look at me, sweetheart, fuck, why did I yell for you?*

And as the gun went off, my life flashed before my eyes, except it wasn't a life I'd lived yet—it was a life I'd stood a chance at, one that was being yanked away from me now that it was within reach.

"Noooo!"

I watched the bullet leave the gun, almost in slow motion, and my heart leaped into my throat, threatening to suffocate me, as I realized she was about to take a fatal shot. I launched myself in her direction, popping off a shot at the man still hiding behind a nearby tree, BlackJack's bullet singing true to the last man, downing him before he could plead for his life.

One blink, one breath in, and it was over.

But she didn't fall. She didn't wince, she didn't flinch, she didn't even reel from a direct hit.

Ace was standing in front of her, his body a shield, taking a bullet for her to make up for the mistakes he made in bringing her here in the first place.

And the blossoming red spot on his shoulder told me that bullet hadn't quite found its mark.

He fell to the ground, our queen's arms around his body, holding him against her as she wailed and screamed his name, and men surrounded her—some hers, some Kings, all concerned for the life of the man who now lay possibly dying on the ground. He coughed and sputtered as she smothered him, his name falling from her lips like a plea to gods long-ago forgotten.

"Kohei, Kohei, please, don't you leave me; Kohei, dammit, if anyone's gonna shoot you, it deserves to be me—"

"I'm not dying, dammit." He grumbled from her arms, wincing as none other than the Soldier poked and prodded at the wound, inspecting the entry wound for any sign of shrapnel. "Fuck, do you have to be so rough?"

The Kings backed up and gave us some space as she looked around, tears shining in her eyes, reaching for all of us at once, and damned if we didn't pile in and wrap her in our arms like lovesick fucking fools, uncaring that a rival gang stood feet away, witnessing our greatest weakness, and our greatest strength.

Our queen brought us together, she made us stronger. She made us whole.

And if that was a weakness, I didn't care anymore. I'd be whatever man she needed me to be.

"Fuck, beautiful, don't scare us like that again. I've only got one heart to love you with; it'd be a shame to lose it to a heart attack—"

Spade punched BlackJack right in the mouth, cutting off his profession of love with a snarl. "You fucking prick! I was gonna tell her first!"

Ace groaned from her lap, rolling his eyes at their antics. "You're seriously fighting over who tells her first? I think it's more than obvious we're fucking head over heels for her by now. *All of us.*"

I smiled and nodded, not as eager as the others to have to fight Spade for the imagined slight. Instead, I kissed her temple, pulling her against my chest, reveling in the way she felt in my arms, safe, where she fucking belonged.

"Still regret answering that call, doc?" I whispered against her hair, a tear falling to the top of her head, one I'd deny until my dying day.

"Not on your life," she laughed, placing a kiss against my throat as I held her closer. "Not once."

"Love's such an overused word, but I'll tell it to you as often as you like, doc," I whispered, meaning every word. "You just tell me when and where."

"How about you come up with a better nickname than doc, Cass? Let's start there."

I laughed through real tears, swallowing them down as she healed my fucking soul once more. "It's a deal, beautiful."

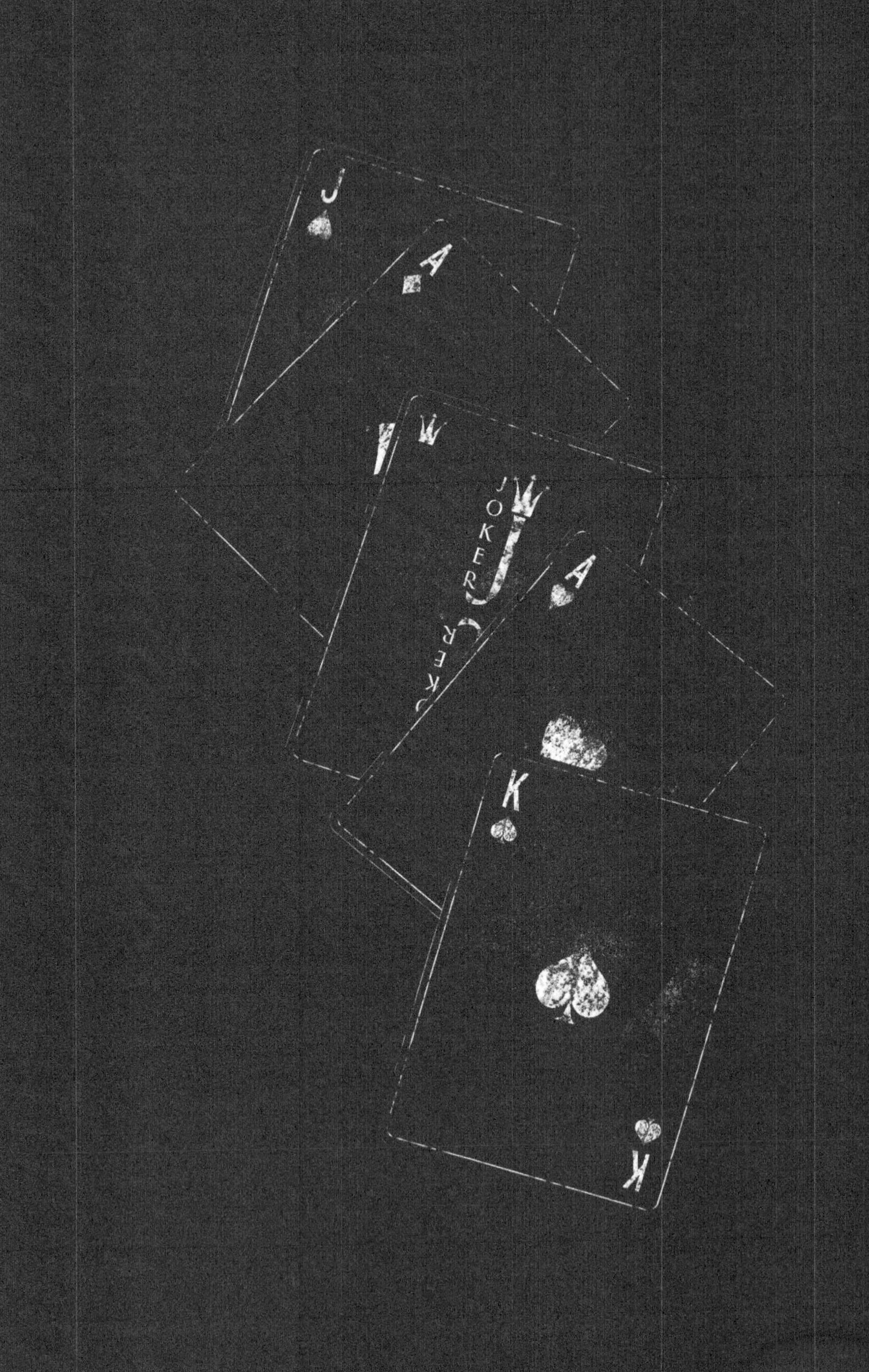
JOKER

CHAPTER FORTY-EIGHT
MALLORY

Ace's wound healed pretty quickly, thanks to the doctor on call at the King's mansion. After a brief interrogation when Ace dropped me on their doorstep, the Kings had put me in a room and left me there overnight. If not for the safety features installed in their home, I'd have been stuck there and likely killed when the intruders showed up, guns blazing.

As it was, I managed to save two of their lives in the process of almost escaping, and in return, a temporary truce was called.

Joker came clean with them about his involvement in the heist, and with the return of the jewels, his part in this whole mess was forgiven.

Ace was a work in progress, and his loyalty to me was still in question, but we were working on it, and taking a bullet for someone went a long way toward working off any forgiveness he needed to earn from me.

Spade calmed down after the first week I was back, though he still took to occasionally stalking me anywhere I went. Especially if it was out of the house.

BlackJack was a solid pillar of support as things evened out, smoothing over relations with the Kings in Ace's stead, serving as more of a leader than I'd expected him to be. He and their ghost, oddly enough named Spectre, traced down the Rossi family members responsible for the hit, and the decision was made to pursue revenge against them.

That wasn't our scene, though. We were white-collar crime. In and out, heists, money grabs, the basics. The Kings didn't shy away from the dirty work, so they could take on that particular wheelhouse.

Speaking of dirty work . . .

I stood on the edge of the new ring the Kings had installed in Spade's gym, appreciating the fine line of his lean but muscular torso, his tattoos flashing as he went toe-to-toe with BlackJack, of all people.

He'd been the first one Jonah let touch him, and after the little near-death fiasco with the Kings and the hit squads, he'd wanted to brush up on his hand-to-hand combat and teach me self-defense, too. I was reluctant to deny him, especially since it meant I got to wrap myself around him—a lot.

Takedowns, you know. They're very hands-on.

Spade stepped in when I started to lag, insisting someone should wear out the man in the ring for me, shooting me a wink and a smile as he hurled his body gracefully up and under the bottom rope in a nice roll. He was on his feet in a flash, reminding the taller man why size didn't always matter, and I couldn't help but enjoy the unintentional show they were giving me.

Fuck, it was so hot when my men went at each other and worked up a sweat. That almost always ended in a shower, and I always got an invite from one or the other—sometimes both, depending on who was playing.

Jonah wasn't there yet, though. Not quite.

"You enjoying your show, beautiful?"

Cass snuck up behind me, his front tucked against my back, hips pressed insistently against my ass as I let my eyes drift closed and feel him. The temptation to turn away and watch him instead of the boys was strong, but I'd promised to pay attention.

I promised, dammit.

"What sort of trouble are you getting up to, Cassian Fontaine?" I teased, my voice dropping low so the others didn't hear me.

His laughter was magical, and it twisted my insides every time I heard it, not that I'd ever want him to stop. "Oh no, not the full name. Somebody's in trouble!"

His fingers traced my spine, and I moaned a little as he ticked off each vertebra like they were a deck of cards and he was about to shuffle. I really, really had to try to focus as Spade ducked a punch and reflected the move, his eyes darting to mine for a split second, narrowing when he spotted his crew brother behind me.

"Leave her alone, Joker. She's busy." Another swerve as a fist came within an inch of his face this time, his grin spreading across that gorgeous face, his newly-trimmed, shoulder-length red hair waving in the breeze. "She'll never learn a thing if you don't stop dragging her off to fuck when she's supposed to be observing."

I could hear the smirk in his chuckle at my ear, could feel it as he placed it against the hollow of my throat, just below my chin. "Well, I guess I'll just have to make sure she doesn't wander off, then, won't I?"

Before I could ask him what he was plotting, he jerked the back of my shorts down, still hidden between my body and his, and slid his cock between my thighs, teasing me, soaking up the slickness accumulating there for him.

Sparring always got me horny. It was something that got me in trouble every time I sparred with Spade.

"I'm going to fuck you while you watch them, and you'd better pay attention, or Spade will fuck *me* next."

I giggled at that thought, then shot a look full of lust over my shoulder. "Ooh, I might pay to see Spade peg one of you guys."

Spade tripped over his own feet as he lunged for BlackJack, his eyes blown wide with arousal. "The fuck did I just hear you say, sweetheart?"

Cass rocked his hips against me and gripped my hips, angling me up on the tips of my toes as he slid in to the base of his cock, groaning. I wasn't sure when he'd snuck the fucker out, but I also didn't really give a fuck.

"Fuck," I muttered, biting my lip as Joker's cock filled me from behind, Spade's eyes on me the whole time. He still traded punches and swings with Jonah, but now his attention was split, and those punches came closer and closer to his face, until one finally connected, and he went down with a groan.

"You hit him!" I accused, my eyes traveling to Jonah, filled with frustration. They were supposed to be playing nice, not actually hurting each other. Another roll of Joker's hips reminded me he was still buried inside me, and I bit my lip to stifle a very wanton groan of approval at the fullness between my legs.

My waist was below the ring, and I was bent forward over the edge, giving him a hell of a shot, but the other two couldn't see what was going on between us. Or at least, I hoped they couldn't.

I should have known better. All this time with the four of them, and I still hadn't learned much.

BlackJack bent over at the waist and met my eyes, holding them for more than was absolutely necessary, a feral grin creeping over his lips. "You're getting fucked right now, aren't you?" he muttered in an amused tone, his brows halfway to his hairline. "Answer me, Mal."

"Yes," I squeaked, nodding furiously as a blush warmed my skin. Joker, no longer hiding, slipped a hand up around my throat and yanked me back, showing off for the others.

In another life, he was a professional exhibitionist, and maybe a little bit of a voyeur.

In this life, too.

I wasn't complaining.

"Look how hard you make him, beautiful," he whispered against my temple, rocking up into me with enough force now to lift me off my toes and drag very aroused whimpers from my lips. "Does watching them fight turn you on?"

I nodded again, closing my eyes in shame. I was *not* supposed to be getting fucked while a lesson was being taught. I was *not.*

But I was.

I had never been much for the rules.

Spade had abandoned all sort of pretense at sparring, his cock in hand already, watching me take dick like a whore, putting on a show for him now, instead of the other way around. I whimpered needily as he flopped down on his ass beside where I leaned against the ring for support, tenderly tucking a stray hair behind my ear.

"Your mouth busy, or can you handle sucking my cock while Joker shows you a good time?"

Holy fuck, yes.

"Give it to me," I growled, hornier than I'd been in a long ass time.

I didn't care that someone might walk in on us, even though the gym was closed for repairs and renovation. The Kings paid well, and now this was Spade's gym, one he treasured almost as much as he cherished me, or so he said.

I wanted to take this to the next level, and here he was, offering something we hadn't done before.

Group sex.

So fucking hot.

"Hang on tight, sweetheart. I want you to fuck me good with that pretty little mouth of yours."

BlackJack stared at us in awe from the middle of the ring, hands on his knees, breathing ragged, pupils dilated til his eyes were nearly black all the way through. He hadn't moved to touch himself yet, but I wasn't about to push him to participate if he wasn't comfortable.

But he was watching, and that made me clench needily around Cass's cock, drawing a groan from him as I leaned forward and put my lips around Spade's thick length, swallowing him as best I could, every little movement behind me sending a vibrating hum through my mouth and down his cock.

Pretty soon, every thrust brought all three of us to a horny, writhing, loud mess, our pleasure echoing off the rafters. I needed more, but the guys had my hands occupied, as well as their own, and the fact that I was so close yet so far away nearly had me in tears, strung so tight I was near to snapping, but I needed that last little touch to send me skyrocketing over the edge.

"Fuck, fuck fuck fuck it's not enough; I need—"

I hadn't even seen him move, but suddenly, there was another person wedged between me and the ring, his head pressed against my mound, a tongue twitching in my folds, seeking my clit with devastating accuracy.

I'd know that tongue anywhere.

"Jonah," I wailed, wishing I could wrap my hand around his arm as he fucked me with his tongue, knowing what I was missing, willing to give it to me even if it pressed his boundaries—

His tongue slid lower, and I felt it probe against where Joker and I were joined, and then his damnable organ slipped inside alongside Joker's cock, and I saw fucking stars.

Pretty sure Cass did, too.

My scream of pleasure rocketed around the room, a beautiful symphony that echoed endlessly, the acoustics in here quite fantastic for a porno. I shuddered around Joker as his cock speared me and spasmed inside my tight channel, filling me with his seed while he groaned and sagged against me.

A second later, Spade's cock was jumping against my tongue, and he was petting my head and reminding me to breathe while I swallowed him down, eyes rolling into the back of my head.

I didn't even have the chance to come down from whatever the fuck all that was before I heard footsteps behind us, and someone pointedly cleared their throat.

"All this fun, and nobody bothered to invite me to play?"

Ace's words might have been harsh, but his voice was teasing, and I smiled, pulling my lips off Spade's now-soft dick with a resounding *pop.* "I didn't even get an invite, pal. I just—"

"—stood there and took it like a good girl, yes, I watched you. Quite a performance, Miss Stanton. Care to repeat it?"

He stalked over and grinned wickedly down at me, his hands fisting in my hair. "Joker's had his fun, as has Spade. But I believe you said something about paying to see someone pegged, isn't that right?"

I watched his lips curl in that wicked grin as Joker stepped back and BlackJack crawled out from beneath me, his hair disheveled, his face covered in my arousal. I leaned down and kissed him, not giving a shit if he tasted like me and Joker, and *fuck,* this was so hot.

When I came up for air, my shorts around my thighs still, his smile damn near speared me in half. "You taste delicious, princess," he whispered against my lips, our eyes dancing with a shared pride in him yet again breaking another boundary.

"I didn't know you were into that sort of thing," I muttered, smiling like a fucking loon as Ace moved behind me to curl against my back.

"Me either," Ace complained, pouting over my shoulder at BlackJack as he stood and dusted off his pants. "Why didn't you tell any of us your door swung both ways?"

His noncommittal shrug spoke volumes. "You didn't ask."

I smiled as Ace dragged me away from the ring and turned me in his arms, tucking away the strands of my hair that had escaped during our fascinating foray into group sports. "Put a pin in that for later, Jonah, and come here. Let me take care of you like you take care of me."

He needed no further encouragement and followed me as the other two slinked off to the showers, leaving us to all our horny escapades.

If this was my life, it was good, and I couldn't ask for better—well, maybe I could. When the heavens opened up and gave you four virile men with insatiable appetites and the desire to mark you as theirs in every way conceivable, I guess there *was* one more thing I could ask for.

But we had all the time in the world for that.

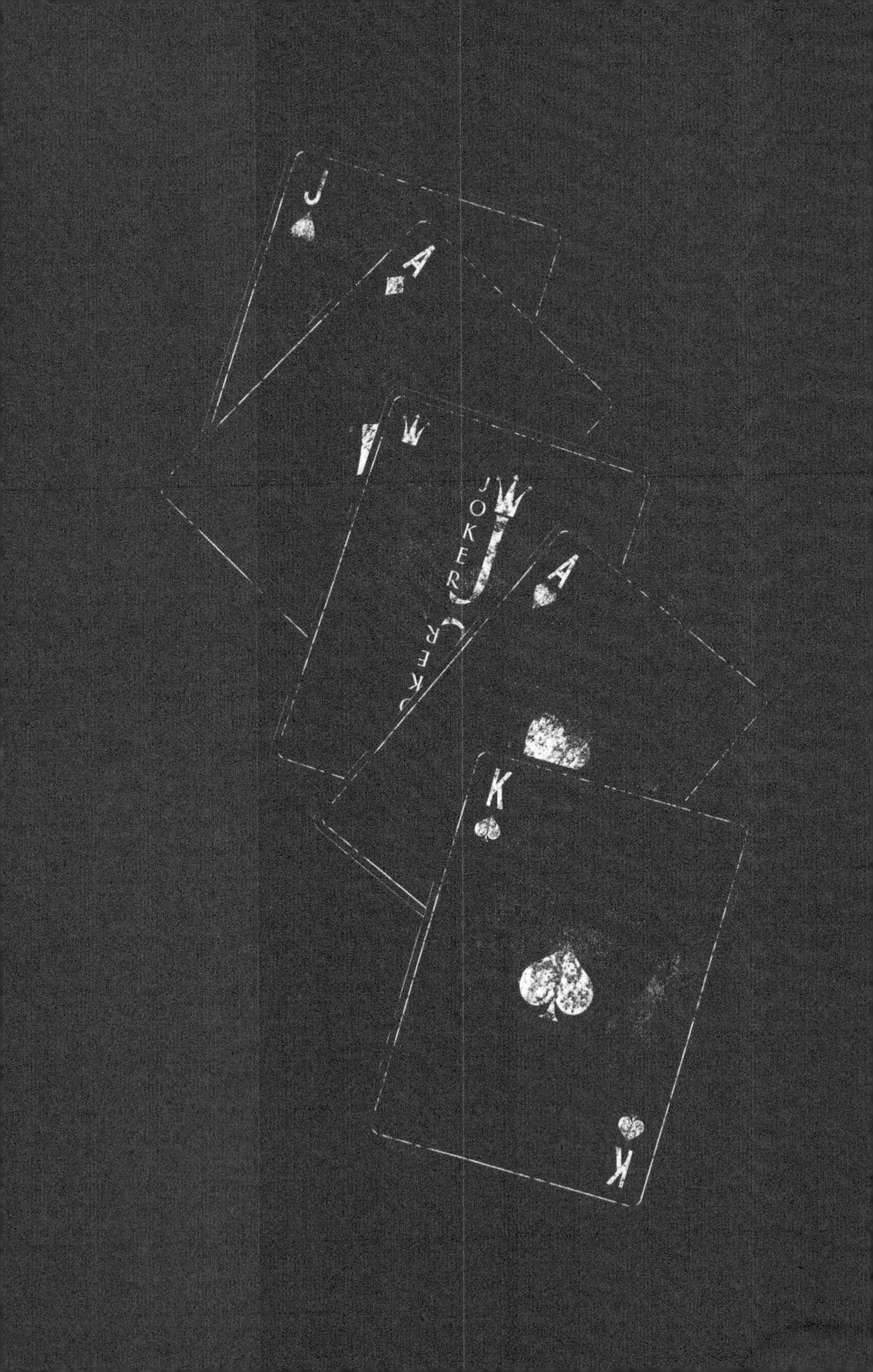
JOKER

EPILOGUE—MALLORY

The Kings made the boys an offer they couldn't refuse—work as an extension of their syndicate to bring down the bad players of the criminal underworld, and reap the benefits of their long arm of protection. Their allyship.

There hadn't been a question of whether or not the boys would take the offer. It would have been stupid to turn it down.

After all, the Wildcards were formidable, but the Kings were at the top of the game, and their reach was unparalleled. Together, we would work in tandem to bring down the mafia family that had threatened to end us all, over nothing more than control and unchecked power.

And I'd do it with all four men at my side.

After all, I was their queen—Queen of the Wildcards—and I had a new title to live up to.

WHO DO I BLAME FOR GETTING ME THIS HORNY FOR CRIMINALS?

Heleva Risque is not afraid to get her hands dirty, and neither are the heroes she writes. From complete alphaholes to grumpy, brooding bad boys, and everything in between, her heroes are walking red flags and trauma-filled shells of their former selves, but by the end of each story, not only will you want to cry for these wounded, unhinged men, but you'll be crawling into their beds, begging to be their good girls.

And you'll love every minute of it.

Ms. Risque has several series on the docket, including her leading mafia romance series, the Khula City Crime Syndicate, and a stand-alone, one-shot romance so dark, so filthy, so *sinful*, that you'll need the confessional on Sunday to cleanse your soul.

If you've got a kindle reads list that would make conversations at Thanksgiving dinner awkward, you're in the right place.

Check out her website at http://www.helevarisque.com